I0678102

This book is a work of fiction, the events are fictitious. Any similarity to a real person, living or deceased, is coincidental and not intended by the author.

ISBN 97809986518-2-8
Published by: Bohlander House Press
Dover, NJ, USA

Www.bohlanderhousepress.com

This book is dedicated to my husband, whose faith and support makes me believe I can do anything.

Adulfwulf Chronicles

Shattered Past
Shattered Dreams
Shattered Ghost

Novella: *Shattered Truth* (Ayden's story)

Other Books by Meg Castro

Fallen Descent

SHATTERED DREAM

By Meg Castro

Chapter 1

Nestled in the mountains of Pennsylvania was a large brick complex that resembled that of a small college campus. There were large dormitories, athletic fields, and green-houses. The campus even had small groups of cottages that all opened onto the same courtyard. However, this was not a college campus or even an exclusive resort; this was Shady Pines Home for the Mentally Ill.

It was a private hospital that provided short term and long term care. Some residents lived in the cottages, while the majority lived in the apartment like buildings where they were under twenty four hour watch and care. All inhabitants could make use of the gardens, athletic areas and classes that were offered. And all inhabitants suffered from mental illnesses that could not be treated in your normal psychiatric facility.

They were brought there as a last resort. They were all brought here because the ailments were caused by the paranormal.

In one of the private apartments was a young woman who had been in Shady Pines for the past ten years. She had been brought there by her family when she was twenty, when doctors could find no cure for her mental state, when no diagnosis could be determined, when she tried to kill her three best friends.

For the past twelve years Susannah Murphy had been locked in a nightmare that raged an ugly war in her mind, her reality and everything in between. When there was no hope for her to get better, her family brought her here so she could live in a comfortable setting. Many thought they were crazy to spend their money; they could afford the best care for their middle child.

The sad part was that it was unlikely Susie was even aware that she had been moved or that she had her own private apartment. The nightmare that raged in her mind kept her oblivious of what was going in the real world, when she did talk it was about demons and things that were so horrible one cringed from hearing the description.

For the moment she was in a sedate mode, which made the staff breathe easy. Susie was sitting in front of one the windows that looked out onto a garden planted by some of the other patients. The morning nurse had fed, cleaned and dressed her in jeans and a sweatshirt.

Susie most likely didn't even notice the flower and vegetables or the other patients walking and working but the nurses and doctors thought it was better than lying in bed staring at the ceiling. The door to the apartment opened up and Olivia, the main afternoon nurse walked in with lunch and medicine.

"Good afternoon Susie," Olivia said in her sing song voice. "I heard we had a good morning with Nancy. I want to introduce you to Joanna, she's my intern for a semester. I'm going to be telling her about you while we get your lunch set up. So don't get upset if you hear me describing your case."

A young woman entered the room after Olivia taking in the comfortable living room with pictures of family, and furniture that was warm and welcoming. Like all of the apartments, there was no kitchen or kitchenette. The cottages were the only living spaces that had a small kitchenette, and those were for the more able minded patients and some staff that lived on site.

"Joanna, Susie is one of our patients that we classify as unknown," Olivia explained as she began to unload the tray on the small kitchen table. "We know why she is in this state but we can't find a way to get her out of it."

"Does she talk?" Joanna asked as she helped the older woman. Olivia sighed looking at the young woman sitting at the window.

"Rarely, and when she does you will hear things that will make the hair on the back of your neck stand on end." Olivia went about the apartment while talking. "However, here instead of letting patients like her waste away in bed, we make sure they got out and about. Sometimes if she shows signs of life we will take her out to the garden and walk her around, or sit and read a book to her. It might be useless but we don't know."

"She's beautiful," Joanna said as she studied the girl with the vacant expression.

"She is, and has a steady stream of visitors. Her parents, two sisters, and two close friends from high school come see her on a regular basis," Olivia informed her intern. "Another friend is on her team of doctors."

"Isn't that a conflict of interest?" Joanna asked as she helped set out the food.

"Not when the friend is Dr. Heinrich who is a well-known name in parapsychology."

Joanna knew the name, anyone who took a course in parapsychology knew Dr. Heinrich's name, even more so since she took down a cult over the summer. "I did a paper on her and her study on the long term effects of spells gone wrong."

"I know," Olivia replied smiling. "That paper is why we selected you."

"Susie, lunch is ready," Olivia said to Susie. "I will be back in ten minutes, if you aren't at the table by then we will have words."

Joanna looked at Olivia, "Will she get up and come to the table?"

"On good days yes," Olivia said. She motioned for Joanna to follow as they left the room shutting the door.

"And on bad days?"

"Let's hope you don't have to see that on your first day," Olivia replied. The door closed.

Slowly Susie turned her head to the door and a slow smile spread on her lips. Behind the vacant eyes, somewhere deep inside her mind Susie sat and waited. She smiled thinking how she was getting stronger each day. Then they would all pay for what was done to her. Betrayed by those friends who came to visit her. Betrayed even more by the one who never did. Soon they would all know the nightmare she was forced to relive each day and night. And when she unleashed it on them they would all tremble. She turned her head back to the garden and stared at the flowers that were bleeding and the trees that were drenched in blood.

CHAPTER 2

Kirsa Heinrich and Sabrina Black didn't need to be asleep to be caught in the middle of a real-life nightmare, they were currently living one. Hurricane Sandy had swept over the Garden State on Halloween leaving millions without power, the Jersey shore decimated, and many feeling grateful they were alive.

The municipal building of Grabenberg was functioning on a generator as Sabrina and Kirsa sat in on a meeting with the mayor. They were all in dirty jeans, sweatshirts, coats, and gloves. They all had barely slept in the last twenty-four hours and were running on coffee.

As Mayor Allan McCore went over the areas hit hardest, Tony placed a pin on the large town map. The door to the room opened, Ayden O'Brian and the local Were Pack leader Phil entered the room. The mayor finished his sentence and looked at the two men.

"Well?" Allan asked. He had sent Ayden and Phil on a search and rescue, hoping to get to the stranded before it was too late.

"Every house has been accounted for," Phil said as he took a coffee someone handed him. "We pulled out about twenty people from homes or cars, they are at the hospital being tended to."

"There are five deaths," Ayden said grimly. He felt Kirsa's hand lace through his. "Sara is going to work identifying them."

"Thank you," Allan said honestly. It was a job he didn't want to give anyone but one that had to be done. "How are we with shelters?"

"The ranch can take another fifty," Sabrina told them.

Her family's ranch was running off of generators, she was even camping out at the ranch because her house was without power and to conserve gas she locked up the manor and was staying with her brother in the old apartment above the ranch's vet office.

"Kirsa?" Alan inquired.

"I got newly turned were-animals and two newbie vamps on the property," Kirsa replied. "I would say only if an emergency."

"How bad was the farm hit?" one of the councilman asked.

Many of the local businesses relied on the Heinrich farm for supplies. Kirsa's was still hurting from the hours of harvesting crops with the farmers and storing them so they wouldn't lose everything.

"As of right now we lost one silo, that we were using for overflow," Kirsa informed them. "Frank is going to let me know but it looks like we were able to salvage about eighty percent of the crops."

Alan nodded. "Everyone but Kirsa and Sabrina are dismissed." The council left the room, when the last one finally left Ayden closed the door. The four took seats at the table and tried not to succumb to exhaustion. "Do you guys need anything?" Allan asked. "I know Phil is making sure his guys are patrolling to help Tony's men."

"Don't worry about us," Sabrina assured Allan. "We are fine, we have supplies and the means."

"Actually Allan," Kirsa began. "Is there anything we can do? This kind of disaster isn't in the budget."

"You two are doing enough," Alan replied. "And if I get any check of obscene amount I will know who it came from and be pissed."

"Well you're going to be pissed because you will be getting one," Kirsa warned. Allan shook his head, he wished every town had someone like them.

"We are blessed to have you both here to help with this. Your families have always been such an asset to our community, not just everyday but in times such as these."

After another few minutes, Ayden escorted the two to the car. He climbed into the driver seat and headed through the chaos. Grabenberg looked as if it was in the middle of a war zone, trees had been uprooted onto cars, homes, buildings. Wires dangled from poles snapped in half, there were no words to describe what the storm had done in the two days it battered the east coast. He had vampires in the city that were stranded, and plans were being made of getting blood to those stranded. It was a nightmare the whole thing. Ayden dropped Sabrina off at the ranch.

"I'll bring Collin over later," Sabrina told Kirsa. "We'll bring pizza."

One of the local pizza places was running on a generator and giving free pizza to anyone who came through the door.

"Sounds good," Kirsa yawned. "You can take a warm shower while you're over." Sabrina laughed.

"I am planning on it."

Ayden took the path that connected the two properties and waved to the two were-wolves who were guarding for trespassers or looters. With the construction site of the old house underway, there was plenty of things looters would want. He pulled the Durango into the garage and helped Kirsa out of the car. Looping his arm around her waist they headed back to the house.

The house was acting as an emergency shelter for the paranormal. It ran on three generators so that blood wouldn't go bad and security could stay in place. When they entered warm air hit them. The pellet stove in the living room was on when they entered through the front door. Zero was curled up asleep in front of it. Ayden headed upstairs to his office to help strategize with the council on how to get to stranded vamps who were running low on blood.

Kirsa walked through the French doors into her office. She turned her iPod dock onto Bruce Springsteen and stared at the pile of boxes that she still had to sort through. One of the ways that Kirsa dealt with the aftermath from the trial over the summer was sorting through boxes that contained her life during her college years. She had finished sorting through her grad school days, now all that was left was undergrad when Sabrina and Sara were in high school.

Letting out a sigh she pulled the top box off the stack and settled on the ground while Bruce sang about the glory days. Pulling off the lid she saw the stack of high school yearbooks that her friends insisted she buy even though she didn't go to high school. She and Sabrina could go through them tonight and have a good laugh.

Under the yearbooks were shoeboxes filled with memorabilia that had once covered her dorm walls. Kirsa had to laugh when she saw pictures of them when they were sixteen. Shaking her head she sifted through the pictures, laughing as the memories came back to her. Kirsa froze at the picture of homecoming from junior year. There were eight of them in the photo; Sabrina and the boyfriend no one liked, Sara going with Brian Black, Kirsa with Thomas Lyon and Susannah Murphy with her boyfriend.

Susannah was the tallest of the four, her hair appeared to be a sunny blonde but when you looked closely it had every color imaginable. Her eyes were a bright green rimmed in blue making them mesmerizing. She used glamour magick on her ears so they didn't appear to be pointy, the telltale sign that she was 100% Faery. Susannah was enchanting, she had a way of always getting what she wanted and had no issue using her charms to do so. Kirsa leaned against the wall and let the memories come.

****

"*You're playing with fire,*" *Kirsa warned a seventeen-year-old Susannah in the old carriage house.* "*We have a gift that shouldn't be abused.*"

Susannah laughed as she reclined on the trunk in front of the window. It was early fall, just after homecoming. Kirsa had been home for three days and had already sensed that something was wrong. Sara and Sabrina were easier to fool; trying to get anything past Kirsa was near impossible.

"*You worry too much,*" *Susannah told her.*

"*You had Ian enchanted at the dance,*" *Kirsa replied.*

This time Susannah didn't laugh. She stared at her friend unsure of how Kirsa knew what she had done. "*It was only for one night, besides what harm is one night?*"

Kirsa stared at the trees outside; they had yet to lose their leaves so they were brilliant shades of red, orange and gold. "*Susannah, you are dealing with dark magick. How do you know you broke the enchantment properly? Do you want him accidentally bound to you for eternity?*"

"*You never can relax, can you?*" *Susannah groaned.* "*Besides Ian as my personal slave has some advantages to it.*" *She saw the color drain from Kirsa's face.* "*Kirsa I'm joking. Seriously we need to get you a man.*"

Frustrated Kirsa ran her hands over her face. Sara and Sabrina didn't see the change in Susannah, but Kirsa had the moment she saw her the first day back. When she brought it up to Sabrina, Brie had told her to relax. Kirsa would be leaving for Cambridge tomorrow and wanted to make sure that Susannah could be trusted with the coven they had started at fifteen.

"Susie, we promised never to meddle in the dark, to only do what was good and right, to never use a spell for our personal gain," Kirsa reminded her.

"You know Kirsa you can be a real downer," Susannah replied her patience clearly had run dry. "Rules were meant to be broken or has Saint Kirsa never broken a rule? I bet you lie about the frat parties you go to? Why would anyone want a bore like you?"

****

Kirsa had never told Sara or Sabrina about the argument that day. It was pointless at the time and afterwards it was meaningless. The following May, Susannah had gone too far into the dark magick and paid the ultimate price. Not death, that would have been more humane.

Instead Susannah was locked in a virtual nightmare that plagued her mind twenty-four hours a day seven days a week. For twelve years she had lived in and out of mental institutions, the last ten at a private one in Pennsylvania. Susannah had gambled that her pure Fae blood would keep her safe and keep her out of harm, instead it cost her her sanity.

A year after the incident, Ian committed suicide. In his note he said he felt lost, like the one thing worth living for had vanished, leaving him alone in the world.

Later and after a long hot shower Sabrina stared at the four yearbooks that now sat on the kitchen island as if they were poison. She poured Kirsa and her both a glass of wine as she looked at the books with a dubious expression.

"Haven't we suffered enough in the last three days?"

"I wanted to share in the misery of going back down memory lane," Kirsa said with a smile. "And who better than my best buddy."

"You got the wrong one, Sara is the one that loves this shit," Sabrina replied. Sara loved everything about high school and going back down memory lane. Sabrina liked her past in the past.

Kirsa laughed. "I was thinking more of burning them later."

"We could use more timber for the large bonfire Brian has going," Sabrina commented with a laugh.

Her brother and his girlfriend had moved-in so she wouldn't be alone at the ranch with the animals and the people that she had allowed to move onto the property to use the water and limited electricity. That moved saved their lives, for a large oak took down the townhouse they had lived in.

Kirsa laughed as Ayden walked in with Colin holding three boxes of pizza. Colin had flown in from

California on a private jet that was loaded with supplies for the ravaged areas. Ayden put the pies on the island as Colin discovered the year books. He flipped one open and groaned as he saw it was from his senior year.

Colin was two years older than them and had graduated during their sophomore year; he quickly closed the cover with a groan. Ayden poured himself some wine then sat at the table watching them get their slices and wine.

"What's the big deal about yearbooks?" Ayden inquired as he looked over the covers.

"They are a permanent reminder of how awkward and uncool we actually were," Sabrina answered. "Of course, at the time we all thought we were the coolest thing ever. Now it's just an embarrassing memory that Kirsa decided to show up with tonight."

"Misery loves company," Kirsa said as she bit into a cheese pizza slice.

"Leave me out of it next time," Colin suggested. He then savored his bite of pizza as if he was in heaven.

"I would think a reminder of your youth would be refreshing and entertaining," Ayden commented. There were times when he wished he had photos of those from his youth; all he had were faded memories.

"A vampire would think that," Kirsa responded. "You would see it as a return to one's glory day. You've had centuries to come to terms with your past so it's easier to look fondly at them."

"A century and a half," Ayden corrected her with a smile.

He grabbed a book on the island and began to flip through it. Ayden began to understand mortal's unease with yearbooks as he saw candid shots of them acting foolish or trying to look as though they were doing work. The portraits, meant to be serious, were hilarious. When he looked up he saw that his three dinner companions were not amused with his reaction. He closed the book and slid it aside.

"So, Colin when do you move into your office?" Ayden asked Colin changing the conversation.

Colin was going to be the first paranormal lawyer to rent out a suite in the new OPIA headquarters in Newark. From what Al said the compound had suffered minor flooding and minimal damage. His suite was the first to be completed, there was already a waiting list for the other twelve office suites.

"I can begin to move in on Monday, once I'm settled then I can start interviewing a staff," Colin told him. "The hope is that by the New Year I'll be fully operational."

"And ready to destroy defenseless planets?" Kirsa asked with an innocent smile.

Colin looked at her and groaned as he threw a crust at her, Ayden caught it before it hit her he then handed it to Zero.

Sabrina held up a hand. "No talking in Star Wars quotes or references, I'm not ready for it."

"Well there goes our conversation," Colin said sighing for dramatic effect.

After dinner Sabrina and Kirsa settled down in her office while Colin and Ayden discussed the storm. Kirsa walked around the room. Sabrina curled up on her favorite sofa and watched Kirsa.

"You want to tell me what's bothering you?"

Kirsa took a sip of wine before answering. "I came across our junior year homecoming picture." It took a moment for Sabrina to remember the photo but when she did she understood.

"Oh."

"I never told you or Sara, but Susie and I got into a huge fight before I went back to Harvard," Kirsa confided, which caught Sabrina by surprise.

"What about?" She took a sip of wine knowing she was going to need it.

"I knew she had Ian enchanted the night of the dance," Kirsa said. She saw the look of surprise on Sabrina's face. "I didn't tell you two then because you both thought I was the one dabbling in the dark arts."

Susannah had begun planting the seeds of distrust while Kirsa was off at college; she was trying to isolate all of them.

"You're right we wouldn't have listened to you. How'd she react?"

"She exploded, told me that I was a bore, that no one wanted me, that I always played by the rules, and so on," Kirsa said sitting down in a leather chair.

Sabrina looked at Kirsa and sighed as she thought of the impact those words would have on her.

Kirsa had always followed the rules that her parents laid down. When their fifteen-year-old daughter went off to college they knew she would drink, they asked her to do so responsibly, that if she was to sleep with a man it would be responsibly. Whereas, Susannah would see rules and promises as a challenge. She always teased Kirsa by telling her she was a bore or dull.

Knowing that in that argument Susannah pulled that out, likely hurt Kirsa more than any action could. "Oh Kirsa, she never understood how you had all that freedom and never abused it," Sabrina sighed.

"I know."

"There is one thing Sara and I never understood," Sabrina began. "We were always allowed to be at the house when Vampires were here. Susannah wasn't. Why?"

"What was her reasoning?" Kirsa asked curiously.

"That your father didn't like her and it was a way to keep you two separated," Sabrina told her. "Which is very unlike your father."

"My parents weren't a big fan of hers, my dad worked with hers on the Paranormal Laws and they were friends, so he knew that they did all they could for her." Kirsa sipped her wine as she explained things to Sabrina. "The real reason was when we were thirteen and Susannah was sleeping over, a Vampire and a newbie showed up looking for refuge from the morning sun. The newbie was cute; Susannah was hitting on him and daring him to drink from her. Dad got there before it was too late and after that she could not be here if Vampires were."

But why?" Sabrina was still confused.

"Fae blood is poisonous to vampires, the purer it is the deadlier," Kirsa explained. "Taking blood from her would be death."

"Did she know that?" Sabrina asked. She didn't want to think that Susannah was conniving even at thirteen.

"She claimed that she didn't, she swore to my father she had no idea," Kirsa said.

"You have doubts though." Sabrina could hear it in her voice that she didn't believe Susannah.

"When it comes to her, Brie, I have a lot of doubts," Kirsa confided. "There are times I wonder if I should have left her there."

"It would have destroyed you Kirsa, if you left her there," Sabrina told her. "We were seventeen and scared shitless by what she did. You brought her Back alive."

CHAPTER 3

A few days later, Kirsa sat in her office at OPIA, the Occult and Paranormal Investigation Agency. In October the UN had officially named her Assistant Director of OPIA despite her not wanting the position. However, telling the UN no was not easy and now once a week she came to headquarters to sort through paperwork and annoy Al, which the only plus to the job.

The other plus was their offices were next to each other with a pass-through window. She had been known to make faces at him through the window when he had his blinds up. However, at the moment Al was pacing back and forth in her office. She swiveled back and forth in her chair watching him, her clear violet eyes studying how tense he was.

"Are you going to talk to me or are you going to wear a path in my carpet?" Kirsa asked leaning back in her leather desk chair.

"What's the status on Murphy?" Al asked flopping into one of guest chairs.

Kirsa was caught off guard by the question. It took her a moment to recover from the shock of it, the only time they discussed Susannah was if she had a psychotic episode at the hospital. Kirsa knew she had not since she had been on the phone with hospital earlier that morning.

"She is in somewhat of a vegetative state," Kirsa answered, her voice neutral. "She still screams sometimes at night, her brain waves are below normal, and no one has slipped her any medicine in about six months so no psychotic episodes. Why?"

"When was her last one?"

Kirsa had to think. "The last one I was called for one was while I was still in Germany," she replied. "Why?"

"Frank handed me a stack of folders the other day," Al began. "He saw a pattern but couldn't place his finger on it."

"That's rare," Kirsa replied.

Agent Frank Willis had an uncanny ability to connect the dots in cases no matter how obscure they were. He was often given the tougher cases to solve because of his ability.

"That's why I agreed to take a look," Al told her. "The four that he gave me occurred in a little over a year. Starting from last Halloween and the last known case this summer."

"I hate when you use phrases like 'last known case'," Kirsa informed him. "What are they about?"

"Four teenagers all about the same age, from different states, different religious backgrounds and family backgrounds," Al explained. "All four end up performing an unknown ritual to heighten their third eye or to gain more power, all four ended up being followed by demons and plagued by nightmares."

Kirsa felt her blood go cold as she took the information in. "You can't give me them."

"Kirs, you're my best demon expert." He hated asking her to do this.

"I'm a lot of experts for you," she pointed out. Sometimes being a genius was not fun especially when one had numerous degrees to go with it.

"Yes and Agent Willis says in his notes he feels you are the only one that can solve these cases."

"What else is in these files?" Kirsa asked raising an eyebrow. She did not like where this was going. "Is this going to be like the phone call I got in Germany that made me come back here because a crazed cult was killing people in my hometown? Because if it is, it's getting old."

"You would have been furious if I brought the Church of Light down without you," Al pointed out.

He was thrilled that the case was done and over with and the Church of Light had collapsed and Kirsa was now safe from the lunatics who had killed almost all of her family. She hated that he was right, even if she still had the scars from the summer.

"Alright, what are in the four files?"

"None of the four teens knew they were calling forth a demon by performing the ceremony. They also won't tell any adult what ritual they performed. The only thing Frank was able to get, was a friend of victim number three said that the ritual apparently came out of a dream."

"And you automatically jump to Susannah as a suspect?" Kirsa went back to swiveling in her chair as she thought about what he said. "That's quite a leap even for you."

"She's been known to mess with dreams and demons," Al reminded her. He got a glare from Kirsa. "And possession, she's big into possession."

Kirsa ignored him. "A demon can only take possession of a body if the body is a willing host, if the body isn't willing it kicks the demon out."

"Then why were the teens followed out of the astral plane by one?"

29

"Simple. The demon wants to know why he was summoned and who is trying to get out of making their payment," Kirsa told him. There was always payment when a demon was called from the demon realm to the realm of mortals. "The demon is hoping the teen will lead them to the person."

"Can Demons enter the dream realm?" Al asked. Al knew how demos of the fae world worked but demons outside of that realm, he was unsure of.

"No, there is something about the dream realm that does not allow demons to enter," Kirsa answered. "So, whoever is giving out the ritual in the teenager's dreams is not a demon."

"Kirsa you know I wouldn't be asking you this if I didn't need you," Al pleaded.

"You will owe me huge if I agree to do this," she warned him narrowing her violet eyes at him.

"I know."

"No, I don't think you do this time," Kirsa said. She finally let out a long sigh. "I want the files to review before I make a decision. Is Frank working on a case at the moment?"

Al laughed at the last part. From September until November First, OPIA was insanely busy. Once Halloween was over, they were quiet until Yule arrived. Which gave them the breathing room to help out with the mess from Sandy.

"He just finished a minor pixie case, why?"

"I want him to go through cold cases in the last ten years and see if there are any that fit the pattern of these four."

"You think there are more that might have slipped through the cracks?"

"It's a possibility." Kirsa tapped a pen on her foot. "You weren't head of OPIA ten years ago. You became head right before South Carolina, so gods know what the old head tossed."

The case in South Carolina was their first case that dealt with the Church of Light. It occurred around the same time she lost both her parents and aunt and uncle. On top of that the former head was an utter moron.

"How soon can you let me know?" Al asked her.

"Give me to Friday to go over the files and make a decision," Kirsa told him.

"I can do that," Al assured her. "Where's Irish?"

"Eileen Brewster needed him to scare some rookies," Kirsa explained.

Eileen was one of the best teachers at OPIA. She had been a field agent up until the new headquarters opened up; Eileen had been offered a position as head instructor for the OPIA Academy. This meant she lived on campus, as a recent widow with two grown children she jumped at the opportunity.

Al laughed at the thought of Ayden going up against some unsuspecting recruits. He didn't look or act like the stereotype of a Vampire. However, when provoked Ayden could become scarier than any stereotype, than any literary interpretation of his kind.

"When is Irish going to stop sending me boxes of Lucky Charms?"

"When are you going to stop sending me Queen of the Damned related stuff?" Kirsa retorted.

"Fair enough." Al laughed. "I got your last medical report."

"What did you think of it?" Kirsa asked.

Kirsa suffered from a rare blood disorder, so rare that it only ran in her family. They had only recently discovered why it only affected her family. Over a thousand years ago an ancestor married and had two children with the head of the sixth bloodline. In their two children was a blended DNA that contained the original vampire DNA mixed with humans. It created a disorder that plagued the line, most died from it before it took full effect.

With modern medicine they were able to control the disorder to an extent. The disorder was slowly changing Kirsa into a vampire; the only problem was that when it finally kicked in she could die from the change. For the moment it was being controlled with use of blood.

"Still stable since Lars," Kirsa replied.

"I have actually cut back on the blood dosage."

"I saw, any idea why?"

"Finn is wondering if it's because of the blood transfusion I received at the hospital," Kirsa said. She failed to mention the other theory.

She had been held prisoner by her former bodyguard, along with her friend Sara. Knowing Kirsa was dying from blood loss and poisoning, Sara was a were-tiger and made Kirsa drink her blood. Dr. Finn believed that the blood was helping keep her disorder calm for the moment.

"Why don't we go check on the class, meanwhile I'll have Frank get the files together for you."

Kirsa nodded as she got out from behind her desk. She smoothed out her black pencil skirt and slipped her blood red heels on. They both shrugged into their suit jackets and attached their id badges back on before heading onto the floor.

Agents were talking with one another and joking around, November was a slow month, a reprieve from the craziness of October and Halloween. Some waved as the two walked toward the back elevators. Swiping his id card the doors opened and he punched the button for cellar.

The training rooms were in building B, but all four buildings were connected by the underground parking lot. Two agents met them at security and escorted them through the garage to building B.

"I take it they are for my own protection?" Kirsa asked.

"I have no clue what you're talking about," Al said trying to sound oblivious to the question.

"Just like the other vampire and numerous were's I smell are just a coincidence not heightened security since the media got wind of me being head of the Sixth Line," Kirsa pointed out.

When she had brought her suspicion to Ayden he pretended to not understand the question. Dietrich changed the topic, so she let them think she didn't know they hired more security. Just like she didn't tell them that in the basement of the mansion she and Tom redid the plan to add an apartment that would be attached to the security room.

Al ignored her and checked the training schedule on the wall to see where Eileen was, they headed down the hall that lead to one of the simulation rooms. Instead of entering the room, they went into the observation room and watched through the one-way mirror.

Eileen stood leaning against the one wall; while the class of fifteen listened to Ayden discuss Vampires. Kirsa immediately picked out the trouble maker; he was in the back whispering to one of the students trying to pay attention. He was tall with dark hair, his clothes were expensive and he wore a Rolex.

"I'm going to take wild guess and say that the Mercedes two door is his," Kirsa said.

"Justin Wembly the Third," Al said growing. "Son of a Senator from Virginia. Old money there."

"He knows we pay shit, right?"

"He knows," Al replied. "He also detests all things paranormal."

"Why'd you hire him?" Kirsa asked.

There had to be a reason because under normal circumstances the kid wouldn't have made it past the interview.

"Because his daddy called me and warned me that his son was applying, he told me to accept him and to teach the kid a lesson," Al replied.

"Wait the Senator knows his son is a dick?" Kirsa had heard horror stories about this kid from Eileen.

"The mother spoils him; Daddy is hoping this will show him that money can't buy everything."

"Oh, this is going to be good," Kirsa said laughing.

Both her and Sabrina had come from money. Neither needed to work a day in their life if they didn't want to. But they had been taught that their position was a responsibility. That though they could live a lavish lifestyle they must also help those in need, to give back to the community. To be leaders. It drove Kirsa crazy when those with money chose the lazy road.

Ayden stood in front of the room talking to the class about what to do if they went up against a rogue vampire.

"You won't be able to beat them in strength no matter how young or old they are," he warned. "That being said, we all have weaknesses. The key is not to make us aware of what you are going to do, our reaction time is quicker than yours."

"What do you suggest?" A student called out.

"Pretend you are going to do one thing and as we react to that movement change your plan of attack," Ayden answered. "Fighting any supernatural being requires you to think and plan ahead while being attacked."

Ayden heard the whisper and had enough of it. "Wembly, do you have something you'd like to add?"

Justin looked at the Vampire with a smirk on his face. "No sir."

"Really?" Ayden asked leaning against the whiteboard. "Because I could have sworn you just said that you could take a vampire with your eyes closed."

Justin blinked at Ayden, he had said those exact words to the guy standing next to him. Ayden smiled. "What they say about our hearing is true," Ayden warned. "Agent Brewster may I use Mr. Wembly as demonstration?"

Eileen tried to keep from smiling. "Go right ahead O'Brian."

"Come here Wembly," Ayden instructed. He slid out of his charcoal suit jacket and rolled up the sleeves of his shirt.

Justin tried not to look nervous as he walked to the front of the room. There were snickers behind him making him furious that people would talk about him behind his back. Eileen pushed herself off the wall and grabbed a box that contained scenarios for students to work with. She pulled one out of the boxes and read it off.

"Wembly, you have been called to a crime scene where a rogue vampire has drained a woman. While at the scene you discover the perpetrator of the crime is still at the scene. When you confront him on your own he becomes hostile."

She looked at the two men. "Do either of you have any questions?" she asked. They both shook their heads. "Good. You start Wembly. Ayden try to keep the blood loss and property damage to a minimal."

"I'll try," Ayden promised with a smile. "Remember I am still considered a young vampire, the older one is the stronger and faster they are."

Eileen motioned for the class to move back a good way, keeping lots of floor space empty for Ayden. She nodded when it was time for Wembly to start and grabbed an evaluation clipboard. Trying to compose himself, Wembly took a deep breath.

"Sir, I have to ask you to come with me to headquarters."

"Why?" Ayden asked lounging against the wall.

He was unaware of his effect on the females in the class as he observed Justin's behavior and movements.

"I believe you have information about what happened tonight," Justin said.

"I don't."

Justin stared at him. "I would still like to talk to you."

Ayden could smell that he was getting frustrated. "Well I don't want to talk to you."

Ayden turned to walk away knowing what Justin was going to do and just as Justin went to lay a hand on his shoulder, Ayden grabbed his wrist and flung Justin to the floor. Justin scrambled to his feet, glaring at the vampire.

"You just assaulted a federal agent," Justin stammered.

Kirsa and Al watched from the viewing room as Ayden half-heartedly broke each of Justin's attempts to get the upper hand. To the human eye, Ayden was moving fast enough that all one saw was a blur of motion. When Justin was curled in a ball bleeding from his nose and a gash on his forehead, Al and Kirsa stepped out into the classroom.

The class turned as the two heads walked to the head of the room. Al put his hand down to help Justin up but the kid refused and instead tried to get up on his own. When the world started to spin, Justin instead sat up and leaned against the wall.

"He broke my fucking nose," Justin yelled as Eileen handed him a cold compress for it.

"You're lucky this was a simulation," Kirsa responded. "Because, in the real world you'd be fucking dead along with that broken nose."

"Oh really, and what did I do wrong?" Justin challenged as he tried to stop the bleeding.

"You never approach a Vampire or any paranormal alone, especially a rogue," One of the students replied.

"You also never lay a hand on a predator for it sets off their hunting reaction," another chimed in.

"You certainly never give them an option to come in for questioning," Kirsa added. "You tell them you are taking them in for questioning."

"You think you know everything just because you're one of those freaks," Justin shouted at Kirsa. He clenched his fist and stepped toward her, Ayden moved in front of Kirsa blocking her.

"Wembly you are on very thin ice," Al warned. "I suggest going to the medical wing to get that nose checked out before you continue this thought track."

"Just wait until my dad hears about this, he's a senator," Justin warned. "He'll see you out of here."

Kirsa raised an eyebrow. "I was appointed by the UN, not Congress."

Once Justin left, Eileen blew a whistle. "Alright everyone show is over back to training," she yelled. "O'Brian, I think you made our point. Thank you."

"I can't take you anywhere can I?" Kirsa joked as they headed out of the training room.

"No, you really can't," Ayden agreed laughing.

****

It was later in the day after Kirsa had retrieved all the files they needed that her and Ayden finally headed home. Kirsa leaned her head back against the headrest of the car; Ayden drove as they headed back to Grabenberg. *Type O Negative* was playing on the stereo; Ayden was drumming along to it on the steering wheel as he guided the car through traffic.

Kirsa shook her head as she tried to keep the headache from exploding.

"You alright?" Ayden asked as he turned the music down.

"Headache," Kirsa responded.

"You're not worried about Wembly's father are you?"

Kirsa laughed at that. "Gods no, his dad had Al accept him only so the kid could fail. He knows his son needs a reality check. He got one today."

"How'd the discussion go with him?"

After the medical team assessed Justin's nose he was escorted up to Al's office for a closed-door meeting with Al and Kirsa.

"We went over comments from his instructors, we then told him how lucky he was that you're a good guy because he could have been killed," Kirsa told him. "When that didn't work we showed him video of a true vampire attack. He threw up then handed in his resignation from the academy."

"He would have been a horrible agent," Ayden replied.

"Trust me, we know. He's arrogant, full of it, not a team player, and hates the paranormal," Kirsa said. "He is everything we don't want in an agent."

"What else did Al want?" Ayden asked. He could tell she was distracted.

"He handed me an impossible case." She sighed as she stretched out her legs. "I need to review the files and see if I can do anything with them. I'm not looking forward to it."

"How come?"

"It deals with demons, teenagers, and the dream realm."

Ayden let out a whistle. "Three things that should never be put together."

"Exactly."

CHAPTER 4

Kirsa shut herself into her home office on Friday morning; she turned her phone on silent and made sure that Ayden was still asleep. She had been putting off going over the case files, but now she had no other excuses, there was nothing else to keep her from doing it. With *Halestorm* on as background music, Kirsa opened the first file along with her laptop so she could input her own thoughts and ideas.

Victim's name is Alexander Jones, age at time of incident 16. Lives in Danvers, Massachusetts. Parents began to notice bizarre behavior around the autumn equinox of last year, he refused to leave the house, when he did he would scream about demons. Parents contacted head of coven he belonged to.

Victoria Winslow agreed something was wrong, his friends would say nothing except that a spell went wrong. OPIA contacted in March of this year. I talked to the parents and victim, Alex won't discuss what happened. Claims there are demons after him, a parapsychologist came to the house and told his parents that he was crazy. They and I agree the para-psychologist was wrong, would like a consultation with Heinrich if she comes back to the states.

The kid is scared out of his mind, I doubt this is a mental illness, truly believe that he thinks demons are after him. Why?

Kirsa went through the rest of the file which was comprised of the interview summaries with the victim and several others. The adults were all in agreement that the teenagers were hiding something. From the interviews with the four students, she agreed that they were deliberately leaving parts out of their story. Opening up the second folder Kirsa began to read.

Victim's name is Mora Anderson. Age at time of incident 17. Lives in Mount Washington area of Pittsburg. Parents are Wiccan, older brother and her raised Wiccan. Warned to stay away from the dark stuff. (Ouija boards, oracle cards, etc.) From talking to her friend Jessica, the incident occurred shortly after Yule, Mora performed a ritual to strengthen her psychic eye, Jessica knew something went wrong when the whole room filled with the scent of brimstone. She quickly casted a larger circle to protect her friend and her, Mora was unconscious at this point. When she comes too she sees demons everywhere.

One-week later Jessica brought her to her Catholic church where Mora has stayed since then. She will not speak of what happened and does not know what Jessica has told us.

This seems similar to the case in Massachusetts.

Victims Name is Kristina Devons and is from the outskirts of Pittsburg, she is 16 at the time of the incident. She is the only child of two very strict parents, have been informed that her father and she do not get along and are often fighting. Grandmother tries to intervene but is voiceless against the father.

Caroline Wilson, friend of Kristina, has given basic information on what happened. They were hanging with a group of friends and decided to use a Ouija board. Their account claims that while trying to commune with the dead an evil spirit hopped on and possessed Kristina. Father committed her to a psychiatric facility after a blessing from the family priest failed.

There is more to this story, thankfully the hospital she is at is run by Kesler who agrees that she and her friends are hiding information. Again, I believe this is related to the other two cases. All are seeing demons after some spell or ritual backfired.

Victims name is Delilah Bartoli, she is 17. Incident occurred this July. She is of Gypsy descent. Decided to dabble in Gypsy magick because of her heritage, comes across a ritual in a book on Gypsy Spells that will increase her psychic awareness, according to friends something goes wrong and when it is over she sees demons. One in particular named Narl.

Delilah's mother, Sophia, summons her mother to help. The grandmother knows a bit of the old magick and is able to help keep the demon at bay, but it is not a permanent fix. We know she is hiding something, the grandmother agrees.

Truly believe all four cases are linked. Hoping that Moore will pass them onto Heinrich for she is the only one that will do this case justice.

Kirsa closed the last file and leaned back in her chair. Frank and Al were right there were definite connections between all four of the teenagers. Three of the four had been practicing the occult while the fourth did it as a form of rebellion which made her a wild card. She texted Al that she was done and wanted to talk about the case then sat back and tried to think. Kirsa picked up her office phone and hit the button for the Black Rose Ranch. Sabrina picked up after the first ring.

"What's up?" Sabrina asked.

It was unusual for Kirsa to call before noon. Her brother sat across from her watching.

"Who has the box from high school that contains the books from our coven?" Kirsa asked.

Sabrina was somewhat surprised by the question and had to think for a minute. "I think I ended up with it. Why?"

"Is there a way to find out?"

"It entails a journey through the attic, but I can check it out, why?" Sabrina asked again. Brian raised an eyebrow; their attic was filled with four generations of crap.

"Al handed me a case and some of the things in the box might come in handy."

"Some of the things or one thing in particular?"

"I need her book of spells."

There was silence for a minute as Sabrina collected her thoughts. "You and Al don't think she's active, do you?"

"I don't know at this point but these cases that he handed me sound like something she would do and has done before, it's going to be hard ignoring her as a suspect completely."

"Have you ever told Ayden about it?" Sabrina inquired.

She wasn't sure how one went about explaining that they took a trip to hell to bring back their friend. Then for that friend's mind to be completely shattered because of the horrors they saw and still see.

"No," Kirsa replied. It was a hard thing to explain to someone who wasn't there. For them to understand that what you were telling them was true and that you were not the one who was insane.

"How soon do you need the box?"

"It's not immediate but at some point, in the near future."

They talked for a few more minutes before hanging up. Brian looked across at his sister, he could tell something was wrong.

"What's up?" he asked his sister.

Now that power was back on, she had moved back into the main house. However, Emily and he had decided after the insurance was settled of moving into the vet apartment permanently.

"Kirsa wants me to hunt down Susannah's book of spells," Sabrina replied.

Brian let out a whistle. "That was not what I expected. Why?"

"There's a case that parallels with what Susie did, she wants it to better understand the case," Sabrina lied. He knew she was lying but he let it go.

"If you need help let me know, parent teacher conferences are next week so I'll be bored those nights."

"Alright," Sabrina said.

"Now back to before she called," Brian said. He watched her eyes darken. "You're not seriously thinking of seeing him are you?"

"Aren't you the least bit curious as to why Anton wants to see me?" Sabrina asked her brother.

In the entire time that their older brother had been in prison he had never once wanted to see any of them.

"No, I'm honestly not interested in what that asshole wants," Brian said crossing his arms over the chest. "He can rot in that cell for all I care."

"He is our brother."

"He stopped being our brother when he killed Kirsa's parents," Brian replied. "Besides when did you get all compassionate?"

Sabrina shrugged her shoulders. Lately she felt like she was suffocating in all her bad judgments and mistakes. Her dreams were disturbing, and sleep wasn't coming easy.

"I guess I'm curious as to why he wants to talk now."

"Probably because our name has been in the media due to what happened over the summer," Brian replied. "Look, Brie I don't like it. I think it's a bad idea and I don't think you should go."

Sabrina nodded. Part of her knew Brian was right, but another part wasn't sure anymore. Lars had shattered her self-confidence and judgment when he betrayed all of them and turned out to be the Head of the Church of Light.Maybe she needed to go back and try and figure things out, that meant talking to her older brother to try and understand how he could become a cold-blooded killer.

CHAPTER 5

Ayden hadn't seen Kirsa since she slipped out of bed earlier in the morning; he knew she was bothered by something. And with life beginning to return to normal he knew it wasn't making schedules with the mayor for warming stations and shower usage. He was pretty certain it had to do with the case that Al had handed her on Wednesday. After sending his own emails o he closed his lap top and headed downstairs. He refilled his mug with fresh blood then followed the music to Kirsa's office.

Godsmack was on, and she was tapping her foot in time while she was making notes. Ayden knocked on the door and entered. He noticed the picture of homecoming hanging up; he studied it before sitting down.

"Two questions: Your parents let you dye your hair purple? And who's the Faery?" Ayden asked.

"They didn't have a choice, I came home with it dyed purple," Kirsa replied, she remembered they weren't pleased but said nothing. "And the Faery is an old friend of mine, Sara and Sabrina's."

"Do I know her?" Ayden asked.

It was odd not knowing someone from Kirsa's past. He knew most of the people that had been in her life so it was strange that there was someone he didn't recognize. The Faery hadn't been at the funerals, nor at the trial. He also couldn't place her at any functions he'd been to at Kirsa's parents house.

"She wasn't allowed over when Vampires were at the house."

Kirsa closed the files she had been reading and pushed it aside. She couldn't help but smile when she looked at Ayden. He was gorgeous, tall, strong and Irish.

Ayden arched an eyebrow at her waiting for more information. While Kirsa was more open with him there were times where getting information from her was hard.

"How did you know she was Fae?" Kirsa asked not wanting to get into why Susannah wasn't allowed at the house when Vampires were over.

"Because I can see her shimmer in the photo," Ayden replied. "She must be close if not 100% Fae."

"She is, her family has ties to the royal court," Kirsa said.

Her coffee mug sat empty, there wasn't enough caffeine in the world that would make her eager to discuss Susannah. Ayden poured some of his contents into her mug.

"Aww, we're sharing blood now."

Ayden's mug paused on its way to his mouth as so, something she had said just clicked. He narrowed his eyes and looked at her. "What do you mean she wasn't allowed over when a Vampire was here?"

Kirsa sighed. Vampires liked to know even the most minor bit of information, they also tended to overanalyze everything. Not that this was minor information, she just didn't want to get into it.

"She stayed over one night when there was a new vampire," she explained. "She flirted with him and offered her blood, Dad got there in time to stop the vampire from drinking from her. The vampire was so new that he couldn't control his thirst when she offered. It was close though after that she was banned from the house."

"What's her name?"

A Fae offering blood to a vampire was a death sentence in the fae court and vampire court.
"Susannah Murphy."

Ayden looked at Kirsa with surprise; now he understood why she was still alive. "Hugh Murphy's middle child?"

Kirsa nodded. "He and dad worked together on the paranormal laws; that's how Susie and I met."

"Isn't she really ill and in some kind of hospice care?" Ayden inquired.

There were other darker rumors about Susannah, that all the shit she caused finally caught up with her. It was a shame because the Murphy's were well known and well liked.

"I don't know, I lost touch with her after she graduated high school." Kirsa did not want to get into what had happened to Susie right now.

Kirsa needed time to figure out how she was going explain it all to him, she had never had to tell anyone before. Everyone who knew was there when it happened or was there during the aftermath.

Ayden watched her for a moment. This was one of the few times Kirsa actually lied to him. With their mental link, it was even clearer when she did lie or tried to avoid a conversation. He didn't call her out on it because he could tell that she didn't want to discuss the Faery anymore so instead he switched over to the cases that Al handed her on Wednesday. He knew she had been avoiding reading them, but it seemed as if she finally had gotten to them.

"You read the cases?" Ayden asked changing the subject. He could hear her mental sigh of relief.

"Just finished," Kirsa told him. "Frank and Al are right, they're all linked. The only clue is from a friend to one of the victims. She said the victim got the ritual from a dream, which seems to confirm everyone's suspicions."

"It has never been a good idea to do a ritual that was given to you in a dream," Ayden pointed out. "Too many creatures have access to our minds when we sleep."

"But not demons, and that's the common thread," Kirsa pointed out.

"Now you have my attention."

"Fae creatures can walk through the dream world like it's nothing, but a demon can't," Kirsa explained. "There is something about the state of our minds when we are dreaming that prohibits demons from entering."

"So then how did demons get connected to the case?" Ayden asked confused.

"After the rituals were performed the teens believed they had fail," Kirsa explained. "Within forty eight hours of rituals is when the demons show up."

"That's odd behavior for a demon, they're more into the possession and domination then stalking."

"Unless the victims unknowingly summoned the demon and now the demon wants to know who is trying to get out of payment," Kirsa replied.

"There is that," Ayden agreed. "And a demon would be furious if someone tried to get out of that, pissed enough to stalk a teenager to find out the source."

"Only I have a feeling the four don't know who the source is," Kirsa said. "Or understand why they have a demon stalking them."

"Which leaves four vulnerable teenagers and four demons that are going to lose patience and try something else to get their payment, not a pleasant situation."

"Precisely."

"You never get handed easy cases, do you?" Ayden inquired.

"No, I don't, which is kind of getting old. Just once I would like a case that involves a were-cat stuck up a tree."

Ayden burst out laughing at the image of Phil stuck up a tree. "Please take me on that call."

She flashed a quick grin. "Anything I need to sign off on or give approval on?"

Ayden and Wyrm were acting as her voice with the council until they figured out the political ramifications of her being head of a sixth line and not being a vampire quite yet. The set up was fine with

Kirsa because it allowed her to focus on the eighteen million projects that she had going on.

"Switching gears, what's your stance on the Russian group that wants to defect?" Ayden asked.

There was a small group of Russian Vampires that wanted to break away and form their own colony. The inner council agreed, only if it was an area in Siberia, that every three months they would be checked on for the first ten years, no humans could be turned unless by council decree and no blood draining. The outer council approved the proposal, but the group declined it, it was either all or nothing.

"They can't be left on their own without any involvement from the council, if they truly want this then they will have to come up with a compromise," Kirsa replied.

"What would you suggest?"

"How about checking into our Caribbean holdings, see if there is an uninhabited island we can send them too, where they can literally start their own colony. Arrangements can be made to deliver blood and supplies, but they have to agree to the Council checking in on them, and no blood draining."

"The Caribbean is worse than Siberia," Ayden pointed out. As soon as he said it he realized what she was doing. "Which is what you want, you want them to see that there are worse places we could send them."

"Exactly. Anything else?"

"They want your date for your coronation ball."

"Ugh," Kirsa groaned. "Tell them that by Yule I will have several dates to run by them."

"It's been two centuries since there was a new head of house, and not just that, but you are the first to sit in the sixth seat so it's a big deal."

"I know and vampires like their ceremonies," Kirsa replied. "Alright go you're distracting me."

Ayden laughed as he left the room after kissing her quick first. They both worked for the remainder of the day.

****

Ayden joined her in the kitchen while she was getting dinner ready after dealing with the Council. They both paused when they heard the sound of a car pulling into the drive. Ayden raised a questioning eyebrow at Kirsa; she wiped her hands off on a kitchen towel.

"Make sure it doesn't boil," she instructed.

Kirsa headed toward the front door and opened it up. She caught a strong whiff of Fae as the car door opened, smiling when Al climbed out of his car. He looked tired, more so than when she saw him a few days ago. Al was in a pinstripe suit with a black dress shirt and a clover pin on the lapel. He headed toward her with his hands in his pockets.

As he got closer she realized the meaning of the pin, Al had been in the fae realm, which explained why she hadn't been able to get a hold of him.

"Ayden break out the honey wine," Kirsa called toward the back of the house.

"Do I look that bad?" Al asked as Kirsa gave him a hug.

For some reason honey wine helped with the effects of the fae realm, Ayden once explained it to them but Al and Kirsa were on to their second bottle by that point. They had rescued a human baby from becoming a changeling, drank two bottles to celebrate getting the child back unharmed and to forget the horrors they saw. Not every place in Faery was nice and inviting. Not every place was that of faery tales, the fae had their own demons.

"No, I could smell the Fae on you." Kirsa shut the door and hung up his trench coat.

They headed back toward the kitchen where Zero was eating his dinner and Ayden was opening one of the bottles of honey wine. His nostrils flared when Al came in the room. The scent of the Fae was like smelling nature in its most perfect form.

"What smells so good?" Al asked as he accepted a glass from Ayden.

"Goulash," Kirsa answered.

She went over to the stove and drained the noodles before pouring them into a bowl. Al sat at the breakfast table and watched as the two worked in unison to finish dinner, he sipped his wine and sighed as it washed away the aftertaste of the Fae Realm. He let the golden liquid warm him up and relax him for the first time all day.

Instead of dwelling on his problems he focused on Kirsa and Ayden. He liked watching them like this, doing domestic things around the house. Kirsa was one of the few people that he trusted. They were friends and close ones at that. After what they went through during the summer: the murders, her being held captive and her injuries, it had only brought them closer.

Kirsa set the noodles down on the table as Ayden brought the red cast iron Dutch oven over. Al noticed that Ayden took a small portion of the beef and vegetable stew. Most vampires, to be polite, would sample food. They didn't need it for nourishment but considered it rude not to taste what had been prepared.

Kirsa waited until Al had a few spoonfuls before she asked, "Do you want to talk about it?"

"I got the call at about two this morning, which is why I didn't answer any of your calls," Al told her.

It was also why he didn't ask her to come with him, he knew she would have. Just as he had dropped everything to be at the funerals for her parents, she would have left her bed at an ungodly hour and traveled to Fae with him.

"They made a decision then?" Kirsa inquired.

She was referring to the Fae court. The realm of the Fae consisted of five courts: Earth, Air, Water, Fire, and the Royal court. Within each of the elemental courts there was a head for each of the different creatures, or houses. Each head made up the ruling body for that element. All of the elemental courts took orders from the Royal Court, or the Tuatha Dé Danann.

Al was a leprechaun; his family was the head of the house for the Leprechauns. The problem was his father had died five years ago, Al's older brother, who should have been the new head, had severe brain damage from being poisoned with iron shortly after their dad died. Since Leprechauns were only male, it meant the next male would inherit the title.

What added to the situation, was that Al's uncle was trying to claim the title. For four years the Fae courts had been dealing with trying to find out who the poisoner was and who in fact was the rightful heir. Al drank a large mouthful of wine before talking again.

"My uncle was found guilty with the murder of my father and attempted murder of my brother," Al began. "He believed that if my brother was out of the way then he would be next in line."

Kirsa stared at him, shocked by the news. "How did that come about?"

"My aunt actually, she handed over his journals and papers without him knowing," Al told her. "That came out after they made me Head of the Leprechauns."

Ayden let out a whistle. "That's rough."

"Not as rough as their plans for my uncle," Al laughed bitterly. "My brother-in-law will act as my physical representation since the five courts agreed that my position at OPIA is too important to leave. They will open a portal for me when I am needed, though once a month I need to go there for official court business."

"How are your mom and sister doing?" Kirsa asked. She had met them at his father's funeral; Kirsa had been given permission to enter the Fae to attend.

"Relieved honestly," Al said. "They are just glad that it's over and they can try to return to normal."

"Is your mom a Faery?" Ayden asked.

"No, she's human," Al responded. He saw the surprise in Ayden's face. Usually the ruling family had to marry a fae. "Leprechauns and Banshees are allowed to marry humans because the line runs pure in the male for Leprechauns and the female for Banshees. It doesn't matter if the other partner is human or not."

"That makes sense then," Ayden answered.

"So, what did you think about the cases?" Al asked abruptly changing the topic.

"That I hate both you and Frank," Kirsa replied. She heard Al's snort of laughter and was glad. "They're definitely connected. I'm going to want to reinterview everyone."

"I have Frank going through our cold cases for the last ten years to see if there are any that slipped past our radar."

"I'll start making the phone calls on Monday and begin setting up interviews," Kirsa promised.

After that they talked about what was going on in the news, what movies were out and everyday things. When dinner was over Kirsa refilled her and Al's wine glasses as Ayden went upstairs to call into the inner council meeting. Al wandered around the living room and her office as she sat on the couch sipping the wine. Zero was curled up next to her, snoring.

"I saw Patrick before I left," Al replied.

It was always hard to see his brother who was forty because now he was more like an adolescent. His sister Brianna went with him to see him, but it was still hard.

"How was he?" Kirsa asked.

Al had the Fae healers send Kirsa his brother's file whenever they updated it she could explain it to his mother in a more gentle way.

"Happy to see me," Al said with a sad smile. "We went to the cafeteria for ice cream which made his day. He was confused about dad but understood that I was head of the house. He knows something happened to him that made him like this. We decided not to tell him about our Uncle, he doesn't need to know and most likely wouldn't understand why."

"Sara went to see Susannah back in September, she wanted to let her know we were both fine," Kirsa told Al. He raised an eyebrow at her. "I doubt Susannah was even aware of what happened to us, but it made Sara feel better. I think in your case Brianna and you are right not to tell him. He won't comprehend why his Uncle would kill his father and then try to kill him, it will confuse him more than anything else."

"I can only imagine Sara's conversation with Susannah," Al said almost laughing. Whenever he saw his brother he reminded himself that it could be worse, a lot worse.

"Very one-sided," Kirsa surmised.

"Do you ever go visit her?" Al inquired as he stared at the homecoming picture. Kirsa let out a laugh at the question.

"Not unless I have to as a medical professional." Susannah was the only patient that she saw as a Parapsychologist. "And even then, it's with extreme caution."

"Why?" Al asked.

"The last time I was called in to evaluate her, she had been in a coma like state for four days," Kirsa told him. "I flew in from Germany to do the consultation. I touched her and was transported into her nightmare."

Al stared at her. "God Kirsa, you mean after all this time she still hates you?"

"Apparently. I know Sara and Sabrina visit her, they can touch her and they are fine. Her family visits her once a week." Kirsa stared at him surprised that he knew that.

Al turned and looked at her. "I get copies of her visitor logs once a month," Al informed her.

"You really do think she's potentially behind all this," Kirsa said amazed. "You give her a lot more credit than I do."

"She broke a cardinal Fae law, and the only reason she is not in a Fae prison is that no innocent's were harmed," Al reminded her. "And what was done to her was a more fitting punishment than the Fae could have handed out."

Each faery court had its demons: trows, phookas, Goblins, boggarts, drakes and more. Being that they had their own demons to summon, it was forbidden for any Fae to summon a Demon from another realm. There were two main reasons for this; a fae was bound to its court so to summon a demon from another realm would put that entire court at risk of being bound to the demon when payment came.

The other reason was that a Fae was an elemental creature, they were from nature, they saw the beauty and ugliness of what nature can do. Demons from other realms were created out of hate, revenge, and greed. They lived in realms that were living nightmares, nothing created from nature. If a Fae was to enter one of these realms their mind would not be able to grasp what it was seeing, it would end up with breaking the mind. In Al's case, he was half and half, his human mother allowed his mind to grasp the concept making him safe when having to deal with demon realms. But a pure Fae did not have that protection.

"She always figured her pure blood would keep her safe from everything," Kirsa said sighing.

"How do you figure?" Al asked. Being of Fae blood he knew the power that went with it.

"She always saw it as a privilege, that she was special because she was not just fae but of the royal court," Kirsa explained. "When she learned that her blood was poison to vampires I think she felt like that meant it would protect her from danger."

"I don't get it, it's not like Hugh and Evegren were irresponsible parents, they always stressed the importance of duty and responsibility," Al said.

He had dated the oldest of the three daughters, Titania, but Susannah had caused a wedge between them, making them walk away from each other.

"Susie always felt that rules were made in order to be broken, that there was an exception to every rule. In the end, it did her in."

"Are you going to be alright working this case?" Al asked her now concerned about bringing her in.

Kirsa was silent. Susannah had been moved to her current facility ten years ago after she had caused Kirsa, Sara, and Sabrina to fall into an unconscious state. It had taken everything that Hagan and Hugh had at their disposal to get the three girls out without causing them serious harm. After that incident she was moved to a more secure and strict atmosphere that specialized in cases like hers.

"I'm going to do some protection spells on myself, Sara and Sabrina tomorrow night," Kirsa promised. "Besides, I sleep with a vampire, he'll smell a demon before it gets into the house, if it can even cross the threshold."

CHAPTER 6

Sara stood looking at the structure that would become Kirsa's new home. Sabrina was with a horse breeder, so she was missing out on some of the decision making. Kirsa had called them when she realized that Ayden was useless with this decision. And they had gotten to that point in the construction of the main house that they needed to make decisions on the siding and colors. He would just shrug and tell her to do whatever she wanted. She also wanted to talk to them without Ayden around.

Sara and Kirsa were both bundled in wool pea coats staring at the choices for the brick that would go on the main part of the house. Kirsa sipped her coffee as they stared at the three piles of brick from three different torn down buildings. All three brick samples came from old buildings or construction sites as opposed to ordering more bricks to be made. Sara found it reassuring to be picking out finishing touches as opposed to finding shelter for displaced were-animals due to the aftermath of the hurricane. It also kept her mind off of Jeff's death.

"Have you seen Susie lately?" Kirsa asked Sara.

Sara turned to stare at her before looking back at the bricks. Sara was helping her to decide the exterior colors. "And what do you think of the yellow?" Kirsa added.

"I'm liking it," Sara said before commenting on the first question. "As to Susie, the last time I saw her was September. Why, do you want me to see her?"

"I thought you went weekly?" Kirsa asked. She was the only one that didn't visit Susie.

"I did, but the last time I went there to see her, I felt like my skin was freezing," Sara replied.

"If you want me to see her I will though."

"I might," Kirsa replied, while she pondered Sara's skin freezing she ruled out the brown siding. "What about the siding for the two wings? White or cream?"

Sara moved to the two siding samples next to the brick they had selected, then stood back to study the choices. "What's going on with Susie, and do we want Sabrina to know?" She asked as she looked at the choices.

"Part of me wants to think Al's paranoid, but another part thinks he could be right," Kirsa said studying the siding choices. "He and Frank handed me four cases that are linked together by a ritual gone wrong. Now the four teens are being stalked by demons."

"Why do you two think Susie might be involved?" Sara sipped her tea, but the tea didn't warm up the chill that had fallen over her. Anything dealing with Susie left her cold on the inside.

"The rituals came to the teens in a dream and they did not know they were invoking a demon when they did the ritual." Kirsa stared at the selection. "The cream siding?"

"I think the cream, with black shutters," Sara decided. Sara thought about what Kirsa had said about the new case. "I understand why the two of you would think of her, it sounds like things that she has done before. Just the crap she's pulled alone with you is enough to convince me she's aware."

Kirsa studied the choice while Sara allowed her to have a moment of silence. "I think you're right with the choice. I'll let Tom know."

"How are you doing with all of it?" Sara asked. Susannah was a bitter pill for Kirsa.

"Friday, I wanted to scream at her for what she did and tried to do," Kirsa sighed as they headed toward the farming section to check out the improvements. "Today there is a bit of guilt that maybe twelve years ago I could have done something to stop it."

"Kirsa how can you be responsible for Susannah?" Sara asked her, her voice full of frustration. "She was the one that craved more power. She was the one who was jealous of what the three of us could do. She was the one that chose to cross the line between good and bad. You didn't force her hand. None of us did."

"Sara, I know that, I know that what she did crossed the line, that she was messing with things she should never have dared to try," Kirsa said. She ran a hand through her hair in frustration sending curls springing out of control. "At the same time, I was there with her in the astral world, I was there when her nightmare became real, when her sanity snapped."

"And at seventeen you knew how to barter with demons? You knew how to make deals with the devil? You knew all the in's and out's of the astral plane?"

"My father always told me that with great power comes great responsibility, I was always careful never to abuse powers. But maybe if I wasn't careful and if I pushed myself I could have learned what she was thinking."

"And invading her mind is so much better?" Sara asked.

There were times when she wanted to shake Kirsa. The only thing that kept her from doing it was a simple fact: Kirsa was the one who found Susannah, she was the one who went to the astral plane to bring back Susannah's spirit, and she was the one who saw what happened.

"Even if I had, she would have denied it, and still have gone through with it," Kirsa added.

"She also would have been more secretive when it came time, which means you might not have been there to save her life," Sara pointed out.

"Some life she is living now."

"And she chose that fate, no one else told her to do what she did, no one held a gun to her head and forced her to summon a demon so she could be more powerful. She did that to herself, neither you nor anyone else is at fault for what happened," Sara said sternly.

"I wish the past could stay in the past sometimes," Kirsa sighed.

"If that was the case then how would we grow and learn? How can we fully appreciate what we have now if we don't look to the past on occasion?"

"You still believe that?" Kirsa asked.

Sara didn't answer right away. "I wake up sometimes thinking he's right there next to me," Sara replied. "It takes a few minutes to realize that he's not coming home. It sucks. But I am learning each day to remember the good times while focusing on each new step as a widow. The house will be ready to become a headquarters for the pack by the new year. I'm looking at places. I'm finding a balance between my past and my future."

"We're here for you."

"I know," Sara assured her. "You're going to have to tell Ayden."

"I know I just can't even imagine how to begin the conversation."

"If he loves you he will listen and try to understand," Sara said. "Since it's pretty obvious that he loves you, I think you'll be fine."

"How did Jeff handle it?"

"The same way he handled me being a were-tiger, it's part of me."

They talked for a few more minutes before Sara got in her car and left. Kirsa sat on the back steps, she texted Tom her decisions and then sat there watching as snow began to fall from the sky. Ayden came out and handed her a mug she took it and drank from it as he sat next to her. They watched as the snow fell, they already had about six inches on the ground from the storm the other night. It was as if Mother Nature decided to see just how much Jersey could take with storm after storm.

"Was she more helpful?" Ayden asked.

"Considerably," Kirsa said. She looked over at Ayden and kissed him on the cheek.

He smiled as he put an arm around her, pulling her closer to him. He was trying to figure out what he had done to deserve her.

"We'll get another six inches by tomorrow morning, "Ayden told Kirsa as he studied the sky.

"Vampire sense?" It seemed like they were just going to keep getting hit with storms.

"It's called being the son of a farmer," Ayden chuckled.

"What were they like, your family?" Kirsa inquired. Every now and then he talked about them in passing. Ayden sipped his blood as he thought of where to start.

"I was the oldest of five. After me came Brenna, Colin, Declan and Eliza."

"It must have been nice to have siblings," Kirsa replied.

She had always wanted siblings, but her mother couldn't have any more children after her.

"Did you want a younger sibling?" Ayden asked her.

"I did, not that I was ever alone. Between the Lyon brothers, Sabrina and Brian it was hard to find peace and quiet, someone was always running through the house."

"My brothers and I were shipped off to boarding school when we each turned eight," Ayden told her. "Not because my dad wanted it but because Catherine wanted it."

"Who's Catherine?" Kirsa knew that many women died during childbirth and that perhaps Catherine was his step-mother.

"My mother," Ayden replied. "She was a hard and difficult woman, which my father made up for with his warmth and attention. I still don't know what my father saw in her. Anyway, off to England we were shipped which meant we were not well liked amongst our Catholic neighbors."

"You're Protestant?" Kirsa asked stunned by the information. She just assumed he was Catholic.

"My last name is actually Molyneaux," Ayden informed her. "Shamus gave me his last name to protect me. I was turned in such a horrific way that I did not remember much of my human life, it took my three days to remember my first name was Ayden."

Kirsa knew that he had been turned by a rogue who had left him for dead and that if it wasn't for Shamus he would be dead. "I didn't know that."

"I had a rough time because of how I was turned."

"What was Shamus like as a leader?" Kirsa asked. "He was from your village?"

"In my village, Shamus did away with religious discrimination," Ayden recalled. "He didn't care if we were Protestant or Catholic or not, all he cared was that we worked hard, we took care of the land, and we fulfilled our oaths. If there was a religious argument he would see to it that it was put to an end. Knowing that we had it far better than others, those types of arguments didn't happen often. If you wanted your child educated, then you either sent him to the school in the village and if you couldn't afford it then Shamus would see to it that one of his children tutored them. Shamus believed that everyone should at least know how to read and write and do basic arithmetic."

"Revolutionary for 1850 Ireland," Kirsa pointed out.

"He thought it was common sense, how else were you to know if someone was screwing you over," Ayden replied with a smile. "He wasn't well liked around Kerry for his ideals but at the same time all the other lords knew if you needed him he'd be there. My mother detested him, thought he was a traitor to his heritage."

"She sounds like a bitch." The minute the words came out of her mouth she almost regretted them until she heard Ayden chuckle.

"That's being polite," Ayden said. "All five of us knew she was horrible, when my brothers and I were

76

home on holiday we protected our sisters as much as possible. While we were at school, our cousins took over for us."

"What did your father do?"

"Da and his brother were both carpenters by trade, when da married my mother he got a portion of farm land with a house and a herd of sheep," Ayden replied. "So he ended up being a farmer, though he'd help my uncle out at the wood shop from time to time. My father liked being a farmer, when the potato famine hit, we had the sheep to keep us going. Shamus and he worked together and orchestrated ways of keeping everyone feed and healthy during it."

"Did you lose many to it?"

Ayden finished the contents of his mug. He had to think it had been so long ago. "I think we lost about a hundred to death and another hundred left for the New World. We were about fifteen hundred before and dropped to just about thirteen hundred after. So not too bad considering."

"Partly because Shamus would see it as his obligation to keep his people safe," Kirsa surmised.

"Shamus always says that with duty comes responsibility. To this day he still looks after the village making sure everyone is taken care of."

"Have you ever gone back?"

He shook his head. "I go to the estate but have never really gone back to my village. Everyone I know is long gone so I never felt the need to revisit it."

Kirsa understood. To Ayden it would be a reminder of a life that had been stripped away from him. For him it would have been a reminder of the people he loved and how they were now lost to him.

"I think that's why Hagan would leave Geheimestadt and stayed away for a century or two, this way when he went back those he knew were long gone."

"Shamus stays because he never had a home prior to becoming a vampire, in his eyes by leaving it would be abandoning those that depend on him," Ayden replied.

"How'd he become a vampire?"

"One of the battles of Ireland, I forget if it was the Norse or the Brits or a warring tribe," Ayden said. "He was mortally wounded. One of the people in the hospital tent was a vampire and saw potential in Shamus. He gave him an option and Shamus, feeling he had more to offer as a vampire then dead accepted. After he turned his maker took him on a trip around Europe, he could see the world and at the same time get used to his new life."

"So ,he's Irish all the way," Kirsa replied. Ayden laughed at that.

"God yes."

"Does it hurt, the change?"

Ayden turned and looked at her. "I'm the wrong person to ask," he admitted wishing he could be more help. "I was attacked, savagely, and then drained to the brink of death. As I felt my heart faltering I vaguely remember being forced to drink blood. As the blood flowed through me, it felt as if the world stopped. Then the pain became amazing."

"How so?"

"I felt as though my blood is on fire, like my heart is going to explode at any moment. Yet at the same time my senses exploded, I began to hear, smell and feel things I never did before. When I opened my eyes that first time it was like I was thinking I never truly saw the world before. Then when the pain increased to such a point that I thought I would die. Then it's gone. For me, there was no one to help me hunt, I couldn't move because of my injuries. So, I learned that starvation was much worse than the pain I had just endured."

"What happened to you?"

"My attacker broke every bone in my body," Ayden informed her. He heard her quick intake of breath. "Even with my new healing ability, I couldn't move or walk. I am sure if I was mortal I would have been dead or paralyzed. So even though I had the urge to hunt I could barely move. As my thirst worsened I hallucinated until I passed out. That's when Shamus found me, he forced me to drink from him, breaking a huge vampire rule. A new vampire's first drink always comes from the sire, but mine left me for dead. When Shamus got enough blood in me, he put me on his horse and brought me to his home. When I awoke I was in his home, I had no clue who I was or where I was. I still don't remember my attacker."

"Ayden, I had no idea." Kirsa kissed him gently.

"What doesn't kill's us makes us stronger." He stood up. "Let's go inside before you freeze to death."

****

Titania Murphy stood in her sister's apartment at Shady Pines trying to stay strong and not give into guilt, not allowing the past to wipe away her future. Her golden blonde hair was pulled back into a simple bun; she wore jeans and a simple green cotton sweater that made her deep blue eyes seem brighter. Her makeup was light and all she wore for jewelry was her family signet ring. Susannah sat in front of the window staring at the snow-covered garden. Olivia and her intern had left to give them a few moments alone. Titania draped her pea coat over the kitchen chair and placed her pocket book on the table. She rarely paid a visit on Saturdays, usually when she came she was with her mother or sister.

Her father hadn't come to see Susie in about five years.

"I know I came on Wednesday with Mom," Titania began. "But how are you doing?"

Susannah just sat in front of the window staring out into nothingness. Titania walked closer to her sister and studied her, wondering where she should begin. Outside the world moved, people readied the garden for winter. Patients walked along a path, but here in Susannah's room it was as quiet as a tomb. Turning she looked at her sister, there Susannah slept so peacefully. It was hard to think of what her sister was capable of.

But, Titania had barely slept after the nightmare; every time she closed her eyes she would see the tortured faces of those she loved. When she finally got out of bed this morning she knew she had to come to Shady Pines. That it was time to stop pretending, to finally come to terms with what she had always known.

"When you first showed signs twelve years ago that something was wrong, I believed you were innocent," Titania began. "That you truly had no idea of the consequences, maybe it's because you're my sister and I knew you knew better than to mess with actual demons. I mean come on, we were raised by the same parents who told us of the dangers, so there is no way you would have messed with demons."

She studied Susannah to see if there was any change before she continued. "When Kirsa, Sara and Sabrina were rendered unconscious ten years ago I thought perhaps it was some coincidence." Titania saw the slight curl of a finger. Perhaps her sister was hearing what she was saying. "Now I know better. You know what's going on, you know exactly what you're doing, and you've always known. Silly of me to forget how you have been the expert at manipulating people since you were small. The problem is that now I am on to it."

A hand clenched the sheets. "I know you weren't innocent," Titania informed her. "That it wasn't all a mistake. I know that you knowingly summoned demons, that you almost killed your three best friends. The next time you think about invading my dream's so I can live through your hell, so help me, I will stake you with an iron nail myself."

Titania went to walk away, but instead was frozen to the spot. She went to scream but nothing came out but her breath. She heard the banging on the front door and the attempt to open it but nothing happened.

The air around her plummeted until it became freezing, until she could see her breath in the air. Until her blood ran cold and frost ran up the windows. Outside patients pointed to the windows of Susannah's room unsure what to think. Inside those rooms Titania found herself in a frozen hell. Icicles dripped from the ceiling, the floor looked like a skating rink.

Susannah floated toward her, her feet not touching the ground. Her blonde hair streaming down her back, her eyes the color of snow, her skin seemed to glow as she stopped in front of Titania.

"You have seen nothing of my nightmares, you know nothing of my pain," Susannah said in a voice that was more dead than alive. "When I am done, you will all be brought to your knees."

The door suddenly exploded open, Titania wasn't even aware of who had come barging into the room. She knew there were hands on her, as other people in white rushed passed her. She heard Susannah scream, heard things crash to the ground.

Someone scooped her up and out of the room, it was only then that she began to tremble. Only then, did she allow the fear to swamp her. Al set Titania down on the couch in Olivia's office. Olivia draped a blanket around Titania then left the room to deal with Susannah.

"*A Ghra*, you ok?" Al asked her as he knelt in front of her. She was freezing, her lips were blue, her teeth were chattering.

Joanna rushed into the office and handed him a coffee mug. "It will help with the chills," Joanna assured him.

Al looked up at the intern. "She tried to freeze me last week when I went to check her stats. My grandmother always said that coffee works to warm the spirit," Joanna informed him.

He nodded, and the young girl left the room. Al gave the mug to Titania then waited until she drank some of the hot coffee. As the chill slowly went away he saw that she began to focus again, the film over her eyes was no longer there. Her lips began to get color, and they stopped chattering. Titania stared at Al, not even sure how they got to be in an office together.

"What are you doing here?"

"We just signed in a prisoner for treatment," Al explained as he sat next to her on the couch. "I was heading up here to get an incident report when I heard your scream. Olivia was already at the door trying to open it."

"I screamed?" She had no recollection of doing that. Titania was convinced her voice had been frozen.

"It took about ten years off my life," Al confessed as he took one of her hands in his. "What happened, *A Ghra*?"

The hand holding the mug trembled; Titania set it down on the end table. "She's been invading my dreams for the last month; I kept trying to tell myself she didn't know she was doing it." Titania took a sip

84

of the coffee before beginning again. "Then last night she invaded my mind and the nightmare was so real, I could smell brimstone, I could smell the incense of the old ones, and then I smelled you."

Al wiped the tear that had started to fall off of her cheek. "Keep talking."

"I was in a room of ice, it was so cold. I walked around and looked through the window," She paused. Al moved to the chair next to her, he held her other hand as he encouraged her to continue. "Each window was worse. The first two were of my parents each chained in irons; the third was Alana. On her head was a crown of iron, she wore an iron mail shirt and was holding an iron sword. The fourth was of you, nailed to an iron cross, with an iron nail through each of your limbs." Titania had to stop to take a breath. "I woke up and knew then that she wasn't unknowing, innocent, or unaware. She knew what she was doing and has known what she's been doing all along."

"Is that why you came here? To tell her you figured her out?" Al asked. They had broken up because of her refusal to believe that Susannah truly knew what she was doing.

"Yes, and to tell her if she ever invaded my mind again I would personally stake her with an Iron Nail," Titania added.

Al smiled at that. "I take it that's when it all went to hell?"

"You could say that," Titania said laughing weakly. He had to think about what to do.

"Where are your parents?"

"They're in Fae, why?" Titania asked as she finished the coffee.

"What about Alana?"

"She's at school, why what's going on?"

"Kirsa and I are working on a case that we think might be linked to your sister, now with what Joanna said happened to her last week and what you just told me, Susannah is up to something."

"What are we going to do?" She was scared now, scared of what her sister was capable of doing.

"I am going to contact your sister's school and arrange for protection," Al told her. "We are taking you home, so you can pack, then you are going to Fae. I want you and your parents to stay there until this is over."

"How long will that be?"

"I honestly have no clue," Al told her.

"Al I can't just run to Fae because my lunatic sister is up to something."

He took her hands in his. "Listen to me, she is messing with demons, and if Frank is right she might be responsible for a few deaths. I will be able to think better if you are safely tucked away in the Fae."

****

Kirsa rolled over in bed and grabbed her phone that was blaring *The Rocky Road to Dublin* by Dropkick Murphys at 3am. Al better have a good reason to be calling her at this time. "It's three am on Sunday, what the hell?" Kirsa grumbled.

"Susannah attacked Titania," Al said.

"Well fuck," Kirsa said sitting up and now fully awake. "When?"

"She went to visit Susannah after lunch; apparently she's been messing with Titania's dreams. Titania finally realized that Susannah is not at all innocent in this and went to tell her so. Susannah did not like it and froze the room, froze Titania to the spot and kept us from opening the door."

"How'd you get in then?"

"I shot the door open," Al replied.

"Wait, why were you there?" Kirsa was now confused. She knew Ayden was standing in the room waiting to hear what had happened. "I had to escort a prisoner there for treatment and pick up an incident report from last week involving Susannah."

"Damn. Where is Titania now?"

"At the family manor in Fae," Al told her. "Her parents were there anyway for the winter. I contacted Columbia and they are going to have Alana watched."

"Al how bad were the dreams?"

"The one that made her realize the truth had her parents, Alana and I are impaled with Iron in different manners."

"Oh Al," Kirsa sighed.

"She's safe, that's all that matters," Al replied."Look email me everything so I can look all of it over when I am actually awake."

"Already did."

"Try to get some sleep," Kirsa instructed before they hung up. Ayden sat on the edge of the bed.

"What happened?"

Kirsa looked at him she was going to have to figure out how to tell him. "Al needed to update me on the case."

Ayden went to say something but knew she was holding back. Instead he kissed her goodnight then went back to his office so he could stew in peace.

CHAPTER 7

Alex Jones stood staring out his bedroom window; his two younger brothers were playing soccer and having a blast. He wanted to be there with them, like he used to be. He wanted to be able to runaround and goof off with them. Or drive into Salem with friends. Yet when he looked outside he saw demons standing on the edge of the property waiting for him to come out, they were always there waiting and watching. He watched as one waved at him with a bloody machete, his younger brothers were oblivious to the demonic clowns that hung out on their property.

Trying to be strong, he refused to close the curtains out of fear. Instead he stared at it then flipped it the finger before closing the curtains, while *Pantera* played in the background. There was a knock on the door, he told them to enter. His mom came in with some fresh baked cookies and a glass of milk. Even at seventeen he still loved cookies and milk. She set them on his desk before sitting on the edge of the bed.

"How many today?" Eliza Jones asked her son.

It killed her that he was a different child now. There was no more laughter in his hazel eyes. No more joking about how long his dark hair was getting, he was now serious and scared. When they had been told what happened they never doubted their son or his friends. Afterwards there had been times when they were outside where they smelled a strong stench of sulfur, where they felt like they were being watched. Sometimes arguments broke out for no reason until Alex pointed out that they were caving into the demons.

"Ten," Alex told her. "Don't worry, Scott and Mike are fine."

Eliza nodded, the last time Victoria, head of Alex's coven, was here Eliza had said something about the fighting, and the circle did a protection ring around the property. According to Alex, now the demons just hung out right on the border.

"Honey, OPIA called," Eliza stated. She liked the woman she had just gotten off the phone with, they had talked for over an hour. The agent was concerned not just about the case but also about her son and his welfare.

Alex groaned as he turned away from his snack, "What did they want?"

"Agent Willis has turned the case over to a senior agent," Eliza told him.

"Told you he was a moron," Alex said. He didn't like Agent Willis, he tried to be his friend. Maybe a year ago it would have worked, but not now.

Eliza stared at him giving him the look that caused her three boys to bow their heads. "Yes well this new agent is not going to take no for an answer."

Alex laughed. Someone was always trying to get one of his friends or him to tell them what really happened. How could they help if they didn't know what happened, but how does one explain hell? How do you go about talking about your inner worst nightmare?

"Her name is Kirsa Heinrich," Eliza continued ignoring her son's silence. "She is Assistant Director of OPIA."

"I'm trembling in my boots," Alex replied sarcastically. He dodged the pillow his mom threw at him.

"Well Mr. Smart Ass, she also has her Ph.D in parapsychology and Cultural Anthropology. She is considered an expert on Demons and she has been treating a patient for the last ten years that went crazy after having her mind invaded by a demon."

Alex looked up from the cookies and stared at his mother. She slid a piece of paper toward him with the agent's name. Eliza got up and headed out of the room, she paused in the doorway.

"When they come up to interview you, I told her not to go easy." With that she shut the door leaving him in his solitude.

****

Ayden walked into Kirsa's office after she was off the phone. He handed her a mug which contained a mixture of coffee and blood. "I saw you were on the phone and didn't want to interrupt. What's up?"

Kirsa took a sip from the mug before she answered. "We are going on a road trip. We leave for Salem on Wednesday and will probably come back on Saturday."

"That will be nice, making headway?" Ayden asked as he read her notes upside down.

He knew that she had spent the day talking to the various adults involved with Alex Jones case. It was fine, he had to do some research for Dietrich on a council member.

"Basically, all the adults think the teens are stonewalling them, they're hiding something but no one can crack them," Kirsa replied with a hint of a smile.

"I have a feeling that smile means you are going to want me to use some of my vampire powers?" Ayden asked.

"I will make it worth the trouble." Ayden's pupils dilated as he smiled,

"You better."

Her phone rang; Ayden leaned over and kissed her before leaving the room. Kirsa waited until the door was shut to pick up the phone.

"Hi Olivia," Kirsa said. "I was just going to call you."

"I got a break, so I figured I'd call, that way they didn't have to track me down."

"How's she doing?"

Olivia let out a long sigh. "One of the Fae Healers came to sedate her, so we have her pretty much out most of the time now. When she is awake she is screaming her head off but no one knows what language she is speaking. The healer said it's ancient but he couldn't understand it."

"Can you get a recording of it too me?" Kirsa asked. "I might know someone who could interpret it?"

"Since we have the mics on in her room around the clock now, that won't be a problem."

"Are the nightmares worsening?" Kirsa asked. Joanna, Olivia's intern, had noticed a pattern. The nights that Susannah had vicious nightmares coincided with a particular evening nurse worked. That nurse was now being monitored closely.

"At this point we can't even tell, Joanna hasn't been attacked since the incident with Titania. That's the only good news at this point."

"Can you send the updates to me so I can add them to what I have?"

"Of course," Olivia said. "Everything is up on the computer anyway so I can get that too you today."

"Thanks Olivia."

"Anytime, I should probably get back to work. I will keep you posted."

Kirsa hung up the phone and walked out into the kitchen. It was too early for whiskey, so instead she popped another vial and downed it. She sensed Ayden walking into the room and prepared herself for his question.

"You must be stressed if you're taking another," Ayden replied from behind her. "You ok?"

"Ask me again in an hour after yoga," Kirsa replied. She couldn't discuss it, not yet. He needed to understand that she would tell him but she needed time to sort through it all.

"Who was on the phone this time?"

"Shady Pines."

"What does a mental hospital want with you?"

"I have a patient there, there was an update that I needed to be made aware of," Kirsa told him.

Ayden studied her. He knew she had a degree in parapsychology but she didn't practice as a therapist. "You don't have patients."

"I have one," Kirsa said and left the room.

Ayden watched as she went up the stairs. She had been putting some distance between them in the last few days.Not in a physical way but more in a mental way, he was completely blocked out of her mind. Grabbing the car keys, he sent a message to her knowing she'd get it.

****

Sabrina was stunned when Ayden walked into the barn she was working in. He wore jeans and a sweater and that was it. No coat, hat, scarf or gloves, just hiking boots and a heavy sweater. She finished talking to one of the employees then turned to greet him.

"What do I owe this surprise visit to?" She asked as she buried her hands in the coat pockets.

"You got time to talk?"

"If we can walk as we do so, or we can wait until we get back to the office," she answered. "Where's your other half?"

"Home, most likely depleting my stock of Jamison while doing Yoga."

Sabrina looked at him for a moment then motioned for him to follow. "Alright what do you want to talk about it?"

She already knew what it was about it. There was only one reason Kirsa, Sara or she ever drank whiskey and it was never to celebrate.

"Kirsa never drinks whiskey, yet a few days ago after Sara had left I smelled whiskey, today I get a mental image of a whiskey bottle. Which, is the first mental image in about three days that I have gotten from her, by the way."

Ayden and Kirsa shared a mental link because of how close they were. It was rare between vampire and human and some-thing that they had grown used too.

Sabrina sighed. "She occasionally drinks whiskey, it's not her first choice but there are times when she will hit it. You're not seriously here to discuss her drinking habits are you? Because trust me there is no problem with that."

A few years ago when her parents were killed followed by her aunt and uncle there was cause for concern, but not now. Ayden was silent as they walked, he liked coming here. The smell of it reminded him of his home sometimes.

"What's Shady Pines Home for the Mentally Ill? And please don't tell me a mental hospital." His accent was getting strong which meant he was annoyed, or pissed or both.

"It's a mental hospital in Pennsylvania. It's privately run, they take in the impossible, the incurable, and treat them as normally as possible. Why?"

"Sounds expensive."

"It is. My question is why the interest in a private mental hospital?"

"They called for Kirsa yesterday, and then today she was on the phone with a woman named Olivia from there. I also believe she might be lying to me."

Sabrina laughed at the last comment. "She can't lie to you Ayden."

"Kirsa doesn't have any patients," Ayden pointed out.

"She has one," Sabrina replied. She saw the surprised look that flashed on his face before it went blank.

"Is this new?"

Sabrina shook her head, "Kirsa has been on the case for almost ten years now. Once a year she goes there for the annual review, even when she was in Europe she would do a video conference. She also goes in if there's an emergency."

"Why hasn't she ever told me about this?" Ayden asked.

"Have you told her everything about your past?" Sabrina inquired. He just stared at her. "I didn't think so. Ayden she loves you, she can't lie to you, which is probably really hard on her right now because she probably wishes she could at the moment."

"And what do you mean she can't lie to me?" Ayden asked.

"When Kirsa was engaged to Anton, she lied to him all the time. It was easier than telling him the truth sometimes. It's how she eventually realized she didn't truly love him. With you, she has always been an open book. In all the time I have known you, which is a while; I have never heard her tell you one lie. She can withhold things from you, but she won't lie."

"I just feel like she's pushing me away to some degree," Ayden said.

"She might be, and she will again," Sabrina took his arm in hers as they neared her office. "I'm going to let you in a tip for dealing with Kirsa. Kirsa has what Sara and I refer to as the fuck off switch, when she gets overwhelmed, or there is too much to handle, she turns off her emotions until she can deal with it. Which means those closest to her get pushed away, but when she is ready she will let you know."

"What do I do?"

"Be patient, she will let you know what's going on. When did you notice it?"

"When she went through her yearbooks."

Sabrina stared at him then mumbled something about vampires. "Well that explains it all."

"Don't give that 'you deserve it look'," Ayden warned her.

"I didn't mean to," Sabrina waived to her secretary as Ayden followed her up the stairs. "Look you have to understand something. High school is bittersweet for Kirsa. On one hand she escaped the chaos of confined overcharged hormones and went to college. On the other hand, she missed the whole confined overcharge hormones. While we had to sneak off to drink, Kirsa could go to a frat party, while we complained about curfews, Kirsa lived in a dorm and had no curfew. She had the freedom of an adult while the rest of us were dealing with being teens. We did include her in the drama of high school by dragging her to homecoming, dances, plays, prom, and everything else."

"So why would it be hard for her to look back at all that?" He didn't understand the whole high school drama.

Being protestant in Ireland he had been sent to a boarding school. For the Catholics that lived in his village, Shamus made sure they were all educated not just in academics but in a trade as well. To him education was a gift, not a nuisance.

"Think back to when you were between sixteen and eighteen, is there nothing from then that you still regret to this day?"

"You have a point."

"And you have had a billion years to come to peace with it," Sabrina pointed out. "All I am going to tell you is that something major occurred when Sara and I were juniors. It was harder on Kirsa then the rest of us and sometimes it comes to haunt her for a bit."

Ayden studied Sabrina. "What happened back in high school?"

"Ayden I can't tell you," Sabrina said. "That is for Kirsa to tell. She will when she's ready, and if you try to rush it she will only close up more."

Ayden ran a hand over his face. "You know there are times when you mortals are so frustrating."

"Right because vampires are so normal and calm," Sabrina replied laughing. "Go home, and tell Kirsa I will watch Zero while you two are in Salem."

Ayden stared at her, "How did you know about that already?"

"She texted me."Sabrina waited until Ayden left the office before she picked up her cell phone.

Kirs, you need to tell Ayden. Sabrina texted.

Why does everyone keep telling me what I already know? I will tell him when I am ready. Right now I have a case I'm working on that is extremely difficult. Kirsa typed back in response.

He's worried about you, he was asking about Shady Pines. What's going on? Sabrina typed.

She's screaming out our names again. I'm doing a protection spell tonight.

You're holding too much in.

TTYL. Kirsa typed simply.

Sabrina sighed and slid her phone into her pocket as she watched Ayden walk toward the Heinrich property. She was going to be really pissed if Susie caused a rift between those two.

Ayden felt the impact of the snowball as he walked toward the house. He turned slowly and did not see Kirsa anywhere but he could smell her. It was hard to stay annoyed when he had snow dripping from him; he studied the white landscape as he silently made his own arsenal. He ducked the next one as he heard it cutting through the air. He heard laughter and sprinted soundlessly through the snow and whirled the snowball at Kirsa. She leapt out of the way and chucked another snowball at him.

Ayden forgot about the were's that were hired for added security and the hidden Shadow that had been sent as a silent guard. Kirsa did not know about them, and for a moment he felt all his stress and worries melt away as they pelted each other with snowballs. They were both running faster than a normal human and throwing faster too. If a normal human was watching all they would have seen were blurry objects moving around. They might be able to make Kirsa out since she was not quite as fast as a vamp yet. He saw her out of the corner of his eye and pounced tackling her to the snow. Ayden stared into her laughing eyes and shook his head; she lifted her head up and kissed him.

He rubbed his nose against hers before he climbed off of her and helped her up. "I can't remember the last time I had a snowball fight."

"Adam and I last Christmas," Kirsa said laughing as they walked arm and in arm back to the house. She could tell by the subtle change in his scent that he was no longer annoyed, which meant her plan had worked.

"I take it then that I should be prepared for another battle in Germany," Ayden assumed.

"Most likely," Kirsa said hanging her wet coat up on the coat rack. She headed into her office and looked at some of the pictures that were there. She had decided to put up the homecoming picture but whenever she saw it new memories floated to the surface.

When Kirsa was fifteen, her father had converted part of the attic into a hang out space for her friends and her. The walls were a sage green with silver and white accents, there had been bookcases, window seats, cream colored carpets, table and chairs. Magazines were often strewn across the floor, and posters of movie stars hung on the slanted ceiling. It was every teenage girls dream come true. At sixteen, Kirsa's hair was short, spiky and pink. Kirsa was laying on the carpet flipping through a magazine while she was on break from college. Sabrina was braiding

102

Sara's hair and Susannah was curled up on one of the window seats staring outside.

"Don't you wanna do anything fun and exciting?" Susannah asked, sounding bored. Her long blonde hair hung to her waist and tonight her eyes were blue.

Kirsa looked up from the magazine, "Susie, I just finished midterms. We could do the movies or something if you want but I just wanna veg and hang out."

Susannah let out a long sigh as she went back to staring out the window. Sabrina looked over at her and tried not to roll her eyes. "What would you like to do Susannah?" Sabrina asked finishing Sara's hair.

"I feel like we do the same old thing, we hang out, read magazines, gossip, go to the movies or the diner," Susannah told them. "It's getting dull."

"I'm open for suggestions," Sara said. "But it's not like there is a whole lot to do here."

Susannah smiled and got up, she went over to her bag and took a book out. "Well I've been thinking that maybe we should form our own witches circle."

The three turned and looked at her, not sure if she was serious or not. Susannah went on to explain, "There are four of us so we have the four cardinal directions and the four elements. Kirsa has been practicing for two years now; I know Sara is good with tarot cards. It would be something different."

Kirsa took the book from Susannah and began to flip through it. Sitting up she looked at the spells and charms. She closed the book and handed it to Sara.

"That book is filled with love spells and love charms," Kirsa replied. "I don't mess with that stuff."

"Why not? It seems harmless," Susannah replied innocently.

"It's not," Kirsa and Sara said at the same time.

"What's so bad about making your crush like you back?" Sara spoke first.

"It's not harmless, you're basically altering someone's emotions to how you want them to be. It's a form of control, and is a short step from black magick. Most practitioners won't touch it because it can lead to all sorts of crazy things."

"What kind of things?" Sabrina asked.

"Well the victim can end up stalking the caster, the caster will be almost violating the creed which is 'Do as you will as long as you harm none' so the caster can get a whole bunch of bad karma on top of being stalked. Plus, you have to maintain the spell for however long you want the person to be enthralled with you."

"But it's for fun," Susannah said.

"Look," Kirsa started. "I have no issues if you guys want to form a circle, but if we do, it will be done so correctly. No love magick or any spells that deal with controlling another person. Magick isn't a joke, it's a privilege and that needs to be respected. "

Susannah slid the book back into her bag and sat back on the window seat. "So if we do this, where would you have us start?"

"At the beginning, you need an understanding of what you are doing and why you are doing it, you also need to understand there are consequences for every action. Whatever you put out comes back to you threefold. So if you send out a curse it is going to come back to you much worse," Kirsa explained.

"You also need to learn how to protect yourself," Sara added. "By opening and closing circles and also how to protect your mind when you explore your third eye."

Kirsa sighed remembering how young they were when starting their own circle. Susannah was convinced that because she was Fae she would be invincible and powerful. Kirsa should have said no from the start, she should have known that Susannah would always want more. But when one was sixteen they tended to not want to see the worst in their friends.

CHAPTER 8

Kirsa stared at the series of crime scene photos that were spread over the conference table in her office. She had gotten a call from Al to come in to headquarters. Now along with Frank, Al and Ayden; they were all going through the gruesome photos before them. It was an apparent suicide from five years ago. It was a grisly photo, the young girl was lying in a pool of her own blood. Her neck and both wrists were sliced open. In the blood around her words were written within.

"How would she have enough time to slit her wrists, her neck and then write a farewell message?" Al asked perplexed. He studied the words and scratched his head. "And how does a mortal know basic Faery?"

"When was the suicide?" Kirsa asked Frank.

"According to the file she was discovered on November first of 2007," Frank answered. "Her boyfriend found her."

"Why was it ruled a suicide?" Kirsa inquired. It was well known that it would be impossible for a person to slit both of their wrists and neck.

"No evidence to prove it wasn't," Frank said. "And they tried from how thick the file was. The coroner put a question mark after suicide because he wasn't certain."

Kirsa sat down and ran a hand through her hair as she thought about it. They had to be missing something. "She had to have help, it's the only way that scene is plausible. Al can you determine what she wrote?"

"I'm going to need some time," Al told her. "It's not clear but I can try and enhance it. I can tell you she mentions an angel and dreams."

Kirsa looked across the table at Al. His look mirrored her own look of horror. Kirsa got up and walked to her desk she grabbed her phone. Susannah had often been described as an angel.

"Olivia post twenty-four hour guards on her room," Kirsa instructed into the phone. "No one goes in alone, and be armed with iron ." She talked for a few more minutes before hanging up.

"I'll call the four families again," Kirsa told Al.

"I'll keep searching through the cold cases," Frank replied.

"Why do I feel like I'm missing something?" Ayden asked to no one in particular.

"I'll explain later tonight," Kirsa promised. She ignored the surprised look on Al's face.

"Kirsa, iron bullets at all time," Al told her.

"How are you going to deal with that?" Ayden asked Al.

"I have gloves that allow me to handle iron, plus I'm half human so it takes a lot of iron to have its effect on me," Al told him."Slightest smell of brimstone, call me."

"I'll be safe," Kirsa promised. It was truth because whatever Susannah was playing at, she wasn't ready yet to face Kirsa.

"Do I need to remind you what happened this summer? Al asked. He was referring to when she was abducted by a suspect and held prisoner and nearly died.

"Smart ass," Kirsa replied getting in the car.

Ayden got in the driver's seat and saluted Al before pulling out of Kirsa's parking spot. "I take it this has to do with your patient?" Ayden asked.Kirsa looked over at him. She laid a hand on his leg then watched the rain bounce off the windshield.

"Yes," Kirsa answered. "Just be patient a little bit more, I will tell you everything tonight."

"I can do that," he promised as he drove back toward Grabenberg.

****

Kirsa sat in Sara's office after viewing the body that was giving her a problem, it was a vampire but the fangs had been pulled making it hard to identify. Sara had been agitated all morning, which was unlike her. Sabrina was the perky friend, Sara the calm one, and Kirsa the serious one. Today Sara decided to be the agitated and annoying friend. Kirsa gave her a view on the body, than forced her to sit down in her office.

"Are you going to tell me what's up?" Kirsa asked Sara.

"I apparently called out her name three times last night and have no memory of it," Sara replied.

"Hopefully it was while you were asleep and not during a more embarrassing moment, because then I would really worry about you," Kirsa joked. She caught the stress ball that Sara threw at her.

"You've gotten quicker," Sara noticed. She didn't mention that Kirsa smelled more like a vampire than a human.

"No changing the topic," Kirsa replied. "Who heard you?"

"I've had Bridgette the last few nights because Phil is in the city for the annual tri state Pack meeting," Sara explained. "She heard me."

"What about the dream?"

"I was skiing down a mountain that never seemed to end, I finally got tired of that one and forced myself out of it," Sara told her.

That was the reason why Kirsa did not have to worry about Sara as much, she was so psychically aware of her own mind and dreams that she often was able to gain control of them without thinking about it. "Try doing a protection spell for when you're dreaming, it should take care of it. You could also buy a dreamcatcher."

"I already have one from the Native American festival last summer," Sara said. "You have any good spells?"

"I'll see what I have, I'll send them to you," Kirsa promised. "Is that all that's bothering you?"

"What if she bound a demon to me?"

"She can't."

"She's a water faery, they excel at dream magick," Sara reminded her.

"Yes but binding a demon in a dream to an unsuspecting host is impossible," Kirsa countered.

"The four teens performed a ritual while they were awake, not while they were dreaming."

"So no demon?"

"Sara you're a weretiger, you would know if there was a demon in the house," Kirsa assured her. "Whether or not you are asleep or awake, their smell would alert you before they could even get near you."

"Ok," Sara sighed. She needed to hear that, to be reassured. "What are your plans for today?"

She knew Kirsa had been at OPIA already that day. What ever happened there had not been a good thing; she could see the stress in Kirsa's eyes.

"I'm telling Ayden tonight."

"Telling him what?"

Kirsa raised an eyebrow at her friend. "About Susannah, about what happened, about how it's connected to the case."

"Oh shit," Sara replied. She had never really had to tell Jeff. He lived in Grabenberg, he saw what happened to Susannah. Besides, Sara didn't go to rescue her so her version was a bit easier to take then Kirsa's side.

"Do you want me or Sabrina to be there?"

"You have enough going on at your house with Bridgette, maybe I'll see if Sabrina wants to come over," Kirsa said. "She might be able to make me sound less crazy."

****

Ayden came downstairs in a jeans and a vintage Doors t-shirt from when he saw them in Florida before Morrison was arrested. He pulled his hair back and as he hit the last step his nostrils flared. Someone was making lamb stew; he also smelled an open bottle of Harp. He walked into the kitchen and saw Kirsa tapping her feet to *Godsmack* as she cooked. Ayden kissed her on the neck as he stole her beer.

"What's all this?" he asked surveying the kitchen. She narrowed her eyes at him as he sipped from her beer. Sighing she went to the fridge and opened a new one for herself.

"I'm cooking."

"I can see that, but I never seen you make lamb stew before."

"That's because I never had a good recipe before," Kirsa told him.

She had gotten this one from Patrick O'Brian, Shamus' oldest boy, who told her it was Ayden's favorite.

He heard the footsteps and had the door open before Sabrina could ring the bell to the back door. He took her coat as she walked in brushing off the snow.Sabrina sniffed the air.

"Is that the recipe?" she asked walking over to the stove.

"Yep," Kirsa said as she handed Sabrina three large soup bowls and spoons.

Ayden was now even more curious about what was going on. He stood out of the way while Sabrina set the table. His eyes widened as Kirsa took homemade biscuits out of the oven and set them in a basket. She handed it to him with a warning look; he had a weakness for homemade biscuits. He set the basket on the table then sat down with Sabrina. Kirsa turned the flame off, then brought the pot over to the table. She ladled out the soup into three bowls.

Ayden took a whiff of the contents on his spoon and his eyes widened. He took a taste and closed his eyes as home came back to him. "How did you get it?"

"I called Patrick and he emailed it to me," Kirsa said smiling.

"He's right it is the best," Sabrina replied. She buttered a biscuit then looked at Kirsa and nodded.

Ayden smelled that Kirsa was nervous. "What's wrong?"

Taking a sip of her beer to calm her down, she took a deep breath. "You want to know what's going on, about my patient at Shady Pines."

"Yes."

"It's a long story and Sabrina is here to help with it," Kirsa explained.

"Kirsa, you don't have too," Ayden told her. He could smell the slight fear in her.

"No I do," Kirsa replied with a long sigh. "Some things have occurred and you need to know before it gets worse, because it's going to get worse before this is done. And you should know it if we are serious about our relationship."

"Alright," Ayden said. He hated seeing her war with so many emotions.

"Do you remember the faery in the homecoming photo?"

"Yes why?" He was getting a bad feeling about what he was going to hear.

"This involves her." Kirsa took a deep breath before beginning. "Susannah's family moved to Grabenberg while her father and mine worked on the paranormal laws."

"I remember," Ayden said. "It was the early eighties, shortly after we came out to the world."

"They decided to stay after the laws were finally written. Sabrina, Susannah and I were all the same age and became friends. When Sara moved to town she fit right in."

"Susannah was never at the house though," Ayden pointed out. He would have remembered a faery at the house.

"Susie was never allowed here if there was a vampire," Kirsa reminded him. "She almost tricked a brand new vampire to drink her blood. After that dad banished her if a vampire was here. Because she was under thirteen the Faery court could do little, but her parents were outraged. They forced her into counseling."

"I take it that was not her first incident?" Ayden asked as he ate the stew.Sabrina laughed at the question.

"Susannah was the middle daughter," Sabrina answered. "They were all raised to respect their heritage and their responsibilities. However, Susannah always saw being a Faery as a privilege, that we should be honored to be friends with her. She also liked to think that rules were meant to be tested."

"I heard tales of Hugh Murphy's middle one being a bit wild," Ayden replied. But it was hard to imagine after having met the other two daughters and his wife.

"That's putting it lightly," Kirsa said. "We put up with her because by the time she started acting wild we had been friends for a while."

"I had a friend like that when I was mortal, we had grown up together but then he became the annoying friend," Ayden said with a laugh. "The one who was often left at the tavern because no one wanted to carry him home or deal with his drunken insults."

"If only," Kirsa sighed. "Things didn't start getting crazy with Susannah until our eighth grade year."

"What happened then?" Ayden asked.

"During our eighth grade year, Kirsa and her parents were called into a meeting," Sabrina explained. Kirsa groaned and drank her beer. "The principals of the middle and high school explained that Kirsa had already taken all the advanced courses at the high school and was worried that she might become bored. He wanted her to take the SAT's and the High School Proficiency test to see if she could test out of high school. If she didn't then they would make arrangements for her to take classes at GU."

"Kirsa how smart are you?" Ayden asked her. It was a subject that they never had discussed before.

"That's a loaded question," Kirsa replied. "We are all brilliant in different ways. An IQ is a number."

"She gets annoyed when her intelligence is brought up," Sabrina said.

"I see that," Ayden observed. "I'm guessing she passed."

"Perfect scores," Sabrina said. "While we entered freshman year Kirsa went off to Cambridge to attend Harvard."

"I was packed off at eight to England to attend boarding school," Ayden replied. He knew what it was like to be sent away from home young.

116

"Harvard was wonderful," Kirsa assured him, knowing that for him being away from home was painful. "There had been other young geniuses that had gone there so they had a program; they also had high security dorms. It was one of the reasons my parents were comfortable sending me there. I pretty much became everyone's little sister."

"So what happened while you were away at college?"

"We hit that age where witchcraft seemed awesome and we all became interested in Wicca and witchcraft," Kirsa answered. "Sara and I had been studying it since middle school, Sabrina was reading about it. By freshmen year I settled on the Norse pantheon. When I came home from midterms Susannah decided we should start a coven, the book she showed me dealt with love spells. We agreed to form our own coven, but no love spells, no manipulation of another's emotions and no dark magick."

Ayden felt the dread begin to surface. Kirsa continued before he could ask a question or she lost her nerve. "I noticed the change in Susannah before Sabrina and Sara, but I wasn't seeing her everyday like they were. When I mentioned it to them they were hesitant to believe me."

"Why?" Ayden asked. He was surprised that the two wouldn't have believed her. The three were as close as sisters.

"Because we thought Kirsa was paranoid and slowly going crazy," Sabrina answered. Ayden looked at her with a confused expression.

"You didn't see what she saw?" Ayden asked.

"It's more complicated than that," Sabrina admitted. "There were moments when one of us would catch her talking to herself. Like she was having a conversation with someone and no one would be there. At first we thought it was ghosts, but every now and then she would say the name of a god and we realized that she thought she was talking to gods."

"You're a god-talker?" Ayden asked Kirsa in awe.

In all the years he had known her, he had never known that. There had been times he caught the hint of a god's scent on her but never connected it.

"That's the name for it?" Kirsa asked. If there was a name, it meant she was not alone.

"It is a very rare trait, the prophets in the bible were god-talkers, so were some of the great seers in the ancient times," Ayden explained. "Those in this day and age are silent for fear of being deemed crazy."

"I understand that sentiment," Kirsa replied dryly

"Have you ever seen a god?" Sabrina asked Ayden.

"Once," Ayden replied, he leaned back in the chair as he remembered. "I was in a bar in Oslo during the winter. This man came over and sat next to me, he was bigger than me. His hair was blonde and he had a huge stein that depicted Norse tales. He told me I was drinking the wrong drink then ordered me Meade. We drank and talked, he somehow knew I had lived many lives and we talked until the bar closed. When we eventually left the bar he looked at me and told me that unlike many of my kind I was blessed. He then walked away leaving behind a distinct scent."

"Snow, evergreen, frankincense, hops and older scents," Sabrina said knowing already.

Ayden looked at her. "How did you know?"

"Kirsa was home for fall break during our junior year. I heard her talking to people in our meeting place. This time I could hear the faint whispers of others, when I walked in that's what I smelled and then I saw them. Freyja, Thor and Frey. They nodded and then disappeared. It was then I realized that she wasn't insane, I also realized that if she wasn't insane then maybe she was right about Susannah."

"So what happened?" Ayden asked. He let Kirsa spoon more stew into his bowl.

"I had just finished my junior year, which meant I was back before they were done with school," Kirsa told Ayden.

"Which always drove the three of us up the wall that she got done before us," Sabrina added as she finished her stew. Ayden got them all another round of beer before Kirsa continued.

"By this point Susie and I were barely talking, we had a huge fight during my spring break. She was convinced that she would be able to talk to ghosts and know things like me or talk to Angels like Sabrina."

"Wait," Ayden said holding up a hand. "You talk to angels?"

Sabrina nodded. "I did, sometimes still do. They're everywhere so I learned how to tune them out, sometimes if one really needs to communicate they will get through the walls I put up."

"What are they like?" Ayden was fascinated. He had never met someone who could see Angels.

"Unnerving, so beautiful your heart aches, they humble you, and you know you're seeing a being that is absolutely pure and good."

"Can you see fallen angels?" Ayden asked curious.

"Only if they want to be seen," Sabrina replied. "They drain the joy and happiness out of the room.

Yet they are as beautiful as Angels but more tempting."

Ayden missed the arch look directed at Kirsa. Kirsa ignored Sabrina and continued. "I told her no spell would be permanent, that it would open her mind during the spell but once it was over she would be back to normal."

"She didn't want to hear that I take it," Ayden replied."But you are born with the ability; it's not something that can be taught."

"We tried telling her that," Sabrina told him. "Sara tried telling her that but she didn't want to hear us."

"Anyway it was late one night and I get this sense that something was wrong," Kirsa began. "I left my bedroom and the house; I headed over to one of the old buildings on the property that we used. Susannah was there, lying in the center of a circle. Candles and incense burning, her eyes were open but vacant. On the floor next to her I saw the ritual. I knew what she was doing, she was going to try and trick three gods into giving her power believing her pure fae blood would keep her safe."

"But it would make it more dangerous for her," Ayden replied. Apparently Susannah lacked common sense. The face were forbidden to perform blood magick.

Kirsa nodded before she went on. "I knew she was in trouble, I knew she was not going to survive when I realized who she was going to trick. I broke the circle, than entered the astral plane. Unlike Susie I didn't need a spell; I could enter if I focused."

Sabrina jumped in at this point. "At this time I felt the presence of an Angel and he would not shut up so I finally woke up and asked him what was wrong. He told me that two of my friends were in danger," Sabrina added. "I called Sara and we rushed over to the meeting place. By the time we got there Kirsa was already unconscious. All we could do was watch and hope all would be alright."

Kirsa sipped her beer before she began to talk again. "When I awoke I was in a large field somewhere. An enormous oak tree stood in the center, a table sat there with five chairs and cups. I headed over to it and saw Susannah standing there with Hecatate and Freya. Freya nodded to me and I knew she was aware of what was going on. Susannah was discussing the deal with Hecatate before she realized I was there. She got angry when she saw me, wanted to know why I came, and that I must be jealous of what she was going to do. I told her that there was nothing to be jealous about when someone thought they were better than gods. Hecate knew, they all knew, they were waiting for confirmation. I gave it to them."

"Who was the third god?" Ayden asked. He noticed she was deliberately not mentioning the name.

"He was beautiful, black hair, and amber eyes. He moved with a grace that one is born with, I knew him of course. Lou and I had a love/hate relationship by this point."

Ayden held up a hand. "Lou? As in Lucifer? The Morning Star?"

"He really hates that name," Kirsa replied. She looked around for a moment expecting him to appear because she was talking about him. "Anyway, he was the one that told Susannah that they were aware of her plans. Something broke in her then, she yelled. She told all four of us that we were all fools, that she had found a way to outsmart us. Then the demons came, she had used demon magick to cover up her faery blood."

"She made a deal with the demon realm to conceal her blood?" Ayden asked in disbelief.

"She knew if the three gods found out they would have to notify her gods and the deals would be null and void," Sabrina explained.

"Alright continue," Ayden said.

"The problem was Lou outranked the demons, he ordered them to remove whatever enchantment they had on her. When the three realized she was a pure faery, they realized they could not bind her without permission from her gods. She laughed and laughed at them. Lou changed," Kirsa looked at Ayden. "Have you ever seen him in his true form?"

"I've heard tales," Ayden replied. "He takes the form of your heart's desire, but if you trick him then the horror is beyond human comprehension."

"There are no words to describe the horror he became. I could see past it, see him in his human form, just like I can see his monster lurking within his human form."

"You knew what to expect," Ayden said softly.

"I did," Kirsa replied. "But Susannah, she's faery. The rest of her broke when she saw him, her fae mind could not grasp what it was seeing so it broke. He wanted her soul as punishment."

"But you wouldn't allow that," Ayden realized. Even though Susannah had done wrong Kirsa would not allow someone to take her friends soul.

"I promised him anything in exchange for me returning with her soul. I knew her mind was broken already. I knew she would most likely never recover. But I had to do it."

"What did you promise?" Ayden asked as a whole new meaning of terror entered his mind.

"He stared at me as he turned back into his human form; when he approached he looked at the two goddesses behind me and they nodded. One drop of my blood. Knowing who I was dealing with,

I told him one drop of blood at that actual moment, not in replay, not in dreams, and not whenever he wanted. He would have only one actual drop of my blood." Ayden took a huge sigh of relief.

"You are smarter than most."

"It's more of understanding who he is. He agreed and the goddesses nodded, Freya took the drop from me and gave it to him. He then helped me bring her back," Kirsa finished.

Sabrina took over. "They had been gone for three hours, by the time they came back all our parents were there. Kirsa explained through tears what had been done. The Murphys were just happy that her soul had been saved."

"What happened with Susie?" Ayden asked. He would talk to Kirsa about the devil at another time.

"Susie, we thought began to recover, she was seeing a therapist to help filter through the nightmares," Sabrina replied. "She finished the school year on home instruction. During senior year there were some minor episodes, she was in and out of hospitals."

"But that wasn't the end," Ayden gathered. If that was the end Kirsa might have talked about it sooner.

"During the summer after we had all graduated," Sabrina began, "Sara, Kirsa and I were rushed to the hospital. We were all unconscious for an unknown reason. Hagan and Hugh went to Susannah, to this day we don't know what they did but after two days of us being unconscious we awoke from a nightmare. She was placed into a mental hospital after that."

"And you became her doctor?" Ayden asked.

"She's why I went into parapsychology with a concentration in Demons," Kirsa told him.

"What does this have to do with your case?"

"The four teens we are pretty sure were approached in their dreams about a ritual to perform. After said ritual they are linked to a demon, they all wanted to improve their abilities. Then Saturday afternoon, Titania confronted her sister about the nightmares she had been having. She told Susannah she now realized that Susannah wasn't the innocent one or the victim. Susannah attacked her in the hospital room. Last night Sara screamed her name out three times."

"Holy shit." It was the only thing Ayden could think to say.

"That about sums it up," Sabrina agreed.

CHAPTER 9

A crown of clear crystals cut into flowers and leaves sat upon Susannah's head, her hair was done in an intricate bun. Gems of every color adorned her ears and neck.Her gown was the color of opals; made of the finest cloth with detailed embroidery on it that would make any Hollywood star weep from envy. The throne she sat on was made of clear crystal, the floors were of white marble, and the walls made of quartz, the room resembled that of an enchanted Ice castle. Susannah stared at the goblin that was bowed before her.

"Narl can't penetrate the grandmother's spell," the goblin informed her.

Susannah toyed with the chalice she held in her hand. "What do you mean?" she asked carefully.

The goblin swallowed. No one liked bringing her bad news, "It's wrapped up in some sort of dream energy and demons can't penetrate that."

If she was stronger she would be able to deal with the gypsy princess herself, but with three of her chosen four having walled themselves off she was getting weaker by the moment. She was tempted to pull energy from her three former friends like she had several years ago or days ago, she really couldn't remember. But they had figured out a way to weaken the connection then, she was sure they would be able to pick up on it again. She would save that parlor trick for another time, somehow she would have to trap the four into their nightmares so she could use them.

****

Ayden was in love with the Hawthorne Hotel in Salem. They had booked one of the suites and he had been in awe of the antiques. He dragged her on one of the ghost tours, and was like a little kid bouncing with excitement. There were a few on the tour that gave him a suspicious glance every now and then but no one asked out right if he was a vampire. For breakfast they went to one of the local bakeries where she was able to have coffee and a croissant while he took in the common square.

The waitress refilled her coffee and watched Ayden, who was outside, "We see a lot of vampires act this way. Apparently because of how well preserved we kept the buildings it reminds them of their glory days."

Kirsa smiled, "He dragged me on one of the ghost tours, and I promised him we would do the witches museum tomorrow. It's like Disney World for vampires."

The waitress laughed, "Do you need a to-go mug or anything else?"

"That and the check would be great," Kirsa replied.

A few minutes later she joined Ayden outside with her coffee, he was sitting on a bench just taking in the sights around him. He put an arm around her shoulder pulling her closer to him, kissing her lightly, he sighed happily.

"I never realized how quaint and charming it is," Ayden told her, his accent thick as he talked. "Or that some of the buildings would be older than me, it's feels like my old village in a way."

Kirsa kissed him, "We have an appointment to keep. I promise we can play tomorrow, today we need to work."

Ayden sighed as he stood up with her. They headed toward the car, once they got in Ayden typed the address into the GPS. About twenty minutes later they were pulling into a private drive that led to an old farmhouse. A woman stood at the front door and watched as Ayden and Kirsa got out of the car.

She opened the door for them allowing them both to enter."Eliza Jones," she introduced herself. "You can call me Liz. I have coffee going in the kitchen and I can make tea if you would like."

"Thank you,' Kirsa said. "Liz, this is my partner Ayden O'Brian."

"It's a pleasure to meet you," Liz replied as they shook hands.

"You have a lovely home," Ayden told her. "I love old farm houses."

Liz looked around her home, "Well this one was built in the mid seventeen hundreds. The original house had been destroyed by the time my husband's family bought the land and built the house. "

They followed her to the back of the house and were surprised by the bright and modern kitchen. There was a fire going in the original kitchen hearth and a teenage boy sat at the breakfast table reading a textbook. He looked up when they all entered.

"Aren't you a little short for an Assistant Director?" Alex asked looking at Kirsa.

"Size matters not," Kirsa replied. Alex stared at her for a moment then smiled when he caught the reference.

"Can I get any of you anything? Coffee? Tea? Manners?" The last one she said staring at Alex with a pointed look.

"Tea would be lovely," Ayden replied. "I'm sure Kirsa would take coffee."

"And manners are optional," Kirsa said.

Liz nodded getting the drinks in order. Alex studied the two of them as his mother moved about the kitchen. He wasn't sure how he felt about another wave of questions by another official. Tonight was his coven meeting and apparently they were going to stay and watch. Closing his school books he leaned back in his chair crossing his arms on his chest.Kirsa sipped her coffee and stared at Alex, watching him with the same intensity as he watched her.

She set her mug down, "Why don't we take a walk around the old farm, Alex?"

He looked at her, "I can't go outside, the demons are there."

"Actually for the moment they aren't," Ayden spoke up. Alex and his mom looked at him. "I'm a vampire."

"So how does that help me?" Alex asked.

"Because everyone, including demons has their own distinct smell," Ayden informed him. "Demons smell like sulfur and burnt frankincense. For the moment you are free of them."

Alex looked at them cautiously, "Alright."

Liz looked at her son, "Honey I'm going to stay here. There's a phone call I'm waiting for."

Alex nodded, Ayden walked out side with the young boy.Kirsa went to Liz and laid a hand on hers, "I'll get him to talk."

Liz smiled, "I meant what I said, be rough if you have too."

Kirsa nodded then followed the men out into the yard. Ayden was talking to Alex about how the different classes of species smelled. Alex was nodding as he listened, Kirsa watched as he kept glancing at an old barn at the edge of their property. They stopped at one of the garden areas that his mother had designed and laid out. They took seats around the fire pit; Ayden knelt next to it to light it to help ward off the chill in the air.

"Alex I can do this three ways," Kirsa began. "I can be sweet and charming, I can be mean or I can have Ayden put you in a trance to pull out what happened."

"He can force me to tell you what happened?" Alex asked nervously.

"I would rather you just tell me."

Alex looked at her then back at the flames. Kirsa studied him knowing that look well. "I know it is not just your secret to share, that it is also shared with your friends. They are protecting you also, but I can't help you if you don't tell me what happened. Trust me when I tell you I know what it is like." Alex laughed, Ayden looked at Kirsa.

"I'm going to introduce myself to Sylvia," Ayden told her. Sylvia was a vampire who lived a few houses down from the Jones'. "See if I can get her to keep an eye out for demons." Kirsa nodded, she watched him walk to the front of the house.

Alex leaned back in his chair and watched Kirsa, "He loves you," Alex replied. "He gives you the same look my dad gives my mom."

Kirsa smiled, "Thank you Alex." She was surprised by how observant and insightful he was. "You still have to talk to me."

"How do you know what it's like to hold a secret?" Alex asked.

"Because when I was your age I was in a coven with three friends," Kirsa began. "One of my friends, a full faery, decided to bite off more than she could chew and got involved with Demons. She tried a spell, it backfired and I had to go into the astral world to drag her back out. Since I did not know the whole situation at the time, things went bad and she is now living in a sanitarium for the rest of her life reliving what we went through. I would wish that fate on no one, Alex."

"I can't tell you the whole thing, my friends can fill in the blanks tonight," Alex told her. "I'll tell them its ok, I know they are trying to protect me."

"I know what that is like; I have two friends that are still protecting me from what happened in high school."

"So it will never end," Alex groaned. He had hoped that at some point they would stop having to shield him and keep him safe.

Kirsa couldn't help but laugh. "I'm afraid not. They honestly mean well. "

"That's why it's hard to be mad at them," Alex replied. He took a deep breath before he spoke again. "What do you know about what happened?"

"I know you were getting frustrated about not being able to do advanced spells and that you wanted to show everyone you could. Then something went wrong and you were brought back to your house."

"What do you think happened?" Alex inquired. He liked her; she wasn't trying to be his friend or his enemy. She was matter of fact.

"I think your buddies and you snuck out of the coven meeting and came back here, most likely to the barn. You tried the spell that you learned and it went horribly wrong. Your friends, doing what they could, brought you back to your house," Kirsa theorized.

"It was in a dream," Alex said nervously. "I learned about the ritual in a dream, the voice pointed me where to look and what to look for. She gave me a name to call out. I did everything the ritual said."

"What happened then?" Kirsa asked gently.

"I knew I would end up in the astral world, but I wasn't expecting to end up in my own nightmare. It was horrible, my worst fear come alive. The next thing I remember I was in my bed. I knew the demon followed me back but it won't cross the threshold because of this being a home."

Kirsa took his hand, "Alex if my theory is right. You truly are a victim in this, that spell would have gone wrong no matter what. I am going to need to see the ritual and where it took place."

"Can we do that with my coven tonight?" he asked. "I can face it with them, and my parents."

"Of course," Kirsa told him. She saw Ayden come back to the yard with Liz and another woman. Alex and she both stood up.

"Alex," Ayden began. "This is Sylvia, she lives two doors down from you."

"It's a pleasure, Alex," Sylvia said shaking his hand. "I have been informed that we are having a slight issue with demons?"

Alex nodded. "Yes, my fault."

Sylvia let out a laugh, "My dear child, it is no more your fault then it is the earth's fault for rotating around the sun. If a demon wants in on this world they will stop at nothing until they are."

Alex looked at her and for the first time felt the guilt he had been holding begins to ease. Liz put an arm around her son, "After Ayden and Kirsa leave, Sylvia is going to help us out by letting us know when the demons are around."

Alex looked at the woman he had just met; he went over and hugged her. Sylvia was taken aback but soon hugged the teenager back. "You're a good person, Alex. Don't let this change you."

Later, Kirsa helped Liz in the kitchen. Sylvia was in the living with Ayden and the rest of the family. In the kitchen, the two were getting the food ready for the coven meeting.

"I can't believe he talked finally," Liz said. She was still amazed that Alex finally broke his silence. When she had seen him in the backyard with Kirsa the haunted look he had for such a long time had begun to fade.

"I can't believe your husband is fine with two vampires entertaining his children," Kirsa said with a smile

.Liz smiled, "I should tell you what my husband does. He helps run a non-profit that helps paranormal's who have nothing find work, housing and vocational training," Liz looked out into her living room, seeing her three sons laughing at something that their father was saying. "I can't tell you how many times he has brought work home with him, and by that I mean a were-animal, a vampire, a witch and even the occasional faery."

Kirsa looked at her, "I will give him my lawyer's number and the number of the pact leader back in Grabenberg. It's a pride, but Phil has been known to take in a stray until a permanent placement can be made. He has a wolf with them at the moment because the local packs are filled."

"That would be nice," Liz agreed pulling out the tray of lasagna from the oven. "I am just grateful that my son has not been given up on."

"If it's one thing Al refuses to do it's give up on a case," Kirsa assured her. "During down times, he will assign unsolved cases to agents who have none. We are hoping to have enough agents one day to have a cold case division."

"He's a good man, your boss," Liz agreed.

The doorbell rang, she heard Alex yelling that he would get it. Liz finished setting up the buffet, "That would be the coven. I will make introductions. And just be prepared for the cold shoulder."

Kirsa walked into the living room and watched the woman who was talking to Alex. The woman turned and looked at Kirsa. The woman was tall; her raven black hair fell straight to her waist with red streaks in it. She wore a bright blue dress that hung to her feet, and her deep brown eyes narrowed in on Kirsa as if she was the enemy.

"You must be the new agent," the woman said.

"You must be Victoria," Kirsa said. They had talked on the phone a few times.

Victoria still was not certain it was wise getting OPIA involved or having another agent to deal with. "What are your qualifications to help with this case? The other agent did not make any headway."

"Let me reintroduce myself," Kirsa said. "I am Dr. Kirsa Heinrich, Assistant Director of OPIA." Several heads turned to look at them. "One of my degrees is in parapsychology with a concentration on how demons can affect the mind."

"And you brought Vampires with you?" Victoria asked, she had yet to meet a vampire she trusted. "I see you do not think witches are capable of protecting their own?"

Everyone in the room was quiet as Victoria challenged Kirsa. Ayden leaned back in the chair watching with amusement. Liz had warned them that Victoria could be headstrong and untrusting with strangers.

"The male vampire is Agent Ayden O'Brian who is my partner, the woman is Sylvia who is a neighbor of Alex's," Kirsa informed her. "Being a practitioner of the Norse tradition for over fifteen years I am well aware of how capable witchcraft is. However, vampires are able to sniff out demons, is there any in your coven that can?"She saw Victoria begin to relax.

"You are a fellow pagan?" Victoria asked. Kirsa nodded. "I did not know that vampires could sniff out demons."

"You can understand then why my being here will be an asset to help Alex," Sylvia spoke. "I can inform them when the neighborhood is clear or when a demon has arrived."

"It will be a great benefit to him," Victoria agreed. To give him some more freedom would help him out more than keeping him stashed away in the house and for that she would be thankful for outside help.

"Now that all the formalities are over, there is food in the kitchen," Liz said moving out of the way of the teenage boys who stormed the food first.

Kirsa walked over to Victoria, "Hi, I'm Kirsa it's a pleasure to meet you."

"And I am a fool," Victoria said laughing at herself. "I am so sorry, I am very protective of my coven and I fear for him."

"I understand," Kirsa told her. "He told me what happened."

Victoria looked surprised then relieved, "I am glad he told someone."

"He wants us all to go to the barn after dinner so he can show us what happened," Kirsa explained.

"I can tell that you have an idea of what went on."

"I do, but I want to see for myself before I make a decision." Ayden walked over, laying a hand on

Kirsa's arm. "If you want food I would get it now before the teenagers eat it all."

"Do you need anything?" Kirsa asked him.

"Sylvia brought synthetic with her, so we are both good," he whispered kissing her head. "I need to make a phone call."

"Is everything alright?" Kirsa asked. "Something about a council vote and needing your vote," Ayden told her. "I'll let you know."

She watched him walk out the front door. She looked at Victoria and smiled as they walked toward the food. "He's also going to make sure the area is still clear."

"He is very handsome, and big," Victoria said. She didn't need to mention that she appreciated the rear view. "I see why they sent him to be your guardian."

"Yeah he is the best," Kirsa replied as she put a large piece of lasagna on her plate. Alex waved her over to where he was sitting with three boys.

She walked over and sat with them, they all eyed her pile of food. "When Ayden comes back in he will nibble off of the plate."

"I didn't know they could eat, cool," said the blonde. "I'm Kyle."

"The one next to him is Brad and the one with blue hair is Dennis," Alex said introducing the rest of his friends

."Alex said it's cool to tell you what happened," Dennis replied. "That we won't get in trouble."

"You won't," Kirsa promised. "The only way we can help Alex is to know what happened."

"He said there are few other cases like his," Kyle added. "We have three similar cases, so we are trying to figure out why demons are becoming interested in teenagers."

"You know we have to deal with peer pressure, drugs, alcohol, sex and now demons," Brad replied. "Can't they play with adults?"

Kirsa laughed. "Usually they do, teenagers tend to be too stubborn, where adults can be easier to manipulate."

"Is that why the four cases are perplexing?" Kyle asked, "Because instead of targeting the adults they are targeting teens."

Kirsa nodded, "Demons are not known for changing their patterns. So we think something bigger is going on."

Ayden came in and sat next to Kirsa; he leaned over and stabbed a piece of lasagna. As he ate the four teenage boys started laughing. He looked at Kirsa, she just shook her head and smiled."I'm missing a joke," he said.

"I'll tell you later," Kirsa promised.

"Can I see your fangs?" Dennis asked. He had never met a vampire before.Ayden thought for a moment, he opened his mouth and extended his fangs. The teens looked at them in awe. He then pulled them back in, and the teens all jumped when he pushed them back out again.

"Mom you gotta see this," Alex called to his mom.

"Leave Ayden's fangs alone," Liz warned from across the room. "They are not a toy."

The off handedness of her comment sent them into hysterics. They spent the rest of dinner arguing over baseball and hockey. Which with them being Boston fans and Kirsa being a Yankee and Devils fan made it a very heated discussion.

After dinner was over and cleared, Kirsa and the group of twenty walked toward the barn where it all happened. Alex took a deep breath before sliding the old doors open, then he went in with the rest of them following. Ayden helped light some of the lanterns they had brought. Victoria, Liz and her husband, and the rest of the coven stood off to the side. Alex and his three friends walked to the center with Ayden and Kirsa. Kirsa took out the recorder and hit start then nodded to Alex to start.

"We used chalk to draw the circle," Alex began indicating to the spot they had used. The white chalk was now charred black. "I thought we had covered all the basic protection spells."

Victoria walked around the circle, impressed with what four teenagers had been able to do. "Alex you did a very impressive job. You even managed to close the circle."

"What happened after you opened the circle?" Kirsa asked.

Alex flipped through his book of spells, "I lit the candles for psychic aid, for clarity and for knowledge. Then I lay down in the center. Once I was situated the three stood at each cardinal point, my head was pointed toward north. After we were all arranged, I began the ritual that was shown to me in the dream."

He handed the book to Kirsa so she could read it. She handed it to Victoria to read and motioned Alex to continue.

"I knew something went wrong the moment I got the last word out," Alex told them. "I was supposed to be transported to a place of learning instead I was brought a place filled with my greatest fears."

Dennis shuddered when Alex said that, Kirsa looked at him. "What's Alex's worst fear, Dennis?"

"Clowns," Dennis replied.

"I can't even imagine a land filled with demented clowns."Kirsa couldn't help but shudder at that thought. "Alright who wants to fill us in on what was going on here?"

Kyle stood forward. "He was shaking, yelling out, we wanted to break the circle but knew that would make it worse. We studied the ritual while he lay unconscious; Brad took out his smartphone and began researching the astral plane and how to get Alex back. He found the spell we used to sever the tie."

"What kind of spell?" Kirsa and Victoria asked at the same time.

Brad tried to remember, "It was a simple chant to get someone out of the astral world if they became trapped against their will. I knew we didn't have everything we needed, but we couldn't break the circle. It said there was a chance that something could follow him back, we figured it was better than leaving him there."

Kirsa walked over to Brad and hugged him; she knew what he was thinking. That he had damned his friend to a lifetime of torment by bringing him back. She made him look at her, "You saved his life, Brad. If you left him there in the astral world, he would have died. We can send the demon back but we can't bring the dead back to life."

"I just wish I could have figured out how to keep the demon in the other world," Brad said.

Victoria stepped forward and took Brad's hand, "In that moment, under those circumstances even the most experienced witch would have brought something back with them."

Liz walked over and kissed Brad on the head, "Thank you for bringing him back. Even if I have a demon that stalks my yard I at least have my son."

"What happened next?" Kirsa asked.

"I had to go in after him," Brad replied. "He was too terrified and we couldn't pull him out by the spell alone. So I had to go in and literally help him battle his demons."

Ayden put an arm around Kirsa knowing this was hitting close to home. They stayed in the barn another twenty minutes. When everyone was leaving the barn, Victoria, Kirsa and Ayden stayed behind.

"You have seen this before," Victoria replied.

"Something similar," Kirsa told her. "That spell he did was to summon a demon. What went wrong was he did not know it. So the spell backfired."

"I don't know much about spells dealing with demons, can you explain?" Victoria asked.

"Let's say you want to become more powerful or seek vengeance," Kirsa began. "The easiest thing to do is summon a demon. Once you find the name of one, you bind them to your bidding. At some point, usually after you get what you want, you have to pay the demon for their power."

"That much I know, but you said he didn't intentionally mean to call forth a demon. How is that possible?" Victoria asked.

"That's where this gets complicated," Kirsa warned. "Someone invaded his dreams gave him a spell that would make him more powerful. They do not tell him it is going to summon a demon, which means he is not a willing participant in the spell. The demon is furious because it means someone is using him to gain his power and not pay him back."

"So he piggybacks with Alex," Victoria said understanding. "In hopes that he will learn who is trying to trick him."

"Exactly," Kirsa replied.

"Could it be another demon?"

Kirsa shook her head. "No, demons cannot go into the dream world, unless they are summoned by the same person. Even then it can only be in their dreams not someone else's."

Victoria thought for a moment, "Liz was told by Agent Willis that there were other cases like this one?"

"I am meeting with the rest of the families next week in hopes of figuring out who could be behind this," Kirsa explained. "Once I know who and why I can figure out how to end it."

"If you need any help you have my Coven," Victoria told her.

CHAPTER 10

Kirsa stared at the blood and horror. She had walked into the room with a detached sense of self. Kirsa knew she had seen far worse scenes then what lay before her, but that didn't make it easier each time you were faced with a violent death. Just this summer she had seen such brutality that nothing fazed her much anymore. But this was close to some of the bodies she had seen.

Joanna had been impaled through the heart and anchored to wall of Susannah's bedroom. Her blond hair had covered her face, her scrubs had soaked up the blood that had spilled from the wound. Sara and Kirsa stood next to each other as they took in the scene. Both were in flannel pajama pants, hooded sweatshirts, and winter coats. It was close to four in the morning, they had only been working on a few hours of sleep when the phone call came. Ayden drove them to Shady Pines, Frank Willis met them there as Al went immediately to the Fae to inform the high court that their worst nightmare had occurred.

Susannah Murphy had escaped and killed an innocent. Sara's intern, began with taking photos as Sara began to instruct the rest of the team. Frank was busy taking statements while Ayden was sniffing around for some type of trail.

Kirsa walked to the body and laid a gloved hand on Joanna, she was stunned at how cold the body felt. From all accounts she had only been dead four hours but her body felt as cold as ice. Sara stood next to her and watched as her friend used her new heightened senses.

"Brimstone, sulfur, rain, fear, joy," Kirsa replied as she took in the scents. "Joanna was terrified while Susannah was joyful at what she was doing."

"She isn't going to get away with murder," Sara replied.

Kirsa walked closer as she took in the scents from the blood, she lifted the shirt that Joanna wore. "She's fucking dead, I'll kill her myself."

Sara watched as Kirsa was already out the door and on her cell, walking over to the body with her stunned intern, she lifted the shirt. *kIrSa* had been carved into the abdomen. As the intern took pictures of it as Sara cursed worse than a sailor.

****

"She had to have gone somewhere," Al replied exasperated as he paced Kirsa's living room. It was close to six in the morning, none of them were working on full sleep. Ayden was the only one functioning.

"I know, however once I left the bedroom all trace of her vanishes," Ayden repeated.

"That's impossible!" Al yelled.

Kirsa came in and set three steaming mugs down on the coffee table. From the metallic scents coming from two of the mugs Al went for the third that smelled like coffee. "Beings don't just disappear."

"They can if they go to the astral plane," Kirsa replied curling on the couch next to a snoring greyhound.Ayden and Al both turned to look at her.

"What do you mean?" Ayden asked.

"Wyrm told me once about a witch that could actually send her body into the astral realm, not just her spirit," Kirsa explained. "She used the ability to kill the wives of her lovers while they slept so that no one would know. It took a vampire to sniff her out, and she only had a bit of fae blood."

"Do you know how?" Al asked sitting in the armchair. Kirsa shook her head drinking her blood laced coffee.

"I can call him later to see if he remembers or if he has records of how."

"How do we beat her if she can do this?"

"I don't know," Kirsa replied. "I think we need more info before we launch a full scale war on her."

"Frank is positive he found three more cases that fit with a potential for two more," Al told her. "That will be nine in total."

Ayden and Kirsa both looked at Al. "Power of three," Kirsa replied.

"Look Al, why don't you take the guest room in the basement," Ayden suggested. "You are both exhausted."

"What if she comes to attack?" Al asked. "You'll be ok by yourself?"

Before Ayden could answer, Kirsa did. "Don't worry we got three were's watching the house and another shadow. We'll be safe."

Ayden followed Kirsa up to their bedroom a short time later. He watched as she got ready for bed as she curled into their bed he watched her.. "I warned Dietrich and Tony that you might pick up on the extra scents," Ayden said. "But I also agreed that extra security was needed."

"As do I, so don't worry, none of you will be turned into toads, Sara maybe for not telling me but the rest of you are safe."

Ayden waited for her to fall asleep before he slipped out his phone. He hit the first number and waited.

"Yeah boss," the gravelly voice replied.

"Let me know the first whiff of anything different, tell the cats the same thing," Ayden ordered. "Oh and Lance, she knows about you."

There was silence for a moment. "She's a smart one. I'll let you know."

Ayden slid the phone onto the bedside table. Kirsa was as safe as she was going to be for the moment. He had someone he trusted with his own life looking out for her yet he couldn't get rid of the nagging feeling that they were missing something.

****

They had left early the following morning, in part to get to their destination before the storm hit. As they entered Pittsburg, the snow had begun to fall harder making travel difficult. Ayden had asked an old friend if they could use his place in Pittsburg, which would make it easier for them to travel to their destinations if the storm hit.

Now, Dr. Arnold Kesler met Kirsa and Ayden at the entrance of the hospital located on the outskirts of Pittsburgh. Kirsa's ski jacket was unzipped despite the snow falling from the sky, Ayden had a black trench coat on more to protect his clothes from the elements then keep him warm.

Dr. Kesler nodded at them both then escorted them to a private office. "I was worried when I heard the weather report for today," Arnold said offering them both coffee.

"We left early yesterday morning," Kirsa told him after thanking him for the coffee. "We rather risk traveling on turkey day then not make it here."

"Smart decision," Arnold agreed. "Is your hotel far?"

"I have a friend who lives close and offered us his home while he is in Romania," Ayden replied.

Arnold absorbed the information and continued on. "Her parents are furious," Arnold informed them as he went back to why they were here.

"We figured they would be," Kirsa responded. "They didn't want this conversation to happen, they hoped the storm would deter us."

"Adding fuel to the fire is the fact that one of Kristina's friends is here to help answer your questions."

"They must be ready to blow," Kirsa said.

"I will go see if the girls are ready then I will come get you," Arnold said as he got up and left the room.

Ayden turned and looked at Kirsa, she looked paler than normal. "You alright?" he asked. When he ran a finger down her cheek he found it cold.

"I think the stress is taking its toll," she told him.

"When we get back to the house we will take care of it," he promised.

Vlad had made sure that his home was a welcome to all supernaturals. It was always heavily supplied with blood, food, and medical supplies. Because of his age, he was deemed safe to all supernaturals. Meaning his hunger was no longer an issue as he only needed little blood to sustain him. It was rumored that he was older than Shamus by several thousand years. And now in his retirement years as he called them, Val made his home a safe house to any in need, whether traveler or stranded.

"Is his name really Vlad?" Kirsa asked.

"Vladimir, actually," Ayden replied. "After he became a vampire it became an inside joke amongst his line. What makes it better is that he had relatives in the Order of the Dragon." Ayden left out the part that Vlad had been changed before he could be sworn into the order.

"Vampires," Kirsa mumbled shaking her head.

Ayden laughed kissing her lightly. The door opened, and Arnold walked in. "One of the doctors is taking her parents to the food court so we can head up without running into them."

"Won't they know when they enter the room?" Kirsa asked as they followed him.

Arnold looked back and smiled, "She refuses to see them instead they sit in the waiting room and pray that she will change her mind."

Kirsa shook her head as they went into an elevator. He swiped his card since they were going to a closed ward. Kirsa had always liked Arnold; he was an Empath making him a phenomenal therapist because he was able to pick up on people's inner emotions and feelings. They had worked together from time to time when he was lost on a case and needed help.

"What is their relationship like?" Kirsa inquired as they got off the floor and waited to go through security.

"From what I have been able to find out, they have never been close. Her relationship with her father is volatile while with her mother she feels pity," Arnold explained. "Her grandmother, who visits three times a week, has never been a fan of her son-in-law but tries to remain neutral."

"Not an easy place to be in," Ayden surmised. "Especially with a grandchild involved."

"Kris' lawyer is working out turning her over to her grandmother until her next birthday, both would be content with that," Arnold told them.

The security guard looked at the gun that Ayden carried and raised an eyebrow. Ayden handed him his paperwork and ID, the guard let out a low whistle as he read it then looked at Kirsa and nodded.

"Try to keep an eye on it," the guard said as he handed back the paperwork.

"Lock is sensitive to my touch," Ayden replied, referring to the locking mechanism on his gun.

"Biometric scanner?" the guard asked intrigued.

"All Shadows have them," Ayden told him. He showed the guard how it worked. "I can get you a name of the guy who makes them for us if you want them for the security team here?"

"I might have my boss talk to you," the guard told him. "We are trying to find ways to keep our equipment safe from the patients."

Kirsa just raised an eyebrow and Ayden smiled as they headed through the last security door. They entered a large common room with bright yellow walls; couches were grouped all around the room. There were two television areas, a bunch of computer desks and bookshelves. Teens were sprawled on the couches or at the computers.

"We have a bunch that went home for the holidays and won't be back until tonight or tomorrow," Arnold explained. "We have a smaller common room for the less stable patients and those that need to be closely watched. We do let them mingle with the others here but we try to keep it more structured then."

"It's happy," Ayden said. The two turned and stared at him. "Well for a mental ward it is."

The two doctors shook their heads, Arnold went down a hallway and knocked on a door. A blonde teenage girl answered all bubbly.

"Hi Dr. K," she said.

"Hi Caroline." He motioned for them to enter. "Girls these are Agent Heinrich and Agent O'Brian."

The two girls nodded though most of their attention was on Ayden. "I will be in the stalking room if you need me," Arnold replied.

Kirsa waited for the door to shut. "Stalking room?"

The brunette laughed. "It's what we call the security room, they have cameras that face all the doors in the hallways, and the intercom system runs through there. In other words we can't go anywhere without someone seeing."

"Hence why you feel so safe here," Kirsa replied as she sat in one of the empty chairs.

"Yeah, I figure someone will see me acting weird or trying to do something that I shouldn't," Kristina said. "I'm Kristina by the way. The perky blonde is Caroline."

They made their pleasantries and got acquainted with each other before Kirsa began with her questions for the teenager.

"Why a psychiatric ward?" Kirsa asked. "Why not a church or even your home?"

Kristina sat cross-legged on her bed and pulled at an imaginary spot on her comforter. "I hated my church, the one my parents dragged me too," Kristina explained. "I hated them, the congregation is filled with self-impressed snobs who do good only because it makes them look good. The minister gives me the creeps. In my research, a demon can enter a dwelling unless it is warded and if a house is filled with love and caring."

Thinking of Alex, Kirsa nodded. "Yes. Love and all the other emotions that go with it can ward a house, protecting it from demons."

"My house has never been a home; it's never been filled with love or caring. Just fear and manipulation," Kristina said. "The demon, it followed me home that night and I knew I wasn't safe. My parents thought I was going insane. They were the ones that brought me here. When I met Dr. Kesler I felt like I could breathe again. I felt safe and secure."

"Why would she feel safe here?" Caroline asked Kirsa.

"A floor like this is filled with a wide range of emotions, feelings," Kirsa began to explain. "Even though these are things that Demons crave, in this amount it is almost too much for them."

"Too much crazy for them to syphon," Kristina said understanding.

"Exactly."

"You want to tell us what led up to us being here?" Ayden asked tapping a pen on his black boots.Kristina looked at him as she bit her lip,

"You have to understand something first. I have never gotten along with my father, despite whatever stories he might try to sell you."

"Can I ask why?"

"Simple, I wasn't born a boy," Kristina said. "He was so sure I would be that he told everyone then I came out a girl and proved him a liar."

"With a mentality like that you would think he came from my time," Ayden replied dryly. "So, because of you being born the 'wrong sex' he has never forgiven you."

"Pretty much, when I was younger I did whatever I could to please him, by middle school I realized that nothing I did would make him happy," Kristina told them. "Anyway, I guess what led to the whole exploring witchcraft was curiosity. I didn't fit in at the church, I don't fit in at my high school, I felt like I was alone and then here was this religion that accepted the loners."

"The Ouija board was not Kristina's idea," Caroline added. "We had both heard stories and really stuck to tarot cards and that kind of stuff."

"Alright," Kirsa said trying to ignore the headache that was pounding between her ears. She felt like someone was trying to get in. "It might go easier if I ask questions and you two answer them."

The two girls nodded, Kirsa went into her bag and pulled out Kristina's folder and opened it up. "Now how into witchcraft were you? Were you in a coven? Was it a hobby? It's fine if it was just a hobby. "

" More of a hobby I guess," Kristina said. "I had bought a few books and read them and found it interesting. I was good with tarot cards."

"Caroline?"

"I like reading about the herbal remedies and what not."

"Ok. So, you are feeling as though you don't fit in any-where and you have a father who doesn't understand you," Kirsa summed up. Kristina nodded so Kirsa continued. "You start reading about witchcraft and Wicca and decided to give it a try on a hobby basis. While doing this you teach yourself how to use the tarot deck. Now how did we go from there to having a demon want your soul?"

Ayden raised an eyebrow at how blunt she was, he could sense the headache that she was battling. Looking back at the two girls he saw a look pass between them and sighed. He also began to smell the faint scent of brimstone and sulfur.

"I don't know," Kristina replied. "It's not like I did something, and it backfired. All I did was play with tarot cards."

"Don't forget the Ouija board," Kirsa replied. She caught a movement out of the corner of her eye and she swore saw a silhouette of Susannah standing near Kristina. "Where were you at the time this all happened?"

Caroline answered, "We were invited to a small party with other students that shared our interests. Kristina had started taking her cards to school, they noticed and then we start hanging out."

"Thank you, Caroline," Kirsa replied. "Alright so you got to the party and at some point, the board gets brought out. What happens?"

"We started with people we knew that were dead, and then when nothing was going on we started asking dumb questions," Kristina replied folding her arms. Kirsa tried not to rip her hair out in frustration, it was like pulling teeth. "Like if there's a demon in the room come forward?"

"Not that dumb," Kristina replied. Kirsa stood up annoyed. "Look ladies, we drove here in the beginning of a snow storm, all because you wanted to talk to us and tell us what happened. Now that we are here I feel like we are playing twenty questions and getting nowhere."

"Kristina do you want help?" Ayden asked.

"Yes."

"Do you want a demon to be tied to you for the rest of your life?"

"No."

"Then you need to answer the question," Ayden said. "If you don't, we walk out of the room and you are stuck with a demon. If you do, then we can help you. Those are your options."

Kristina looked out one of the windows in her room be-fore she said anything. "Look I don't know what you want me to say. I mean we played with the Ouija board and the next thing I know there is a demon trying to possess me and the only place I feel safe is looked in this hell hole." Caroline went to say something but closed her mouth when Kristina shot her a dirty look.

Kirsa looked at Ayden, "Then we are done here. "

"You're just going to leave?" Kristina asked surprised.

"You aren't telling us anything important, now we move on to the next person on our list and hope they will have more information," Kirsa told her.

Ayden followed her out of the room, before they could say anything the door opened, and Caroline slipped out.

"I don't know what's wrong with her," Caroline apologized. "Yesterday she was all about the meeting today, then when I got here she was all against it and how we all were turning against her."

"Caroline do you know what happened?" Kirsa asked.

"All I know is that when we were asking the board questions she asked to speak to a specific person," she said. "I don't remember the name, but it was a strange one. It was after that when she went crazy."

"Could you ask the others if they remember?" Ayden asked. "Even if it's not the exact name it would help."

"I will do anything to help her," Caroline promised.

Kirsa handed her a business card. "Can I ask what happened to the Ouija board?" Kirsa asked.

"We burnt it the next night, then Skylar and I buried it on sacred ground and sprinkled holy water over it."

"Good thinking," Kirsa said surprised how quickly and thoroughly they had acted. "Call me anytime if you need to talk."

Caroline nodded then slipped back into the room. Kirsa and Ayden walked down to the security room. Arnold was watching the camera that was hidden in Kristina's room. They watched as she paced the room obviously talking to someone, Caroline was trying to engage her in conversation, but Kristina was acting like she wasn't even there.

"Is there audio on the tape?" Kirsa asked.

"In order to give privacy, we turn it off unless a threat is posed," Arnold replied.

Ayden focused on the screen, "She's talking to someone that's not Caroline. Something went wrong or didn't go as planned and she's trying to apologize."

Everyone in the room, including Kirsa, turned to look at Ayden in amazement. He looked at them and shrugged his shoulders, "I can read lips and even though it's on mute I can pick up some of what they are saying."

"Can you get us a copy?" Kirsa asked the security guard.

He looked at Arnold before answering. "Yeah I can send it in a media file then mail you the hardcopy."

"Perfect," Kirsa said. "Arnold I'm sorry about today."

"I should be the one apologizing," he told her. "Let me walk you two to your car. It has gotten pretty bad out since you arrived."

"We don't have far to drive," Ayden assured him as they entered the elevator.

"After he transcribes the tapes can you send me a copy for her file?" Arnold asked.

"Of course," Kirsa promised.

"Did she give you anything?"

"Caroline snuck out after we left and told us that Kristina asked for a specific person to come forward," Kirsa informed him. "She's going to ask the others who were there if they can recall the name."

"Caroline and a few of the others have come every week to visit her," Arnold told them. "They have all tried to rationalize with her, their parents alternate who brings them and who picks them up."

"And of course on days like today she is oblivious to it all," Kirsa said.

"Exactly. I will let you know if I learn anything in the meantime," Arnold said as they reached the entrance doors. Taking a look at the white outside he nodded to them, "Drive safe."

CHAPTER 11

Like many wealthy vampires, Vlad's home was found in a gated community filled with large estate like homes and property. Ayden's name was on the list of visitors letting them through the gates. Kirsa could barely focus on the homes and well-maintained lawns as they drove toward the end of the development. Ayden pushed the button on the remote and the garage door slowly opened so that he could pull in alongside Vlad's Jaguar. They climbed out of the car and walked into the mud room where they stripped off their winter gear.

"Why don't you go change and I'll get food," Ayden suggested.

Kirsa nodded as she moved sluggishly toward the back stairs that led up to the second floor. Ayden watched her with a look of concern. Even when dealing with the horrors of the summer, he had never seen her so tired and sluggish. But during the summer she had been drinking more blood to compensate for her disorder.

Now she was on a smaller dose. Walking to one of the two stainless fridges, he pulled out two bottles of blood and poured them into glasses. He then went to the other fridge and sorted through the food that Vlad left for his staff. Vlad was in Romania dealing with some issues on his ancestral estate, he had sent Ayden a text that he and Kirsa were welcome to stay at his home while they were in Pittsburg.

Ayden pulled out a homemade turkey pot pie and followed the directions that the housekeeper had written on it. He then helped himself to the wine selection and pulled out a nice cabernet. When Kirsa came downstairs in black stretch pants and an oversized shirt, the wine had been poured, the blood had been poured and the pot pie was on the table.

Kirsa looked around the dining room as she took a seat, "He likes the dark and dramatic doesn't he?"

"I think if he could walk around in a black cape he would," Ayden said with a smile. "Vlad likes the theatrical version of our life."

"I see that," Kirsa said as she drained the goblet of blood in seconds then waited for the head rush that would come.

In moments her senses became heightened and all the fatigue and stress began to melt away. Ayden watched as her violet eyes became darker and clearer and the dark circles vanished. He smelled the change in her emotions as she became calmer and more grounded.

Smiling she took a sample bite of the pot pie and savored all the different flavors she was picking up. He sat back and sipped his wine enjoying watching her eat. When she offered him a bite he accepted then went back to the comfortable silence that lay between them. He refilled their wine glasses and laid a kiss on her head as he walked past her.

He picked up her mood an instant before she got out of a chair. Smiling at him she took their wine glasses and toward the door. She paused in the doorway and threw a look at him from over her shoulder. He knew right then he was a goner. That at that moment he would do anything for this woman, that she was his fate. He followed her to the grand staircase and then up to their guest suite.

She set their glasses down on an antique end table the turned to face him. Without saying a word she pulled her t-shirt off revealing a black bra edged in red lace, when she slowly pulled off her stretch pants he found out she wore matching panties. That was the final straw that snapped his control as he moved toward her.

****

"Holy shit," Ayden said as he lay on his back and pulled her against him. "You bit me."

Kirsa nodded then kissed the puncture marks that had not healed all the way. "I've never been able to do that before."

He kissed the top of her head as his hand traced circles on her back, "You weren't able to pierce skin the other night."

She laughed, "Yeah sorry about that."

He tilted her face so that he could look into her eyes, "Kirsa you are the only person that has bitten me like that and made it feel erotic. "

She knew he had lovers before her, but it was nice to know that she was different. "Maybe it was the blood at dinner, maybe it recharged my system?"

"Maybe we got a preview of what you'll be," he pointed out.

Sorrow filled her eyes, "Ayden we don't know if I will survive this."

He kissed her nose, "You have no choice in the matter."

She laughed and was comforted by his certainty. Sighing she curled closer to him and let sleep wash over her. He lay there for an hour before sliding away from her; he kissed her bare shoulder before he pulled the blanket over her. Ayden pulled on his trousers then stepped out into the sitting room. He closed the double doors before he placed his phone call. P

Patrick O'Brian picked up on the second ring, "Its wee bit early, Ayden."

"I need to talk to you," he said responding Irish.

Patrick knew when his blood brother spoke in their native tongue that it was serious. "What's up?" he asked as he poured himself some blood.

"It's Kirsa."

"She hasn't taken a turn for the worse, has she?" Pat asked pausing.

His biggest fear was Ayden losing Kirsa to the blood disorder. For if she died from it, Ayden had made Patrick promise to stake him and then bury his ashes with Kirsa in her family crypt. No one else but Pat knew of the plans since he was executor of Ayden's will.

"No," Ayden assured him. "Here's the thing, she's been really run down lately so tonight when we got back from the interview I had her take a glass of blood."

"It makes sense, with how she's been working the case I can see it taking its toll. How'd the interview go?"

"Horrible, which didn't help," Ayden said. "I had her take the blood during dinner, and I watched as she changed before me."

"Define changed," Pat inquired becoming more interested. He locked his door so that his baby brother Daniel wouldn't barge in. Daniel was a pest on his best days and a nightmare on his worst.

"The dark circles vanished, her eyes became darker and clearer, I could smell the change in her emotions; she became calm and more at ease. The agitation was gone; it was obvious that her senses were heightened."

"During the summer when Finn had her on the bags regularly didn't you say her senses became more pronounced?"

"They did, Pat she drank from me."

There was silence as Pat absorbed the words that Ayden had said. Ayden had never allowed another vampire to drink from him, unless it was a life or death situation.

"What do you mean drank? Like you slit your wrist and she drank from your wound?"

"No like in the middle of sex she bit my shoulder and fangs broke the skin and she drank from the wound," Ayden said.

"She's never been able to do that before has she?"

"No, it was like I got a preview of what she will be like as a vampire."

"Well shit," Pat replied as he pulled on his chin. "You gotta call Finn and let him know, because you need to know if this is going to lead her to changing the old fashion way."

"Will he talk to me about it?"

Now Pat knew why Ayden was calling. "Let me check, give me a minute."

Pat walked over to his laptop and pulled up the file he was looking for. He was known as the Vampire's lawyer as he held many of their wills and bequeaths on his lap top. Going through Ayden's and Kirsa's he found what he was looking for.

"Yes, she signed off on her last visit that he can discuss her medical history with you," Pat replied. "His office sent me a scan of the document."

"Thanks," Ayden replied. "What are your thoughts?"

"Knowing her history, she's been showing signs for months now, maybe this is another step toward her changing," Pat theorized. "But I'm not a doctor according to today's standards so I would still call Finn when you get a chance. He will probably have better answers than me. It's been a few centuries since I practiced medicine."

"Thanks Pat," Ayden said.

"Anytime, you know that," Pat told him. "Since I have you on the phone, when are you two coming to visit again?"

"We'll be in Germany for Yule and Christmas, I'll see if we can figure something out."

"Maybe we can meet up in Germany at the estate since you were not there the last time we were all at the there," Pat said.

Daniel would not let any of them forget that Ayden got out of going to the estate for protection over the summer. He also ignored them when they explained that Ayden was off dealing with a sociopathic vampire.

"Yeah you know I was just dealing with nut jobs and people who wanted me dead," Ayden laughed.

"Alright I will talk to you later."

"Sounds good."

Ayden hung up the phone then checked his messages to see if he missed anything important. It was another two hours before he returned to bed, Kirsa curled up right against him and he held onto her. He hoped that his brother would not have to follow through with his decree; he hoped that Kirsa would beat the disorder that threatened to kill her.

****

The following day, Frank met Ayden and Kirsa at the old row house in one of the neighborhoods in Pittsburgh. Since they were there dealing with Kristina they figured they could stop in on one of the old crime scenes. Frank handed her a steaming cup of coffee as they looked at the house.

"Seventeen-year-old honor student," Frank began. "Her name was Marissa Allen. Her parents moved out of the home about six years ago, after the death. Now they rent it out. They are in between tenants at the moment."

"Let's get this over with," Kirsa said as they headed up the steps.

The front door opened, and a small woman came out, she was a bit heavy but it worked for her. Her white hair was pulled back as she studied the three of them.

"I'm Martha," she said shaking their hands.

"I'm Kirsa Heinrich, this is Ayden O'Brian, and you talked to Frank Willis before," Kirsa introduced them.

"Why don't you come in, I arrived early to turn the heat on," Martha told them as she ushered them over the threshold. She guided them to a sparkly furnished living room. "Frank said you reopened Rissa death."

In the car they had decided that Kirsa would do the talking. "I am working on a case with Ayden and

Frank," Kirsa began. "There are some similarities between the current cases and Marissa's."

"They wanted to rule her death a suicide," Martha said. "We knew she didn't kill herself and fought it until they left the death as unknown. I think they wanted to rule it, close it, and forget it."

"I know it's been six years, but can you tell us about what happened?" Kirsa asked.

Martha nodded. She needed to move while she talked, it kept her calm and centered. "Marissa was a junior, an honor student and president of the student council. Our oldest was in his senior year of College," Martha told them. "It was after Christmas that we all noticed the change."

"What kind of change?" Kirsa asked gently.

"She was still bringing home A's and being active in school. But something about her changed. You would be talking to her and gets this feeling that she was off somewhere else. Sometimes if you walked by her bedroom you would hear her talking to someone. You would almost be certain you heard a second voice, but when you went to check there was no one else there."

"Did she change any friends?" Kirsa asked.

"No, and she didn't lose any either, she didn't break up with a boyfriend, or go through any trauma," Martha replied. They had answered similar questions six years ago.

"I know these are similar to ones you have answered in the past," Kirsa apologized.

"I understand, you are new to the case, so you need the background," Martha replied. "If it will help Rissa then I'll repeat my answered every day for the rest of my life."

Kirsa laid a hand on Martha's. "Did she mention any new interests? Like Witchcraft, tarot, Ouija board?"

"None," Martha told her. "After we cleaned up her room, we found the Tarot Cards and her journals. I couldn't read them; I didn't want to know what was in them."

Martha walked over to a box in the corner and picked it up. She handed it to Kirsa, "We thought it might help with answers. You didn't know her so what you read won't affect you."

"Thank you," Kirsa said. "Can you bring me to where she was found?"

Martha nodded and led them to the basement door. "She was found down there near the back of the basement. I just can't go down there."

Kirsa laid a hand on Martha's arm letting her know she understood. Kirsa headed down the stairs with the two men following her. Ayden turned on the overhead light; it did nothing to get rid of the gloom. The walls were cinder block, the floor cement, the air was damp. Kirsa walked around and as she headed toward the back she felt like she had walked through a wall of ice. Ayden caught her before she hit the ground.

"Who are you?" Marissa asked. Her red hair was a mess; mascara was running down her face, she was in her favorite pair of pajamas.

"I'm Kirsa." Kirsa could see the fear in the young girl. "What's wrong Marissa?"

"She won't leave me alone," Marissa told her.

"Who?"

"The woman," Marissa said. She looked around frantically as she hugged herself tightly. "She's everywhere, in my sleep, in my head. I turn a corner and I see her. How can she be everywhere and no one but me see her?"

"Tell me about her," Kirsa said calmly.

Marissa shook her head. "If I talk about her she'll get angry. She needs me for something but won't tell me what."

"I want to help you," Kirsa told her.

Marissa laughed cynically. "No one can help me."

She looked off toward the corner. "Did you hear that?"

"Hear what?" Kirsa asked. Then she heard it, a soft voice calling out Marissa's name.

"Ignore the voice Marissa. If you give her power it will make her stronger, if you ignore her it will make her weaker."

The voice got louder; Marissa's eyes began to dart all over the place as she backed toward the corner of the room. She was trembling and Kirsa knew she could do nothing.

"She's here, you need to leave or she'll get you too," Marissa pleaded.

Then she went very still. "No please don't, I promise the next time I'll have it. I won't fail you; I've never failed in my life."

Kirsa then watched in horror as a silhouette appeared with a long sword. Before Marissa could scream the sword went through her pinning her to the cinder blocks behind her. No blood poured from the wound even as the body convulsed. Kirsa watched as the body slowly slumped forward. The person pulled the sword out and laughed. When the person turned toward Kirsa, she screamed out in recognition.

Kirsa awoke lying on the old couch up in the living room. Martha came out of the kitchen with a cup of tea and handed it to her as she sat up. Ayden held her other hand while she sipped the tea to calm her stomach.

"She didn't kill herself," Kirsa told Martha.

"Then how?" Martha asked. The doubt she had tried to ignore for the last six years vanished with that simple statement.

"I don't know but I have a feeling the journals will tell us something," Kirsa assured her.

"If you need anything further, please don't hesitate to call," Martha said. "And thank you, thank you for not giving up on Rissa."

CHAPTER 12

At thirteen Kirsa had read It by Stephen King and had seen the movie. The book thrilled her to the bone and the movie freaked her out for a long time. Neither prepared her for the hell she awoke to. When she had gone to bed, she was home in her own bedroom with Zero snoring next to her on the floor. They had gone to OPIA and updated Al, then came home and relaxed. Now, she somehow found herself in what she could only assume was Alex's nightmare, there were clowns everywhere. And not your "happy spray you with water from a flower clowns", but demented and terrifying clowns.

Clowns with their makeup streaked and blood splattered, clowns wielding bloody machetes and all laughing. They were making Pennywise look happy and kid friendly. Kirsa stood hiding behind a ruin that was crumbling and covered in cobwebs. She tried to figure out how she had ended up here, all she remembered was a blinding headache and then she woke up here. Silently she peered out and saw clowns with running face paint carrying machetes and other sharp implements, they looked as if they were hunting for someone or something. She tried to get her bearings as to where she was and where she could go.

All she knew for certain was she was never going to look at a clown again in the same way. She almost screamed when a bloody clown head came flying at her followed by a blood dripping axe. Closing her eyes she tried to calm her heart rate and tried to formulate a plan to get her out of this hell hole. Focusing on the movement that the clowns marched in, the seconds between swinging axes, she began to make her plan on getting through the obstacle course of hell.

Ayden held onto Kirsa's hand while machines beeped, and conversations occurred outside her room. She had woken up screaming at two in the morning, Lance had broken through the back door as soon as he got the first whiff of sulfur and was in the bedroom as Ayden was shaking off the trance he had been put under. Now Lance paced the room as Al

180

and Frank tried to get information on what the hell was going on.

"Al's stalking the nurses' station for details," Frank replied as he entered the room. "I really hate this place," he said as he took in Kirsa laying deathly still in her hospital bed.

"It seems to me you guys are prone to hospitals," Ayden observed.

"When you deal with the nightmares and those that chase them hospitals become second homes," Frank informed him.

"Any word on the others?" Lance asked as Ayden traced a finger over Kirsa's face.

"Sabrina has Zero and is fine, as a precaution though, Brian and Emily are staying at the manor with her and Colin. Phil is sending two guys over there just to make sure." Frank relayed. "Sara is fine also thought Phil and Kirsa's cousin Laura are staying at their house. Bridgette is home with them, she told her coach that she was needed at home, so she has been helping out."

"What about the teens?" Lance inquired as he stopped pacing. Ayden had filled him in on what was happening.

"I called and left messages so now we'll wait to hear back and hope no one else is like this."

Ayden nodded, glad that he did not have to worry about anyone else at the moment, and he could focus on Kirsa. He hated seeing her like this, in a hospital bed hooked up to machines. Al walked in thrusting a black thermos into both Ayden and Lance's hands.

"Got it from the night nurse," Al said unbuttoning the top button. "They have a supply for such moments so if you need more just hit the call button."

Ayden nodded unscrewing the cap. He drank some of the contents before he said anything, "Any word?"

"According to her brainwaves and heart monitor, she is fine," Al said. "Which is the good news, the bad news is Finn and the neurologist have no clue why she won't wake up. Finn's going to analyze her blood see if it has anything to do with the disorder but from your report he is inclined to agree with you."

Before they could continue the conversation, Dr. Finn walked in and shut the door. He walked over to the bed and checked on Kirsa before turning to the two men.

"Alex slipped into a similar unconscious state about six hours ago," Finn began. "I just got off the phone with his doctor. Same thing, he complained of a vicious headache then the next thing his father knows is he began to collapse."

Al grabbed his phone, "I'm getting guards posted on Sara, Sabrina and the three other victims."

Finn waited until Al left the room, "Ayden I don't even know what to do here. Neither does the neurologist, everything indicates that she's fine."

Kirsa ripped a piece of her shirt and tied it tightly around the wound on her thigh; she tried to catch her breath as she reloaded the rifle she had found. Leaning against the run-down amphitheater, she tried to focus on what was going on. She felt like she was living in a sick and twisted video game, some place ancient where clowns walked around heavily armed and thirsty to kill. Tucking hair behind her ears she began to listen to her surroundings, the wound in her thigh was going to slow her down so she was going to have to rely on her senses to help.

Cocking the gun she took a deep breath then jumped from her hiding spot and charged for the crumbling rope bridge. She fired as clowns began to converge on her trail, she blew one's arm off with a single shot but it kept coming at her. As one reached for her she jumped onto the bridge.An arrow landed in front of her, she then heard someone yell for her to hurry across. Not wasting time she began to run over the bridge. She looked back when she heard a large explosion; she froze when a limb shrouded in cheap shiny satin landed in front of her still smoking. Regaining her composure quickly she sprinted across the bridge jumping over the missing sections.

A hand reached out and grabbed hers as she reached the other side. The hand was human and not clad in a clown costume. Looking up she almost smiled in relief when she saw Alex standing in front of her. She hugged him; he grabbed her hand and pulled her in a direction. Kirsa followed him until they reached an old silo, he opened the door to it and helped her in, he climbed in after her. He made sure he barred the door before he lit a small candle.

"What the hell are you doing here?" Alex asked as he looked at the wound on her thigh.

"I was going to ask you the same thing?"

"This is my nightmare," he replied as she tried not to grimace while he cleaned out the wound.

Ayden woke up when the door to the hospital room opened, the night nurse Maeve slowly entered. She handed him another thermos as she checked over the machines. Making a note on the file she turned and looked at the vampire. The other one was asleep outside in the hall. She had met them earlier, both picking up on her scent when she had entered the room.

"She hasn't changed, we can't decide if that's good or bad," Maeve informed Ayden.

He nodded studying her while he drank. She had pulled her hair back, and looked a little more tired than she had a few hours ago.

"I know you are aware of what I am," she replied sighing.

"Does that bother you?" Ayden asked drinking. Maeve was a Banshee. "I was startled but now am fine. It's hard when we come across a vampire."

"I can imagine."

"Can you?" She asked doubtful.

"You are there to warn that death is on the horizon and also help mourn, yet here I am. I died a horrible death but yet I still walk this earth, it must throw off your senses," Ayden surmised.

"It does," Maeve nodded smiling. Shocked that he understood. "It's the initial shock then once it's past I can focus again."

"I was born and raised in Kerry," Ayden told her. He hesitated a moment before he went on. "I heard a banshee the night I died."

She looked surprised at first then smiled a sly smile. "Then you are a unique man."

"Why?"

"No one I know, man or vampire, has heard their song and lived to tell such a tale," Maeve replied, she saw the question in his eyes. "The song of the beensidhe is supposed to be final, so to hear yours and then survive is a one of a kind situation."

"How do you know it was my song that I heard?"

"It leaves a mark that only a banshee can see," Maeve replied. She turned to leave then paused. "He is a leprechaun is he not? Al from OPIA?"

Ayden just smiled knowing whatever answer he gave would confirm her suspicion, he just raised his thermos in thanks and watched the banshee nod and leave the room. He finished the contents then set it on the nightstand. Ayden took Kirsa's hand in his and watched her as if she was sleeping.

"What is going on in there, Kirsa?"

Kirsa awoke to Alex moving around in the small space. He smiled and then handed her a backpack and a handgun.

"They retreat during the day, they have the barn heavily guarded but during the day they are weaker," Alex informed her.

"The barn? As in the one on your property?" Kirsa asked.

"The exact one," Alex told her. "I came across it when I was running from a bunch of the orange wig ones, that's when I realized it all."

"The barn is the center of the spell," Kirsa said understanding. "They are protecting it because if anything disturbs the power then..."

"Bye-Bye nightmare realm."

"What's your plan?"

"For some reason spells don't work as well in sunlight here," Alex told her. "I figure it has something to do with dreams being night based."

"Pretty much," Kirsa said. It was more complicated than that but that was the easiest way to explain it.

"If we can get into the barn before nightfall we can get some footing," Alex told her. "I am sure there are guards in there as well."

"It's smarter to get through as much of their defenses when they are at their weakest then to wait."

"Alright, the backpacks have water, power bars, a walkie talkie in each, and ammo."

"Where did you get all this stuff Alex?" Kirsa asked him in amazement at what he had.

"The silo was filled with it," he told her. Kirsa nodded looking around the space; she didn't get the sense that this was a trap.

Instead she felt as if someone was trying to help them get out here. Alex carefully unbarred the door then slowly opened it, they saw twenty demons dressed as clowns standing in the shadows of the trees watching the barn. The majority had their backs to the silo, unaware of what was going on there.

"If we lure them into the sunlight it will make them easier to kill," Kirsa told him.

"Then we run for the center of the field and fight," Alex told her.

She grabbed his hand before he could run, "No. I run for the center of the field. While I distract them, you run to the barn. Don't do anything once you are in there until it's dark, I will meet you there."

Alex didn't like the idea of one of them running into the middle of the demons, but he also understood that one of them had to make it into the barn to get them the hell out of the nightmare.

Sabrina walked into the hospital room and saw Ayden talking to a raven-haired woman. Ayden saw Sabrina and waved; she went to the bed and stared at Kirsa while Ayden finished up the conversation with the nurse. Sabrina stared at Kirsa lying in the bed, she tried to shake off the chills she was getting but it wasn't helping. Ayden walked up and laid a hand on her shoulder causing her to jump.

"What's up?" he asked her.

"Ten years ago, Susannah showed signs of improving," Sabrina began. "She was talking about topics other than demons. We actually thought we were getting her back, that maybe whatever had been done was being undone. When you mentioned Kirsa's name, she seemed remorseful not agitated nor furious. Even the doctors thought she was better."

"What happened Sabrina?"

"She fooled all of us but Kirsa," Sabrina said. Sighing she walked to the windows and looked out.

"The three of us were all in different locations, all doing our own thing. Then instantly we were all screaming in pain then silent. None of us remembers where we were or what happened while our bodies laid unconscious."

"How did you awake?"

"Hugh and Hagan went to Susannah and told her that if she did not release control on the three of them they would see that she was bound in Irons."

Ayden let out a whistle. "How did they figure out it was her?"

"Hugh smelled the spell on his daughter and knew her past history; he connected the dots and told Hagan. Afterwards the Fae courts ruled she was better here than in Fae, so she was placed into Shady Pines with the warning that if she ever pulled the spell again it would be life in a Fae Prison."

"Will that work this time?" Lance asked joining the conversation. He had met Sabrina on his patrols of the estate.

"No, someone needs to go in and get her out," Sabrina answered. "The only way to end it is to defeat Susannah in the astral plane."

"Then why haven't any of you or Kirsa done that?" Lance asked. "I mean if it's a battle in the astral plane then the three of you could do it."

"Kirsa has the strongest connection with the astral world; however there is a problem with that. She made two deals the night she saved Susannah, the drop of blood and a promise never to return on her own to the astral plane."

"But she's there now," Ayden pointed out.

"Not of her own free will," Sabrina replied.

"So, who the hell do we get to do this?" Ayden asked frustrated.

Sabrina turned and looked at him; she slowly shrugged out of her coat and laid it over a chair. Taking a deep breath Sabrina answered, "Me."

CHAPTER 13

Kirsa stood in the middle of the field firing round after round of iron and silver bullets at the demonic clowns approaching her. Out of the corner of her eye she kept watch on Alex as he made his way to the barn unnoticed. Every now and then she would feel a ripple in the world, ignoring it she kept shooting at the clowns who seemed oblivious to the black blood gushing out of them. Grabbing a grenade that would release a whole bunch of iron nails, she pulled the pin and then sprinted to the barn. She leaped through the open window just as the grenade exploded.

Alex helped pull her through as they hid under the sill. They could hear the screams of death and those dying, and then the smell of burning flesh began to filter through the opening. When the last scream become silent, Kirsa looked around and saw they were in what would have been the tack room of the barn, there was a faint humming sound and she could feel the power surrounding the place. There was a ladder that went up to a hay loft. She pointed to it and Alex nodded.

Going first, she slowly climbed up, peeking her head over the edge she saw the loft was clear for the moment. She climbed over and set her pack down as she tried to get her bearings. Alex came over a minute later; he looked out of a small gap in the boarded windows and gagged. Clown body parts were sprawled all over the field still smoking from the iron. Turning away he went over to Kirsa.

"Do we wait until night?" he whispered.

"I want to get the feel of the place before then," Kirsa answered.

Walking to the door she slowly opened it trying not to groan as the door squeaked open, when there was enough room for her head to stick out she looked around. There was a ladder that led down to the main part of the barn; the other lofts were vacant and so badly dilapidated that no one could hide there. There was no one but them on the top level. Cautiously she slid through the slit and motioned for Alex to stay.

She crouched behind some boxes and looked down below. In the center of the room was a circle outlined in blue fire, a pentagram was etched into the center of it. Demons surrounded it all armed and all alert; Kirsa *counted the demons and made more mental notes before sliding back into the loft.*

"There are thirteen well-armed demons surrounding the circle," Kirsa said.

"Are they dressed as clowns?"

"Thankfully no," Kirsa answered. "Let's see what we still have then we will begin to formulate a plan."

Alex nodded as they opened their packs and took stock of what they had. He watched as she went through their ammo, weapons, and grenades.

Alex went to eat an apple when Kirsa knocked it out of his hand. "Don't you know your Greek myths?" She asked him as she continued taking stock.

He thought about it for a moment, "Persephone and Hades."

"Apple, Pomegranate. I doubt they will care."

She tossed him the protein bar. "Eat that instead."

They ate in silence. Alex studied the water bottle not recognizing the symbol on the label. "How do you know we are safe with this?" he asked Kirsa.

"I know who the symbol belongs too and trust me when I tell you he wants me out of here."

She finished the bottle then looked around their space. "Alright there are thirteen guards, just before evening we should begin knocking down that number," Kirsa said. "We don't know how many more are going to be joining them once darkness comes. "

"How do we plan on doing this?" Alex asked.

"Bow and Arrow," Kirsa said handing it to him.

"Do either of us know how to do that?"

Kirsa looked at him with a smile, "We can if we think we can," Kirsa replied. He looked at her skeptical. "It's the astral plane. Do you think that grenade I threw was really filled with iron nails originally?"

"Then why can't we think ourselves out or them away?"

"Limitations," Kirsa said.

"Weird," was all Alex could think of to say.

Handing him the quiver of iron tipped arrows, Kirsa edged out of the door and he followed. They made it to their position behind the crates as they waited for dusk to begin to descend. When the sky began to turn purple the first arrow hit its mark causing the demon to squeal as it crumbled to the floor dead. The two near it went to investigate the smoking body, before they made it they were both dead. Alex handed her more arrows as he took out the crossbow and loaded it. Within another few minutes they were down to the last two who had retreated to the shadows of the barn.

Kirsa focused on them and felt her eyes begin to adjust to the dark; loading two arrows she pulled back and then let them fly through the air. They heard the screams then silence signaling the arrows had found their mark.

Alex and Kirsa smiled at each other as they reloaded and waited for what was to come. Slowly they watched as the sky outside darkened. Kirsa watched as the blue flames surrounding the circle rippled and then flared as if signaling something was approaching.

Outside she heard loud talking and then a woman screaming about something. The words were not clear, but someone was obviously not happy. Kirsa figured it had something to do with what was left of the demons outside. The doors to the barn blew open and Kirsa swallowed her gasp when the person entered.

Susannah stood in the doorway wearing a pale blue dress; she wore sapphires and diamonds, a tiara that looked to be of ice. She was not alone, three demons were with her, waiting for her next command as she took in the scene before them.

"I thought you told me that they had them captured?" she screamed.

"That's what the last word was, the girl was injured, and the boy was running out of speed," Narl told her. He was the tallest of the three demons.

"Well obviously that information was wrong," Susannah remarked. "Otherwise your friends got bored and killed themselves."

The three demons said nothing; Susannah tapped her foot on the ground as she tried to formulate a new plan. She hadn't wanted to make a move this soon, but time was running out. She only had a few more full moons to pull off the impossible. If she could get Alex trapped in the nightmare realm then she would have half the power she needed. She had not planned on Kirsa being sucked into the realm shortly after Alex. That was an added bonus, one that she was going to exploit.

"Begin the preparations for the binding ceremony," Susannah ordered. "Even if they are not present I can still filter their power."

The demons grunted and began to prepare for the circle and the ritual that would be performed. Kirsa watched from behind the crate as one of the demons made a clay figurine that looked like Alex. Another was setting up an altar, while the third began to light candles.

Susannah walked to a large wooden cabinet in the corner that had an intricate designs on it. She pulled out several bottles, a flat stone and a box. Alex and Kirsa looked at each other, both understood that one of them was going to be bound to this place and another banished.

"Where's my sulfur?" Susannah yelled, demanding an answer.

The three demons looked at each other before looking at her all shrugging their shoulders. She stormed toward the first and slapped it then turned on the other two demanding an answer to her question. "Sulfur does not just get up and walk away?"

"It would be funny to watch though," a voice said from the shadows.

Kirsa smiled as she readied her cross bow, she saw movement out of the corner of her eye and recognized one of Alex's friends jumping from rafter to rafter. Kyle winked at them as he positioned himself above one of the demons.

Susannah slowly turned around toward where the voice came from. It was not a voice that she was expecting.

"You surprise me Sabrina, coming all this way."

"Why so surprised?" Sabrina asked. There was no fear in her voice.

"I warned you if you ever tried anything like this again I would help to stop you," Sabrina replied emerging from the shadows.

"Why does she have wings?" Alex whispered to Kirsa.

Kirsa looked at Sabrina and saw the wings, "She can talk to Angels and for some reason when she comes to the astral plains she gets wings."

"Cool," Alex replied, he wanted wings.

Kirsa noticed the three demons beginning to move toward Sabrina, she then watched as Kyle swung down taking two out as he landed. Alex shot the third demon with his rifle. Sabrina and Susannah looked at the mess before them.

"Looks like your henchmen are of no more use," Sabrina replied.

"Perhaps," Susannah replied with a smile. She would miss Narl, he was the most capable of her army of demons. And was pleasant in bed. In the end They could all be replaced.

Kirsa felt Susannah begin to cast a spell that would use the blood of the demons. She jumped off the loft and tackled

Susannah, they hit the ground hard. Kirsa was pretty sure she heard her arm break but with Susannah underneath her it was hard to focus.

"I can't cast," Kirsa yelled to Sabrina.

"Kyle, Alex I need you," Sabrina said. Alex climbed down the ladder and joined them. "She's going to start summoning more demons while I bind her; I need you guys to kill as many demons as you can."

Alex tossed Kyle the crossbow then they took position Kirsa battled Susannah on the ground. Sabrina cast the circle then began the simple binding spell that would temporarily bind Susannah back to her body. Kirsa plowed a fist into Susannah's jaw as demons started to rise from the ground. She vaguely heard Alex take a deep breath, meaning some were dressed as clowns.

Susannah found Kirsa's broken arm and smashed it harder into the ground. In a haze of pain Kirsa's instincts took over, moving faster than what the others could see, she pinned Susannah under her, driving her knee into Susannah's stomach.

Susannah looked up at her with slight fear, Kirsa smiled displaying her fangs. Susannah started to laugh in triumph, but Kirsa remembered what Ayden had told her about fairy blood. Kirsa felt the spell that Sabrina was casting gain power, Susannah began to move frantically under her.

Susannah reached with her fingers to grab the hilt of the ceremonial dagger, when she got a handle on it she grabbed it and went to shove it into Kirsa's stomach.

Kirsa caught her hand and twisted it; they struggled for control, as the spell took hold Kirsa fell onto Susannah as her injured arm gave out. She heard the sound of metal sliding through skin and saw the shocked look on Susannah's face.

Hands pulled Kirsa up, standing with Alex, Kyle and Sabrina, they stared at Susannah with the knife sticking out of her abdomen.

"Is she dead?" Kyle asked.

"We could only be so lucky," Kirsa said holding her arm.

"We'll have to ask Al about the rules concerning Faeries in the astral world," Sabrina replied as they watched the body shimmer out of sight.

Kirsa looked over at Sabrina and smiled. "Thanks."

"You think Sara and I would leave you here?" Sabrina asked.

"What now?" Kyle wondered. "Is this over?"

"Who knows but I have a feeling the answer is no," Alex answered. "I think this is just the warm up."

CHAPTER 14

Al stood with his back toward his office door; he was staring out the windows watching recruits running in the slush that was falling from the sky. Ayden and Kirsa sat waiting for an answer, Kirsa's arm was in a sling out of precaution, by the time they had gotten her to x-ray the break had begun to heal.

"The Astral Plane was at one point a portal between the worlds," Al began. "It linked the world of humans, the fae, demons and other realms together. About a thousand years ago there was a power struggle for control of the portal, for the one in control would have ultimate power."

"What happened?" Ayden asked.

"The god's of the human realm intervened," Al answered. "They realized that no one deserved to hold the power of the portal over anyone. So, each group involved in the war, the humans, the fae and the demons, were each handed restrictions. The humans, who caused the most bloodshed, could not enter the portal by their own means. If they were injured on that plane then that injury would carry through to the real world, if they died then they would be brain dead here. The demons, causing the most damage, could only travel if they were summoned. A death in the astral plane was a true death for them," Al explained.

"And the fae?" Kirsa inquired. "What was their punishment?"

"The rules of Iron applied when before it had not, the one exception was if non-iron related injury occurred it would not carry through entirely into the real world," Al answered. He saw the confused look and continued. "If let's say a fairy lost an arm but the sword was silver than in the real world they would have a cut instead of loss of limb."

"So, if the knife I used on Susannah was silver then it would be minor damage," Kirsa surmised.

"Exactly," Al replied.

"Yeah well if I came back with a broken arm and bruised ribs then she should suffer also."

"Any word on Alex and Kyle?" Ayden asked.

"Fine, no demon has been sighted or sensed since that night. He isn't plagued by nightmares anymore and feels like whatever bonds were there are now gone," Kirsa told him. "He even went to the coven meeting last night."

"At least we know that in order to sever the tie, we battle her in the astral plane."

"Yes, but I can't do the ritual or cast the spell, or set foot willingly in there," Kirsa reminded Al.

"Do you think Victoria could?" Ayden asked.

"After the holidays we are going to talk about it in detail, she said she would be willing to do it but wants to know fully what she will be up against," Kirsa said.

She glanced at her watch, "Anything else? I'm meeting with Frank to go over the case."

"I think that's it," Al went to say something else but stopped when there was a knock on the open door. Titania stood there. "What are you doing here?"

"I have two guards outside don't worry," she promised Al. "I'm sorry if I'm interrupting," she said taking in Kirsa and Ayden.

"We were just leaving," Kirsa said. "I'll let you know what Frank and I decide on," Kirsa told Al heading to the door.

"Good, Ayden what are you doing while they're talking?"

"I figure I would go scare the shit out of some of the recruits," Ayden replied with a smile.

Titania watched them leave before turning to Al. "I was going to call first but figured you would tell me not too."

Al motioned for her to take a chair. "Do you want coffee, tea or water? For the harder stuff you have to wait to end of business hours."

Titania laughed as she sat. "Tea is fine."

Al used the intercom to tell his secretary he needed a coffee and tea. "What can I do for you?"

Kirsa watched as Ayden listened to the conversation through the wall, she got the files ready for the meeting with Frank. Arlene, the secretary, walked into the room with two steaming mugs she set them down on Kirsa's desk.

"There is a woman in his office," Arlene informed Kirsa.

"Titania Murphy, older sister to our suspect," Kirsa replied. Kirsa sipped the mug as Arlene tapped her foot.

"I just brought them tea and coffee, they were speaking that weird language that he speaks with the walking dead over there."

Kirsa couldn't help the smile, "Irish. It's why Ayden's eavesdropping and not me."

"Hmm. Let me know what he learns," Arlene replied.

She went to leave but stopped. "He took his coat off and is sitting in the chair next to her."

Al was a creature of habit, he always wore his coat and always sat behind the desk in front of a client. If it was a casual meeting with an agent then he sat on the edge of the desk, still with coat on.

"This should be interesting. Send Frank in when he gets here."

"Will do, and there is a joint training session with the wannabes, they've requested the walking dead."

"I'll let him know," Kirsa replied.

Arlene always referred to Ayden or any vamp as the walking dead. She walked over and handed Ayden his mug then stood next to him while he wore an expressionless look.

Frank walked in and raised an eyebrow at Ayden's still form then smiled, "This has to do with the mystery woman doesn't it?"

"Does the whole campus know?" Kirsa asked as she walked to her desk.

"That there is a beautiful woman in Al's office who told security her reason for visiting was personal? Yes."

"This is all going to be blamed on me," Kirsa warned sitting down.

"Probably," Frank agreed. "How's the arm?"

"Stiff, I can get rid of the sling tomorrow," Kirsa told him. "Alright so what have you found out?"

"According to Kessler and the friend, Kristina is getting worse," Frank said. "The transcription from Ayden helped and confirms the audio they have been able to understand. She is now speaking in Latin sometimes."

"No name yet?"

"None, and when the friends try to recall the name their mind goes blank."

"A security measure most likely."

"Delilah's nightmares are increasing, and Mora is the same."

"Let's pay attention to Delilah, the nightmares could be a sign that she might be next. I have a feeling though that Susannah won't try anything so soon," Kirsa replied.

"He asked her out on a date," Ayden said resurfacing.

He drank the contents of the mug then joined Frank and Kirsa. "Does Al go on dates?" Frank asked.

"Apparently he does."

"What else were they talking about?" Kirsa inquired.

"Fae politics, apparently one of the subgroups wants to break off and be their own group," Ayden explained.

"Fun. That will go over well."

"That nurse Maeve smelled like her, think she's Fae also?" Frank asked.

"Possibly," Ayden replied. "So, what am I doing?"

"Breaking in wannabes," Kirsa told him.

"Then I will leave you two to the detective work," Ayden said. "Come find me when you are ready to head out."

****

After returning from OPIA, Kirsa headed upstairs to get out of her work clothes. After a shower and a quick change, Kirsa went on the hunt for Ayden. She found him in the living room reading a book with Zero was curled up in front of the pellet stove. Handing him a wine glass she curled next to him on the couch. Ayden set the book down and sipped the wine.

"What didn't you want to say in front of Frank?" Kirsa asked as she sipped her own glass.

He turned the wine glass in his hands. "When you were next to Maeve what did you pick up?"

"She's definitely fae, hints of candles burning and rain falling. I figure she's from the water branch," Kirsa reflected.

"She's a banshee."

Both eyebrows shot up, Kirsa set her wineglass down on the end table. "How can she be?"

"A banshee is in a sense a female faerie, that's the original meaning."

"Don't they bring death or something like that?"
"

"Their song signals that someone in your house is about to die, you could also find them mourning for the dead in the hills surrounding themselves with candles."

"Wow, I've never heard a banshee song," Kirsa said in wonder. "Which when you think about it is kind of amazing on it's own."

"I have," Ayden confided. He took a sip of wine.

"When?"

"I was going to the tavern with some friends, the famine was beginning to end, and we all could breathe a sigh that we survived. There was a lot of rebuilding, other towns had lost so much yet we survived. So, we were going to raise a pint in celebration and in memory."

"What happened?" Kirsa asked softly.

He didn't speak of the night he was turned, and when he did it was brief. "I heard this beautiful voice singing off in the distance, as if the voice was being carried on the breeze. I stopped to listen, no one else heard it. I knew then it was a banshee crying for someone. We went to the tavern and drank with all the other men in the village. It was very early morning when I stumbled out of the tavern that night. I was attacked a few streets from the tavern, dragged to the woods and slowly drained. It was the song that kept floating through my head and drowned out the laughter. Even as I lay dying I could hear the song, it brought peace to me."

Kirsa took his hand in hers, "Ayden?"

"When I awoke, which was a surprise, Shamus was sitting next to my bed. Candles lit everywhere," Ayden recalled. "He asked my name and when I told him he smiled and said 'Gideon's oldest boy'. He then went on to explain what happened, how he found me and what he had to do. I was so weak from being left to die that it was a week before I began to fully feel the power that I now had. It was then that Shamus and I left for the continent. "

"What of the song you heard?" Kirsa asked.

"According to Maeve, it was my death the Banshee was mourning. I was supposed to die that night, but Shamus changed my fate. She said it left a mark, the song. That only a banshee can see it."

Kirsa leaned over and kissed him softly. "I'm thankful for Shamus finding you and saving you."

"I always wondered why I was spared then I met you and I knew my reason for it," Ayden said as he brushed a curl out of her face. "Kirsa you're it for me, there is no one else and has never been another before you that I have loved fully. If I had a ring I would ask you now, but I want it to be special and planned not because I got sentimental."

"I don't need a ring or promises," Kirsa assured him.

"Yeah you do," he said as he gently pushed her down on the couch and kissed her. "And I'm going to make those promises to you."

Kirsa went to say something but he silenced her with a kiss as his hands began to roam over her. Giving up she wrapped her arms around him and surrendered to him.

****

Colin walked into the library of the Black home and found Sabrina curled up in front of the fire with one of her dogs sleeping next to her. She was drinking wine when he walked in; she looked up at him and smiled faintly. Colin sat in one of the leather chairs and sipped his brandy.

"Wanna talk about it?" he asked.

"Is it horrible to hate someone you once thought of as a sister?" Sabrina asked.

"Not if they have done everything they can to destroy that relationship and trust," Colin assured her.

"I always got so mad at Kirsa when she would feel as though it was her fault for what happened to Susie."

"Why?" Colin wondered. Sabrina turned and stared at him. "Why did you get mad at her for feeling guilty?"

Sabrina thought for a moment before answering. "I guess I figured that Susie deserved what she got for making deals with demons, which she did. The other part is I wasn't there with Kirsa when she had to go in and find Susie."

"I'm sensing that's changed."

"Susie still got what she deserved but now I understand better the weight that Kirsa took on at such a young age," Sabrina confided. "I was only in there for what seemed like a few minutes and it took everything I had to keep from messing up something. And there was that thought at the back of the mind, what if I screw up? What if something I do hurts the three of them?"

"I agree with you on Susie, she dabbled in shit she should never have touched especially since she's a faery," Colin said. "Part of me understands the guilt that Kirsa felt; she went in there to save her friend and came out with her friend being crazy."

He held up a hand to silence Sabrina's retort. "I also understand where you come from. Susie preyed on her friendship with Kirsa and Kirsa fell into her spell in a sense. Instead of letting her face the consequences, she instead went in and tried to save her friend. She should have been relieved that she wasn't trapped there as well or injured beyond repair."

"Have you ever been betrayed like that?" Sabrina asked.

Colin smiled coldly. "Yes." He took a sip of his brandy before explaining. "It was one of the reasons I decided to come back to Jersey. One of the associates at the firm I worked at got a bizarre case, I was asked to help her on it."

"What kind of case?"

"The accuser claimed the defendant raped her in the astral plane," Colin said flatly. He laughed at the dubious look on Sabrina's face. "Our thoughts exactly. They were engaged by the way, he had broken it off when he found out she was pregnant with his younger brother's child."

"Oh shit!" Sabrina exclaimed.

"He kicked her out of his townhouse, took the engagement ring back and took her name off all the joint accounts. He then went and wrote her out a check for all the money she had in those accounts and even for a portion of the ring value."

"Nice guy," Sabrina replied.

"Elliot is, to a fault at times," Colin told her. "Samantha needed help with research; we needed to find out if her claim could be proven or if this was an attempt to ruin his name. Late nights and lots of wine lead to us to become intimate. When it became obvious that it was more than sex we agreed to be exclusive."

"What happened?"

Colin swirled the brandy in his glass and thought. "The case got thrown out, there was no way it could be prosecuted plus a friend came forward saying she was trying to ruin Elliot. Samantha and I moved in together, she moved into my Condo with me."

"Wait, Barbie, the one we all hated? That's the one you're talking about, she's a lawyer?"

"Yep, anyway we were going strong," Collin continued ignoring Sabrina's face. "I met Elliot at the bar for drinks one night; she was going to hang with some friends of hers at a club. Let's just say I got back earlier then she thought and found her in bed with our boss. The next day I was called into his office where I was told that she was being given the promotion I was promised and that I was not to speak of what I saw. He told me she worked her ass off for the promotion. I handed my resignation in at the end of the day. I went home boxed up all her things and piled them in the hallway and returned the engagement ring I had bought. Then Elliot and I went out again and got shit-faced."

"Oh Colin," Sabrina said taking his hand in hers.

"Hey, it could be worse," he told her.

"True, your ex could be a serial killer locked up in a doorless, windowless and sunless cell for all eternity."

Colin laughed then leaned forward and kissed her gently. "You never asked me the other reason I came home."

"What's the other reason?" Sabrina asked softly.

"I was going to fight for you." Colin got up as he finished the brandy. "I'll see you in the morning Brie."

Sabrina nodded as she watched him leave the room. She had been betrayed twice in her life by two people she had trusted and loved dearly, one a friend and one a lover.

The wall she had built around her heart over the summer was critical in helping her deal with the betrayal. She needed to be sure that she could trust herself again with people, if she could learn to trust her heart again. Kirsa had told her not to overthink matters of the heart, the brain tended to get in the way sometimes.

Now she had Ayden, Kirsa had completely opened up to him revealing sides to Ayden that she had never shown anyone. Sabrina wanted that but at the same time she was terrified of screwing up again. Sighing Sabrina got up from the couch, it was time for bed where she could dream away the fears and thoughts.

Dreams

CHAPTER 15

Kirsa stood on the wall of her castle in Germany staring down at the bustling village before her. The castle and town were all decked out for the holidays, snow had fallen and children of all ages were playing in it. Kirsa closed her eyes as she smelled hot chocolate coming her way. Wyrm handed her a mug and stood next to her as he pulled the hood up on her coat to keep her warm.

"You look too serious for the holidays," he told her.

"Too much on my mind I guess," Kirsa replied sipping the warm liquid. Yule was next week; they had arrived early due to what had happened with Susannah.

"I can understand that," Wyrm said as he watched Matthew playing with some of the village kids. "You spent a few days in the hospital, upon your return the reporter was at your doorstep. I can see why coming back here would be an ideal solution."

"Wyrm I want to get into the archives," Kirsa said. Wyrm looked at her in surprise.

"You don't have to ask to enter the family archives."

"Not those archives."

There was silence as understanding dawned on Wyrm. "Why?"

"You once told me a tale about a Faery who hid from the world in the Astral plane," Kirsa explained.

"You think Susannah accomplished this fete?"

"In the hospital, her scent ended at the bedroom door," Kirsa told him. "There are no windows in the bedroom, no vents, no access panels, nothing. Yet she vanished without a trace. No one has picked up her sent or trail anywhere surrounding the facility."

The archives she was talking about were the complete Vampire archives. However, it was not just vampire history that Wyrm and those that came before him reported. It contained the history of every human group on the planet: humans, ware's, witches, vampires, the Fae. There was a joke that it was harder getting into the Vampire Archives then it was to get into the Vatican's. No one sitting on the cur-rent

Inner Council had stepped foot in the archives. Though Victor had desperately wanted too, since Wyrm did not trust the man he refused all one hundred and seventy-three requests.

"Very well, but Ayden will not be allowed to enter," Wyrm informed her.

While Kirsa was talking with Wyrm, Ayden walked with Dietrich through the woods outside of Geheimestadt. Ana and the kids were due in a few days making Dietrich a bit more restless than usual. They were discussing Kirsa and wanted to be well out of hearing range so as not to let her know.

"She looks amazing, Ayden," Dietrich told him. "Happy, content, and so sure of herself."

"It's been amazing to watch the transformation," Ayden agreed.

"You always knew there was an amazingly strong woman under the frailty and uncertainty," Dietrich said.

"I did. Despite everything she saw and had happen to her, she never gave up no matter how weak she thought she was. She left her home to take time to heal and find a place to stand and I think when she realized that she could be her own foundation she began to realize how strong she was."

Dietrich nodded. "What of this reporter?"

"She's been bothering Sabrina and several members of the Church of Light. Colin and the church's former lawyer are working on some type of joint statement or possible press conference to discuss it once and for all."

"It was smart to bring her earlier than planned," Dietrich said. "She was the one that thought of it which made life easier for Lance and me not having to convince her."

"How are they getting along now that we all know she has been aware of him from the beginning?"

"She thinks he looks like the painting of a medieval knight," Ayden said laughing at how accurate the description was. "At which Lance explained that he got his name because of how lethal he was with a lance."

Lance was from the English branch of the O'Brian line, he and Ayden had always gotten along. When Ayden had been nominated for a Shadow, Lance vouched for him and had become one of his tutors.

"Dietrich there is something I need to ask you," Ayden said.

Dietrich turned and looked at the young vampire and noticed he looked a bit paler than usual.

"Is everything all right?" If he was alive he would have taken a deep breath before beginning.

"I love her; I think I've been waiting for her since the gypsy woman first told me I would live twice."

When Ayden was human his sister Brenna dragged him to see a Gypsy woman living on the outskirts of his village. She had told Ayden that he would live two lives and that in his second life he would find his true mate. The eerie part is the woman described a dark-haired woman with eyes the color of heather.

"It often takes a vampire longer to find their true match," Dietrich told him.

"Her father is dead," Ayden said. "But you have stepped in to be there in his place. It makes sense that I should ask you for permission to marry her."

Dietrich stopped walking and stared at him, not finding the words to say what he felt he hugged Ayden. "Of course," Dietrich said thickly. "You have always had it."

"Now I just have to find a ring," Ayden said.

"I might have something in mind," Dietrich told him.

Most of Kirsa's family's jewelry had been destroyed in the explosion six years ago. "I will have my secretary bring it with her when she comes tomorrow."

"I guess I should call Tony and ask him as well?"

"That would be a good idea," Dietrich agreed. "Otherwise neither of us will hear the end of it if you ask only me."

CHAPTER 16

Sabrina stared at the foreboding structure as the armored car made its way across the bumpy road. She had seen paranormal prisons before, the one in Upstate New York looked like a prison, however the structure before her was more of a fortress built with the intention that its inhabitants were forgotten about. Sabrina wiped sweat off her brow as they drove deeper into the jungle of the uninhabited island. Kirsa was going to kick her ass if she ever found out that Sabrina was doing this, Sara wouldn't be too far behind her either. Large gates moved on their own, squealing as the unused motors protested.

The car moved forward before armed men walked over to surround it.

Eztil stepped out of the car first, her jet-black hair was pulled back in a tight bun, she brushed her black suit off so the wrinkles vanished. She was second in command of the Sachin Line, Victor's trusted advisor. Turning her dead black eyes on Sabrina she nodded for the woman to exit the vehicle. She spoke to one of the guards in a language that had not been heard for a few centuries.

Sabrina followed the woman as they were flanked by the soldiers as they headed to the heavy metal doors without handles or windows.

They opened from the inside, Eztil entered and Sabrina followed listening as the terrifying woman barked out commands snapping men to attention as they walked down the hallway. There were no windows, the doors were so seamless that it took you a moment to notice them, there were no handles or locks on them, nothing that showed anyone lived in this prison.

The only indication that prisoners were here, were the narrow food slats at the bottom of the doors. Sabrina was cold for the first time since landing on the brutally hot island where the humidity was close 100%, if it was wasn't from the air conditioning. Sabrina now understood the whole purpose, this is where you sent the most vicious to be forgotten and to die slowly.

They walked for what seemed like forever until Eztil stopped and pulled out a single key, she inserted into the wall and a retinal scanner came out. A door slid open and the two women walked through, Sabrina jumped when it slammed shut behind her. She looked ahead and saw Lars standing behind a twenty-four-inch-thick bulletproof glass.

Eztil turned and looked at Sabrina, "You have all the time you will need." She then turned and left leaving Sabrina alone with Lars.

****

Kirsa was about to enter the vault when her phone went off. Ayden and Wyrm looked at her as she picked it up from the bin. It was Colin calling her work phone.

"She vanished," Colin said his voice in a panic.

"Who vanished?" Kirsa asked silencing the panic that wanted to flow through her veins.

"Sabrina."

Wyrm and Ayden could hear the conversation and the name made them more alert than they were a moment before. "Ok explain what happened."

"Brian, his girlfriend Emily and Sabrina were supposed to fly to the Carolina's for the holidays," Colin explained. "Sabrina changed her mind and said she would get a later flight. She's been so secretive since you left like she's been planning something and not telling anyone."

"Alright did you go through her desk, her appointment book?" Kirsa asked. Sabrina wrote everything down in her appointment book.

"I did but nothing was there," Collin replied. "There are two tarot cards she had shoved in this week's pages."

"Which ones?"

"The chariot and three of swords," Colin said.

"Did you say three of swords?" Kirsa asked as her mind began to formalize a theory.

"Yeah."

"Are they both upright? Or is one reverse?"

There was silence for a moment. "No, they are both upright."

Kirsa flipped through her memory of the cards. The chariot usually meant that in order to move forward down a path one must overcome the obstacles in their path. The three of swords was one of the more dreaded cards in the tarot. It represents new and raw pain, that the truth will be more hurtful than not knowing.

"Colin call Upstate and see if she is going to visit him," Kirsa said as she ran through the possibilities. "She did a reading and something about her past is nagging at her."

"Alright I will let you know what I learn."

They hung up and Kirsa handed her phone to Ayden. "Keep it on you in case he calls back."

He nodded then kissed her goodbye as she followed Wyrm into the archives.

****

Lars was thinner than he had been in August, his hair was dull-brown and his eyes seemed dead. The lights only made him seem paler than he was. His muscles were still there, perfectly etched in his white skin. He looked at her and smiled a devilish smile.

"You look amazing," Lars said. His Norwegian accent was thick.

It was one of the things that had first attracted Sabrina to him was his accent.

"You look horrible," Sabrina answered back.

"Well you know the accommodations are a bit primitive here," Lars replied laughing. "So, what brings you here my love?"

"I need answers," Sabrina told him.

"What kind of answers?"

"Why choose me?" She asked.

Lars's mouth formed a slow smile as he looked her over. "I chose you because you are beautiful and smart. I chose you because I find you attractive and you found me attractive. I chose you because you being her best friend was an added bonus."

"So, I was convenient," Sabrina said dryly.

"No," Lars said as he examined his broken nails. "You were useful."

"What every woman wants to hear, they were useful." Sabrina studied the area as she focused on why she was here. "Why target Kirsa and her family? Why didn't you just go after the heads of each house?"

"Vampires love their lore, their history and their past," Lars reminded her. "The sixth line has been a fantasy, a myth, it has also caused turmoil and strife."

Lars paced the small area as he talked. "There were always rumors that the Adulwulf's were the legendary line, even when they became the Heinrich's in the new world the legend still attached itself to them. Killing the five heads would have certainly caused pandemonium, but to target the one family that signified our past, legend and myth would be more of a blow."

"Did you know the truth?"

Lars nodded. "I connected the dots long ago and waited until it would be of use. Allowing a non-vampire to sit on the council is idiocy and should never happen. I knew at some point the truth would come out and when it was going to I would strike."

"Does that mean Hagan realized the truth behind the myth?"

"He had begun to read the journals in the vault of their house," Lars explained. "He knew how to read old German; he was unaware that I knew what he was doing in there. Everyone else thought he was cataloguing the contents. It was during the cataloguing he found the ring. He knew at once when he saw it. When he came out that day I smelled the knowledge on him and knew that the time had come to start the plan."

"So why kill all those people if you were targeting Kirsa and her family."

"Distraction at first," Lars admitted. "The deaths in South Carolina were a distraction to keep her unaware of what was going on. She had always suspected the explosion was the work of someone who knew her parents intimately. Then when she left for Germany and showed no signs of coming back I needed to tempt her to come back. The only way I knew how was to bring murder and chaos to her hometown. She would feel honored bound to end it."

"You really are sick and twisted," Sabrina said disgusted. Lars laughed at that, his laughter bouncing off the walls.

"Oh? Did you come here to see if I really am the monster or if it was all some kind of delusion of grandeur? Because I really am this bad and evil."

****

Wyrm and Kirsa sat at one of the long wooden tables set in the center of the large central room of the underground archives. There were five locked rooms off of the central room, within the main room were row after row of shelving units holding all sorts of artifacts, books, ledgers and boxes. Wyrm had figured out that he heard the story around the 1500's during one of the witch trials. They were now going through the ledgers from that time period hoping to locate any mention of the tale.

"How important is this tale?" Wyrm asked trying to keep her distracted from Sabrina.

"From what we have learned, no faery has been able to do this in living memory," Kirsa told him. "Al's family vaguely remembers it happening centuries ago but can't recall the details. If we can learn how she did it, then we might begin to construct a plan of attack which is better than stumbling around waiting for her to attack."

"How are you doing after the last attack?" Wyrm asked.

She looked at him then back at what she was reading. There was something she knew that she had yet to tell Ayden. At the same time, she couldn't keep it too herself. "If I tell you something in confidence you won't speak of it to anyone?"

"You have my word that I won't," he assured her. "What is it honey?"

"I didn't even know at the time, it was so new I don't think Ayden even picked up on it," Kirsa said. Wyrm laid a hand on hers to give her strength.

"Apparently I was pregnant, about five weeks, Finn believes."

"You were?" Wyrm asked cautiously.

"I was, the trip to the astral plane and the trauma my body took on terminated it."

"Oh sweetie," Wyrm said pulling her to him. He held her tight as she centered herself and dealt with the grief. He tipped her face up to his and smiled at her. "Take heart in knowing that if it was meant to be it will happen."

"It also makes me want to end this even more," Kirsa said.

"You will have to tell Ayden at some point, he needs to know," Wyrm told her. Wyrm squeezed her hand. "Let's get back to the task at hand."

Three hours later Kirsa jumped up in excitement, rap-ping her bad knee on the table as she did. Wyrm slid his glasses off and stared at her.

"You found it?"

"I did," she said excitedly.

Wyrm got up and walked over to where Kirsa sat and leaned over her shoulder to read what she found:

"Ciaran the Fae had been accused of thirteen crimes of witchcraft in Scotland in 1568. On the date of her questioning she vanished from sight, with no trace or hint of scent to be found. It was found later that she sought refuge in the astral realm, not just her spirit form but she was able to bring her physical self with her. Vampyres,

Weres, and her own people sought her out for her crimes were cruel and true. A powerful witch was able to enter the realm and battle her there, with an iron sword she killed Ciaran in the astral plane. She brought the body back to the realm of the living and it was burnt on pyre for all to see. The ritual was burnt so that none could try to repeat what she did. "

"If they burnt it then how did Susannah find it?" Kirsa asked to no one in particular.

"I have learned that not everything stays forgotten," Wyrm told her. "Perhaps she was also told in a dream how to do it."

Kirsa looked at him, "That really doesn't help. All I know is that it's possible, but the ritual is lost."

****

Sabrina opened the front door to a pissed off weretiger. Sara stood there in her winter coat with a look that could kill. Knowing better than to dismiss her she let Sara enter.

Sara didn't even bother to take off her coat instead she grabbed Sabrina by the throat and pulled her so close their noses were touching. Inhaling the scents off of Sabrina, Sara felt her anger rise. Without saying a word, she threw her friend across the foyer and walked out of the house slamming the door behind her. She waited to call Kirsa until she pulled into her driveway.

"Well?" Kirsa asked when she picked up on the second ring.

"It's worse than you thought," Sara replied as she walked up the front steps.

"Do I want to know?"

"No, you really don't," Sara said the anger was still driving her adrenaline crazy. "She went to see him."

"I figured she went to see Anton."

"Oh no, that is not who she saw." It took a moment then Sara held the phone away from her ear as Kirsa cursed out every possible thing imaginable.

"I'm going to kill her," Kirsa said through clenched teeth.

"Calm down, I am sure there is a perfectly logical explanation for this," Sara said.

"There better be because I don't want to think of how many laws she broke by seeing him," Kirsa replied.

"I hadn't thought of that," Sara replied as she stepped in her living room. "Oh my god, you're right she broke laws."

"Several serious ones. The more interesting thing is how in the hell did she get there, I don't even know where the prison is."

"What are we going to do?"

"I don't know, I'll talk to Dietrich and see what he says, I don't know how much I can protect her from the outcome. No one is to know where he is and he is not supposed to have visitors."

Kirsa walked back into the family room where Wyrm was getting ready to read some of the papers regarding her family. Kirsa had come across them while reading the journals. Adam and Anne had just put the kids to sleep, Adam handed her a wine glass as she sat next to Ayden on the couch.

"You can start Wyrm," Kirsa replied.

"The day after Hagan died, Kirsa planned for his entombment. A priest from the neighboring town had arrived to give condolences and to offer any help. A young brother joined the priest, when the brother learned that there was more to Hagan, he declared him the child of the devil and that he could not be buried in a sacred place," Wyrm began.

"I'm sure that went over well," Ayden replied draping an arm around Kirsa's shoulders.

"The priest tried to reason with the young brother saying that from what he heard Hagan was a kind and good lord not just to his wife and children but to his people as well. He protected them, kept them fed and even helped with clearing ditches, and cutting down trees. The brother told the priest that if he did not report this to the bishop then he would, the priest bid the brother farewell and continued to help Kirsa."

Adam booed the monk and got popcorn thrown at him by his wife. Wyrm continued on. "The day after the burial the priest received a letter from the bishop, a formal inquiry was to be done on the whole town. The priest knew what that meant and warned Kirsa, he also told her that he could be there when the Bishop and his men arrived."

"Smart priest," Anne replied. "He warned Kirsa when he didn't have to."

"What happened?" Kirsa asked.

"Her younger brother and she talked things over with the heads of the town; they would wait until the bishop got here and hear his say."

"When did the shit hit the fan?" Adam inquired. He knew something huge was going to happen.

Moving past some paragraphs Wyrm found the spot, "The Bishop arrived a week later. When he learned that Kirsa was running the town in a sense, he was furious he refused to speak to a woman. Kirsa called for her brother to mediate the talks. The bishop explained that each villager and town's person would be called before him to testify; as long as they gave satisfactory responses they would be fine. Those that did not would be forced too."

"In other words, they would be tortured until they either died or gave in," Kirsa replied dryly. "I can't see this going over well."

"It didn't," Wyrm agreed. He knew this story, it had been told to him a long time ago. "Kirsa apparently was able to keep her temper and when the Bishop left to prepare for the following day she called the entire town and farmers to her home for a town meeting. She explained what had transpired with the Bishop and that by all townspeople he was including the elderly, the ill and children."

Wyrm paused to take a sip of his tea before continuing. "There were already other supernaturals living in the town by this point, so they had more to hide then just Hagan. Kirsa apparently gave them a few options, they could allow the Bishop to interview them and possibly be tortured to death. Or they could close the gates at dawn and refuse the bishop, which would most likely lead to battle."

"Now I know where you get your sense of justice from," Adam replied with a smile to Kirsa.

She rolled her eyes and Wyrm continued. "The town agreed that anyone who did not go along with the rest would have to leave otherwise they were endangering everyone else. Everyone but one family agreed to lock the gates. The one family was sent under escort to their home to pack up their belongings and then was escorted to the gates which were closed behind them."

"I can't imagine the Bishop was happy the next morning," Ayden said.

"No and calling his soldiers he tried to break through the walls, he went to burn the barns and stables only to learn that the livestock had been moved as was the grain and food," Wyrm went on. He flipped through a few passages. "After a week of trying to get over the walls, of shouting prayers, threats and gospels, he suddenly died in mid sermon from most likely a heart attack. The soldiers packed up and left after stealing the gold he carried in his chest. The town decided that only those willing to keep the secrets would continue to live in the town. That the gates would be closed at night and any threats would be dealt with on their own."

"That explains why it remained secluded, why the Council could be safe here, and why everyone was afraid of here," Ayden replied. "There were always rumors the Geheimestadt was the hunting grounds of the devil and the residents were his servants."

"They encouraged the rumors," Wyrm replied. "I just know this town was considered our safe house if we ever needed to escape like we did this past summer."

"Dietrich will be excited about the find," Kirsa said yawning.

"You alright kiddo?" Wyrm asked.

"Just tired," Kirsa replied.

"Why don't you head up to bed, between jet lag and the excitement from today you need some sleep," Ayden told her. She nodded kissing him goodnight, then she head up to their room knowing that sleep would hit as soon as she climbed into bed.

Dreams

CHAPTER 17

Kirsa dressed in a black pinstripe skirt with matching jacket, she wore a deep purple shell under the jacket and slid on her heels. Looking into her jewelry box she pulled out the reproduction signet ring that she had yet to getting used to wearing.

Tonight, was her first council meeting as head of the sixth line. She slipped it on then selected the pearls her parents got for her when she graduated college. Putting them on she took a deep breath trying to steady her nerves.

Ayden knocked on the inside of the door, he wore a charcoal gray suit with a black dress shirt and striped tie. His hair had been pulled back into a braid. Kirsa smiled at the sight of him in a suit, she knew they would make use of the tie later but for now he was here to escort her to the meeting.

The meeting, which was usually held in Austria, was being held in the old throne room of the castle. Ayden kissed her on the forehead before he led her from their rooms.

Two other shadows joined them as they walked down the hallway to the stairs. Even though she was in her own home, there was protocol and she needed to be escorted by guards just in case someone tried to attack her in her own home in the tiny village in Germany.

A table sat in the center of the throne room, each of the six chairs had the emblem for the head of the blood line. A bear for the Nacht line, red fox for the O'Brian, wild boar for Aldruic, jaguar for Sanchin, caribou for Annushka, and the wolf for Adulwulf.

Dietrich stopped talking to Dimitri when Kirsa walked in, Ayden kept her arm in his as he guided her toward the two men. Dimitri held out a hand to Kirsa and smiled as he pulled her into a hug.

"Welcome daughter," he said with a thick Russian accent. "We are joyous that you are now with us."

"Dimitri let the poor girl breathe," Sebastian ordered as he took Kirsa from him and held her tightly. "Thank you, for all you did," he whispered.

He knew the others heard it but knew they would pretend not to have.

When he let her go he passed her to Shamus who spun her in a circle. "You treat my son well," he said kissing both her cheeks. He then went off to talk to Ayden in their native tongue.

A man approached with stark black hair and piercing black eyes, despite being a vampire his skin was still tan.

"Kirsa this is Victor Sanchin of Argentina," Dietrich introduced them.

Of all the members of the council, he was worried most about Victor. Victor tended to not play well with others; he liked keeping his vampires to himself and out of the council's control.

"It is a pleasure to finally meet you," Victor said kissing her hand. He ignored the hint of fangs from Ayden and kept holding her hand in his. "I have heard much of you but none spoke of your beauty and grace."

Kirsa felt the pull and knew he was trying to charm her, thankfully her psychic abilities made it difficult to seduce her mind.

"Thank you for your help in placing my last prisoner," Kirsa said smoothly as she gently extracted her hand from his.

"It is also an honor to finally meet you as well."

Dietrich motioned for everyone to take their seats, the shadows and body guards took their positions around the room. Kirsa had to keep a laugh to herself over the thought of anyone trying to break in at that moment.

She knew Ayden heard her thought because he smiled at her and nodded. She took her seat in between Shamus and Sebastian, knowing they put her there to keep her away from Victor. Dietrich took his spot at head of the table and stood looking at the five members.

"This is the first council to have all six head of houses," Dietrich replied. "I would like to formally welcome and announce Kirsa Heinrich as head of the Adulwulf line."

The men bowed their heads for a moment to signify their acceptance of her. Dietrich continued, "There are two situations that need to be discussed before we break for the ball. Dimitri what is going on with your trouble makers?" Dietrich asked.

Dimitri groaned not wanting to think about it. "They have at this point rejected all terms and continue to give me a headache."

"Even when shown there were worse places they could be sent?" Shamus asked. "We all agreed it was the most reasonable of the ideas."

"Too reasonable if you ask me," Victor mumbled.

"We are not killing one hundred vampires just because they want to try their hand at self-rule," Dietrich said to Victor.

"And that is why you are the head of us," Victor said with a sneer.

Ignoring Victor, Dimitri continued. "I have asked their representative for an alternate proposal and gave them until the first of the year, if not then the discussion is closed. If they don't want the deal then they will get nothing, I am tired of their bull-shit."

"I agree," Sebastian said. "If they don't want to compromise then we end discussions."

"Sounds good to me," Dietrich agreed. "We can show that we tried to work with them, but they were the ones that chose to not compromise." Dietrich looked around, "Is there any other news that needs to be handled before we leave for the holidays?"

"What of Ayden O'Brian's position as Miss Heinrich's shadow?" Victor asked. "It was left to be decided until after the trial and has not been discussed since."

"Kirsa what are your thoughts on the matter," Dietrich inquired.

"Though I live in a small town, after the events of the summer I think it shows that protection is required for me," Kirsa explained rationally. "There are reporters who show up unannounced, I still receive the occasional threat. He is used to my routines, works well with my agents at OPIA I think the situation can stay as it is. I do not see a need to change it."

"Then I say we move for permanent installment," Dimitri replied. "We each have a permanent Shadow so it seems only fair that Kirsa does as well. Especially since she is more fragile than we are."

"We have never given a mortal a permanent Shadow," Victor roared standing up.

"Actually, on two occasions a permanent shadow was assigned to a mortal," Kirsa corrected Victors rant. Everyone looked at her. "My namesake was given protection shortly after Hagan's death and her daughter as well. Adala was threatened on two separate occasions by hunters, when she was actually staked, thankfully she survived, a shadow was placed on her until she died at an old age. Same with Thorrin, Hagan and Kirsa's son. One of his sons was threatened and was granted protection until he died. So, it has been done."

"Then I see no need to argue it further," Shamus agreed. "Unless there are more objections?"

Victor remained silent. Dietrich smiled, "Then I will have the paperwork ready for tomorrow, as of now and until your death Kirsa Heinrich, Ayden O'Brian of the O'Brian bloodline will be your Shadow. May he protect and keep you and all that come from you safe."

Kirsa smiled and knew that Ayden was as well. The meeting ended, and Victor stormed out, Kirsa waited until he was out of earshot. "What is his problem?"

"He has no heir, no successor, and he is single," Dietrich replied. "You are quite the catch in the mind of some."

Kirsa laughed, "Wait until they know me better. That thought will change. If you will excuse me I would like to congratulate my newly appointed guard."

****

The grand ballroom was lit up with tea lights, garlands, and a huge Christmas tree in one of the corners. The state dining room had tables set up to go with buffet tables; there was a bar set up there and a small trio of musicians.

Kirsa wore a red ball gown with black and silver bead work, her hair was up in a twist, she wore her mother's diamond earrings and necklace. She stood talking to the mayor of the town, vampires, and wares mingled throughout the main floor of the castle.

"It is good to have the castle back," the mayor told Kirsa.

"It was something Adam and I wanted to do," Kirsa replied. "I think it makes a nice new chapter, don't you?"

He nodded then laughed as his wife dragged him to dance he set his champagne down on a table and waved goodbye to Kirsa. Ayden came over and handed her a new glass. He looked stunning in a black tux, he wore a red tie and red vest to compliment her gown.

"Would you like some fresh air?" he whispered.

"Gods yes," Kirsa answered.

Taking her hand, he led her through the crowd and out into the hallway he grabbed her black cloak and draped it around her, then guided her out into one of the gardens.

It was the winter solstice, there was a dusting of snow on the ground, and it scented the air around them. Kirsa stared up at the night sky taking in the moon and stars. Ayden smiled and kissed her lightly.

"I was going to wait to give this to you," he said taking a small box tied in ribbon out of his pocket. "But tonight, it seems magical and I have never been good at waiting."

She smiled at him taking the small box from him, he watched as she undid the gold ribbon. She opened the box and gasped at the ring that lay nestled in the center.

A diamond lay in the center of the setting, it was surrounded by elaborate filigree work with small sapphires centered in the work. She could tell by the gold it was old, Kirsa looked up at Ayden who had gotten down on one knee. All the air in her left as her heart began to pound.

"You are my life now," he whispered. "Take this ring and be mine."

"I already am," she laughed as she hugged him.

He slipped the ring onto her trembling finger and kissed it there, then spun her around kissing her. When he set her down they both felt as if they were being watched, turning to the left they saw the couple watching them with smiles on the face. The woman looked identical to Kirsa, the man tall with long black hair, they nodded then disappeared.

"I guess I got their blessing," Ayden replied in awe. He looked down and kissed Kirsa again.

"Ayden, the ring. It's old," Kirsa said staring at it.

"I wanted you to have something that was not purchased in a store," Ayden told her. "It came with Dietrich's blessing."

She laid a hand on his cheek and smiled, she kissed him lightly one more time. This time they heard footsteps as her cousin Adam approached.

"Sneaking out to neck I see," Adam replied. Then he saw the ring glittering in the moonlight. He hugged Kirsa fiercely and then hugged Ayden.

"Welcome to the Adulwulf's."

"We should go back in before everyone notices we are missing," Kirsa said laughing.

"Yes, we can't have both hosts skipping out on their own ball," Adam joked.

He looked at Ayden, "So whose permission did you get?"

"Dietrich's and Tony's," Ayden replied. "I am glad that I never have to do that again."

"I can only imagine," Adam said.

Kirsa stopped them, "Adam do you have your phone?" Understanding he took it out and snapped a picture of the ring on Kirsa's finger, he then sent the image to Sabrina, Sara, and to Tony's wife Donna. "We will hear their squeals from here probably."

"There are times when I really don't like you," Kirsa replied even though she couldn't help but laugh.

When they arrived back into the ballroom everyone was talking a mile a minute, Ayden tried to pick out what they were all saying. Anne came running over. "You missed it," she whispered. "They appeared out of nowhere, nodded their approval and vanished."

"Who appeared?" Adam asked.

"The original Kirsa and Hagan," Anne explained. "Victor stormed out of the place shortly after."

"We saw them too," Kirsa said laying her left hand on Anne's.

Anne went to say something, but her eye was caught by the glimmer on Kirsa's finger. "You're engaged!"

CHAPTER 18

Kirsa sat in Sabrina's office, Sara sat to her left while Sabrina finished up on a phone conversation. Kirsa had only been back for two days when Sabrina issued her summons, now here she was in some sweater and gray slacks waiting for Sabrina to get off the phone. It allowed Sara time to ogle her ring. Sabrina hung up the phone and looked at her two friends.

"Let me explain everything at once then you can scream and yell at me all you want."

Sara and Kirsa looked at each other than at Sabrina. "This is going to be interesting," Kirsa replied getting comfortable in her chair.

Dreams

Sara did the same as they both waited for Sabrina to speak.

"While Kirsa was off getting engaged and Sara was off with family for the holidays I did two things, well three actually," Sabrina began. "The first is the least of my crimes. I saw Susie."

"Like in a vision?" Kirsa asked raising an eyebrow. "Because I'm pretty sure I told both of you to call me if she came to visit."

Sara laid a hand on Kirsa's leg. "Kirsa we promised not to interrupt, besides Sabrina is too smart to do something like visit a deranged psychopath who has demons living in her head."

"Are you two done?" Sabrina asked, they nodded so she continued.

"No, it wasn't a vision or a dream," Sabrina admitted. "She was at the barn. And before either of you jump down my throat. Ever since I went to help Kirsa and Alex defeat her in clown hell, I couldn't get her out of my head. She asked to seek refuge here and I told her no. But I was able to say everything that I have wanted to say to her."

"Alright I can understand the motivation, it was still dangerous to see her," Kirsa replied. "Now if that was the least of your crimes, I am worried about your next two."

"We know it isn't that she saw Anton or Lars because that would be more than stupid," Sara replied. They watched Sabrina blanch at the comment. Confirming their worst suspicion.

"Tell me you didn't? Because we were really hoping we were wrong." Kirsa rubbed her temples as she felt the headache forming, "I don't even want to know but explain anyway."

"Anton's lawyer contacted me about the fact that he wished to speak with me," Sabrina replied. "I know I mentioned it to Kirsa. I have been going back and forth about it and decided that I would go and hear what he had to say. I didn't even tell Brian that I went because I knew he would chain me to up to keep me from going."

"That's because Brian has sense," Sara replied folding her arms over her stomach.

Ignoring the comment Sabrina continued. "I had the family lawyer come with me and sit in on the meeting. He wanted to express his sorrow that Sara was a victim of the cult's crimes and that he hoped she was doing well. He asked how Kirsa was doing but I did not answer those questions, I didn't want to give him any ammunition."

"At least you used some of your brains," Kirsa said.

"Basically, the point of the meeting was to see if he could sweet talk me into funneling some money into his account at the prison. I smiled and told him no at which point he ended the meeting."

"Ok so what's your third and final crime? The one that you really don't want to tell us but are going too," Sara inquired. "Because part of me is afraid of what it could be if you told us about Susie and Anton first."

"Just don't interrupt, storm out, or yell until I get it all out," Sabrina said. Kirsa and Sara both promised. Wringing her hands, she began. "I took a two-day trip to an undisclosed location in South America. I needed to see him and say my piece."

"Wait," Kirsa said. "If you are talking about who I think you are, he's not allowed visitors so how'd you get in?"

"I went through the representative for Victor and she got me in," Sabrina replied. She saw the anger flash into Kirsa's eyes and began to explain. "Eztil was able to charter a flight and get me into the prison so that I could talk to him. They tapped audio into his room so he could hear and talk back. I never got to face him after all, I never got to tell him how I felt or ask him questions. I needed to know if he had used me from the start or if he ever had feelings for me."

"And you honestly think he would tell you the truth?" Sara yelled.

Kirsa yelled surging up from her seat. "Are you out of your fucking mind, Sabrina? Do you have a death wish that we don't know about, because I can come up with better ways to die!"

"Kirsa let me explain," Sabrina replied. She looked at Sara for help who just sat there and narrowed her eyes at Sabrina. "You were able to tell him how you felt, you were able to close that door I never had that opportunity."

"That's because he had me abducted, drugged and tortured me! He attempted to rape me but couldn't get it up because I kept mentioning his sister's name!" Kirsa yelled back. For the first admitting what Lars had tried to do her.

"You have to understand Kirsa."

"No, I really don't," Kirsa replied softly.

Grabbing her coat she stormed out of the office slamming the door so hard pictures fell off the wall and a crack formed down the middle of the wood door. Sabrina looked at the door then at Sara.

"Can you talk to her?"

"Oh no this is all on you," Sara replied. "You went and saw him. Maybe you needed to have your say but to me and Kirsa it's betrayal, Sabrina. You went to talk to the guy who held us prisoner and tortured us and would have killed us. How are we supposed to handle this?"

"Am I not allowed to have peace in this?"

"Kirsa and I are never going to have peace with what we went through," Sara replied getting up and putting her coat on. "We both will be living with not just the mental scars but the physical ones from him for the rest of our lives. I lost my husband to that monster. My tiger has scars from the silver."

"My priest said we must all find peace," Sabrina replied.

"Yeah well obviously he was never chained to a damp stone wall and had things that could kill him dripped on him or injected into him. Because if he did, he'd be singing a different tune real quick."

With that Sara walked out leaving Sabrina alone in her office. Colin was not speaking to her for what she had done and now Kirsa and Sara weren't either.

****

Kirsa called Dietrich once she crossed onto her property with Zero close behind her. Dietrich picked up on the third ring.

"Lars is banned from visitors, right?" Kirsa asked not even saying hello.

"Well hello to you too," Dietrich replied. "And yes, he is banned from any interaction at all. Why?"

"Because while we were in Germany, Sabrina went to visit him." There was silence on the other end as the words sunk in.

"How?"

"She said she talked to one of Victor's people, an Eztil, and they got her in and out," Kirsa replied.

"Which mean she now knows the location of the top-secret prison for the most dangerous," Dietrich replied. "This is more serious than she could even imagine."

"I know, I also want to know how the hell they got her into the prison and if Victor is aware of it."

"Let me handle this, I will call the other three and see how they think we should approach this," Dietrich assured her. "I will let you know what we come up with."

"Thanks," Kirsa said.

"Is she still alive?" Dietrich asked.

"I didn't kill her, but I walked out so Sara could've eaten her," Kirsa replied. "This was also after she informed us that she talked to Susannah and Anton, so I want you to be impressed with my restraint here."

"I am actually stunned by it," Dietrich replied. "Alright let me see what I can do, I will talk to you or Ayden later."

They hung up, Kirsa decided to follow the path that lead to the main house and began heading that way. She couldn't help but smile as Ayden met her in a green Irish sweater and jeans, his hair was pulled back and the sleeves on the sweater were pushed up to his elbows.

He kissed her lightly as he fell in step with her. "Sabrina's went that badly?" Ayden asked.

Kirsa had sent him a mental message about meeting her outside. Even in his head he could tell how pissed off she was.

"I need to calm down before I can discuss it otherwise I'll just end up going back and hitting her," Kirsa replied. "So we are going to check on the progress of our home."

Ayden smiled, "I like how that sounds, our home."

He kissed her left hand then held her ring as they walked to the building sight. The exterior walls were completely up along with the frame for the roofs, tarps were draped over the roofs to keep the elements out of the house. Kirsa and Ayden made their way through the piles of construction debris and supplies.

Tom noticed her as he talked to one of his guys, when he finished he headed over to where the two of them stood.

"Hey, congratulations you two," Tom said. "The word is all over town."

"Thanks Tom," Kirsa said. "How are things?"

"Come on inside and see," Tom said.

They followed him in through the front door cutout and then stood in the grand foyer and just stared at all the progress that had been made. The rooms were completely framed out, wires hung, pipes came up from the floor.

"My god, Tom it looks fantastic," Kirsa replied in awe.

"Drywall is up in the family wing," Tom said with a smile. "So you might want to finalize colors and flooring because I think in month we will be good to start that phase."

Ayden laid a hand on Kirsa's shoulder, he could tell the range of emotions that were surging through her at the moment. Kirsa went over and hugged Tom who looked startled by the reaction.

"Kirsa it's going to be amazing when it's done," Tom promised as he patted her back.

They were there for an hour as Tom showed them all the progress that had been made on the house while they were gone. Zero seemed to even approve of the lay out as he pranced around the workers begging for pets. When they left, they walked in silence back to the guest house; Ayden knew she was gathering her thoughts. She hung her coat up on a peg and then hung up Zero's lead.

Ayden walked to the fridge and pulled out a bottle of wine and poured two glasses.

Kirsa took the glass and sat on the counter not even sure where to begin. "I have never been so furious at her in my life. I don't even know where to begin with what she did while we were gone."

"The beginning is usually the best place," Ayden suggested leaning against the other counter. He had called for Chinese to be delivered around six so they had some time.

"Then will start with Susannah appearing at the barn, since that's the least of her offenses," Kirsa replied.

"Shit I kind of don't want to know what the others are," Ayden realized.

****

It was almost eleven at night when Kirsa punched in the security code at the Black house. She walked into the kitchen and saw a startled Colin sitting at the island eating ice cream.

"I take it she doesn't know you were stopping over?" Colin replied.

"No she doesn't," Kirsa answered. "You're going to want to be in on this conversation."

"I stay out of female drama," Colin told her. "You ladies get vicious when pissed off."

Kirsa rubbed her temples as the migraine she had been fighting off decided to make an appearance. "Colin I am not in the mood so please just follow me up to her office and be present during the conversation, so I can tell the grumpy old men that I followed protocol."

With that Kirsa turned and went up the old servant's staircase to the second floor where Sabrina's office was located. She knew that Colin followed her, knocking on the open office door Kirsa saw that

Sabrina had her glasses on and a glass of wine sat next to her.

"Come to argue some more?" Sabrina asked sitting back in her desk chair.

"Don't start with that," Kirsa replied walking to the small dry bar and pouring herself whiskey.

She walked over and sat across from Sabrina. "I'm not apologizing because of what I said to you, you needed to hear it. You were reckless and put yourself in a very dangerous situation that I might not even be able to get you out of."

"What are you talking about?" Sabrina asked her.

"I'm ignoring Susannah because she came here, and you said no," Kirsa went on. "As to Anton, you did tell me when he contacted you but you never mentioned it again, so I figured you were ignoring it. You caught me by surprise; part of me can also understand why you needed to see him. With everything that happened over the summer it brought back a lot of memories for all of us and I can understand wanting to see him just to reassure yourself that you didn't make a mistake there."

"At least you, unlike some people, are beginning to understand," Sabrina replied.

"Yeah well that is where my understanding ends," Kirsa warned as she drank her whiskey. "Because when we came to Lars I just can't even wrap my head around why you would even want to go see him. And I understand what it's like being in love with someone who killed people and never have I wanted to visit him."

"That's not true Kirsa, you have paid him visits," Sabrina rebutted.

"Not social visits, I went to see him because he was a potential lead in the case, I wasn't going to tell him how I felt. I did all that in a letter and then burnt the letter like any sensible person does," Kirsa replied.

"I really figured you would understand me wanting to talk to him," Sabrina sighed.

"Really? Whatever gave you that impression? I never wanted to talk to your brother again and the only reasons that I have is for work. I, unlike you, never broke several paranormal laws and vampire laws in doing so."

It took a moment for the last part to sink in and when it did Sabrina paled. Collin now was paying attention to the conversation. "What do you mean?"

"The prison that Lars is housed in is a top-secret facility where only the most dangerous go," Kirsa explained. "The location is classified to such a degree that Victor is the only person that knows the whereabouts of it. Well that is until you. You also visited a prisoner that is banned from visitors and did not get the nearest head to approve of the situation."

"I don't understand," Sabrina said confusion clear in her voice. "If that's the case then why was I allowed to go and see him?"

"That is a very good question, one that has the grumpy old men fighting over who gets to ask Victor that very question."

Colin spoke up for the first time, "If Victor was aware of this then how is Sabrina still responsible?"

Kirsa looked directly at Sabrina when she spoke, "Because she was not tricked or coerced. She voluntarily made the calls to find out if she could see Lars."

Draining the rest of her whiskey she looked at her best friend. "When your punishment comes I suggest following it without complaint."

"You sit on the council now; can't you do something?" Sabrina asked not bothering to hide the fear in her voice.

"I already did," Kirsa said getting up.

"Well if they're going to still punish me then it wasn't enough obviously."

Kirsa turned and stared at her friend. "I got them to spare your life."

With that Kirsa turned and walked out of the room. Sabrina looked at Colin with fear in her eyes.

"Collin..."

"She's right," Collin said hating to admit it. "The laws are clear, to know where one of those prison is a death sentence. She has most likely used up all her debts to get them to spare you."

"But they shouldn't have ...."

"You should never have even thought that this was ever a good idea!" Collin yelled. It startled both of them. "Brie, you have been locking all of us out, keeping us at a distance. I get it, your trust has been shaken badly. But this, what you did? It's suicide."

"Why can everyone else get peace but not me?"

"Not everyone gets peace," Collin corrected her. "Sara and Kirsa will never get peace for what was done to them. You were wrong in this."

Sabrina felt her world around her crumbling. When she heard Collin sigh, then felt arms wrap around her she wanted to fight him off. But he held tighter resting his chin on top of her head. "I might not agree with you but I'm here for you," Collin told her. "Just as Kirsa and Sara will when they calm down."

****

Ayden heard Kirsa's phone go off, pulling away from her sleeping form he climbed out of the bed. When he saw it was Al, he pulled on a pair of jeans from the pile of clothes then walked out of the room.

"It's three in the morning Al," Ayden said as he headed to the back door.

"You are not Kirsa," Al replied annoyed. "Where is she?"

Ayden pulled open the French door and walked out into the cold night air. A thin layer of snow lay on the ground as he stood barefoot and shirtless on the deck. "She's sleeping. What's up?"

"How's the case going?"

"Getting more complicated by the minute," Ayden answered. He thought the question odd since Kirsa had talked to Al after coming back from Sabrina's.

"Look I need to talk to her, it's about her patient," Al said abruptly. Ayden looked out at the sky, "I will let her know when she wakes up."

"Fine if you are going to be protective, tell her that she needs to meet with the doctors at noon," Al informed him.

"Sounds good, should I have her call you?"

"No," Al said.

Ayden heard the phone disconnect. He looked out into the sky and thought about the conversation he had with Al. Looking at the phone he hit redial.

"It's 3:15 in the morning why in god's name are you calling me," Al growled into the phone.

"So that wasn't you who just called Kirsa's phone," Ayden replied.

"I was actually sleeping, something you should try Irish. Besides why would I call Kirsa at this ungodly hour?"

"To inform her that she needs to meet with the other doctors about her patient," Ayden informed him.

There was silence for a few moments before Al answered. "What do you know about Susannah?"

"Everything."

"You didn't let 'me' know that you knew?"

"Nope I played dumb. Think it was Susannah playing a trick?"

"Mind game more like it," Al replied. "Alright tell Kirsa in the morning then have her call me after the interview with the gypsy."

"I will pass on the information."

CHAPTER 19

Kirsa sat at her desk, she was in dark brown dress pants, a baby blue cardigan set, her hair was still wet from her shower. Ayden was filling her in on what occurred while she was sleeping, she tapped a pen on the edge of the desk as he told her about what happened. When he finished he leaned back in his chair and sipped from his mug. This morning he had gotten up with her so that he was ready for the interview with Delilah.

"Al isn't even on the contact list for Susie," Kirsa replied as she thought about the two phone conversations.

"Could she even manipulate a phone like that is my question?" Ayden inquired.

Kirsa thought for a moment, "Yes, in theory. Technology and electronics are easy to manipulate, spirits don't need a lot of energy to use them. To do something physical, like manifesting that takes a lot more."

"But can she do it? She's not a spirit or ghost?"

"She's done things like this before," Kirsa told him. "Little mind tricks to let us know she is still there somewhere inside the chaos."

"Why doesn't she do it all the time then if she's bored?"

Kirsa laughed, "She would if she could, however being on the run she's gonna be hard press to find drugs. Back at the hospital, she was good at manipulating new staff into getting her sleeping pills."

Ayden raised an eyebrow confused now. "Why would that work?"

"Susie is pure faery, which means the medicines used by mortals affect her in a completely different way," Kirsa explained. "In her case, human medicine make it easier for her to enter the astral plane, people's minds."

"But she was on medicine," Ayden pointed out.

"The medicine that she does take comes from the fae world," Kirsa replied." This is why on all her charts it stated to check with me before giving her a new drug. When and if she can get her hands on additional drugs they allow her to completely separate her mind from her body. Giving her the extra boost to go play games and wreak havoc on the astral plane."

"That makes sense," Ayden said as he finished the contents of his mug. Kirsa's desk phone rang, Ayden held up her mug and she nodded for a refill as she answered.

"Hello Olivia."

"Hi Kirsa, I was hoping you would be up and about," Olivia replied.

"I have a victim interview in an hour coming to the house, so Ayden and I are up earlier than usual," Kirsa explained. "So what kind of havoc did she do last night?"

Olivia chuckled, "We had a feeling you would know. It seems she hit Alana, Sara, Sabrina, two of her doctors and I am going to assume you unless the others filled you in."

"She got me at 3 am, Ayden picked up my phone, so I was not aware until just a few minutes ago."

"Even though she escaped she still has us running around in circles and keeping us on our toes," Olivia replied. "Can I ask what she did to you?"

"Pretended to be Al and told me to be to the hospital for noon to meet with her other doctors."

"Not as creative as some of the others, I think she took five years off of Sabrina's life before she realized it was Susannah."

"Now I am going to have to call her and find out what she was told," Kirsa said laughing.

After they hung up Kirsa called Sabrina who answered on the first ring. "So, what did Susie say to you?" Kirsa asked.

"That I was pregnant," Sabrina replied. "She pretended to be the nurse from my doctor leaving a message on my voicemail. I bought it for a few seconds before I realized why the hell was my doctor calling me at two in the morning."

"Wow, all I got was Al," Kirsa said. "She must have exhausted herself with you."

Sabrina laughed. "When I got my voice back I informed the nurse that if I was pregnant then it was a case of Immaculate Conception because I have not been with anyone since Lars."

"Do you know what she said to Sara?"

"Sara caught on right away, so when she was informed that Bridgette's mom was suing for custody she hung up. Who else got hit?"

"Two of the other doctors," Kirsa told her.

"How are you doing today?" Sabrina asked. She was liking how they were almost back to normal.

"I'm doing alright; I've got the interview so that will keep me busy."

"I know I tell you that you shouldn't feel guilty, but I wasn't in there with you," Sabrina began. "As long as you now understand there was nothing you could do then it's a start."

"Why don't you call Sara and we can all have dinner here tonight, bring Colin," Kirsa suggested.

"Sounds good, oh have Ayden bring Delilah's siblings over to the office when they arrive. I can show them around the horses."

"Sounds good."

They hung up after that. Kirsa left her office making her way toward the kitchen, there was a fire going in the pellet stove giving the living room a comfy feel to it. Zero was curled up in front of the fire snoring away. Ayden was at the counter pouring coffee into her mug, he handed it to her along with a vial of blood.

She took the vial as if it was a shot then chased it down with coffee. "Susie told Sabrina she was pregnant."

Ayden almost spit out what he was drinking, "She must of have nearly died."

"She did, apparently Sara caught on right away and hung up on her. They're going to come over for dinner. Should I count you in for eating?"

Ayden smiled making his blue eyes twinkle, "I'm still stuffed from earlier, but I might nibble depending on what you make."

Kirsa shook her head; she put a tea kettle on the stove to boil then brought down four china cups from the china cabinet. She could not wait until the main house was done, when she could finally settle into a house. Walking to the tea cabinet, she grabbed two tins of tea.

"You're making tea for company?" Ayden asked.

Kirsa nodded getting out the tea tray, "I figure it will help calm everyone down."

He leaned against the counter watching as she gathered everything together then he followed her into the living room. She set the tray on the coffee table just as the doorbell rang.

Zero got up and stretched before following Kirsa to the door. He cocked his head as she opened it sniffing the strangers as they walked in.

"You must be Kirsa," Edwin Bartoli said. "I'm Edwin. This is my wife Sophie, our children Delilah, Dante, Lucas and Gabbriella, and the most important person in our home Grandma Nadya"

"The dog sniffing you is Zero," Kirsa informed them as Zero walked around the family sniffing their hands. "Come in we have a fire going."

Ayden walked into the hallway, "Good morning," he said putting emphasis on his Irish brogue.

"You're the vampire," Nadya said with piercing green eyes.

He smiled at the old woman, "You're the gypsy."

She cackled at that, "I like him."

With that Kirsa moved them into living room sitting on the couch, Zero followed her laying his head on her lap when she sat down. Edwin looked at Kirsa and they followed.

"If you would like Edwin," Kirsa began. "I have made arrangements with my business partner to take you and the rest of the brood on a tour of our ranch. Ayden can give you directions, there's a drive that connects us to the ranch."

"That would be wonderful," Edwin agreed. "Sophie you can text me when you're done."

"Of course," Sophie said sitting next to her mother. "Just remember Dante, no rides on a horse."

The older of the boys rolled his eyes. Edwin kissed his wife, oldest daughter and mother in law before leaving with the rest of the children. Ayden followed him out.

Kirsa looked at the three woman and the eerie similarities between the three as if they were the perfect example of maiden, mother and crone. Sophie and her daughter had rich brown hair, and olive skin, where Nadia's hair was pulled into a white bun. They all had green eyes with gold specs, which brought out their complexion even more.

"Let me explain first bring you up to date on what's been going on since we last talk," Kirsa began as she poured the tea. "As I told your mom, Delilah,

Director Moore, handed me a pile of files that he wanted me to look over. He and the other agent believed there was something linking the cases together but could not figure it out. After looking over them I agreed that there was something similar between the four files and agreed to look in on it. After you, I only have one more victim to talk to."

Ayden came in and sat down next to her. Kirsa continued, "I am interviewing each of you because I want to hear for myself what happened and to see if I can fill in the gaps."

Delilah looked at her mother and grandmother who both were fixing their tea. "I'm not sure what else I can tell you that I didn't already tell the other agents."

Kirsa smiled gently, "Humor me and just go through what happened again."

Delilah sighed rubbing her hands on her jeans. Her grandmother patted her knee. "Well I guess it started when one of my friends bought a book on Gypsy Magick," Delilah began. "She lent it to me because she knew I would be interested in it."

"This would be Vanessa, right?" Kirsa asked, making a note. Delilah looked startled that she knew the name. "I talked with Vanessa and her dad last night."

"Oh, yes Vanessa lent me the book. I knew that our family was tied to an old Romany tribe known for their seers."

Nadia spoke, "My family had come to America in the 1800's, they wanted to get away from the stigma and start a new life. We became farmers but kept the traditions of our ancestors."

"My family did the same thing in the 1700's," Kirsa replied. "Does your family produce seers?"

"Only on the female side and all too varying degrees," Nadia answered. Kirsa motioned for Delilah to continue.

"I wanted to be a great seer," Nadia admitted. The grandmother rested a hand on her granddaughters. "I wanted to be the one who could see the future in crystal balls, know when people are coming, and pick up on things. My mother always knows when the phone is going to ring and usually who is on the other line."

"You want a job screening my phones?" Kirsa asked. "This way I know when it's the press?"

Sophie laughed. "It does have its uses, but as I have always told Delilah it has its downsides as well."

Delilah shot her mother an annoyed look, "I don't get how knowing things is a bad thing."

"Because sometimes you learn things you don't want to learn," Kirsa said before Sophie could. "I had a friend who thought the ability had to be the greatest gift in the world, the true measure of power. I used to have to try and convince her that it was more a curse then a gift."

Shaking her head not sure she agreed with either of them, Delilah went on with her tale. "Anyway, I found a spell and tried it out. It backfired and well you know what happened. I became tied to a demon and here we are."

Kirsa nodded and got up. She walked through the French doors and into her office, Delilah watched as Kirsa searched through a bookshelf, moving her finger over the spines. She selected a book and walked back into the living room. Kirsa handed Delilah the book.

"Show me what spell you used," Kirsa replied. The book was the exact same one that Vanessa had purchased.

Kirsa had already been through it and knew that the spell was not in there. She also had informed Sophie of what she would be doing. Delilah's hand shook as she stared down at the book. She looked at her grandmother and mother who both smiled at her as they sipped their tea.

"It's not in here," Delilah mumbled.

"Oh?" Kirsa asked. "Well I have three other texts on Gypsy Magick if you want you can look through them to find it? But that would be a waste of time wouldn't it?"

Delilah did not know what to say so she said nothing, hoping one of the women flanking her would. Neither said a word as they drank their tea. Kirsa leaned back in her chair.

"I'm going to wager that the spell that you used was not found in a book," Kirsa began. "I will also make an assumption that you did not find it on some online site either?"

The young girl continued to say nothing. Kirsa took the book from Delilah then spoke. "Delilah, have you ever done any sort of binding spell before?"

"No, why?" she asked confused.

"Usually when you do a binding spell, whether for good or bad, you need to know something about the person," Kirsa explained. "When you are doing the type that your grandmother did and one that I had to do on a friend of mine years ago, you are given insight into what occurred, like how a demon became linked to you. The only questions left are why and where did you get the spell?"

Kirsa saw the color begin to drain from the girl's face. "For example, your grandmother knows you did a spell that borders on dark magick, she knows it involved calling forth a demon to use its power, she knows it backfired and instead of staying in its realm it followed you here. She also knows that the spell she put on you is not a cure nor is it a permanent solution. So, unless you want a demon to follow you around for the rest of the life we would like you to fill in the blanks."

Delilah remained silent, Kirsa sighed. "Look if you want a demon hounding you for the rest of your life then we will be taking a field trip to a private sanitarium where you can see firsthand patients that have been driven insane by spells backfiring," Kirsa replied. "Where up until a few days ago a friend of mine laid locked in a nightmare state, had no clue what reality is. It's not a fate I would wish on my worst enemy. We have two options. You can tell us without help or the handsome vampire next to me can charm you into telling us and then we go visit Susie just to make sure you told us everything."

Delilah looked at Kirsa then to the man next to her. She then looked at her mother and grandmother they both nodded at her, neither saying a word.

"I learned about the spell in a dream," Delilah finally said. "I had been having these strange dreams about a fantasy world. There was this woman, I never saw her, but her voice was soothing, almost hypnotic. She told me she had the answers for me, a simple spell that would open up my third eye."

Kirsa wrote down what she said, Sophie now had an arm around her daughter and Nadia was holding her hand. "You had no idea you were summoning a demon?"

Delilah shook her head, "Nowhere in the spell did it say anything about summoning or even naming a demon. If it had I would never have crossed that line, I would never have opened myself up to that kind of power."

"Why hasn't the demon possessed her if she summoned it?" Sophie asked rubbing her daughters arm.

"Because she was not willingly summoning it," Kirsa replied. "Even Demons have rules and because she had no clue that she was summoning a demon her body and mind were not open for possession. The demon followed her back not to possess her but to find out who summoned it."

"You said there were others?" Nadia asked.

"We talked with a young man whose story is almost the exact copy of yours," Ayden replied. "A spell was told to him in a dream, unknowingly summoning a demon; however up until a few weeks ago he couldn't leave his house because of the demon that is lurking around him."

"What happened before the holidays?" Sophie asked.

"The person responsible for this pulled us both into his nightmare," Kirsa explained. "Her goal was to bind us to the nightmare so that she could use our energy to make us stronger."

"My darling one," Nadya said to her granddaughter. "You have two choices: Stay a victim or become a fighter.""

I'm scared," Delilah admitted.

"So are we," Sophie told her daughter. "But we can't fight this for you."

"You will be interviewing more?" Delilah asked Kirsa.

"Later this week," Kirsa told them.

"Do you think we could have the boy you talk to already information, it might help them if they could talk to each other?" Sophie inquired.

"His mother thought the same as well," Kirsa said. She went into her office to get the letter they had Alex write. She brought it out and handed it to Delilah. "He thought you might want to read about his experience."

Delilah took the letter and held is if it was fragile and would break. She smiled weakly at Kirsa, "What happens now?"

Kirsa sat down and looked at the three women sitting across from her. "Well you can take a deep breath and try to relax," Kirsa began. "There is a tea blend I like that helps with sleep but at the same time won't heighten your third eye. You want to stay away from using any herbs that could enhance the third eye or dream states for a while, just in case."

"Grandma said the same thing, I haven't even done a tarot reading since then," Delilah sighed. "I apparently have a knack for it."

"And yet you don't see yourself as a seer?" Kirsa asked.

Delilah looked at her as if a light bulb went off, "You're right, it is a form isn't it!"

Kirsa laughed, than poured herself some tea.

"As for the case, I will keep interviewing anyone involved. We will be talking again because the only way I know of how to defeat what is going on is to actually travel with you the astral plane. But that is down the road, not in the immediate future. There are a lot of maybes and what if's at this point."

They talked for another hour before Sophie let her husband know it was ok to come back to the house. When they left Kirsa collapsed on the couch, Ayden sat next to her as she curled her feet under her.

"What are your thoughts?" she asked

."Running along the same line as yours," he replied stretching out his long legs. "That the reason the demons are sticking around is to find out who is trying to get away without paying their dues."

Kirsa rested her head in her palm and stared at Ayden. "This is going to be a long one," Kirsa agreed. "Even if their stories match we still have to figure out who, why, how, and where it is all centered. Then there is the how do we break what has been done to them without injuring their minds, and deal with the culprit without them knowing what we are going to do."

****

It was a few days after her interview with Delilah; Kirsa was sitting at her desk consumed with demon research when there was a knock on her door. She looked up and saw Sabrina standing there; she was in a suit, not her usual look. Her bright red hair was bound up in a twist and she was wearing pearls.

Kirsa leaned back in her desk chair and motioned for Sabrina to come in, "I feel so underdressed."

"I was at a horse auction and luncheon," Sabrina sighed sitting down and slipping off her heels. "We sold three studs and have one signed up for breeding with two farms in Virginia."

"Go us," Kirsa said. "I am so glad you deal with all the horse stuff. However, I doubt you came here to discuss horses and business, what's up?"

Sabrina knew there was never getting anything past Kirsa, it was pointless. She would find things out one way or another.

"A few things actually," Sabrina said. "Is it too early for a drink?"

"It's gotta be five somewhere, but I am not serving you a girly drink. We got wine and beer," Kirsa said.

"Wine, it goes better with the outfit," Sabrina laughed.

As Kirsa got up to hit the kitchen Ayden appeared with two glasses of wine, "Were you reading my mind again?" She asked.

"No, I just got an image of two glasses of white wine. I also picked up on Sabrina's scent." He kissed Sabrina hello and handed her a glass, then gave Kirsa hers.

"You want to order out or should I thaw out a Mrs. Hanson meal?"

"Mrs. Hanson," Kirsa replied.

He nodded then left. Sabrina turned to appreciate the retreating view then sipped her wine and set it down on the edge of the table.

"Talk," Kirsa said.

"The first issue the reporter is back sniffing around, wanting to do a cover story about Lars and what happened with the church," Sabrina began.

"Please tell me you have not spoken a word?"

"Hell no," Sabrina laughed. "Though Colin said a press conference might have to happen. "

"And here I thought sexy Irish vamp would keep the unwanted away."

Sabrina laughed at that. "You two have really settled down and seem to be in a solid place."

"Scary huh?" Kirsa said smiling. "So, what's the second issue?"

"Colin and I went on a date."

Kirsa almost choked on her wine. "Seriously?"

"Yes and we even slept alone. No sex."

"I'm speechless."

"I can see that." Sabrina leaned back in the chair and sipped her wine. "Was it hard to trust again after Anton?"

Kirsa laughed, "Oh my god yes. Especially because I had held back parts of me with him, so it was the thought that if he couldn't love me for the parts I showed him how could he love all of me?"

"What changed?"

"Me." Kirsa to a sip of wine as Sabrina looked at her. "I changed. I grew up; I took the lessons of the past and learned from them. I began to have confidence in who I was, I began to like who I was again, and eventually realized that settling for something that wasn't what I wanted was not fair to me or anyone. Then Ayden came to the castle, it was pouring, there was lightning and thunder. He was drenched to the skin, I was yelling and laughing at him as I brought him up to the family wing and sat him by the fire. He made me laugh; everything was at my pace and not his."

"What made you realize that you could trust him completely, that he wouldn't break your heart?"

"When I realized that he could shatter my heart completely," Kirsa told her. "Your brother never had that much power over my heart. Yes, I was broken when I ended the engagement with Anton, but it was more exhaustion from years of mental abuse. With Ayden, he could shatter my heart. Plus getting shot at by a lunatic in an abandoned farmhouse filled with biological ickiness doesn't hurt either."

Sabrina laughed, "Bullets flying would help with the whole knowing you could trust someone thing. Alright, I need to get home before my housekeeper sends out the National Guard."

"I'm here if you need me," Kirsa told her
. Sabrina gave her a hug then left. Kirsa pushed her work aside and made her way to the kitchen. One of Mrs. Hanson's stews was simmering on the stove. She closed her eyes when his scent passed over her, then his arms were around her waist and he just held her as she took in his scent. He kissed her neck then nuzzled her ear.

"What's with all the mushiness?" she asked as he kissed her jaw.

Ayden slowly turned her around and kissed her softly, "I heard what you said to Sabrina."

Kirsa couldn't help but feel the blush come over her face. "Ahh, yeah what can I say I was having a mushy moment."

"No, not you," Ayden chuckled.

CHAPTER 20

Kirsa awoke to violin music being played somewhere in the manor. Climbing out of the stunning hand carved four poster bed with red satin sheets; Kirsa pulled on a satin robe and headed out of the bedroom. She knew she wasn't home, yet everything was familiar, she had been here before. Descending the stairs, she followed the heart wrenching music to the large music room.

There he stood, the man who stole her breath and haunted her dreams when she was a teenager, and even occasionally as an adult. He was tall, well over six feet, his black hair was short and spiky. The black suit was finely tailored and still managed to showcase his muscular body. Kirsa felt the ruffle of a breeze and saw that she was now wearing a stunning blood red gown.

The man turned and faced her, his beauty still taking her breath away, his amber eyes were like molten gold in the candle light. He wore a black button down shirt and a tie that matched the color of her gown. Gracefully, as if floating, he approached Kirsa and kissed her hand.

"It has been far too long," Lou replied as he escorted her to a table for two.

"You're the one that made the decree that I was never to set foot in the astral plane," Kirsa reminded him.

She sipped the fine champagne that appeared on the table. "I take it this is a dream?"

"Bringing you to the astral plane is too dangerous at this point," Lou said. Servants brought them their appetizer. Kirsa actually detected a note of concern in his voice.

"Are you concerned for me?"

"Concern is such a strong word," he said thoughtfully waving his hand in illustration. "More of unsure of how things will play out."

"What has you so unsure?" Kirsa was aware that he like a few others knew all that was going to happen to every person on the earth.

"At this point even Odin has been blocked out what might occur," Lou informed her, he saw surprise flash in her eyes. "He was going to come to you but it has been decided that I would be the last one she would think of."

"Susannah," Kirsa replied. "This is larger than messing with a few teens heads isn't it?"

"That is only the start of what she is trying to do," Lou replied.

They finished their appetizer and he waved a hand making them vanish. Kirsa leaned back and sipped her Champagne.

"How serious?"

"The All God council was called," Lou answered. Referring to the rare meeting between every head deity's including himself.

"It must be serious if the Gods held a council meeting."

"Even the boss of all of us is concerned," Lou told her. "And you, my love, are in the cross hairs."

"Why me?" Kirsa asked. She was getting tired of always being the cause or reason for something.

"Don't you understand your family history?" Lou asked raising an eyebrow. "Or are the vampires lost as to what your very existence means?"

"Now I am confused," Kirsa said. She was not sure she was going to like the answer. "If you tell me and I don't want to know it can you erase it from me?"

Getting up from the table Lou walked over and pulled her from her seat and held her. "Your humility has always made you the most beautiful creature I know."

Sighing, as she breathed in frankincense, myrrh and hellbane, she felt safe and protected. "What is it Lou?"

"You know of the vampire lore?" Lou asked as he led her to one of his gardens.

"There was a woman named Eve, she bore six children, each child held a particular power, but all had the thirst for blood, those six children began the six bloodlines we know today. The line I come from is believed to be from the original son and he never turned anyone."

"Let me fill in the blanks," Lou said as they walked through the garden path. "When Adam and Eve were cast out of the Garden of Eden they go and populate the earth with their children."

"I did attend Sunday school," Kirsa reminded him. "I know the whole tale."

"No one knows the whole tale," Satan corrected her and continued as flames danced around him. He took a deep breath returning to normal. "After they had settled, a fallen angel descended to their home. To this day no one knows who he is or what group he belongs to. He was not one of mine for if he was I would have killed him outright for what he did."

"It must be bad," Kirsa said.

"Though they were cast from Eden, all the gods and fallen angels knew not to touch them for they were protected by the Abrahamic god. This fallen angel, he acted on his own. He tried to seduce Eve, but she refused all his advances."

"Aren't fallen angels impossible to resist?"

"Cute and you should know that is not the case," Lou commented before continuing. "Furious, that she would choose a mere mortal over the likes of him, he rapes her and impregnates her. He then lays a curse onto the unborn children that they will have the power of the gods, but only blood would sustain them. They could live for eternity, but silver would be poison, a weapon through the heart or decapitation would be the only ways to kill them."

Kirsa sat down on a nearby bench; Lou summoned her champagne glass and handed it to her. He sat next to her on the bench and continued with his tale. "Nine months later Eve gives birth to six babies, they look beautiful and perfect. They hope that the curse is not true. I'm going to skip ahead a few decades," Lou informed her.

She nodded to let him know it was okay, that he could continue. "The six children watched their parents die and then their siblings and yet time had barely noticed them. They decide it was time to leave their home and explore the world that lay before them. As they each traveled on their own they became lonely and wanted a family of their own. From that desire came the first true vampires."

"What happened to the six children?" Kirsa asked captivated by the tale.

Lou had to think for a few minutes before he answered. "Ogma died during the early days of Christ, he pissed off the wrong tax collector and was crucified in the traditional method," Lou recalled. "His son eventually makes it to the British Isles and settles there. Anya made it to what we call France, but due to her blood thirst she is murdered during the reign of terror, however her sons stay for they enjoy the people and the culture."

"Gotta love the Reign of Terror," quipped Kirsa.

"True," Lou chuckled. "If I were to believe the rumors, Maria is still alive. She made her way to Latin America long before the conquistadors and blended in with the natives there. She had a severe dislike for those who were unfaithful and fed off of them. There is no report of death and she has not turned up in any underworld dominion, so she is unknown."

"If she is alive she has to be several thousand years old," Kirsa said.

"That she would," Lou agreed. He tapped his glass recalling who was next. "Grigor is next; he made it to Eastern Europe long before the czars. He liked the dark and the cold, he is the reason people think vampires burst into flames if they walk into the sun. For he spent almost a millennium in darkness then decided he missed he sunlight and went to see a sunrise and his skin caught on fire like old parchment."

"That kind of sucks," Kirsa said.

"But his last sight was the sun," Lou pointed out before continuing. "The next to last is Dorin who ends up in Scandinavia; his line gets their mental gifts from him. He was so renowned as a fortune teller and prophet that during the inquisition he was burnt at the stake, his head cut off and placed on a spike for all to see."

"And then Hagan," Kirsa realized.

Lou nodded. "The youngest one, who never turned another being into a vampire. He never even killed a human from taking too much blood. But we know what happened to Hagan, he ends up in Germany to become Lord of a small village. He would come back every few centuries to take back power and reestablish ties. His last homecoming, he fell in love with a young village girl, a gifted healer. They marry and have two children. That is the blood that runs through you. Now do you understand why you are so special? Because the rumors are correct, the blood that flows through you is from one of the original six children and from Eve."

"Does Susannah know the truth?" Kirsa asked. Fear tried to creep up but with Lou holding her hand it was chased away.

"No, she might suspect that you are more powerful and that makes you unique, but we have spread rumors for centuries that it is due to your unique blood."

"Which is true," Kirsa replied with a slight smile. "So, knowing why you all fear for my safety in this, the question is what is she planning?"

"Because of what Susannah did all those years ago, she knows an iron prison is waiting for her once it is known what happened," Lou explained. "She is trying to raise an army of demons to take on that challenge."

"She wants to rage war with faery?" Kirsa asked skeptical.

"That would be foolish, everyone knows not to mess with the fae," Lou laughed. "No, she is going to rage war against all who know the truth about her. By making you all crazy or dead no one would believe the stories. And you are her final target. The problem is her mind is fractured so she does not have the strength to call forth an army of minions."

"Hence why she is using teenagers," Lou told her. "Their minds are pure and moldable and perfect target for what she's doing."

"Why is it backfiring?"

"Because all but one, are unwilling to share their mind with a demon, not that I blame them. I hate sharing my mind with a demon."

"You are a demon, Lou," Kirsa said dryly. "Any advice?"

"Focus on the ones that you can save first, get them demon free then use what they have to offer," Lou suggested.

"It's going to be hard to fight a battle when I can't be on the battlefield."

Lou ran a hand down her cheek and stared into the violet eyes. Eyes that haunted his sleep and waking thought.

"I have thrown the bargain out."

Kirsa froze Satan didn't just do something like that for no reason. "And what do you want in return?"

"I will erase our bargain, and take away the conversation pertaining to your bloodline, you will remember everything else," Lou told her.

"See this is where I get nervous about what you're going to ask for," Kirsa informed him.

"No sacrificing your first-born son," Lou promised. "All I want is a kiss and for you to answer a few questions."

"As long as the kiss has no strings attached or hidden agendas," Kirsa said softly.

"None."

"Alright."

He smiled softly making him all the more stunning. Lou cupped her chin and tilted her head up to his, slowly he bent down and found her lips with his. The kiss was soft and gentle; he wrapped his arms tighter around her as her hands ran through his hair, he deepened the kiss. Lou knew he had to stop before he could not, so he pulled back and kissed her nose. She smiled and touched a hand to his cheek.

"I would have become mortal for you," he whispered.

She was the only woman he had ever truly cared for and not wanted anything from. He refused to use the term love because what he felt was so strong and pure. He held it close for he knew if he ever said those words others would hear and she would be in far more danger then she already was.

"I know," Kirsa told him as their foreheads rested against each other.

"Why him?" he asked kissing her forehead. "I know his feelings are as deep as mine and as true as mine. But why him? Is it because you saw my other form?"

She looked up at him and smiled softly. "Lou I always saw your other form whenever you got angry or mad it was always there lurking over your shoulder."

"Then why?"

"Because he will tell me his secrets if I asked him, because he will share his life with me, because I will be the center of his world, and because I can have all of him," Kirsa answered honestly. "I know that with you I can never have all of you, I can never know all your secrets, and that even if you were to become mortal you will always wish to be back here I could never have asked you to do that."

"He is the luckiest man in the world, I hope he knows that," Lou said swallowing the lump in his throat. "If he ever hurts you I will build a special place for him in hell."

"I would be disappointed if you didn't," Kirsa replied as they walked to the entrance of the garden. "Please don't let this be goodbye again."

"Whenever you need me I will be there, no strings attached," Lou replied. "Even in monster form."

"If you ever need someone to listen you know where to find me," Kirsa said kissing his cheek. "Oh, and if you ever pull that crap again like you did ten years ago you will wish you never met me."

"Hell hath no fury like a woman scorned," Lou said laughing. "Goodbye my dear."

She watched him walk back to his manor with his other form showing in his shadow. Sighing she walked through the gate.

****

Kirsa woke up to Ayden staring at her. She sat up in bed and tried to focus on everything that had just happened in her dream. Kirsa looked at Ayden and realized he had heard her dream, she never even thought that he would be able to hear. Ayden kissed her gently, relieved that she didn't taste of brimstone or hellbane. He then pulled her close just to make sure she was truly there and his.

"I could hear you but you couldn't hear me," he whispered.

"I didn't even know that you would be able to," Kirsa said. Then she thought of Lou and their kiss that was not one of friendship. "Ayden, I don't even know how to explain anything."

He brushed a curl out of her face, "You came back to me. I don't care that the Devil and I fell for the same woman. You chose me and everything else is moot."

She kissed him again then sat back against the headboard. "Did you hear everything about Susannah and what she is trying to do?"

"I did," Ayden told her. He left out the part that he still remembered the origin tale and the truth about her blood. "How do you want to proceed?"

"In the morning I'll call Al and Frank, I think the four of us need to sit down and begin hashing out a plan. He said to focus on those that we can help first."

"I'm guessing that Kristina is going along with Susannah," Ayden said.

"So we focus on Delilah and Mora, and work with Kristina's friends."

"Sounds like a plan," Ayden agreed laying back down in the bed. "Are you going to tell Sabrina and Sara?"

"I will, he said she is planning a war against all who know, that would include them," Kirsa replied yawning.

Ayden kissed the top of the head and watched as her body slowly began to fall asleep. He just held her for a long time before he was able to rest.

CHAPTER 21

They gathered in one of the conference rooms at OPIA headquarters. Coffee and pastries were set out on a side table. Allowing Sara, Sabrina, and the others to get comfortable before it was time to work. Al walked in with Kirsa and Ayden.

"Alright there is a reason, other than a headache, that I called you all here today," Al began as they all took their seats. "We are all aware of the conversation that Kirsa had with a certain individual the other night. After talking about it briefly it was decided that in order to move forward with this case, Frank and I need to know everything that happened during those last two years of high school and what happened when Susannah tried to attack you a few years later."

"What do you want to know?" Kirsa asked as she drank her coffee.

"Everything," Al replied.

"That can cover a lot of grounds," Sara warned. "You might want to be more specific."

Al knew this was not going to be easy and that the three best friends were going to form one unit making it hard to get through. "When did you start practicing witchcraft?"

The three women looked at each other and Kirsa took the lead. "Sara and I were the first," Kirsa answered. "We both grew up in the paranormal world, and gravitated toward the pagan religions and witchcraft. For me it was learning how to control my abilities. For Sara she felt more accepted then she did at the churches in the area."

"Even though the paranormal laws had come out before I was born," Sara replied. "Some of the churches were not thrilled with allowing monsters into their sanctuaries. Even if they said they accepted you I could tell they were still weary of me. That they liked us better when we were a myth or a fable."

"You weren't the only person to feel that way," Ayden replied. "When the groups decided that it was time to come out there was concern for how we would be accepted. Even though we had been living with humans for centuries they didn't know and didn't want to know."

Frank knew they were getting off track but now he was curious. "Why come out at all then?"

"Technology," Ayden said simply. They all looked at him confused. "With the invention of the computer we knew our time was limited until we would be forced to reveal ourselves. It allowed us time to discuss privately with world leaders of politics and religions. It was the religious leaders that had the most concern, not because they didn't want accept us because they already had without knowing, they were more concerned with how the congregations would accept us."

"The minister tried to make me feel welcome but the looks from the rest of the people were enough to make me not want to go back," Sara said. "My grandparents and father never forced me. My minister was great though, he felt that as long as I didn't give up on faith, that i found a faith where I could find a place that I was accepted he was happy."

"What about you Sabrina?" Al asked.

Sabrina closed her eyes and took a deep breath. "I see angels." She looked at the stunned looks on Frank and Al's face.

"Run that one by me again?" Al asked. He wasn't quite sure if he heard her correctly.

"You know how Kirsa sees ghosts and can talk to them," Sabrina asked. They nodded. "Well it's like that but instead of dead people I see Angels. Though I really don't talk to them because they aren't big on being noticed."

"You mean like angels from heaven?" Al inquired.

"From heaven, from hell, I have even seen Valkyrie's on occasion," Sabrina replied. She remembered the Valkyrie, stunning beauty, strength and grace that she had never seen replicated. The Valkyrie came to take the Jeff's soul the day of his funeral to his place with the other fallen soldiers.

"I have never heard of such an ability," Al replied in awe.

"Dietrich said it's like only two people a generation have the ability, and no one knows why," Sabrina told him. "It doesn't stay with a family even."

"Are there Angels in this room right now?" Frank asked.

"Every being has one protector spirit," Sabrina said dryly. "Except vampires. So right now, there are five in the room along with us."

Al and Frank both looked at each other and then at Sabrina in fascination. "Like Kirsa I wanted to have a better control of it," Sabrina said continuing with the topic at hand.

"What about Susannah?" Al asked.

"Well as you know she is Faery and comes from one of the royal courts," Kirsa began. "They worshiped the old Irish gods, so she grew up as a pagan and around magick. She never really talked about it until freshmen year; she came to me with a book she found that was on Faery and love magick."

"None of those books are actually written by a fae," Al grumbled. He hated those books, all they did was cause trouble and get people involved in something they knew nothing about.

"I took a look through the book and told her it was a bit dark for my taste," Kirsa replied. "She then wanted to know if I practiced, who I prayed to, what I could do. From there it just kind of escalated, we had our own little coven of four."

"Kirsa was away for chunks of time," Sara added. "When she would come home for breaks we would do something big, like a ritual or summoning. When we realized that Kirsa could walk the Astral world without so much as a spell we began to experiment with that. She was the one that first noticed the change in Susannah."

"You two didn't?" Al asked.

"They were with her every day, I was gone for a month at a time," Kirsa reminded him. "So I was able to see the change more clearly. However once I said something they both thought about it and realized that I was right to be concerned. We tried to talk to her but the more jealous she became of what I could do the darker she became."

"Did you have any inclination that she was messing with demons?" Frank asked.

"No," Kirsa laughed. "She was Fae, my dad wrote the laws on the paranormal, so I knew all about how if a Fae wanted a demon they used their own and didn't go into the demon realm."

"Why is that?" Sara asked. "Why don't the fae and demons mix?"

"It's how we are made," Al answered. "Fae are creatures of nature and of dreams. We live on beauty and grace. Demons are creatures of nightmares and hate. Though Iron is lethal to both of us, we do not cross paths. A Fae who sees a demon in true form, well their mind cannot wrap around it, it destroys their mind. Once that mind is broken then the demon can do what it wants with the host body."

"But you're Fae," Sabrina pointed out.

"I'm only half," Al told them. "My mother is human. Since the leprechaun gene runs in the male line we can marry whoever we wish. So, the human part of me is able to grasp the horrors of the demon world."

"Susie though is 100% fae," Sara realized.

"Which means she wouldn't be able to handle it."

"And she didn't," Kirsa said. "The second Lucifer became his true form she broke."

"What happened that night Kirsa?" Al asked cautiously. He knew what was in the file, what he had been able to gather from Kirsa, but never heard the whole tale straight from her.

"I had come back for summer," Kirsa said. She felt Ayden's hand on hers to give her strength. "I knew something was wrong when I got home. There was this old cabin on our property at the time that we would use for rituals. I went there and found her. She had already cast the circle, had said the spell and was lying unconscious in the middle of the circle. I saw the spell on paper and knew what she had done. She had made a deal with three gods, each one not knowing about the other. I broke her circle and casted my own around us then sent myself into the astral world. I was able to locate her, by that time Hecatate and Freya had figured out her deception."

"Really she tried to pull one over on Hecatate?" Frank asked amazed. "I even know not to mess with her."

"Susannah was convinced that her faery blood would keep her safe," Kirsa informed him. "When I got there, they had informed Susannah that since she broke their contract by going behind their back they would not aid her. Then the third appeared."

"Who was it?" Al asked. He had a pretty good idea as to who it was but had to ask.

Ayden squeezed Kirsa's hand letting her know he was there. This time Kirsa took a deep breath. "Lucifer. "

"Was he in his human form?" Frank asked. He had stories of people meeting the morning star.

"Yes," Al answered, surprising even Kirsa. "He has his normal human form; he can also appear as your heart's desire. He doesn't show his other form unless you manage to let loose his fury which is a lot harder than you would think."

"Can I continue?" Kirsa asked looking at the two of them. They both nodded letting her know they were done. "Anyway he shows up and informs Susannah that the deal she made with him was null and void, that she still owed him her price. It was then she summoned the demons. Once they saw Lou though they submitted to him and showed her in her true faery form. Lou in his fury became his monster form, it shattered her mind. I offered to make her payment."

"Why would you do that?" Frank asked.

"I've always wondered why myself, but she won't tell," Sabrina replied.

"Because I knew I was safe, I knew that I would not be harmed, that unlike Susannah my blood would protect me," Kirsa replied. "And I know that sounds naïve and egotistical but it's true."

"You went up against the devil and were convinced he wouldn't hold it over you," Al yelled. "That's beyond stupid."

"She's right," Ayden said before anyone else could jump down her throat. "Her blood, unlike Susannah, protects her."

Al looked at Ayden and saw meaning in his eyes and knew to drop it. "Alright."

"So, what happened when you offered payment?" Frank asked.

"I had to give each of them an offer to be accepted, Hecatate was to continue making offerings to her. To Freyja my soul when I die," Kirsa said. "Lou wanted a single droplet of my blood. I also promised to never enter the Astral Plane again. Even in her broken state, Susannah still tried to kill me. Lou reverted back to his monster form and threatened her that if she ever harmed me again he would allow me free reign in the astral world."

"I told you Frank, inflict his wrath and you get his other form," Al reminded him.

"What did Susannah do?" Frank asked.

"She broke," Kirsa said simply. "You could see it on her face and how she held her body that her mind just broke into thousands of pieces. Knowing she was broken, Lou helped me bring her back."

"We could tell from just looking at their bodies," Sabrina replied. "When we found them they both looked as if they were in a deep sleep. But then Susie's face contorted to show a look of absolute horror, we knew then that something had happened. Kirsa came back first and tried to wake up Susie but nothing."

"All our parents were there when they woke up," Sara added. "Evegren was able to do something to get Susie to wake up but the damage was done."

"She was in a state hospital until they moved her to the private one," Frank said checking over the files.

"Why?"

"Because the doctors were trying to cure her or fix her," Sabrina replied. "There is no fixing a broken mind. Not to mention that when you gave her drugs she became more dangerous. Her parents moved her to a place that was started to help those damaged by the paranormal, who were permanently scarred."

"What happens when she is given drugs?" Frank asked them.

Sabrina laughed at the question. "You explain it Kirsa, you're the doctor."

"I hate you sometimes," Kirsa mumbled.

Sabrina smiled at her as she drank her coffee. "When Susannah is given drugs, they sever the few ties she has to her body and allow her free reign in her world that she has created. When that occurs, she tends to wreak havoc on those she knows. It's not pleasant or pretty. Ten years ago she was able to get sympathy from a nurse who began to slip her meds, it went unnoticed for two days but the damage was done. "

"That's when she took the three of us out of commission," Sara said. "She was draining our energy, so she could build up her own energy."

"It was after that attack on the three of us that they moved her to Shady Pines," Kirsa explained. "It was a more secure setting and there was no experimenting with drugs."

"Do you still have the spell she did?" Ayden asked out of nowhere. They all looked at him. "You said she had it written down, do you still have it?"

Kirsa and Sabrina looked at each other. "If it wasn't destroyed in the explosion, and it wasn't in the boxes that I have then it would be at Sabrina's," Kirsa said.

"I've been going through my boxes and haven't found it yet," Sabrina replied.

"Alright we'll start there," Al replied. "If we can find out the original ceremony then we might be able to come up with a counter spell to deal with our last three teenagers."

The meeting went on for another hour, when it was over Kirsa walked with Sabrina and Sara to the garage. Sabrina unlocked the doors to her car then leaned against it.

"So, is Lou still hot?" she asked Kirsa. Sara chuckled as she slid into the passenger seat.

"Why am I friends with you again?" Kirsa inquired.

"Because I'm awesome," Sabrina reminded her.

Kirsa laughed at that and felt all the tension drain away when she did. "Yes, he's still hot."

"Like mouthwatering and want to jump his bones hot?" Kirsa just stared at her with a dangerous look.

"I think she is choosing not to answer," Sara warned.

Sabrina nodded at the comment; she figured he still would be. "Alright, I'll let you know when I start going through the boxes."

"Shout if you need help," Kirsa told her.

CHAPTER 22

Caroline watched as her best friend paced the hospital room while she carried on a conversation with herself. The Kristina she had known had begun to vanish, her beautiful brown hair now hung in matted clumps, her face was covered in scratches she inflicted on herself. Caroline sat in one of the chairs and wondered what was going on in her friend's mind.

"Kris, what's happening in there?" Caroline asked.

Kristina stopped pacing and looked at Caroline, for a moment it seemed like she didn't know who she was. "I'm being given orders."

"What kind of orders?" Caroline inquired trying not to cry over the state of her friend.

Kristina held a finger to her lips giggling as she looked around the room. "It's a secret," Kristina whispered.

"Krissy, don't you remember, we tell each other everything," Caroline said laughing. "When we were smaller we would stay up late at sleepovers whispering over secrets."

Kristina shook her head as she banged her fists against her head. "She'll get mad."

"Who'll get mad? You can tell me, I want to help you?"

"No you can't," Kristina said shaking her head. "She only can help me."

"Alright," Caroline sighed. "How can she help you if I can't?"

"Because she is all knowing, she truly cares about me," Kristina replied standing straighter. "I have a place beside her."

Caroline went to argue but sighed. Nothing she said was going to change what was happening. "Kristina I'm not coming back after today," Caroline said.

Skylar, her boyfriend, was right the visits haunted her more and more each time. "You have chosen your path and I must choose mine."

"We all have paths to choose," Kristina intoned. "We all have a place; we all have blood to spill. It is through the spilling of blood that we are truly free."

Trying not to show how freaked out she was by that last line, Caroline nodded sadly to her friend. Caroline doubted that Kristina was even aware that she had slipped out of the room, or that the nurse had slipped back in. Skylar was leaning against the wall waiting for her, he put an arm around her shoulder as they headed to one of the group therapy rooms.

Kirsa got up from her chair when Caroline and Skylar walked in; she went over and held on to Caroline.

"Up until this last time, every time I came here I would be so upset when I left," Caroline replied breaking the silence. "But today I realized that Kristina was lost to us that night."

Skylar took a folded piece of paper out of his back pocket and handed it to Kirsa. "This is what we remember from that night," he informed her. "I know it took a while but the group of us wanted to make sure that what we gave you was as close to the original one as possible."

"Thank you," Kirsa said.

"You're not saying it but you can't save her can you?" Caroline asked.

Dr. Kesler went to speak but Kirsa answered. "Out of the four, she is the only one that has succumbed to the desire of what is offered," she explained. "I honestly don't know what will happen to her when we break the link. It could heal the damage done or it could make her worse."

"Why is she different from the others?" Skylar asked. They had talked to the other three, all who seemed cool and normal.

"Unlike Kristina, the other three come from happy and loving homes," Kirsa answered. "That bond protects them from the worst of the demon's tricks."

Caroline looked at her boyfriend then smiled weakly at Kirsa. "And we all know she has never had a loving home."

Skylar looked at Kirsa. "Look the group of us talked about it, we know it might be too late to save Kristina but if you need our help let us know."

"We'll keep in touch," Kirsa promised them.

Dr. Kesler walked the two young kids out leaving Kirsa and Ayden alone. He studied her face before he spoke. "You can't save her."

"No, I can't. I think she had all of us fooled from the beginning." Kirsa had known from the moment she got Caroline's frantic call last week that Kristina was lost to them. "When we sever the connection, it will cause her to spiral deeper and deeper."

"She made a statement that was similar to two of the suicide victims," Ayden pointed out. "That blood will purify."

"You think Kristina might try to harm herself or others?" Arnold asked as he came back into the room.

"It's a possibility," Kirsa replied.

"I'm going to go discuss security, you two stay as long as you need," he told them.

Ayden pulled her onto his lap and just held her. He knew that losing Kristina was rough for Kirsa. "What time do we meet Mora?"

"I'm going to call her parents after lunch," Kirsa said glad for the change in topic. "Then they will let the church know we're coming."

"Why don't we go out to dinner when we are done here?" Ayden asked. "I'll let Vlad know we won't be stopping in."

"He'll be fine with it?"

Ayden laughed. "Vlad hates company. But for his future leader he is willing to put up with us."

"A night alone, away from everything would be nice," Kirsa agreed.

"Then let's go," Ayden said as he gently slid her from his lap and stood up.

The *Fairmont* hotel was located in the downtown section of Pittsburgh. Ayden had reserved one of the one-bedroom suites with the view of Mount

Washington. Kirsa stood in front of the windows staring out at the view, he handed her a glass of champagne that he had ordered up to the room. She smiled as she took it from him.

"You didn't have to do all this," she said after sipping the champagne.

"We haven't had much time to celebrate us being engaged," Ayden replied. He kissed the finger that bore his ring. "I thought it would be nice to splurge even if we are working."

She followed him to the table that had been set up with their dinner. He was right, it was nice to sit down and just relax for a while. After dinner he uncovered the chocolate bomb for dessert and Kirsa groaned. It was chocolate cake with the middle oozing out of the top, and then topped off with vanilla ice cream, hot fudge and chocolate shavings.

"So where do you want to get married?" Kirsa asked him after sampling a forkful.

"I figured you would want get married in Grabenberg or Germany," Ayden said surprised by the question.

"I've thought about it." Kirsa took another bite knowing she was going to regret the dessert later. "If we get married in Grabenberg the media is going to be all over it. I feel if we got married in Germany I am going to be handing the wedding over to the inner council and it will be more political than anything."

Ayden tried a small sample of the dessert. He sipped his red wine to wash down the richness. "I hadn't thought about those aspects. Where are you thinking then?"

"O'Brian Castle."

He stared at her for a moment. Deep down he had wanted to be married where he had been born. Now Kirsa was letting that dream come true.

"Are you sure?"

"Only if you wear your family's colors."

Ayden got up and pulled her off the chair and into his arms. He kissed her pulling her closer to him. He then rested his forehead on hers and just stood there with her. "You are the answer to all my prayers and dreams."

****

The following morning, they braved the cold and walked around downtown grabbing breakfast at a small café. After lunch they headed back to the hotel to call the Andersons and set up the interview. Kirsa changed into grey slacks and a purple sweater set to set off her eyes. Ayden pulled on black trousers and a steel gray sweater. Grabbing her black pea coat and bag they headed out of their room. Ayden had called down for their car so it was waiting for them when they hit the lobby. It took them about twenty minutes to find the small brick church in the Mount Washington neighborhood.

Father Patrick stood outside the church doors and waved to them he then showed them where to park. He was short with graying blonde hair and twinkling blue eyes.

"You must be Kirsa and Ayden," he said shaking their hands. "Please come in out of the cold. Mora has talked much about you."

"She seems like a wonderful young woman," Kirsa said as they entered the sanctuary.

It was an old church, with stunning glass windows, long wood pews, and alcoves that held statues of saints. It didn't feel stale or stuffy but instead full of life and energy.

"She really is," Patrick laughed. "At first the members thought I was crazy for letting her stay here but she has won them over."

"Where does she stay?" Ayden asked as they walked to a side door. He had his answer when they walked through the door and into the house attached to it. There was conversation and laughter coming from the back of the house.

"I have a guest apartment upstairs," Patrick explained. "One of the young novices has moved in to help Mora out. My apartments are on this main floor. It has been nice to have the house filled with young energy."

They headed to the kitchen and Ayden stopped when he saw the woman talking to a young teenager. Both had flaming red hair that was wild and curly. When the mom turned he stopped short, she reminded him of his baby sister. She had the same bright green eyes and scattering of freckles over the nose. Kirsa looked at him for a moment as he tried to regain his composure.

"This is Dr. Kirsa Heinrich and Ayden O'Brian," Patrick introduced. "These are the Andersons. Josh and Brenna, Mora is the younger version of her mother and Jordan is the one buried in my refrigerator."

"Did you say your name was Brenna?" Ayden asked his voice rough.

"Yes, why?" Brenna Anderson asked in a beautiful faint Irish brogue.

"Sorry it's just you look so much like someone I once knew and share her name," Ayden replied. "It caught me a bit off guard."

Kirsa had never seen Ayden like this before. She took his hand in hers and squeezed it as they sat down.

"I was born in Ireland and came over when I was just a baby," Brenna told him as they sat at the table. She studied Ayden and focused on his eyes. They reminded her of her fathers.

"Where in Ireland?"

Brenna let out a laugh, "No one has ever heard of my town. We still speak Irish there."

"Try me."

"Ayden is originally from Ireland," Kirsa explained.

"Ah," Josh said. "Her family is from south of Kerry, I can't even pronounce the town's name."

Ayden froze and then recited the name with a flawless accent.

Brenna looked at him, "How did you know?"

"It's the town I was born and lived in until I became a vampire," Ayden replied.

Mora found the whole conversation exciting. "This is amazing."

"Are you an O'Brian by birth?" Brenna asked.

Now she was intrigued by the large Irish man who came from her town. "No, it's the name of the man who took me in after I was turned," Ayden told her. "My last name is Molineux."

The Andersons all froze as they stared at Ayden. "You're him!" Brenna exclaimed, jumping up and hugging the startled vampire. "You were the first victim."

"What do you mean I was the first victim?" Ayden asked confused by her reaction.

"I don't know the details, by Great-Grandpa always told us that his uncle was the first murder in a string of murders that have gone unsolved, no matter how much money the O'Brian's put into the search."

"Wait," Kirsa replied. "Ayden would be the Uncle to your great grandfather?"

"Yes," Brenna said. "Great-Grandpa is the youngest son of Declan Molyneux."

Kirsa looked at Ayden who was in shock. "Why don't you and Brenna go talk and I will handle this."

"You sure?"

"This is important for you," Josh agreed with Kirsa. "You both need to learn about this connection."

Everyone watched as Ayden and Brenna left the room. Mora spoke first. "Does that happen often? Vampire finding lost family?"

"Not when you are talking about a vampire Ayden's age or older," Kirsa replied. She took a moment to compose herself. "Alright Mora, aside from family reunions, I need to know what happened that night and what led up it."

Josh squeezed his daughter's hands letting her know he was there for her. Mora took a sip of water.

"I grew up in a pagan household," Mora began. "I knew what to stay away from and avoid. Mom's Irish and Dad's grandparents came over from Norway so I always gravitated to the Irish and Scandinavian Deities."

"Even though you knew better it was tempting to experiment?" Kirsa asked.

She had heard the tale often enough; a teenager is told to stay away from something but the lure is almost too powerful to ignore most of the time.

"Not really. I stayed away from the Ouija board and would only do tarot readings on myself," Mora replied. "It's odd because I remember this clear as day. I was at a bookstore with some friends and while they were off in the romance section I was in the occult section. This book seemed to fly out of the shelf and landed at my feet. It was on faerie magick, mom always said to be careful with the Fae, but the book was so enticing. I flipped through it and bought it."

Kirsa felt her blood turn cold when Josh slid the text across the table. The cover had changed but the title and authors name were the same. She closed her eyes before she opened the book; it was identical to the book that Susie had shown her all those years ago.

"The spell you used that night, was it in here?" Kirsa asked. She was pretty sure she knew the answer but wanted to make sure.

Mora shook her head. "I had done one of the spells to bring psychic awareness in dreams. In my dream it was like I was really in the realm of the fae."

"Tell me about it," Kirsa said.

"The colors were more vibrant and rich, your senses were so much more aware, it was like being in the most perfect Fairy Tale setting but surpassing even that," Mora said sighing. "At the same time, I felt as though I was on the outside not able to fully appreciate it what it all had to offer. Then I heard the voice. It told me that it knew how to cross the barrier, how to make it so that anyone could enjoy the world of the Fae. I heard the ritual then, when I woke up I wrote it all down."

"Do you have it? The ritual?" Kirsa asked hoping the excitement was not in her voice. She didn't want to get too excited that the ritual was still intact or that it might be the one that Susannah tried all those years ago.

"I wrote it in my grimoire," Mora replied.

"Could I get a copy of it?" Kirsa asked.

Josh looked at Kirsa for a moment. "You know the ritual she's talking about."

"I might, a friend of mine dabbled in the darker Fae magick. She believed that her Faery blood would keep her safe," Kirsa explained. "She showed me that same book over fourteen years ago."

"What happened to her?" Mora asked.

"She escaped from a mental institution even though she is still plagued by nightmares," Kirsa replied. "The blood she thought that would protect her actually caused her condition. Her faery mind could not grasp the images and horrors that she saw so it broke."

"I had to read Dante's Inferno this year, where I was dragged to in that ritual reminded me a lot of his description of the worst levels of hell," Mora stated.

"I thought the same thing when I had to go in and drag her out of there," Kirsa told her.

"Dad, it will be on the last two pages," Mora told her father.

"I can scan it into the computer tonight and send it to your email," Josh told her.

"That would be perfect," Kirsa said. For the first time since Al handed her the files she felt like they were making headway with this case. For the first time in months she was able to finally take a breath.

CHAPTER 23

While Kirsa was researching spells and rituals with Sabrina, Ayden went upstairs and called Shamus. They had returned from Pittsburg the day before and he had questions he needed to answer. Closing the door to his office he called Shamus' personal number. He didn't want to talk to anyone else at the moment.

"Ayden, what do I owe this call to?" Shamus replied as he sipped his evening blood.

"Questions," Ayden replied.

Shamus heard the serious tone in his adopted child's voice. He set the glass down and motioned for his oldest son to leave the room. "What's wrong?"

Ayden ran a hand through his hair as he tried to formulate a thought. "Kirsa and I went to Pittsburgh this weekend to talk to two of the teens involved in her case. Mora Anderson is the one living in the Catholic Church."

"You went into a Catholic Church? I'm shocked," Shamus said chuckling.

"I met Mora's family," Ayden continued. "Her mother is Brenna Molyneux."

Shamus sat still as stone as the name hit him. "A relative?"

"The great-great granddaughter of my brother Declan. His son, her great grandfather is still alive."

"My God, Ayden," Shamus replied in shock. "How did she handle it?"

"She wants me to meet her parents."

"That's wonderful," Shamus said. He meant it.

"The question I have is that according to family legend I was the first of series of murders," Ayden began. "Is it true?"

Shamus sighed as he leaned back in his chair. "The night you were turned against your will I was coming back from Dublin," Shamus recalled. It was a memory he did not like to dwell on. "I found you and knew that what you experienced was absolute horror, that you made no choice, and were left for dead. I brought you back to my home, after we bathed you and fed you it was then I realized you were Gideon's eldest."

"You didn't recognize me before?"

"Ayden, you had been beaten to death, every bone in your body had been broken. Your face was unrecognizable," Shamus replied. "Your sire then turned you so that you would feel the pain of the healing and then die from hunger."

"Were there others?"

"When I realized you were from the village, I had a carriage take us to Dublin once you were fit," Shamus told him as if not hearing the question. "While we traveled, Patrick kept me informed of what was happening. Six other bodies were found while we were abroad. All had been drained of blood, but none were strong enough to survive the beating and then the transformation."

"He's never been found?" Ayden asked. He was numb to all of this. His emotions were all over the place that it was easier to turn them off then focus on them.

"No and I don't think he likes that I took you under my wing because on the day you should have died I always receive one black rose," Shamus told him.

"Is how I was turned why I didn't remember who I was?" Ayden asked.

When he awoke as a vampire he had no memory of his mortal life. It didn't take days to remember but decades. And when the memories came they came crashing wave after wave of emotion as he remembered the family he once had.

"Ayden," Shamus sighed. "I have talked to older Vampires and how you were turned was atrocious and beyond comprehension. You should have died that night, those that I have consulted agreed that due to the trauma you experienced that night your brain blocked it out but in doing so, blocked everything else out as well."

Ayden was silent unsure of what to say or think. "Mora told me that even after my death, Catherine still made everyone's lives hell."

Catherine was his mother; she was a horrible human being he had yet to meet someone as horrible as her.

"Catherine could have been queen of the world and still have been the bitterest person alive," Shamus sighed. How are you handling all this?"

Ayden looked out the window taking in the trees and other surroundings. "I am letting them decide how to handle it, I've gone a hundred and fifty years without them, if they decide they want me then I will welcome them. If they decide it is all too much, then it will be disappointing but life goes on."

"Keep me apprised of the situation," Shamus said.

"Shamus, I might meet the son of my brother."

Shamus heard the catch in Ayden's voice. It was slight, but it was there. The reminder that this path was not one that Ayden had chosen, it had been one forced upon him. "I hope you do, son."

"Do me a favor, Brenna said her parents came over because of financial issues with the family."

"They never recovered from World War II," Shamus said. "The land went barren and they are just barely making ends meet. Why?"

"Pay off their debt in my name, buy back the house from the man who is renting it to them, and the land."

"I will have Patrick access your accounts and make the transfers," Shamus told him. "You don't have to do this."

"Yes I do," Ayden said simply. "I was the oldest and it would have been my burden, by dying it fell to Colin and Declan."

He hung up with Shamus after that. For a moment he thought that he wanted to be alone but then he heard Kirsa laughing and realized he needed to be with her. Ayden found Sabrina and Kirsa pouring over old note-books. Kirsa looked up and smiled at him as he sat next to her on the couch. She squeezed his hand; he let her know he would tell her later. He kissed her forehead before relaxing into the cushions.

"How's it going?" Ayden asked.

"Josh emailed me the ritual that Mora used," Kirsa informed him. "From what we have seen it is almost exactly like the one that Susannah tried to perform, though it is a bit different."

"It gives us a starting point at least," Sabrina interjected. "We at least have a better idea of what we are looking for."

"How does it differ?" Ayden inquired as he glanced over the printout.

"In Mora's she is asking to be a vessel to funnel the power to another source," Kirsa told him. "In Susannah's, if Sabrina and Sara are correct, she asks to be the direct conduit of power. "

"Alright so how do we undo the one that Mora did?"

"I have Alex and his coven working on that," Kirsa said. "This way we can focus on locating the original ritual."

Ayden nodded as he looked over the pile of books that had taken over the living room. "I regret ever telling you to go through your high school things."

Kirsa laughed. "Al still would have handed me the case, at least with me thinking about Susannah I was more open to the possibility then I would have been."

Sabrina rolled her shoulders and glanced at her watch. "When is Sara getting here?"

"In a little bit," Kirsa said looking at the clock. "She was picking Bridgette up from practice then dropping her off at Phil's."

****

Later that night Kirsa laid in bed with Ayden, her head rested on his stomach as he stroked her hair with his hand.

"What were your plans before you became a vampire?" Kirsa asked.

Ayden had to think. "I told you I was the oldest and that we had a few options." Kirsa nodded loving how when he talked of his family his brogue came out more. He continued, "I was getting to the marrying age, there was one girl who was relentless in her pursuit of me. It didn't matter that neither family wanted the match, including me."

"Why?" Kirsa asked.

He laughed, "Because my family was protestant, and her family from the next town over was Catholic."

"Did you have your sights set on anyone?"

"Don't laugh when I tell you this," he warned with a finger, Kirsa nodded her head solemnly. "There was a group of gypsies camped outside our village, my younger sister Brenna dragged me to one of their shows. She brought me to a fortune teller and told her that I needed a bride."

327

"I am sure you were thrilled," Kirsa said trying to hide the giggle that was threatening to escape.

"Overjoyed," he responded dryly. "The gypsy woman told me that I would live a long life, though one filled with blood, wars, and also peace. I would see new lands and sail the ocean."

"Well she was correct."

"Oh, just wait," Ayden promised. "I remember the next part exactly, she gazed into her ball and consulted her cards. The tent, filled with incense, was quiet while she looked like she was solving a riddle. She then told me that I would meet a woman from a different age, her hair dark as night, eyes the color of heather; she would carry the gifts of the wise. "

Kirsa stared at him, he smiled and kissed her lightly then continued. "My sister asked when we would meet; the gypsy asked if she could wait outside. Rolling her eyes, Brenna, got up and stalked outside. The gypsy told me that the life I knew would be over in a fortnight and a new one, the one I would meet my soulmate in would be beginning."

"If you tell me you became a vampire a fortnight later I will hurt you," Kirsa said.

"It was three weeks actually after that meeting that I was attacked and turned into a vampire," Ayden told her.

He felt the chills that ran through her. "If you now tell me that you fell in love with me when we first met I will be freaked out," Kirsa warned. She was in elementary school when she first met Ayden.

"God, no if anything I thought of you as my baby sister," Ayden laughed. "It wasn't until I saw you when you turned twenty-one that I knew you were it."

CHAPTER 24

Sabrina knew she had to be dreaming. It was the only explanation for her to be wearing a wedding gown. She ignored, or tried to ignore, that her roses were bleeding, but the blood was not staining the gown. The odd thing was, she wasn't in a church or even in a field of flowers, she wasn't quite sure where she was due to the fog. Trying not to panic, Sabrina instead took in her surroundings.

The fog was making it difficult to make sense of where she was, it was as if someone hadn't completed painting the back drop. Sabrina began to walk to see if it would get her anywhere, as she did she realized that surrounding her were pictures of her life.

"I know I'm not dead, bitch," Sabrina called out.

She was answered with laughter.

"Oh no, when I am done you all will be begging for death," Susannah's voice replied. "When I'm done you all will be begging for mercy."

Now Sabrina realized that Susannah had taken her into the nightmare realm. She remembered that when Kirsa was dragged into the realm she met up with Alex. Sabrina began to think of the other three that were alive. She ruled out Kristina based on her willingness to listen to Susannah.

"Delilah or Mora, I'm here, my name is Sabrina and I am friends with Kirsa," Sabrina said calling into the wind.

****

Kirsa, Ayden and Frank Willis stared through the hospital room window as they watched Carlotta Louis talk to someone that wasn't there. The doctor had entered the room to try and explain their purpose to her. Ayden rested a hand on Kirsa's back knowing she was worried about Sabrina, Collin had called on their way to meet with Carlotta to tell them that it was Sabrina now unconscious in the hospital.

"Which one is this?" Ayden asked.

"She murdered her family in order to purify herself," Frank reminded him.

"Right," Ayden said suddenly sorry that he asked. "Why did I get dragged here?"

"You are going to use your charms," Kirsa said. "Her guardian ok's you entrancing her to get answers."

"Great," Ayden replied.

The doctor walked out. "I'll be watching in our security booth, press the button if you need assistance. But the three of you should be fine."

Kirsa walked in first, Carlotta had a shaved head because with the hair she ripped out she tried to make a noose to strangle herself with. Her brown eyes were dull and lifeless as she watched them enter the room. She wore white medical scrubs and sat crossed legged on her bed.

"Hi Carlotta, I'm Kirsa," Kirsa said as she sat in a chair next to the bed. "Those men are Ayden and Frank they are friends of mine."

Carlotta cocked her head to the other side as Ayden and Frank both leaned against the wall.

"Pretty," Carlotta replied.

"Carlotta, I want to talk about your family," Kirsa began.

"They should be here soon," Carlotta replied looking around the room. "It's almost time and they're never late."

"Are you celebrating something?" Kirsa asked silencing Frank with a look. Carlotta nodded earnestly.

"Oh yes, we will be celebrating her rebirth. Aida and Aria will be so thrilled to witness it."

"Whose rebirth?"

"I can't tell you," Carlotta whispered holding a finger to her lips. "If I tell she won't come."

Kirsa and Ayden looked at each other. They had heard a similar line a few days ago. "You don't have to tell me," Kirsa assured her. "Carlotta can you talk to me about what happened your senior year of high school?"

"No."

"How come?" Kirsa asked pretending to be confused.

"Bad things happened then," Carlotta said frowning.

"What happened?" Kirsa asked gently.

"She told me, said their blood would clean me," Carlotta said rocking back and forth. "She lied, they found me."

"Who found you?"

"The demons," Carlotta whispered.

Kirsa watched as Carlotta rocked back and forth. She knew she wasn't going to get anything more out of the girl; she nodded to Ayden letting him know it was his turn. He took her seat then focused on Carlota who watched him with curious eyes.

"Hi Carlotta," Ayden said with a smile. "Can you look into my eyes for me?"

When she did, Frank watched as she went under the trance within a second. He looked at Kirsa and she signaled for him to get the tape recorder ready. She then took her seat next to Ayden.

"Carlotta," Kirsa began in a nice even tone. "What happened four years ago on Halloween night?"

"I was walking home from a school party," Carlotta began in a neutral tone. "I didn't notice the four guys following me from the school to my house. They attacked without warning, dragged me into the back of a parking lot. They each took turns raping me next to the garbage. They left me for dead. A patrolman found me and brought me to a hospital, he was nice stayed with me while they did tests. They contacted my parents. They were furious."

"Why?" Frank asked.

He thought furious was an odd word to use for the fact their daughter had been raped.

Carlotta turned her head to face him. "Because they believed it was my punishment for celebrating an evil holiday. That I now had disgraced the family." The three looked at each other as Carlotta continued. "They would not press charges because they believed I deserved what happened. It was discovered at the New Year that I was pregnant. They wouldn't even let me put it up for adoption; they were going to force me to raise it on my own without their help. They told me it would be a constant reminder of what happens to those who sin."

"What did you do?" Kirsa asked gently.

"I began to have these nightmares of giving birth to a demon child. Each night I prayed that someone would help save me from my fate. Then she came, the angel."

"What did she look like?"

"Beautiful like an angel should," Carlotta said in as if in awe of it all. "Her hair was long and blonde but shined like the rainbow. Her eyes were the color of the ocean and her gown was silver. She shimmered in gems, she listened to my anguish and my horror. She promised she would make it all better, that she could help me. She told me to recite: *Now Anger melt in tears of salt, now sadness freeze in winters breeze, I bind my soul to thou who comes, I bind my soul to myself, so none shall harm it more.*"

"What happened Carlotta? What happened after the ritual?"

"Nothing," she whispered. "The nightmares still came; I was still pregnant, my family refused to look at me. Even at the breakfast table no one, not even my younger sisters would talk to me. The angel came back and visited me in a dream. She told me that perhaps it hadn't worked right because I was no longer pure. She gave me another ritual to perform. It would require the cooking of fresh hearts wrapped in thorns and impaled with iron."

No one spoke as the girl went on. "I killed them while they sat at dinner all telling each other how wonderful they were. Then I cut out their hearts and boiled them. She was there with me the whole time, she's never abandoned me."

Ayden cut the connection there. He looked at Kirsa who nodded, they left the room as she began to rock back and forth. Her doctor met them in the hallway. Dr. Allen had been working with Carlotta for the last three years; he knew her case inside and out. Frank went to interview some of the nurses and other staff that interacted with her.

Kirsa and Ayden followed Dr. Richard Allen to his office so they could talk in private.

"You made more progress then we have since she came here," He told them as they took their seats.

"Her brain is damaged beyond repair," Kirsa said.

The secretary came in with a tray of coffee and set it down on the desk. Richard waited until she left before beginning. "Carlotta was damaged long before the gang rape," Richard explained.

"What do you mean?" Kirsa asked as she sipped the coffee.

"Since taking over her case three years ago, I have done some research into her back ground prior to her senior year. I interviewed relatives, friends, classmates. Basically, anyone that remembered her or her family," Richard explained.

"What did you learn?" Ayden inquired. He had set his mug aside after taking a sip to be polite.

"Her parents, especially her father, were hard people to know and to live with. Her mother was a classically trained pianist and her father was a composer," Richard told them. He pulled her file from his cabinet and handed it to Kirsa. "All their children have opera or musical names."

"I picked up on that with her sisters Aria and Aida," Kirsa said.

"She also had two brothers named Sigmund and Wagner," Richard added.

"I thought she only killed four people?" Ayden asked confused.

"The brothers were from her father's first marriage," Richard explained. "If anything, they were the only two that gave her any kind of love and respect. They pay for her to be here, for any type of additional treatment or therapy, they visit when they are in the area."

"Are they involved in the music area?"

"No, much to the fury of their father. Wagner is a para-normal lawyer in Canada and Sigmund teaches Medieval History at Seton Hall."

"So, what was different with Carlotta?" Kirsa asked. "I take it both parents wanted a child prodigy."

"And they got one with Carlotta." Richard went on his lap top and hit play on his iTunes folder. Soon an angelic voice began to sing Ava Maria. "That's her at eleven singing at Carnegie Hall."

"Holy Shit, she's phenomenal," Ayden explained.

"I vaguely remember her name now," Kirsa realized. "My parents donated a lot of money to the arts and I remember talk of this operatic prodigy."

"By fifteen she was accepted into Juilliard but for some reason her parents would not allow her to attend," Richard informed them. "Instead she was enrolled in the private school in their town and had private lessons before and after school."

"If they sent her to New York it would be releasing control and it sounds like neither would do that," Kirsa surmised.

With her parents, it was trusting their daughter enough to let her move all the way to Cambridge at the same age.

"Wagner has a similar theory as well," Richard agreed. "She was not allowed to partake in any school activities, when she toured there were private tutors. During school breaks she performed, they never allowed her to take a day off."

"A lot of pressure to put on someone so young," Ayden stated.

"You were never pressured by your parents were you?" Richard asked Kirsa.

She smiled softly at him. "They wanted me to be as normal as I could for as long as possible," Kirsa explained. "There were lots of therapists involved to make sure I grew up normal. I was given the choice as to whether I should try to test out of high school and go to college or if I wanted to attend high school with my friends. They always supported me."

"Carlotta didn't have support at home, she didn't have choices," Richard replied. "Sigmund and Wagner both agree that there was something off with her after turning down Juilliard, that a part of her broke afterwards."

"She probably saw it as a chance to get away from her parents and when they refused she became hopeless," Kirsa said. "Which fits the pattern."

"No one is saying it explains what she did, but it helps understand her psyche at the time," Richard added. He then slid over the sealed envelopes that contained the photos from the crime scene. He kept it sealed so that no one could accidentally see the horrors.

Kirsa slid open the top and took the photos out. Ever since the summer when she found Isabella nothing surprised her anymore. However these came close. There was no way of knowing who was who; the bodies had been butchered beyond recognition. Kirsa knew that they had to do DNA testing to determine who was who. She imagined what would have been a spotless kitchen was covered in blood and other gore.

Body parts were strewn across the floor, table and counters. Kirsa shivered at the bloody footprint marks throughout the pictures. She felt her stomach turn at the large pot on the stove with bloody contents in it.

"She confessed to the murders," Richard stated. "In a monotone voice she detailed the crimes and how she went about it."

"The rape destroyed whatever was left of her," Kirsa said. "Richard what happened to the child?"

He looked surprised at the question. "She had a miscarriage, if you ask her it happened after she visited her faery godmother in the dream world. Some suspected she did something to terminate it."

Kirsa and Ayden both looked at each other, the grief flashed quickly in their eyes before it vanished. "I have learned recently that traveling to the astral plane while pregnant does something to the pregnancy and causes a miscarriage."

"Really?" Richard asked fascinated. "It would make sense if early in the pregnancy, at that development period it is susceptible to everything."

"Between turning down Juilliard, the rape, the fury of her parents, and the loss of the child, that's enough for even a sane person to snap," Kirsa pointed out. "If we go with the fact that there might have been something wrong to begin with then it explains her being chosen."

"It's also similar to Kristina's background," Ayden added.

"If there is anything else please let me know," Richard told them. He then bit his lip before speaking again. "I was hoping not to do this, but it is an honor meeting you Kirsa. Your work is what inspired me to go into parapsychology."

Kirsa smiled at him. "Thank you, it's nice to hear things like that."

They met up with Frank in the cafeteria before heading to the car. Lance opened the car doors letting them all in. Frank sat up with Lance as Ayden and Kirsa slid into the back of the Durango. They waited until they were in the car before anybody spoke.

"You recognized the spell didn't you?" Ayden asked Kirsa.

"The first one Susannah used was twisted to bind Carlotta's will to hers. It actually is a quite harmless spell, used to help do away with negative thoughts," Kirsa explained. "She added to it, twisted it so that it became a binding spell."

"What about the last ritual?"

"A very dark ritual, I've never read all the way through it," Kirsa answered. "It's to summon a demon for each heart given."

****

Kirsa sat with Sara in the hospital. Ayden was on the phone with Dietrich giving him the latest information that they had, Lance stood outside the private waiting room monitoring who was coming in. While they waited for an update, Kirsa filled them on their visit with Carlotta. Al walked in.

"Titania is going to search for the ritual, the royal court has given her access to the archives in Fae," Al began as he sat down. "Delilah is unconscious; Alex and his family are driving to Warwick as we speak to see if they can help in anyway."

"How do we get her out?" Collin asked as he stopped pacing.

"I'll go," Kirsa said. "The problem is we have no idea what Delilah's nightmare realm is. We did with Alex."

"Why is that important?" Collin asked frustrated. This whole situation was spiraling out of control, and he could do nothing but sit there and watch.

"Because if Kirsa doesn't have an idea of where to start she will have to search the entire plane to find them," Sara answered. "Delilah's best friend is reading her journals and when Alex gets there he is going to go through her book of shadows to see if they can find anything out and let us know," Kirsa told them.

"Collin, take Sara to the manor both of you get some sleep. Ayden and I will stay here until morning."

****

Sabrina stood before a beautiful cathedral, one that belonged in a European city in a stunning wedding gown. She could hear a violin quartet playing inside and watched as people in their best entered the building. Walking across the street in the warm summer day she hesitated before opening the large doors. As her hands touched the handle she was transported inside.

The church was a glow with candles and beautiful flower arrangements. Sabrina was looking down on it from the balcony that housed parts of the organ. She studied the people recognizing many of the faces down below. It was the figure standing with the priest before the altar that shocked her. Lars stood there looking stunning in his tux with a look of excitement on his face.

"You could have had him. He could have been yours for all eternity." Susannah said in her mind. "Look how in love you both are, how happy and content."

"It was a lie Susie," Sabrina replied, she ignored the pain in her heart. "He never loved me, I was just part of his plan."

343

The music changed to that of the wedding march, which caused Sabrina to groan. Then she watched as her father walked her down the aisle to the now glowing Lars.

"You could have ignored that voice telling you something was amiss, you could have gone on pretending."

"And live a lie?" Sabrina laughed at the wedding below. "I'd rather be alone and know the truth then live a lie."

"What has that brought you, being alone? Your friends hate you for going to see Lars, no one can trust you. What joy is in that?"

"They were angry, and they had a right to be, I understand that," Sabrina replied. She knew Susannah was trying to cause doubt. "I am rebuilding the trust that I caused to slip. I am not alone."

"Look and see which of your friends is not there celebrating with you, the happiest day of your life and she couldn't even make it. Sabrina studied all the familiar faces. "

Sara stood with Jeff in one of the pews; her face was crestfallen with sorrow as her husband confronted her more like they were at a funeral rather than a wedding. As if this wedding signified something far greater than a joyous occasion. Then she realized who wasn't there. Kirsa was nowhere to be seen, nor was Ayden.

"She couldn't even come to your own wedding."

"If she isn't here then perhaps Lars' plan worked and she's dead."

"Her life could have meant your happiness. She ruined it all."

Sabrina felt cold at the thought. "No, she showed us the truth even though it almost killed her. I would rather have her then the man of my nightmares."

A silver staff appeared in her hand and using it she swung the intricately carved staff at the glass causing it to shatter. As the pieces fell around her the image faded until there was nothing.

****

Delilah stared at the Gypsy camp before her, wagons and tents made up a small transient village. Gypsies called out their wares to pedestrians, some inviting those to get their fortune told or buy a love potion. Delilah looked down at herself and saw she was in a skirt of blues and greens swinging around her, bracelets covered her arm, hoops dangled at her ears and scarves tied her hair back. She shivered as she heard her name being called out, and then there was silence.

"They are your people. This is where you belong instead of ignoring your heritage."

"My people came over long ago to settle down and create a life," Delilah replied. It was true her ancestors tired of the wagon trains, of the nomadic lifestyle and sought out a new life.

"They ignored the magick in their blood, turned their back on their people. But you, you could show them how strong you are."

"Let me guess I could have all this power but at a cost? So what is it selling myself to Satan or to a demon?"

"There doesn't have to be a cost, I can show you how to have others pay your price. "

"No deal, I would rather have no ability then have someone pay for my own stupidity," Delilah said.

"But you could have the knowledge of all the great seers; you could be worshipped as a god. "

"Or be thrown in the loony bin like you," Delilah pointed out.

She watched as a silver coin fell into her hand. A scream filled the air as the scene before her crumbled to the ground. Once again, she heard her name, this time it was clearer. She followed the direction it came from.

CHAPTER 25

*T*he smell of coffee radiated from one of the conference rooms at OPIA headquarters. Ayden, Al, Frank and Kirsa were trying to connect the dots while Sabrina lay unconscious in a hospital. Lance was with Colin at the hospital, he would be able to pick up the slightest change in scents.

Kirsa couldn't sit at the hospital and wait, so instead she poured through the files trying to find a link, a missing piece.

"The four suicides each took place on a Friday," Frank pointed out. "As did Carlotta murdering almost her family."

"What about the current Four?" Al asked.

Kirsa flipped through the files and checked the dates with the calendar on her phone. "Friday as well."

"Alright our first major break, they all happen on a Friday." Frank wrote it down on the whiteboard. "Now with two of the suicides not cooperating, we can still safely say that everyone got the ritual from a dream. The description fits Susannah."

Two of the victims' families refused to answer any questions or calls. Kirsa ran a hand over her face. "The question is what happened five years ago and why she tried again now."

Al tapped a pen on the table as he looked at all their notes scrawled over the white boards. "Kirs, you said ten years ago she tried something on the three of you, but Hagan and Hugh threatened her."

"They threatened to steak her with iron nails if she ever tried it again," Kirsa replied. "Why?"

"She knows your dad is serious because she is not allowed at the house when vampires are there," Al said. "Five years ago, there was a slight power struggle in the water branch. Two of the smaller houses were vying for more power, the Faeries had to keep peace and try to negotiate a deal."

"She would be aware of it because Titania and Alana talked to her as if she was part of the conversation," Kirsa added. "Which means, she knew that her father was occupied keeping peace instead of watching her and making sure she didn't attempt anything."

"Your parents are both still alive, but with a power struggle that means the Fae become a bit weaker, not as many eyes to watch her." Al tapped the pen on the table as he thought through it. "But how do you go about picking five random people to possess? None of them have any ties to her or to any fae."

"It's actually not hard," Kirsa replied. Three heads turned to look at her. "The astral plane is basically one giant dream realm in a sense. You have creatures that live there full time, and portals to other realms. Dreamers stick out; they glow to indicate they don't truly belong there. "

"Does everyone have the same glow?" Al asked as he wrote down what she was saying.

"Kind of. Let's say you are in good state of mind but want to work through a dream you had to see what message was there, you would glow a bright white to show you were stable. However, if you were going there to escape, to ignore the pain in the real world, you would have this black nimbus around you."

"So, all Susannah would have to do is pick out those with the black nimbus, locate where they are from and then target their dreams," Frank replied putting it all together.

"It would still take time to find all that out, but the black nimbus would narrow things down quite a bit," Kirsa explained. "You are talking thousands of beings and countless areas to sort through."

"It's not like she had anything better to do with her time," Frank pointed out. Kirsa nodded in agreement.

"What about now? Anything going on in the Fae this time around?" Ayden asked Al.

"Nothing major," Al replied. The only thing he was aware of was his father's murder and him being promoted to head but that wouldn't cause a power fluctuation.

"So why this time?" Frank asked. "If there's no power struggle what happened to make her think she could try again?"

"She started a year ago, so it's before I came back to New Jersey," Kirsa said. "But she hasn't grabbed anyone else since July which is when I get here."

"Kirsa when was homecoming?" Ayden asked. He knew schools had homecoming in the fall.

"It's usually around Halloween, why?"

"Because Alex is targeted in October," Ayden reminded her.

"Last October was also the ten-year reunion from high school," Kirsa said jumping up and walking over to the whiteboard. "She wouldn't be able to go obviously but she would have known. She would have been furious that she couldn't go and show people what happened to her."

"All that anger finally culminates, and she starts her plan," Al said. "Now what do we do with the information?"

"Ten years ago, I graduate with a bachelors and masters, they graduate high school. Sara and Sabrina go off to college," Kirsa said as she began writing on the board. "Susannah instead of going off to NYU is locked up in a mental hospital. She hears about the ten-year reunion and realizes that while she has been trapped in her nightmare we have moved on."

"The big thing is Hagan is no longer here to make his threat come true," Ayden said gently. "She can now target the three of you without fear of his threat."

"Because you know she won't think her father will harm her," Al added.

He knew for a fact that wasn't true. He had paid them a visit last night and it was taking everything to keep Hugh from ripping the astral plane apart, so he could get his hands on Susannah. They had started the process to renounce her from their line and house, it was the worst thing you could do to a Fae was to strip them of their house and line. Kirsa went to say something but her work phone went off. She saw it was Alex.

"What's up Alex?"

"I think I know what her nightmare is," Alex said. The excitement was in his voice.

"Alright I'm putting you on speaker, I'm here with Al, Frank and Ayden," Kirsa told him. She set her phone in the middle of the table and turned the speaker on. "You're on."

"Delilah used her book of shadows also as a dream journal," Alex told them. "She keeps referring to these nightmares where she has to relive an event that caused her embarrassment or pain. She writes that if her psychic ability was strong enough she would be better prepared for those dreams and be able to defeat her demons."

"That would mean that Sabrina would be going through the same thing," Al said.

"You were catapulted into Alex's clown nightmare. It would make sense that Sabrina was having to face her own demons as well."

"Lars and Anton," Kirsa said. Ayden was at the door before she got to it and had it open as they rushed out of the office.

****

Dietrich sat in his office in Austria, he was trying not to focus on the hell that Kirsa was dealing with in New Jersey. Which is why he called a meeting with Victor. Now, Victor sat across from him.

"Tell me Victor how a mortal learned how to get in touch with you?"

"Perhaps Kirsa left the number to my office lying around," Victor said dryly, trying not to act surprised by the question.

Victor studied the office in Dietrich's home and thought it was rather bland.

"Kirsa does not leave things lying around for others to see," Dietrich informed him.

He leaned back in his leather chair and studied the South American vampire that sat across from him.

"I hope you're not implying that I had something to do with this," Victor replied. "What evidence do you have?"

"Your second in command brought her to the prison and to the room where Lars was."

"And?" Victor was losing patience with this meeting.

There were other important things he needed to do then be lectured by Dietrich.

"I am sure you read Lars' sentence."

"Of course, I needed to know how to outfit his cell," Victor answered briskly.

"Then you would have read over the part where it states no interaction with any being, not visits or conversation," Dietrich answered. "And yet your second in command had no qualms on bringing a mortal to the prison and allowing her to speak to the prisoner in question. Either you allowed this, or she acted on her own."

"Obviously she acted on her own," Victor said aghast.

He acted as if he was horrified by the idea that he would have anything to do with violating a prison sentence.

Dietrich studied him. He knew Victor was lying through his teeth; however, he could not prove his involvement. Opening a folder, he took out a paper with the seal of the Inner Council, dipping his pen in ink he signed the bottom of the document. After applying fine sand to the ink to help it dry he then folded it and sealed with wax.

"That is all I needed to hear," Dietrich replied standing up. It signified the end of the meeting.

"What's the document that you signed?" Victor asked suspiciously, not getting up from his seat.

"Eztil's death warrant," Dietrich answered with no remorse in his voice. He watched the shock flash through Victor's eyes.

"Her death warrant? Why?"

"Why? It's obvious, instead of informing you of the situation she chose to act on her own. That alone deserves punishment, added to that she brought someone to our prison which only you are supposed to know the whereabouts of, and violated a prison sentence by allowing Lars to have a visitor. Those three crimes call for death."

"But she's my second," Victor said. He was stunned that they would take this path, it was a path he never even considered they would take.

"Yes, and as your second she knows proper protocol and what to do in situations like those. Instead of informing you of the request, she acted on her own and broke several laws in doing so." Dietrich studied Victor, he was not taking the news well.

"And what of the mortal?" Victor asked in a near whisper.

"She will have her own punishment don't worry," Dietrich promised. Unless Kirsa was right and Susannah somehow implanted the urge to see Lars into her head. "We are currently looking into our jurisdiction over the mortal and what punishment we can give."

"She should also be killed."

"If she was aware of the protocol and blatantly ignored it like Eztil then she would be, however she was unaware of the proper way of things," Dietrich told him. "And she is not a vampire."

"How long do I have until I have to kill Eztil?"

"Oh no, you won't be killing her," Dietrich said and saw that he truly caught the asshole off guard with that comment. "Nor will you know when. Someone will be assigned to the detail."

Victor went to walk out of the office, but Dietrich called him back for a moment.

"A warning Victor. The inner and outer council are quite disappointed in the behavior of your vampires, this is not the first time such action has been taken in regard to one of your children. If another vampire steps out of line, you will be removed from the inner council and as Head, and someone else will be appointed."

****

"Really? Senior Prom?" Sabrina asked into the night.

The banquet hall was decked out in silver and black. Stars hung from the ceiling as candles glittering all over the tables. Meatloaf's Paradise was playing, and everyone was dancing, not even paying attention to Sabrina in her wedding dress.

"Are we doing the Christmas Carol thing? Because that's been overdone!"

"I forgot how annoying you are", Susannah replied, frustration evident in her voice. "I'm trying to show you how much better your life would be without Kirsa in it. Senior Prom you broke up with your boyfriend after Kirsa and Sara saw him kissing someone else. If they hadn't told you, you would never have known, and prom would not have been ruined."

"You are wrong on two counts, Susie," Sabrina pointed out. "The first is that living a life of ignorance is not living. Though I was pissed that he was cheating on

me, I had more fun after pushing him into the pond outside and with Sara and Kirsa then I did before they told me. I would rather know then ignore what is going on."

"Sometimes ignorance leads to happiness. "

"No ignorance leads to compliance, not happiness," a voice said from behind Sabrina.

Sabrina turned to see a dark-haired girl with golden skin standing before her. "Delilah?"

"Sabrina?"

"Yes," Sabrina said. "Welcome to Prom."

Delilah looked around taking in all the late 90's fashion and music. "Seems more fun than my junior prom."

"Well it seems you two found each other, I was wondering if you would, however unlike the other time, there is no one location, no demons to battle, no one to come saving the day. "

"There are always demons to battle, even if you didn't send them," Delilah replied. "You think by making us face ours we will succumb to you. We're both stronger than that."

At her words prom faded from view leaving them in the middle of nothingness. Delilah took in Sabrina's wedding gown and silver staff.

"I don't even know where to begin," Sabrina said laughing.

"That's fine because I have a silver penny and am dressed like its Halloween," Delilah replied.

****

Kirsa paced the hospital room as she talked to Victoria on the other end. They were discussing what to do.

"I don't think you can go in there," Victoria said as she slammed a book closed on her end. "I think if you misjudge you might cause more damage than doing any good."

"That was my thinking as well," Kirsa replied. "We are going to have to let them battle this one out on their own."

"Not necessarily," Victoria replied. "What if you entered the astral plane and created a dream realm that was a room of prayer and positive thoughts? You could send them positive thinking and try to break through that way. Alex might be able to help since you two have linked before."

"Tell him to be ready in an hour," Kirsa said as she hung up.

Ayden and Colin watched as she shrugged out of her suit jacket, took her watch off and emptied her pockets. There was another hospital bed in the room for Colin to sleep on, instead Kirsa hopped up on it.

"What's going on?" Ayden asked as he walked to the edge of the bed.

He took the watch and other things from Kirsa and slipped them on to the bedside table.

"I can't enter her memories for risk of damaging them," Kirsa told him. She saw Colin wanted to argue so she continued. "What I can do is create a room where I can meditate and send her grounding thoughts. Alex is going to attempt to meet up with me and help."

"You think it will work?" Colin asked.

"It's either try this or have them walk through every bad memory and hope they come through unscathed."

Ayden pressed his forehead to hers knowing what this had cost them last time. He kissed her gently then nodded as he watched her close her eyes. Within moments she was cold and still. Ayden would not let go of her hand, not until she came back to him.

****

Kirsa opened her eyes to a bright yellow room with candles burning everywhere. Large windows showed different forest scenes and soft music was playing in the background. Looking around Kirsa began to add pictures of Sabrina just to give it that bit of a personal touch. When she was satisfied she slipped out of her shoes and sat down on the overstuffed purple floor cushion. A green one appeared a moment later for when Alex joined her. She sent a message to him then began to focus on Sabrina.

CHAPTER 26

The jungle was hot, humid and dense with plants.
Delilah and Sabrina hacked their way through it with a
rusty machete they found impaled in a tree. They had
learned the blade was iron when Sabrina decapitated a
demon with it and the blood smoked. They had also used it
to cut away at the bridal gown that Sabrina was still stuck
in, it now hung in tatters to her knees and Delilah gave her
one of her scarves to tie her hair back with. When they
could no longer hear the demons behind them, they both
stopped, leaning against the trees to catch their breath.

"So, whose nightmare is this?" Delilah asked panting
between words. "Because it's not mine."

Sabrina looked up at Delilah and rolled her shoulders, hoping to loosen the ache that had settled between them. "Well it's not mine."

"Then if it isn't either of ours, whose is it?" Delilah wondered.

"Excellent question," Sabrina replied.

Realizing the pain was not going to subside anytime soon she pushed herself off the tree. "Let's keep moving before they catch up."

All Sabrina knew was they were stuck in a tropical jungle that was sweltering hot and humid. The only weapon they had was the single machete, neither of them could perform any spells, and she was responsible for a terrified seventeen-year-old girl. As she hacked away at the foliage she tried to figure out why they were here.

Susannah might be nuts but there had to be a reason she chose this location. They came across a stream and both knelt down on the ground drinking from the water and washing themselves to cool off.

When Sabrina looked up she felt her blood run cold. Through the foliage she could make out a ten-foot-high electric fence with automatic weapons and sun lights positioned on all the posts. Slowly she pushed herself off the ground and walked across the stream, as she got a better view. Delilah, noticing something was wrong, stood next to her.

"I know where we are," Sabrina replied.

"I take it that it's not a good place" Delilah stated as she watched the color of Sabrina's skin pale.

Sabrina shook her head. The most secretive and heavily guarded of all the paranormal prisons, where all the most dangerous criminals were housed was now looming in the distance. And she had no wings.

"Delilah we are on an island where one of the paranormal prisons are," Sabrina told her.

She would not inform the girl that only the worst of the worst was here. Sabrina ignored the fear that tried to paralyze her as it dawned on her that she was stuck on an island with the scariest and deadliest villains on earth. All she had to protect Delilah was a rusty machete.

"Lovely," Delilah said swallowing the lump of fear that wanted to lodge in her throat.

Sabrina turned to face the olive-skinned beauty, "Let's settle here and come up with a plan. She's up to something, and we need a plan and weapons."

Delilah looked around, "I can gather branches and rocks and we can figure out what we can do with them."

"Alright, I'll try to map out what I remember," Sabrina said. Grabbing a stick, she began to trace out a rough map of the area.

Doing something kept both of them so occupied that the fear they had been feeling could be ignored. They had a purpose and for now that purpose was keeping them thinking, not dwelling on the impossible. Delilah was drenched in sweat when she added the last of what she found to the pile. She washed her face in the stream then leaned against a large rock as Sabrina studied the map.

"If we follow the stream it should bring us toward the only entrance," Sabrina told Delilah.

"You're not thinking about storming the prison, are you?" Delilah asked in a small voice.

"No," Sabrina assured her. "But we can follow the road, I remember seeing a ruin somewhere along the way to the prison we can hold up in there and bring the battle to us."

It was far-fetched, but it was the only thing she could think of.

They heard laughter fill the air, Delilah jumped up and Sabrina put an arm around her as they both looked around. The laughter got louder but no one appeared.

"You think a pile of sticks and stones will save you from what is waiting for you?" Susannah's voice asked them. "I'm going to enjoy watching him drain you!"

"And I'm going to enjoy Kirsa shoving an Iron stake through your heart!" Sabrina yelled back.

"You really think she is going to come rescue you after what you did? You came here without her knowledge. How can she trust you now? Face it you're alone, like you always will be."

"I'd rather be all alone then be a crazy bitch who gets her kicks from invading other people's dreams! All because you're too chicken shit to face people in the real world!"

Delilah watched in horror as Sabrina was picked up by invisible hands and flung into a tree. Delilah ran to the crumpled body as the laughter faded away. Gently rolling her over onto her back, Delilah checked her over for injuries. Sabrina opened her eyes and smiled weakly at Delilah who helped her sit up.

"Well at least we now know what she is up to," Sabrina said.

"She's right we're all alone," Delilah replied softly. "We're going to die here."

"Delilah, Kirsa and Alex were alone when they were stuck in Clown Hell," Sabrina pointed out as she took inventory of what Delilah had found. "And if they both got through that experience we can deal with this."

Delilah sat on the rock finding it hard not to brood about how unfair life was, she was going to be stuck here miss her prom, Alex's prom, graduation, missing out on going to Suffolk University in Boston. Sabrina sat next to her and held her hand; Delilah rested her head on her shoulder and sighed.

"As long as we do this together we're not alone," Sabrina whispered. "We'll get out of this. I promise."

It was then they noticed a black shape falling from the sky and landing before them. Sabrina slid off the rock and approached the bag with suspicion. She motioned for Delilah to stay where she was, there was a note attached to the bag.

Hope this helps. By the way use the black grenade only when you need us the most. Alex and I have one shot at this so don't blow it- Kirsa

P.S. Delilah we're going to make it to prom and college- Alex

Sabrina handed the note to Delilah as she opened the bag and smiled up at the sky. On top of the small arsenal of weapons were two sets of t-shirt, jeans and sneakers. Clean clothes. She handed the ones for Delilah to her then continued to go through the bag.

Automatic weapons, two vests lined with silver and iron stakes and vials of holy water, two swords, and a belt of grenades. The two stripped out of their dirty rags and quickly bathed in the stream before they put on fresh clean clothes. When they were dressed, Sabrina began dividing the weapons. Delilah folded the note and slipped it into her bra to help remind her they were not alone.

Sabrina smiled at her before she found a map at the bottom of the bag .

Brie, if you can cause a diversion at the gates it will give you a head start to the ruin. I would suggest saving the black grenade until then. The stream will get you to the front entrance, then follow the road for about a mile that will lead you to the ruin.

Sabrina folded the note and map and slid it into her back pocket. She handed Delilah one of the vests as she slipped her own on. Once the weapons were divided up *they began making their way toward the entrance. Using the machete to cut down foliage, Sabrina tried to ignore the fear that was making her blood cold as ice. The sun was beginning to descend when they hit the entrance. She stopped in the tree line and knelt to the ground.*

Taking their old clothes, she soaked them in holy water and gasoline that was in the bag. She told Delilah to run down the road at her signal. They needed to be to the ruin before night hit. Delilah readied herself as Sabrina lit the bundle and chucked it.

Delilah was off the moment Sabrina launched the ball of flame. She ignored the screams and voices as she bolted down the dirt road. Delilah jumped over any obstacle in the way, soon Sabrina was catching up to her. When they heard guns being loaded they pushed themselves faster, both ignoring the muscle burn, the shortness of breath and the fire in their lungs.

Even as bullets fired into the dirt at their feet they zigzagged along the road until they hit the landmark on the map, Sabrina grabbed a grenade, pulled the pin and launched it behind her. They dove into the foliage as the grenade went off; Sabrina pulled Delilah up as they rushed to the ruin that had been overtaken by the jungle.

They climbed through the window and moved leaves to conceal it. Sabrina searched through the duffle bag and pulled out a medical kit and two flashlights. They took care of the injuries caused by shrapnel, then leaned against the walls and tried to catch their breath.

"How long until nightfall?" Delilah asked as she massaged the cramps out of her legs.

"I don't know," Sabrina said.

They both jumped when they heard the explosion, Sabrina pulled Delilah under her as the ruin trembled from the impact. She covered Delilah's mouth to muffle her crying as other explosions were heard off in the distance. Sitting up she raised a finger to her lips, Delilah nodded and Sabrina removed her hand.

Sabrina took a peak out the window and red eyes stared back at her. The scream was caught in her throat as Delilah pulled the black grenade off the belt and threw it right in the face of the monster. Grabbing Sabrina they dove under the table and felt the heat of the explosion. They heard a commotion in the room and watched as Alex and Kirsa dealt with the demons dressed all in black.

"Cutting it close don't you think?" Kirsa asked as she killed the demon with a sword. Sabrina got up with the help of Alex and hugged her friend.

"You said to wait until we needed it most."

Alex pulled Delilah out from under the table and tried not to blush when she threw her arms around him.

"They are setting off landmines," Alex told them.

"How do we get out of here?" Delilah asked.

"Very simple," Kirsa replied. "Follow me."

Alex positioned himself so that Sabrina and Delilah were between Kirsa and him; they headed out toward the road where an army of prisoners were marching. Susannah *wore an army green gown and a tiara made of grenades. Susannah stopped in her tracks when Kirsa emerged out of the woods. Kirsa smiled at her as the army stopped behind her.*

"How are you here?" Susannah demanded. "You made a deal with the devil that you would not willingly step foot in the astral plane."

"I did," Kirsa said. "But he has done away with it; decided he'd rather me be here than you. Surprise!"

Susannah raised the rocket launcher, Alex grabbed Sabrina and Delilah so that neither could stop the inevitable. Pulling the trigger, Susannah fired off the rocket aimed right at Kirsa and laughed when it hit her right in the stomach.

CHAPTER 27

It took two days of observations before doctors would allow anyone to be discharged. Finally, once all the paperwork was signed along with the promise not to do anything like what they did again, everyone was sent on their way. Those in New Jersey headed to Kirsa's home to decompress, while Alex and his family went back to Delilah's house to recuperate before heading back to Massachusetts.

"So how the hell didn't you get blown up again?" Sabrina demanded. Kirsa was at the stove finishing the beef stew.

Al, Colin and Ayden were sitting at the table drinking beer. Kirsa put the lid back on the pot and watched as the snow was coming down hard outside.

"Al do you want to explain it?"

"Oh no this was all Lou's idea, so you get to explain, even though it was brilliant," Al told her with a smile as he sipped his beer.

"I couldn't actually enter one of your memories for fear of messing with them, so Alex and I created a meditation room where we could focus on the two of you," Kirsa explained. "This way we could focus on you and Delilah and try to help with motivation."

"That explains us hearing our names occasionally and feeling rejuvenated," Sabrina replied.

"Susannah then broke her own rules that she set up when she brought you into the memory of the prison."

"How?"

"You and Delilah were supposed to be facing memories and dreams where you had to make a choice that was not the easiest," Kirsa told her. She sipped the honey wine and continued. "The memory of the prison was not a decision you made apparently, it had been suggested and implanted in your mind. When she sent you there and sent demons after you she broke her own rules."

"Which meant what exactly?" Ayden asked.

"I want to know what you mean by me not making the decision to go to the prison," Sabrina added. "I'll get to your question at the end Sabrina," Kirsa promised. "When she broke her own rules it meant that I could enter your memory without ruining it. Lou supplied the weapons because Alex and I could not figure out how to bring weapons into a room made for peace."

"That could be a problem," Sabrina said. She wasn't sure how she felt about Lou helping.

"We came up with the plan of how he could get them to you," Kirsa explained. "He also explained that if I in theory sacrificed myself he would be there to sever the three of our ties to her. Hence the black grenade."

"Wait, so when you willingly stood before a rocket launcher you were aware that he might not be able to save you but were willing to risk it just so she couldn't fuck with us anymore?" Sabrina asked just to clarify.

"Basically."

Sabrina sipped her wine as she thought about it. "So, you, me and Sara no longer have any ties to her."

"Neither does her family," Kirsa added.

Al looked up from the table. "He apparently did such a good job it severed the ties to those that had been closest to her."

"Do they know?" Al asked Kirsa.

"I told Titania this morning."

"Now I have two questions," Sabrina interrupted. "Why didn't I have my wings and what do you mean she implanted the prison idea into my head?"

"Wings?" Colin asked confused.

"Sabrina has wing in the astral plane," Kirsa replied.

"Cool," Colin said.

"You couldn't summon your wings because you didn't willingly enter, so they couldn't come out," Kirsa explained. Lou had explained all the rules and regulations to her while he was amassing a small arsenal for them."

"That makes sense in some way," Sabrina replied.

"You told me that she paid a visit to you, right?" Kirsa asked.

"Yeah just after you left for Germany," Sabrina answered.

"How soon after that did you start thinking about seeing Lars?" Al asked this time.

Sabrina leaned back in the chair and thought about it. "I guess the next day it started to bother me and the more I thought about it, the more it felt like I had to do it."

"How'd you get the information from Victor?" Ayden wondered.

Sabrina stared at all of them as she tried to remember. "I was able to bypass Kirsa's security on her computer and went in through there, I think."

"I'll let Dietrich know," Kirsa said to Ayden.

"Alright, so now what?" Colin inquired.

"Kristina is slipping deeper and deeper into craziness," Kirsa told them. "So, our next move is Mora. Ayden and I have been talking and we might have a plan."

"Why do I have a bad feeling about this plan?" Al said to no one in particular.

"How could it be any worse than having Kirsa getting help from the devil," Sabrina asked him.

"You need some back story," Ayden began ignoring Sabrina and Al. "This remains between us and no one else until this is over. "

The three nodded their heads; Kirsa smiled and sat by him. "When we went to interview Mora we found out that I am related to her mother."

"How related?" Al asked, all of sudden interested.

"I think we figured it out that I am Mora's great-great-great uncle or something like that," Ayden informed them. "My youngest brother is her great-great grandfather."

"That's bizarre," Sabrina said in awe.

"Wow," was all Colin could say.

Al began to catch on quick. "This means the same blood runs through both you and Mora."

Ayden smiled at Al. "Exactly. Brenna, her mother, called last night to tell me the nightmares are getting worse. More and more pressure is being put on Mora to cave in to Susannah."

"With Alex and Delilah out of the picture she's running out of bodies," Colin replied. "It would make sense to start targeting Mora more intensely."

"The thing is, I found the ritual," Kirsa said. Everyone but Ayden stared at her. "It was in the journals of two of the suicide victims. They match exactly."

"So, what does this ritual call for?" Sabrina asked. She had a feeling she was not going to like the answer that Kirsa was going to give her.

"For the person to offer a goblet of their blood to be bound to the power source with," Kirsa told them.

"Don't tell me you want Mora to offer her blood," Colin said getting ready to argue.

"Not Mora's," Ayden assured him.

Al studied him. "You sure you want to do this?"

"The poison works both ways," Ayden reminded him. "She won't die from it but it will weaken her enough that Kirsa can go in and end it."

"I'm coming with you," Sabrina said. "You're not going in alone this time."

"You're talking about having your blood in the goblet," Colin replied understanding. "Won't she know?"

"Not until she drinks," Al pointed out.

"But she's Fae, won't she know it's vampire blood?"

"Fae can identify other Fae by sense of smell," Al explained. "We know humans because they are muskier and try to cover their scent with various other scents, so it is all confusing. We can sometime tell with were's if one is around but that's only after it rains and they were caught in it. But vampires are human, so they smell human to us."

"So all she'll know is the blood smells like Mora," Sabrina said.

Kirsa got up to check on the stew. She turned the burner off and brought it to the table. Al spooned out the stew for everyone and refilled everyone's drinks.

Ayden looked out the window as the snow was getting heavier, "You better plan on staying the night, Al."

"It is getting bad out there," Al agreed.

The conversation returned to the ritual. "When do we do the ritual?" Sabrina asked.

"The next full moon," Kirsa answered.

"Alright, so we have a plan," Colin replied. He liked having plans. "Let's just hope she doesn't act before then."

Kirsa and Al both cursed when their cell phones buzzed, they then groaned in unison as they read the text.

"You are not going out in this weather, "Ayden told Kirsa.

"It was Adam saying they are going to set my date if I don't," Kirsa replied.

Al laughed, "Titania texted the same thing for me."

"Wouldn't it be funny if you did a joint ceremony," Sabrina said laughing. Al and Kirsa looked at her with huge smiles on their face. "Kirs, no way would both councils allow it, I was joking," Sabrina replied.

"Would they?" Kirsa asked Ayden.

"It would actually make sense to do a joint one since Al's Head of OPIA and you're his second in command," Ayden said thinking it through. "They wouldn't have to orchestrate two different ceremonies."

"Now we just have to agree on a place and a date," Al replied. "It should be in Germany," Ayden said. "That's where your seat is from Kirs."

"I am fine with that," Al said. "I know we can do a portal there, it's been done before."

"Now a date," Sabrina said. "Just think, after this you can pick out a wedding date."

Kirsa looked at the calendar on her phone and smiled. "Walpurgis Night."

Ayden and Al both stared at her then burst out laughing at how perfect it was. Sabrina and Colin both raised their eyebrows in confusion.

"April 30th, the eve before Beltane," Kirsa explained as she hit the number for Dietrich.

"Brilliant," Ayden replied. Kirsa nodded as she waited for Dietrich to pick up the phone.

Dietrich saw his cell phone vibrating on his desk, he was going over the file that had been delivered.

"Nacht."

"Hey Pop," Kirsa said.

He couldn't help but smile at her voice. He pushed the file on Victor aside so that she would have his full attention. "Hello, *liebling*. What can I do for you?"

"I got the text from Adam and a date has been selected," Kirsa told him. "I just have two requirements."

"Alright I shall see what I can do."

"I want it at the castle and Al and I want a joint ceremony."

Dietrich thought for a moment, a dual ceremony would be entertaining. It would also show the alliance the Vampires had with the Fae and the strong ties between Al and Kirsa. "It can be arranged now what is the date?"

"April 30th of this year," Kirsa replied.

"That is perfect my dear," Dietrich replied smiling. "I will let the others know at our meeting tomorrow."

CHAPTER 28

Frank watched the snow fall outside the windows of his condo. Kirsa was ok, both Sabrina and Delilah had come out of their comas alright. Kirsa had called and invited him over for dinner. Tonight, he wasn't in the mood for company.

His ex-wife wanted more money, his lawyer assured him he had nothing to worry about, but here he was in the middle of January watching the snowfall, drinking alone, and plotting her death.

Ever since the divorce he had come up with unique ways of killing her, he knew he would never do it, it wasn't in him, it just helped with the anger. She had cheated on him with his brother then couldn't understand why he wanted a divorce. Now he had been disowned by his family and was alone.

He sipped his whiskey, mesmerized by the falling snow. When the balcony doors opened and the most beautiful woman he'd ever seen stepped through them he almost dropped his glass. Her blood red lips smiled as she caught the glass for him as it slipped from his fingers.

"You wouldn't want to drop the glass," she said in a sultry whisper. She took a sip from it before handing it back to him.

He watched as she took in his condo, her hair was almost white matching her porcelain skin. The gown she wore was silver and clung to her curves. He tried not to drool as she walked around his space.

"It's must be hard to be all alone," Susannah whispered as she walked back toward him. "I can make you no longer alone."

He tried to swallow as she ran a red tipped nail down his shirt. "I can make you hard," she whispered in his ear as her finger continued lower.

"Who are you?" he asked as he felt his pants fall to the ground.

"I am your greatest desire," she replied stepping back and allowing the gown to fall to the floor.

Frank couldn't think anymore. The woman was stunning, her body perfect, her hair flowed over her shoulders like waves of gold. She walked toward him and brought her mouth to his.

"I am the answer to all your desires," she whispered as they kissed.

He didn't know how he managed to get out of his shirt and tie, but he did. He stepped out of his pants then grabbed her by the waist. Frank carried her to his bedroom where he placed her in the center of the bed, she looked like a goddess lying there looking up at him. He came down on top of her, his hands hard as he explored her skin. He kissed her breasts as he roamed down her body, intoxicated by her scent.

Susannah ran her hands down his well-muscled back as his hands found her ready. She was surprised by how in shape he was in as she traced the ridges of muscles. When he brought his mouth back to hers she rolled them over.

She trailed a line of kisses down his chest, smiled at his quick intake of breath when she took him into her mouth. Just before he exploded she sat up and slowly guided him into her. She had planned on setting the pace like she often had with the men she tricked into her bed.

He surprised her when he rolled her onto her back and set the speed. She hadn't planned on having an orgasm, so when it hit causing her to scream out, it was all the better. When he emptied himself into her she smiled running a hand down his sweaty back. She kissed his neck as he rolled off of her.

"You are an amazing man."

"You are a gift," Frank whispered.

"A gift should never be wasted," Susannah said running a hand down his chest. "I have a very important job for you Frank. I need you to deliver a message for me, can you do that?"

****

Kirsa and Al arrived at the crime scene in one piece thanks to Ayden. He was parking the car where a detective showed him, letting them off. One of the detectives noticed Al and headed over toward him, his face grim.

Robert Shaw was a Jersey City Detective, he had seen his share of horror on the streets. The body at his feet was one of the worst, they covered it so as not to make everyone sick.

"Hey Shaw, what's going on?" Al asked as they shook hands.

"I hate to call you both out in the middle of a blizzard, but when I saw who it was I figured you'd want in," Shaw told them.

They were in the middle of a state of emergency but knew that these two would want to know, would want to be part of it.

"Who is it?" Kirsa asked as she pulled the hood up over her head to keep the snow off.

382

Shaw just motioned for them to follow. Kirsa couldn't help the block of ice that now sat in her stomach. It was close to five in the morning, they had made it to Jersey City in half an hour thanks to no one being on the roads and Ayden's driving. Ayden joined them as they stopped by a body that had been covered up by a white sheet. It didn't cover the gore that had escaped the body when it met pavement.

"It's bad," Shaw warned before pulling the sheet down.

Neither had been prepared to see the mangled remains of Frank Willis lying on the sidewalk outside his condo. Ayden caught Kirsa when her knees gave out; Al had to swallow the bile that had risen in his throat. He was unrecognizable as he lay naked on the pavement. A message had been carved into his flesh in Fae. Al let out a string of curses as Shaw pulled the cover back over and stood up.

"Once I realized who it was I knew I had to call you in," Shaw said.

"How?" Al asked as he tried to comprehend what he was seeing.

"I don't know," Shaw said honestly. "There's no suicide note. No sign of a forced entry."

Shaw walked with them into the building and took the elevator up to the fifteenth floor. When the elevator door opened they were met with curious neighbors and cops everywhere. Shaw motioned and soon the cops formed a line to keep onlookers from spotting Kirsa as they headed to the door.Kirsa was the first to notice how cold the condo felt, she was still in her pea coat and felt a chill in the air.

Rubbing her arms with her hands she walked around the living area while Al and Shaw talked. Ayden walked toward her then stopped short in the middle of the room. Kirsa turned and watched as he sniffed the air.

"I smell Faery," Ayden said looking around.

Al and Shaw stopped talking and looked at Ayden.

Al took a sniff of the air, "Water Faery."

"She came in from the balcony," Ayden replied as he walked to where the balcony doors were.

"How can you tell?" Shaw asked.

"It's where her scent trail begins," Ayden told him.

Kirsa stood in the center of the modern living room, she noticed how around where she stood the scents became mingled and entwined. She headed toward the bedroom, seeing her head toward the hall Ayden followed with his hand on his gun. This was all too convenient for him as if they were walking into some kind of trap.

A tangle of sheets showed that Frank had company before walking off his balcony. Kirsa studied the bed and walked over; taking tweezers from the evidence kit she picked a single strand of blonde hair and held it up to the light. It reflected every color in the rainbow.

"She's dead," Kirsa said as she passed the bag to Al.

Al studied the strand of hair in the bag and closed his eyes. He had just lost one of his best agents to a psychopathic faery. Ayden ran a hand down Kirsa's back; she leaned into him trying to focus on everything.

"You know who else was here?" Shaw asked coming into the room.

"A suspect from one of our cases," Al replied.

"I'll have everything sent to your lab of choice," Shaw promised.

"Keep men posted outside and in until this is solved, "Al said.

Shaw nodded then headed out to start giving orders.

"This is a trap, a set-up," Ayden pointed out.

Al handed Ayden the sheet of paper where he translated the message on the chest. "I agree."

I am the vessel, I am the spreader of news, the time is close. Ayden showed it to Kirsa.

"You don't go anywhere without both me and Lance," he said pointing a finger at her. "I want you armed with iron bullets at all times, you hear me."

"I hear you," Kirsa said.

It was pointless to try and reason with an angry and protective vampire. They were at the crime scene for another hour before heading back to headquarters where they set up in Al's office. Ayden poured a shot of whiskey into three coffees, Kirsa and Al were sitting on the couch. He handed them their coffee before getting his own. After sitting down across from them they toasted their coffees and drank. It was seven in the morning; the office was deserted.

Al had no clue how he was going to deal with telling his agents about Frank. Liza, his ex-wife, had just left sobbing into her sister's shoulder. They were no closer to figuring out why he had been picked.

There was a knock on the door, Eileen stood there in sweatpants and a t-shirt. She lived in the dormitories and had run over when the rumor hit her door.

"Tell me the rumors are wrong?" Eileen asked.

When she saw their faces she knew the answer was not the one she wanted. She walked over and poured herself coffee with a shot of whiskey.

"He jumped off his balcony," Al said in monotone. He left out the part about him being completely naked and semi-aroused.

"I won't believe that he committed suicide," Eileen said fiercely. She and Frank had gotten along, often hanging out after everyone went home for the day.

"He didn't," Kirsa said and sipped more coffee. "He was coerced."

Eileen understood that this had to do with the case the three had been working on. "What do you need me to do?"

Al ran a hand over his face trying to figure out his next step. "I need you to go through his things, try to locate anything that seems off."

"Of course," Eileen said. "Does Liza know?"

"Yeah," Kirsa replied. "She'll pass on the arrangement information. She's in shock."

"She never understood the divorce, it had come out of nowhere," Eileen told them. "He never even told her the reason why, she just came home one day, and he handed her the papers."

"That doesn't sound like him," Ayden said. Frank was a pretty laid-back guy and didn't give into impulse.

"No one ever understood the divorce," Al told Ayden. "We were all caught off guard especially when he cut ties with his family. God, I have to call his mother."

"I'll do it," Kirsa volunteered.

"Thanks, but I need to do it. It goes with the job."

****

Three days later Kirsa, Al and Colin poured over the coroner's report, courtesy of Sara, and the evidence. They had overtaken one of the conference rooms, where two vampires and two agents stood guard. Colin was going through the evidence report.

"Why a strand of purple hair?" Colin asked. A strand had been found inside a locket at the condo. "I don't get it."

Kirsa stared at him with raised eyebrows, he just looked at her even more confused. Before she could speak the door opened and Sabrina walked in carrying Mrs. Hanson's lasagna.

"I figured the three of you would be working late so she made me bring it," Sabrina told them as she set it on a side table. She kissed Colin before sitting down. "Sara told me she completed the report."

"Maybe you can explain why Ayden is flipping out over purple hair and DNA being run on it," Colin asked her.

"Junior year Kirsa dyed her hair purple," Sabrina replied. "It actually looked good on her."

"Was that before bubblegum pink hair or magenta?" Colin inquired. Kirsa had changed her hair color a few times in undergrad before going back to her natural color.

"It was the first color," Kirsa replied. "The magenta was my favorite, maybe I'll get magenta highlights?"

"So where was this hair found?" Sabrina asked getting back to her original question.

Colin tossed her the evidence bag with the locket in it. "It's the locket we gave Susannah for her sixteenth birthday."

"I recognized it also," Kirsa said as Sabrina gave her back the bag. "Did you drive here by yourself?"

"Bridgette has therapy tonight, Phil has a new were-cub and a guest, and Sara is pouring over all the evidence at the lab," Sabrina replied. "Which means I am playing the role of Aunt Sabrina."

"Whose Phil's guest?" Kirsa asked, though she had an idea of who it might be.

"Your cousin," Sabrina said with a smile.

"What about tomorrow?" Colin asked. He would be staying in the dorms with Al, Kirsa and Ayden.

"Bridgette is staying with me tonight, as well as Zero, plus between the men Tony has posted and Phil's cats I'll be secure." Sabrina thanked Al when he placed lasagna in front of her. "What about you guys?"

"Everyone attending the funeral and burial is staying here tonight," Al explained. "This way we will leave in one group. I'll be in the Durango with Kirsa, Ayden and Colin."

"I still don't think it's wise to have the director and assistant director driving in Kirsa's car," Colin replied.

"Nothing will happen to them," Sabrina promised.

"Why because a vampire will be driving?"

"No because my car is armored," Kirsa replied as she signed off on something for Al. She looked up into Colin's shocked face. "After my parent's death and aunt and uncle's, Adam and I both have armored vehicles."

"Is that why you can just go through security?" Colin asked. Every morning every car entering had to be inspected before pulling into the underground garage.

"It's kind of hard to get the scans to see through all the stuff," Kirsa said. "By the way it's classified."

"Sabrina knows?" Colin asked looking at his redhead.

"And Sara," Kirsa said. "But other than the three of you, Dietrich, and Adam, that's it."

"I never fully understood what being who you are entails," Colin said. She had a state of the art security system; she currently had at least five armed guards at all times. He knew at some point during the day she had to check in with both Dietrich and Tony, and now this.

"Ayden still thinks Frank's death is a trap for you?" Colin asked.

"I am tending to agree with Irish," Al replied. "Susannah would know that Kirsa would have to go tomorrow regardless of it being dangerous. Not just because they were friends, but because it's part of our role as heads."

"Is that why you are all going as one tomorrow?" Sabrina asked.

"For logistic and security reasons yes," Al replied.

Sabrina looked at her watch. "I should head back to building B." She gave Kirsa a hug. Colin got up and followed her out into the hall.

Colin walked with her toward the lobby, so they would be out of earshot of Ayden and Lance. He brushed a strand of hair out of her face as he kissed her lightly.

"You'll be safe?" he asked.

"Bridgette and I are planning on girl's night in the family room, which means the four dogs will be in there with us. Not to mention the guard outside. Mrs. Hanson and her husband are in the old Carriage house with their own guards. Try not to worry," Sabrina said.

"I'll worry less when this is all over," Colin told her.

****

The following day was clear and in the high thirties. After the private service for family, friends and coworkers, the police escorted the caravan of mourners to the cemetery where Frank would be interred with the family gone before him.

The security was high, several packs had loaned out members to help keep a psycho-faery away. The family sat in the first ring around the burial site while agents and friends stood behind them. Kirsa hid her grief behind sunglasses, this was personal now.

She stood with Al's hand on her shoulder as they listened to the minister say a prayer over the grave. Ayden and Lance were patrolling the area while the service continued.

Kirsa watched as each family member laid a white rose on top of the casket. The minister gave his last words of condolences, before being escorted to his car. Kirsa and Al were the first to speak to the parents, as Kirsa talked to Mrs. Willis she heard the click of a gun and shoved Liza and Mrs. Willis behind the tombstone, Al followed her action with the father and brother.

The first bullet took a chunk out of the tombstone. Kirsa caught the scent.

"We got Silver," she said into the walkie at her hip.

Another bullet hit the dirt right by her feet. Eileen rushed over and crouched behind her. "I'm the target," Kirsa whispered. "Cover me as I go to another tombstone."

Eileen nodded and readied her gun to cover as Kirsa bolted to the next headstone. Al joined her a few moments later. "She wants to draw you out," Al said.

"It's working," Kirsa said taking the vest an agent handed her. She slipped off her trench coat and slipped the vest on.

"The bullets are coming from the woods, have everyone cover and meet in the woods."

Before Al could argue he watched as she sprinted toward the tree line. All she looked like was a blur of movement as he began to issue orders. Ayden was already cursing at him for letting her run off like that. Kirsa dove for cover behind another tombstone.

She smelled brimstone, "We got demons, Al!"

"I'll try and get the civilians out of the line of fire," he answered.

The fire hit her shoulder from the side, ignoring the pain she rolled over and shot the demon between the eyes. Getting up she ran to the trees. A bullet took a chunk of bark off a tree as she hid behind it.

"Come out, come out wherever you are Kirsa," Susannah said in a sing song voice. "It's play time."

Kirsa said something as she controlled her breathing making it quiet and steadier. She had Ayden yelling at her in the head for being stupid, she ignored him as she quietly made her way through the trees.

"Hiding isn't very lady like," Susannah called again. "I had this gown especially made for today. I was going to make it out of his flesh but decided raven feathers were better."

Kirsa refused to let the rage give off where she was. She located where Susannah was and sent the information to Ayden since she had turned off her radio. She was trying to ignore the string of curses in his head while they relayed information.

"I'm disappointed in you," Susannah replied pouting now. "I had hoped for a meeting before our final battle."

Susannah felt the cold metal against her temple and the click of the trigger. Using what power she had gathered she froze Kirsa to the spot much like she had done to Titania. In her gown of black feather's she walked toward Kirsa who was trying to move.

"I'm not done, not by a long shot," Susannah whispered. "I have been planning this for ten years. No one, not even you, will stop me."

"What do you want Susie?" Kirsa asked ignoring how numb she was feeling.

"I want everything you took from me."

"And what about what you took from me?" Kirsa asked.

Susannah formed a sword of ice and shoved it through Kirsa, she laughed as she silenced the scream.

"I took nothing from you, but I will."

Susannah went to say something but saw the blur that moved through the air and tackle her. Ayden plowed his fist into her jaw. With a thought she flung him against a tree and stood up.

"I am invincible," she yelled into the wind. With that she vanished.

Lance caught Kirsa before she fell. Her teeth were chattering, lips were turning blue, one of the weres came over and took her knowing their body heat would help.

While Al ordered security checks, in the distance the sirens of ambulances were heard. The first ambulance that arrived Al ordered to take Kirsa. Ayden rushed inside with Kirsa as the paramedics began to take her stats, Ayden listed off all of her medical information as they put pressure on the shoulder wound.

Al poked his head in the open door, "Three cars are ready to escort you to the hospital."

Ayden nodded and the paramedics slammed the door shut. Later Kirsa sat on the hospital bed while Dr. Allen Finn checked her over. Ayden was leaning against the wall with a gun at his hip. There were two dead, ten injured and about one hundred demon corpses. Allen finished with the bullet wound before he said a word.

"Your body temperature has stabilized," Finn told her as he washed his hands. "However ,if it goes above 99 I want you at the emergency room."

Kirsa nodded as Ayden helped her pull the surgical scrub top over her head. Finn took his tablet and began making notes.

"The bullet that struck you wasn't silver, so it should heal in no time, stitches to keep it from bleeding. They're dissolvable so you don't need to have them removed."

"Anything else?" Ayden asked.

"It's February 1st," Finn replied. "I need you in my office on March first to draw more blood."

"You just took three vials," Kirsa pointed out.

"I know, and I want to take more," Finn told her. "Other than staying out of the way of bullets and trying to avoid hypothermia you're good to go."

He nodded to Ayden before leaving the room. Ayden rested his head on her forehead and just stood there breathing her in. He needed the connection to reaffirm that she was alright.

"I wish I could promise I'll be safe," Kirsa whispered.

"In order to do that you would have to resign and move to an unknown spot," Ayden said. He brushed a curl out of her face and kissed her gently. "Just try to not get shot again."

"I'll do my best," Kirsa promised smiling.

"Let's go home," Ayden said.

He sent a message to Lance to ready the guards. Throwing his black trench over her head, he put his arms around her to guide her. Lance took the other side as they were surrounded by a mixture of paranormal guards.

Kirsa didn't need to see, she could hear the clicking of cameras and the reporters throwing questions out. When they began to shove, Ayden swooped her up into his arms and they ran to the waiting car. Lance hit the top of the car with his hand signaling time to go. Lance was talking to someone on the phone, Kirsa knew it had to be Dietrich as he tried to assure him she was fine. Ayden pulled her closer to her, resting his head on top of hers.

"What of everyone else?" Kirsa asked.

"Being taken care of," Ayden assured her. "The Fae have handed over their elite guard to help with protection detail."

"We buried one of our own only to lose several more," Kirsa said trying not to let the grief swallow her. "More blood on her hands."

"Remember that," Ayden told her. "The blood is all on her hands, not yours, and not Al's."

CHAPTER 29

Mora stepped out of the shower; using her hand she brushed the fog off the mirror as she stared at herself in the mirror. Her eyes seemed bigger than they did a year ago, they seemed more cautious and wary. But then a year ago she wasn't worried about demons or living in a catholic church to keep her family safe.

Sighing she turned away and began to dress in jeans and a white tank top. She braided her red hair, not wanting it to fall into her face or into candle flames. Carefully she hung the towels up before leaving the bathroom. The house was so quiet, she was all alone. They had learned to trust her and believed she wouldn't do anything inside the sacred walls.

Barefoot, she headed toward the room that had become her bedroom. It was small, but it had what she needed. Clearing off the window seat of the cushions, she set down two candles.

Next, she placed a bowl of water and a small plate of sea salt. She uncovered her athame that her brother had smuggled to her and laid it down next to the offerings. Flipping through her book of shadows she found the ritual.

Tonight it would end, how fitting that the full moon fell on Imbolc.

How fitting that, tonight she would begin her new life. The faery was too powerful, too tempting, it was time to give her what she wanted. Before lighting the candles, Mora set the goblet filled with blood on to the makeshift altar. Her thigh was still bandaged from where she had cut it earlier in the day, no one would know she had cut herself. Before casting a circle, Mora went and got the last two things she needed before the ritual could start.

****

Dr. Kesler ran down the hallway of the psychiatric ward. He was followed by four orderlies and three nurses. He and three men ran full force into the door that belonged to Kristina's room, but they bounced off of it. On the other side they heard the wild laughter that made their skin crawl.

"We have to get in there," Arthur said as he looked around.

"What about through the windows?" A nurse asked. "The ledge is wide enough that one of us could make our way over there."

"No, not after what happened to Frank Willis," Kesler replied. He was not risking any of his staff. "We have to try to get through the door."

"And if we can't?" an orderly asked.

"Then we hope and pray we get through this alive."

****

Carlotta imagined herself center stage singing for royalty. Her gown would be a beautiful rich color, cut low enough to tantalize but not scandalize. The lights would cause her jewels to glitter, her hair would be perfect, not a strand out of place.

As the curtain rose, the crowd would fall in love with her before she began. Nodding to the conductor, she began to sing. She had the crowd in the palm of her hand as she sang the first note.

"She's been singing for hours, Dr. Ryan," a nurse said as they rushed to the room that held Carlotta. Dr. Ryan stopped and listened to the singing.

"She's singing Musetta's Waltz," he said.

Her voice was hauntingly beautiful, one that should have been on stage not locked away in a fractured mind. They were met by a handful of security guards. Dr. Ryan took the keys from one of the guards; he inserted the key into the hole. They watched in shock as the key melted, he pulled his hand away before it was burnt.

"What the hell is going on?" a guard asked. "I wish I knew," Dr. Ryan replied. He took out his cell phone and called the only person who might be able to help.

****

Kirsa sat with Al at the podium in the public room at the OPIA headquarters. They were giving their first press conference since the massacre at Frank's funeral. The room was heavily secured as each press member was signed in, patted down and equipment was checked. Al waited until everyone was seated before he spoke.

"Thank you for coming today," Al began. "This press conference was arranged so that information could be given to the public and to correct any misinformation that might be out there."

Al looked at his notes and continued. "Two weeks ago we buried Agent Frank Willis who had been with OPIA for ten years. He was an amazing agent and an all-round good guy. He never let a woman leave the office alone if they were working late, he always made sure the coffee pot was on and full."

That got a few chuckles. "I don't know anyone who thought negatively about him, not even his ex-wife." Al took a sip of water before continuing. "As to his death, Frank did not jump, he did not commit suicide. He was murdered during an ongoing investigation, pushed from his condo balcony. The person responsible then ambushed his burial, killing two more of our agents and injuring ten people in the process. Because of this person, Assistant Director Heinrich and I have attended three funerals in two weeks. Something neither of us would like to do again. We are releasing a photo to the public, if this woman is seen please contact authorities immediately, do not even approach her."

The news that it was a female sent shockwaves through the press as they murmured to each other about it. Even more of a shock was the female in question was beautiful. Al answered some more questions about the suspect in question, giving information regarding height and age.

"Dr. Heinrich can you tell us about your relationship with the Church of Light?" a familiar voice asked from the crowd.

Kirsa narrowed her eyes at the female reporter.

"I take it that you would be the one that has been calling my house twenty times a day and sending double that in emails."

Everyone turned and stared at the young reporter who now seemed nervous.

"You wouldn't answer my calls."

"No but my lawyer did," Kirsa replied. "This press conference isn't about me or the Church of Light. However, if you really want an answer then I will give it to you."

This time all eyes focused on Kirsa. "I have been in contact with several former members of the church. The church no longer exists; all paperwork regarding it has been destroyed. The former members and the survivors are trying to move on with our lives which is hard to do when one is constantly calling us about it."

"Will there be any civil suits against them?" The same reporter asked.

"No," Kirsa said. "Those responsible have been punished."

"As a victim yourself, are you ok with the results?"

Kirsa laughed. "Oh honey, I'm not a victim," Kirsa corrected her. "Victim is a term we throw around at people who have suffered something horrible. Where we can talk about them in hushed tones and watch them waiting for them to break. I'm not a term nor am I statistic. I'm a survivor. I survived the crime done against me and now I have moved on with my life."

The reporter stared at her in shock at her answer. Another reporter stepped forward.

"Agent Heinrich is it true the Fae are helping with the current case?"

"Yes, the suspect is using Faery magick and is posing a threat to the Fae as well," Kirsa explained. Ayden signaled to her and she looked at her watch. "I'm sorry, I have a pressing engagement to attend too. Director Moore will take over for me."

"Congratulations by the way on your engagement!" Some of the press called out as she headed toward where Ayden stood. Kirsa smiled and nodded before they ducked out of the room.

"What's up?" Kirsa asked as she pulled on her coat.

"Mora started the ritual," Ayden informed her. "Around the moment she started, both Carlotta and Kristina began to show odd behavior changes. Carlotta has been singing Musetta's Waltz for the last two hours, Kristina has been talking in Latin."

"We suspected that when she started the ritual that those two would feel it," Kirsa reminded him. "The doctors?"

"Both are observing what is going on while trying to keep others safe, we have given orders not to interfere unless it puts other's at risk," Ayden said. He opened up the passenger door for Kirsa and waited for her to slide in.

"What about Delilah and Alex?" Kirsa asked as he started the car.

"Both are fine, showing no signs of anything."

Kirsa nodded as they headed out of the garage. She texted Sabrina and Sara to let them know what was going on Ayden drove.

****

Mora sat in the center of the circle clearing all thoughts from her mind. She asked for protection, she asked for strength, and she hoped this would be the end of it. Closing her eye's she focused on silence as she gained control over her thoughts.

Once she was centered and sure of herself she recited the words that she had memorized. With the candlelight flickering against the walls she offered herself to Susannah, binding her will to that of the faery. She felt the ripple of power and swallowed back the fear and uncertainty that this would work.

Having faith in her blood she opened her eyes as Susannah stepped out of the astral plane.

"Well this is a surprise," Susannah said as she walked around the circle.

"I hadn't counted on you."

"Are you disappointed?" Mora asked raising an eyebrow. Her glass green eyes watched the woman carefully.

The silver gown she wore whispered as she moved around. "Not disappointed just surprised, I had counted on two, prepared for two but to have three makes it all the better."

"What happens now?"

Susannah laughed as she flipped through the book of shadows. "Anxious are we?"

"I only have a few hours before they return."

"Darling, in a few hours nothing will matter," Susannah told her. She took in the altar and looked at the contents.

"My, you did do your homework."

"What's the point of doing something if you don't do it right?" Mora asked.

"I am going to like you, you remind me of an old friend," Susannah replied as she ran a finger down the goblet. "Not that I don't trust you, but I want to see where you got the blood from."

Mora looked at her as the panic flashed in her eyes. Swallowing hard she unbuttoned her jeans and slid them down past her knees, when she stepped out of them she raised her leg so that Susannah could see the bandage high on her inner thigh.

"Curious place for it," Susannah replied.

"I didn't want anyone to know about it, anywhere else it would have been noticed," Mora pointed out.

"You really did think of everything," Susannah said smiling. "Well then I guess delaying this is pointless."

"Probably," Mora agreed.

Susannah took the goblet off the altar and nodded to Mora.

"Do you give this goblet on your own free will?"

"I do," Mora said.

"Do you give the gift of blood of your own free will?"

"I do."

"Then may the blood bind us and unite us so that we may move together through the realms," Susannah said.

Mora expected her to take a sip from the goblet and that she would know the truth from that sip. Instead Mora watched with eyes wide open as the woman in the elegant gown and stunning jewels chugged the contents of the goblet. Not a drop dribbled down her chin as she drained the goblet of its contents.

"There," Susannah said as triumph filled her eyes. "Now my pet we have much to do. Come here."

Mora stood where she was and smiled as Susannah watched her with a confused look.

"I said come here," Susannah repeated as she felt her heart beat faster.

"No thanks I'm good where I stand," Mora replied. She watched as the woman's pale skin became flushed.

"I didn't give you a choice," Susannah yelled as she felt her lungs burn.

"You sure about that?"

"Why you insolent little fool!" Susannah went to step forward but instead fear grabbed her throat as pain began to fill her body. "What was in that goblet?"

"Blood."

"Your blood?"

"Of a sort," Mora replied. "It came from a relative of mine."

Susannah's eyes went wide as the pain increased. "Whose?"

"A vampire," Mora answered. "You might have heard of him. His name is Ayden."

Susannah went to lunge at the fool but instead she felt herself being pulled somewhere. She tried to struggle but felt the burning of poison run through her veins.

She landed with a thud on moist ground. Slowly she stood up looking around as she did, it looked familiar. There was a wooded area, crops grew in the distance, in another direction horses roamed. She heard dogs barking in the distance.

"So, we finally get to meet," a deep voice said behind her. "I've heard so much about you I feel as if we already know each other."

Susannah slowly turned around and saw a tall man walking toward her. His blonde hair hung in curls to his shoulders; he wore a goatee accenting his roman like nose. It was his blue/green eyes that drew her in.

He wore a black sweater and faded blue jeans but no coat to fight against the chill in the air. Maybe she was the only one that felt the chill. She pushed a strand of hair out of her face and tried her best seductive smile.

"Do I know you?" she asked in a sweet voice. He smelled like Mora.

"No but I know you," Ayden replied stopping before her. "Hello Susannah."

"How do you know me?" She hoped to look innocent.

"I heard about you from some mutual friends," Ayden said.

"Kirsa, Sara and Sabrina send their best by the way."

"Ayden." She had seen him in Kirsa's mind. Which meant he was also the vampire that Mora was speaking about.

Ayden smiled as comprehension dawned in eyes that were haunted and a bit crazy. "Put it all together now?"

"This is all a big misunderstanding," Susannah began. "I just wanted to show them I was alive and aware of what was happening."

"Interesting way to go about it don't you think? What better way to show friends that you're alright than by possessing their minds and causing them bodily harm?"

She glared at the vampire. "How would you feel if you were trapped for ten years and when you learned how to escape no one rejoiced? No one even cared? Instead they attack you like you're a criminal."

"Then I guess you don't recall the three agents you killed, or the four civilians that you killed five years ago? They were all just part of this plan that we should be rejoicing about?" Ayden inquired.

Susannah shook her head and walked around in a circle taking in the scenery. "I knew no one would understand my plan, my methods. People needed to be taught a lesson; they needed to understand the pain I was going through. They needed to see that I was the victim all along."

"Killing people, causing others to go insane seemed like a good way to go about it?"

Ayden watched as she paced back and forth mumbling about how no one would understand.

Babe, she's crazy, he told Kirsa.

I realize that. Just keep her talking or something.

Susannah stopped and stared at him, she cocked her head to the side realizing he could communicate with Kirsa. "Her blood is tainted you know."

"Whose? Kirsa's?" Ayden asked. There were a few other people she could be referring too.

"Yes Kirsa," Susannah said frustrated. She then smiled seductively running a hand down her body. "Why choose her when you could be with someone untainted?"

"Let me go out on a limb here and say you're nominating yourself?" Ayden inquired. "Because if that's the case then hell no."

"But I could give you so much more, you could rule all the vampires and I all the humans."

"Don't crazy people get tired of the whole world domination thing? It's got to get a bit old."

"It's not world domination," Susannah snarled. "I see it as more mental enslavement."

"Oh, so you do recognize that you're crazy and admit to wanting to enslave people. That's kind of funny."

Susannah began to curse at him in Irish unaware that he was following along with what she was saying. He watched as she paced and talked to herself, as her hands moved about while talking, it was almost entertaining if one forgot that she was a complete psychopath.

"I'd rather be staked then be your sex slave," Ayden replied in perfect Irish. Susannah whirled around.

"I can arrange that."

Ayden caught her in mid jump and snapped the wrist that handled the silver stake. He threw her into the nearest tree causing it to crack up the length of it.

You almost ready? Ayden asked as he walked toward Susannah's crumpled body. *I hate for you to miss out on all the fun.*

Don't worry we'll be along shortly.

Susannah lunged at him with a sword; he jumped out of the way as it sliced through the air. He let out a low growl when she tried to freeze him to the spot and when that didn't work she threw ice shards at him. One caught him on the cheek as he sprinted to the trees. Kirsa had given him the go ahead, so with a pissed off faery close behind, he ran toward the old barn. He leaped through the barrier and landed in the barn in the physical realm.

Susannah came crashing through after him. When she looked around all the color drained from her face.

CHAPTER 31

*T*he barn was a glow with hundreds of candles, a large circle made of salt encompassed the entire building. Incense burned, honoring the gods of old. Susannah stood up, blinking against the flickering light. As her vision cleared she realized three things: the first was she was now in the physical realm body and all, second was she knew where she was, and third what true fear felt like.

Kirsa, Sara and Sabrina stood before Susannah.

"It's been a while since we've all been together like this," Sabrina said dryly.

"I thought this had been destroyed," Susannah whispered with a hint of fear in her voice. There was still power in this room.

"Just the main house was," Kirsa replied.

"Beautiful full moon isn't it?" Sara asked.

Susannah looked at the three people that she once thought of as friends and wondered how she could trick them, how she could use them against each other. She had come too far to admit defeat, she had done too much to just give up.

"So, what now, a dramatic battle to the end?" Susannah asked as she began to whisper to the two that had called to her.

"Or you could turn yourself in," Kirsa said. "That would be the easiest and the best scenario."

Susannah glared at all of them as she summoned her magick and threw shards of ice and silver at them. Kirsa dove for the nearest cover.

"I guess no is her answer," Sabrina called from behind some boxes.

"Did you think I'd be that easy?" Susannah asked trying to locate the four of them.

"Only with men," Sara commented.

She ducked lower as the ball of fire hit the metal box she was behind. "With the blood of the offering, I take thee power and bind it to me times three," Susannah mumbled.

She repeated it and repeated it. "May the magick of the fae protect me against all that bring harm. "

"Still trying to win this?" Sabrina called.

She could see Ayden and Kirsa preparing their shots. "Brie, she could never admit when she was wrong," Sara pointed out.

Sara smelled the grenade and dove toward the other side of the room. Sabrina grabbed her and pulled her under her, allowing all the silver to pour down on her instead of Sara.

"May the blood given freely grant me the power to bring them to their knees!" Susannah yelled.

Sabrina focused on the pain while Sara focused on her beast with in. They both fought the urge to go on their knees. The first shot caught Susannah in the knee bringing her down to her knees.

"May the power of Dana's cauldron heal me," Susannah mumbled.

She felt like she was going to fly apart from all the power that was flowing through her. She could not loose when the gods were on her side.

Kirsa watched in horror as the iron bullet was pushed out of Susannah's knee and the wound began to heal. She looked at Ayden and he nodded to her.

"You are going to have to try better than that Kirsa," Susannah laughed. She stood up, the power radiating off of her.

Sabrina kept Sara pushed to the floor as Susannah unleashed the elements. Curling them in a ball she draped her leather coat over what was exposed of Sara. Together they began to whisper protection spells.

Sabrina felt wings surround them and knew if she focused she would see guardian angels surrounding them. Sara poked her head up from the cocoon.

"I can protect myself," Sara whispered. "Focus on keeping Kirsa safe."

Sabrina went to argue but Sara just shoved her head down. They both cringed as they heard something get thrown across the room. There was a sickening crunch as a body hit the wall causing the place to shake.

Kirsa shook herself off as she tried to pull herself up after Susannah threw her into the wall. She and Ayden were waiting for the order from Al, who was waiting to hear from the two mental facilities and the fae court.

Seeing what Susannah was going to do, Kirsa bolted across the room and took her friend down in a simple dive. Susannah used her power to throw Kirsa off of her.

A beautiful white tiger leapt out from behind the crates and snarled at Susannah.

"Oh, has kitty come out to play?" Susannah taunted the tiger.

Sara, in her tiger form, responded with a huge roar. Ayden helped Kirsa up then headed to Sabrina. With Sara keeping Susannah pinned to a spot Kirsa approached.

Kirsa bashed Susannah's head into the floor, and then punched her in the jaw as her former friend struggled. Susannah clawed at Kirsa's eyes then shoved her off with a simple wind enchantment. Kirsa tasted blood.

"You won't kill me Kirsa, you don't have it in you," Susannah yelled as she called on more enchantments. "You're too soft, too righteous to allow blood to dirty your hands."

This time the tiger lunged and took Susannah to the ground. Allowing Kirsa time to reload her gun.

Kirsa saw Ayden look at her and nod. Kirsa aimed her gun at Susannah.

"Maybe when I was seventeen, but things have changed in the past twelve years."

Susannah laughed at that. "You could never kill a friend."

"Never say never," Kirsa said. Susannah heard the click of a gun, she heard the bullet leave the chamber.

She saw the look on Kirsa's face, she watched as Sabrina was ready to let loose an army of angels.

Preparing for the impact, Sabrina grabbed the tiger by the neck. The impact flung them backwards into the door causing it to crash open. She blinked a few times only to see that Kirsa now knelt next to her.

"You're the one with blood on their hands," Kirsa whispered as she closed Susannah's lifeless eyes.

"Kirsa," Ayden said gently.

Kirsa went to ask him what but he was pressing his jacket on a wound on Sara. Her tiger form had vanished, she lay on the ground, with blood surrounding her.

"Sara, no," Kirsa whispered as she crawled to her friend. Ignoring all her own injuries as Kirsa gathered her in her arms.

"I'm fine," Sara assured Kirsa as she coughed up blood.

Ayden radioed to Al that they need help now. Sabrina came to Sara's other side. Kirsa looked at Sabrina and mouthed that the dagger in Sara's side was silver.

"We're getting you help," Kirsa told her as she took one of Sara's hands in hers. It was already cold.

"You and Kirsa can compare scars," Sabrina joked trying hard not to cry. Sabrina pushed some hair out of Sara's face.

Sara smiled weakly as her color began to fade. "I'm going to see Jeff. It's going to be alright."

Kirsa choked back a sob as she brushed a kiss on Sara's forehead. "Kirsa, you don't have to be tough all the time," Sara coughed.

Ayden stayed back, when he saw Al's car followed by the ambulance. As people piled out of vehicles, he motioned for Al to give them all a moment.

"Brie, keep her grounded," Sara instructed.

"I will," Sabrina promised.

"Go see Jeff, I promise I won't become a hermit again," Kirsa whispered.

"You better not or I will haunt you," Sara whispered faintly. "I love you."

Sabrina and Kirsa sat there holding onto Sara's hand as they watched her take her final breath.

There was movement all around them but neither paid any attention to it. When the paramedic came to move Sara's body, Kirsa wouldn't let them touch her. She pulled Sara close to her and wouldn't let anyone near them.

"Kirs," Ayden whispered kneeling down next to her.

"They can't Ayden," Kirsa said through tears. "They can't just take her."

"Do you want me to do it?" Ayden asked her.

Kirsa nodded as Sabrina came around to hold on to Kirsa. Ayden looked at the paramedic, who also nodded. Wrapping his coat around Sara, he closed her eyes, then picked her up in his arms as if she was sleeping.

The cops, agents, and paramedics formed two lines as he walked with Sara to the awaiting ambulance. No one spoke as Ayden laid her down in the ambulance. As the doors closed he felt the anguish that flowed through Kirsa. When he turned around Sabrina and Kirsa were wrapped up in each other. This was their moment to grieve.

CHAPTER 31

Kirsa sat curled up in front of the pellet stove. Ayden came in, he sat next to her. She hadn't said much in the last day. The news didn't ease the pain that Kirsa felt. Collin had just left, taking Sabrina back to the ranch to at least shower and change. Neither of them had wanted to be apart. Sabrina had slept with Kirsa last night with Ayden and Lance standing guard.

"Susannah's breathing on her own," Ayden said kissing her on the forehead. Kirsa looked up at him. "Al just called."

Kirsa said nothing as she stared into the flames of the pellet stove. Ayden brushed through her curls with his fingers.

"So, did you purposely shoot her in the one spot of the brain that wouldn't kill her?" Ayden asked her. Hoping his question would distract her for even a moment.

"She needs to answer for what she has done," Kirsa replied. Her voice hollow, void of all emotions. "Killing her would have been too easy, an escape from judgment."

Ayden knew that Kirsa would feel as though she had killed Sara, Kristina and Carlotta, that she was as responsible as Susannah was. They had learned that both had slit their necks at precisely the same time in the same manner.

"You did all you could," Ayden told her.

"Two more died because of her," Kirsa replied.

"For Kristina and Carlotta they were already lost when we found them," Ayden told her. "Nothing you did was going to save either. Carlotta was already shattered, and Kristina craved what Susannah promised."

"And Sara?" Kirsa asked her voice cracking. "There were four of us, then three. Now there is only two."

Ayden said nothing as he pulled her to her side. Kirsa looked up at him. "Does it get easier? Seeing death after death?"

"Not easier, you begin to accept it, appreciate the fragility of it. Even vampires die eventually," Ayden said.

CHAPTER 32

Court Suite 1 looked like your typical courtroom. The judge's bench was front and center, the witness stand was off to the right. There was the thirteen seat Jury box, the prosecution table, defense table and a podium in between.

Behind the tables was the public gallery that was separated by bullet proof glass. There were six rows of chairs on either side of the center aisle. Outside of the main courtroom was the press box, where the press were allowed to wait during trial, there was also a conference room and small bathroom for those involved.

Kirsa and Al sat in the front row of the public gallery, the families of those involved filled in the rest of the seats. The press had been barred not just from the courtroom but from the press box as well.

This was not a trial session, instead it was an extradition hearing to decide if Susannah should be tried here or moved to the realm of the Fae and face her punishment there. It made things simple in some ways, there was only one lawyer and one judge, there was also no jury.

Titania sat in the witness seat while Colin went through the basic questions. When he finished with them he moved on to the more difficult ones.

"How dangerous is Susannah?" Colin asked her.

"Extremely," Titania said.

"Can you explain to the court how dangerous she is?" She nodded.

"My family are water Faeries," Titania explain in a calm and clear voice. "We are able to manipulate the elements of water. We also excel at dream work. I am very strong in elemental magick where my younger sister Alana excels at Dream Magick. Susannah could do both but not strongly, she wanted to be better than us. Through the use of dark magick she was able to fulfill that desire. Susannah can enter your dream, she can shape it to however she wants it to be without you knowing. She can manipulate water as if it was a simple trick, forging weapons out of ice."

"Have you experienced any of these dreams or weapons yourself?" Colin asked.

He could tell the judge was greatly interested. "You have to understand that up until this point I believed her that she was innocent that she didn't know what she was doing," Titania stated. The judge nodded his understanding. "I had a nightmare, in which my family was killed with the use of iron in some horrible way. She also showed me Director Moore impaled on an iron cross with iron nails. It was then that I realized that she knew what she was doing, that she knew what was in my mind."

"That must have been difficult to realize," Colin said encouragingly.

The door to the courtroom opened and a man walked in with a visitor pass on. They waited for him to sit before Titania answered. "It was," she agreed.

"What did you do after the nightmare?"

"I confronted her, told her I knew now that she was responsible. She was supposed to be comatose; she was supposed to be in some type of vegetative state. Yet the moment I turned my back to her I was frozen to the ground, and she created a blizzard right there in the living room of her hospital suite. It took Director Moore firing iron bullets into the door knob to open it. So yes, I have firsthand experience to know just how dangerous she is."

"Is there a way to keep us safe from her?" the judge asked. "Iron, lots and lots of iron," Titania said.

The judge signaled for her to step down. One by one Alex, Delilah, Mora, Caroline and some of the other victim's families spoke out about what happened. How their children changed, how their lives had been forever altered. When the last one left the stand, Colin stood at the podium.

"I would like to call Wagner Louis to the stand," Colin said.

He heard the murmur's and knew he had caught Kirsa and Al off guard. Carlotta was the tragic tale that needed to be told, more so than Kristina. Kirsa watched as the man who came in when Titania was speaking stood up.

He was of average height with light brown hair and hazel eyes, he wore an expensive cut suit. But he walked with care and with grace as he nodded to Colin. When Wagner sat at the stand, Colin began.

"Please state your relation to the case."

"I am the half-brother of Carlotta Louis, she died on February 15th," Wagner explained. The judge nodded allowing Colin to proceed.

"Can you explain the relationship you had with Carlotta?" Colin inquired.

"My brother Sigmund and I came from our father's first marriage," Wagner explained. "Our mom divorced him when I was three and Sig was only three months old."

"That must have taken a lot of courage on your mom's part to divorce with such young children."

"Derek was a difficult and hard man," Wagner replied. "He strove for perfection, when he didn't get it he became angry, not violent but vocal. Mom had had enough of all his anger and divorced him. He remarried when I was ten, I was twelve when Lottie was born."

"Did you see her often?"

"We were required to see him two weekends a month and every other holiday," Wagner recalled.

"When Lottie was born, Sig and I fell in love with her. She was perfect in every way, always smiling." Wagner smiled as he thought of his sister. "Even when they pushed her, she was a happy kid."

"What changed?" Colin asked.

"It was after Aria and Aida were born, that Lottie saw how different she was treated from them," Wagner replied.

"How so?"

"Aria and Aida were able to take part in activities, they were able to have friends, they bragged about the money the family had."

"How did that make your sister feel?"

"Lottie began to feel as though her only purpose was to make money. Which was true, she was an opera prodigy and had tours and cd's. She had no life outside of making money. Sig and I tried to help her; we tried to take her away on little trips without the rest of the family. By the time she tried out for Juilliard she had begun to lose that spark."

"That happy little girl had begun to fade?"

"She became invisible," Wagner corrected. "All my father and step mother saw was the prestige and money when they looked at her. When she got accepted to Juilliard they said no, they only had her try out so they could say she had been accepted at such a young age."

"That had to be devastating to a fifteen-year-old," Colin replied.

"I think a part of her died that day," Wagner said. "The rest died after the rape."

"She was gang raped and became pregnant as a result, what support did she have?"

"None at home," Wagner answered feeling the anger still rise in him. "Sig and I tried to do what we could. They thought she deserved it for sneaking out to go to a senior dance. That it was punishment for defying them," Wagner explained. He felt the outrage in the room. "After the rape, Sig told her he would adopt the baby, I would pay for the medical bills, and our mom would take her in. She felt free like she was finally going to get away from them, and then those dreams began."

"What happened?"

"She began to tell us about these dreams, about this faery godmother who would hold her and tell her it would be alright. We didn't think much of it, but then Sig found books on dark magick in her room. We took her out to dinner and asked her, she said she was doing research and that her faery godmother could help erase everything that happened. That is when she took a turn for the worse. She was barely eating and sleeping; she was talking to herself, laughing when no one else was around. We tried to talk to Derek about it but he ignored it. Then she did the first ritual, she called me hysterical the next day that it hadn't worked."

Colin handed Wagner a glass of water, so he could collect his thoughts. The courtroom was silent as he explained the downhill spiral of his sister. Wagner finished the water before he spoke.

"Sig, Mom and I were going to drive down and just take her. We had it planned, lined up the therapists, had everything in place. Then we got the phone call from the police. She had confessed, I talked to her and acted as her lawyer. She wasn't competent to stand trial; everyone saw it when they looked into her eyes. They were dead. I asked what happened; Dad read her journal found out about our plans. Told her she was his, that she would always be his, that she would never leave that house."

"When he confronted her, she snapped. Said the Faery appeared and helped her with the ritual. That she helped kill them, helped boil their hearts."

"Who do you think killed your father and his family?"

"Lottie did, I know that, but I know that if it wasn't for those dreams, for that faery the idea would never have been planted," Wagner replied. "In my mind they are both equally responsible."

The judge had asked for a recess, so he could go through all the information. When he returned he asked for Al and Kirsa to step forward.

"Director Moore how many prisons are there in Fae?"

"Five, one for each branch," Al replied. "The fifth is the most secure calling for only the most dangerous of prisoners. It's made entirely of iron."

"How does a faery work there?" the judge asked out of curiosity.

"Special clothing," Al said.

"I see the high court of the Fae has signed off on allowing the prison transfer?"

"They have, they understand the danger she possesses."

"It wasn't until Mr. Louis that I was truly convinced of how dangerous she is," the judge admitted. "If she can prey on the most innocent and fractured of minds and make them commit such horrible acts then I fear what she could do if she was to ever be released. I allow the transfer on one condition."

Al and Kirsa both looked at each other wondering what the condition would be. "Yes, your honor?"

"You and Assistant Director Heinrich are the two that escort her to the High Prison."

****

Ayden paced Kirsa's home office. Al was on the phone in the living room, Lance was fending off reporters outside while Colin dealt with the press conference back at OPIA headquarters. The media had just learned that a ruling had been made two days before and were having a fit that they hadn't be notified. The reason for that is because everyone involved needed to prepare statements to release. They had camped out on the road leading to Kirsa's home.

"This is going to be a logistical nightmare," Ayden replied.

Kirsa looked up from applications for a housekeeper.

Her hair was pulled back and she was in t-shirt and ripped jeans, thrilled not to have to wear a suit for a while.

She was trying to focus on something normal and not focus on Sara's memorial service tomorrow.

"It will be a dry run for the coronation ceremony and our wedding."

"I can't wait to be in the new house with the new security system, then we don't have to worry about the press," Ayden said sitting down in a chair.

"Tony's sending some cops over to clear them off," Kirsa reminded him. "Lance is having a blast baring his teeth if they get to close."

"You really are calm about this whole thing, aren't you?" Ayden asked studying her carefully.

She closed the file knowing she would not be getting back to it anytime soon. "Ayden, it's over. Yes, it is going to be a pain in the ass to get me into the high court of Fae but it will be done. Yes, there is the chance that you and Lance might not get cleared, these are all things that are out of our control. In another two months we will be moving into our new home, those decisions I can control."

"How can one so young be so wise?" Ayden asked kissing her lightly.

"My dad once told me that age does not make one wise, it's the experience we live that give us wisdom."

"Then not only are you the fairest of all but the wisest too," Ayden said with a wicked smile.

"That was way too corny," Kirsa said laughing as he kissed her again.

Al knocked on the door frame. "I hate to interrupt but I am anyway."

"What's up?" Kirsa asked.

"Ayden and Lance can go as far as the entrance into the High Court," Al said. "I have been promised the High Royal Guards as protection for Kirsa while we are there."

"I'll go let Dietrich know," Ayden replied.

Al sat down exhausted from the last few days. "Titania should be here in an hour to help go over what you need to wear and bring."

"I've been to Fae before," Kirsa reminded him. He shook his head.

"Kirsa most faeries never see the Royal Court, you will be in the presence of Tuatha Da Danaan. You have no idea the protocol that is expected and demanded. This is not a simple drop off trip."

CHAPTER 33

They all met at Sara's home. It was a mix of cops, were animals, and those who knew Sara. Her family had come from New England. Kirsa hugged Sara's brother and her grandparents. When she was done Phil came over to pay his respects. Kirsa spotted Laura and walked toward her.

"How's he doing?" Kirsa asked her cousin, noting that he was wearing sunglasses.

"As well as Sabrina and you," Laura replied. "Bridgette is keeping him going, she's giving him a purpose to get out of bed."

"He lost his female counterpart, even though they weren't romantic, there was a bond there," Kirsa answered.

"I just hate not being able to help any of you," Laura sighed as she looked at Kirsa. "Honestly, how are you doing?"

"I'm about to give a eulogy for my best friend," Kirsa replied. "I'm numb. Then it all crashes into me and it's reliving mom and dad again."

"Now you have me and my family, so you aren't alone," Laura remained her. "You have Adam and his tribe. You have Ayden."

"I know," Kirsa replied.

She caught Phil's signal. Ayden found her and handed her a candle than they all formed two lines. Phil led them into the woods that the pack ran in. A podium had been set up in the center of an open field and chairs were set up for everyone. Kirsa walked to where Phil stood.

"I know," Kirsa whispered as she hugged the large man.

He couldn't even say Sara's name without crying so she agreed to speak. He squeezed her hand and went to stand next to the podium. Kirsa took a deep breath and walked to the podium. She tried to smile as she took her speech out and laid it on the surface.

"We are all here to celebrate the life of Sara," Kirsa began. Her voice faltering on her name. She took a deep breath as she played with her signet ring. "I had no clue what to say today. I was going to say something witty, tell a funny story, maybe say a poem about love and loss."

Carefully she unfolded the paper. "This all began because I opened my yearbook and found a picture of four friends," Kirsa started. "So, I actually went back to that dreaded senior yearbook, which I was not in but Sara and Sabrina still forced me to buy."

Sabrina half snorted and cried as she nodded from her seat, with Collin there next to her as support. "We did," she agreed.

"I am going to read what Sara wrote me," Kirsa went on. "Kirsa, we're seniors. When I first moved here I was scared and terrified that no one would ever accept me for the monster I was. Then I met this tomboy with skin knees, braids falling out, and these purple eyes that were big and bright. She knew what I was, but she never once treated me any different then she would a friend. When our parents were asleep on the night of the full moon, she would sneak to the basement where the safe room was and curl up in her sleeping bag and read to me whatever book she was reading at the time. I began to not dread the full moon anymore. And slowly over time I began to see myself no longer as a monster but as Sara, the girl who could be a white tiger. With Sabrina in our circle, I knew I had my family. The two of you always making sure I was okay leading up to a change and after a change. My father no longer lived in fear of what could go wrong, instead he could finally live as well."

Kirsa had to take a break because the next part was rough. "We are seniors. And our life is before us. It is going to take us to so many different places. We are going to go on journeys that will help shape who we are. All I know is that you have always been my beacon, whenever I needed you, whenever I doubted myself, our friendship shined the way back. I hope one day that I could be the strength for you that you have been for me, for Sabrina, even for Susie. You are our heart and soul. No matter where we go, know you will always have a white tiger as your protector."

CHAPTER 34

Glastonbury, England was a town filled with legends. It was the rumored burial site of King Arthur, the location of the legendary Avalon, Merlin was rumored to have lived there, and there was even a well believed to be where the chalice from the last supper was buried. It was filled with quaint shops, new age stores, tea shops and tours that would bring you to the legendary Tor where you could hike to the top and see the most stunning views imaginable.

Lance pulled into the parking spot outside the tourist information center and pulled his sunglasses on. People were milling around, annoyed that there would be no tours to the tor today. Al got out of the passenger side and looked around; it had been awhile since he had come to Glastonbury.

Nodding to Lance he headed into the gift shop, the head of OPIA for the UK walked over to AL. No one else knew that the Head of OPIA and his second in command were in England.

"It's been ages," Louis Donnigan said as they did a one arm embrace.

"Since our last summit a year ago," Al replied. "We all set?"

"Pissed off the tour groups but everything is in order," Louis assured him as they headed out of the building. He nodded to Lance and smiled as the passenger window on the second car rolled down; he leaned in and gave Kirsa a kiss on the cheek.

"We had bets going on how many limbs Al would lose when he offered you the job."

Kirsa laughed. "Please tell me you won it?"

"I did," Louis replied. "I'll hop in with Al and you can follow."

Kirsa nodded and rolled up the window. She looked and Ayden, he squeezed her hand. "We're heading out boys," she called into the back of the large armored van.

There were a few grunts as Ayden pulled the van out of the spot. Concealed in the back was a 100 percent iron portable cell containing Susannah. There were five were-wolves, two vampires and three faeries riding along all armed with iron weapons.

Ayden followed Lance out of the parking lot and noticed the cop cars pulling out with lights flashing to escort them to the Tor. Tourists and residents alike watched the procession as the caravan moved through the main part of town and headed toward the Tor. The well-worn path that wound around the hill was visible from the road.

"Tell me we are not walking the path?" Ayden asked.

"No, we are taking the steps that lead straight up," Kirsa promised.

They had slowed to a crawl as they drove over the country roads. Farmers nodded to them as they drove past. It took an hour to reach the Tor, when they did the cop cars formed a half moon around the two official cars. Kirsa and Ayden jumped out of the van meeting up with Lance, Al and Louis.

"How are we doing this?" Lance asked. "This is a steep climb."

"We have a special cart made for this," Louis told them. One of the cops got it out of their van and brought it over. "We attach the portable cell to it and it makes it easier than having to carry it."

"Everyone has iron bullets?" Kirsa asked the police officers as they began to ready themselves.

The ten in her van would be pushing the prison. The cops were there to make sure Susannah didn't attempt anything. The cops nodded, everyone began the last minute preparations.

It took a half hour to hook the cage to the cart, which involved a complicated pulley system. When everything was locked, Louis gave the signal and the procession of thirty began to make the slow ascension up to the top. The single tower loomed ahead of them as they walked up the rugged terrain. Farms were seen at a distance with sheep and other animals looking like small dots on the horizon.

After they finally reached the summit they put the brakes on the cart and AL and Kirsa began to get ready for the trip. The black covering came off the cell revealing to Susannah where they were.

"No," Susannah whispered as it dawned on her where they were. "You can't be serious."

No one listened to her as Al and Kirsa changed into more formal clothing. One of the officers stared at Susannah not sure why someone so beautiful was trapped in such a deplorable prison. She was too beautiful to be trapped there. Slowly he began to move toward the cell while others talked about what was going on.

When the officer got within range, Susannah grabbed him by the collar and pulled him up against the cell. Before she could do anything, she felt the burning on her temple before she felt the pressure of the gun.

"Let him go or I will splatter your brains all over this spot," Lance said as he clicked the bullet into the chamber.

Susannah looked at him from the corner of her eye and saw that not only was his gun trained on her but so were thirty other guns as well. She released the officer who collapsed to the ground. Two officers ran to gather up their buddy still keeping their guns aimed at her.

"That's why I told you all to ignore her," Louis yelled. "She might be beautiful, but she is even more dangerous."

Lance stayed as he was while Kirsa and Al went over plans with Louis and Ayden. When they were done Ayden looked down at Kirsa and smiled sadly.

"She's going to try something," he whispered kissing her cheek.

"I know."

"Be safe, come back to me," Ayden said kissing her one last time.

"I'm not letting you get out of marrying me that easily," Kirsa told him as she twirled a strand of his hair between her fingers.

Louis motioned to the ten supernatural officers to move her into the center of the tower, those authorized followed while the police formed a tighter circle around the outside. Once the cage was loaded off of the cart and the cart moved away, everyone but Kirsa and Al moved outside of the Tower.

Ayden kept his focus on Kirsa while Lance kept his gun aimed at Susannah.

Al took Kirsa's hand in his and she laid a hand on the cage. She nodded to Al who just closed his eyes. Kirsa felt the ripple of power surround them; she felt her senses go haywire as everything disappeared around her. Al kept a firm hand on hers forcing her to keep a firm grip on the cage. What felt like an eternity was only a matter of seconds.

****

"You can open your eyes," Al replied in a hush tone. He positioned himself so he could see her reaction.

Kirs opened her eyes and stood stunned. It was as if they never left the Tor, the only way she knew they had was that Ayden and everyone else was gone. She stared at Al confused.

"Welcome to Avalon," Al replied.

Kirsa was speechless as she looked around, it was stunning. Twenty guardsman appeared outside of the tower all of them saluting Al.

"Welcome home," the leader said to Al.

"Thanks Balor," Al said as they hugged. "Balor this is Kirsa Adulwulf. Kirsa, this is my distant cousin Balor, he's head of the Royal guard."

"It's a pleasure," she said as he shook her hand.

"It's an honor to us to have you here," Balor told her. He motioned his men to take their things and for another group to deal with Susannah.

"I will escort you to your lodgings."

When they had left the larger group, they were able to speak more freely.

"What are we dealing with?" Al asked.

"Tonight, is the welcoming dinner," Balor explained as he nodded to novices. "There you will present Kirsa and the reason for you being here. They know of course but it has to be official."

"Just like we had to hold a trial even though we knew she would be sent here," Kirsa replied.

"She grasps politics well," Balor said smiling.

"She deals with the grumpy old men on a regular basis," Al reminded him, causing him to laugh.

"Does everyone refer to the five of them as the grumpy old men?" Kirsa asked. They were referring to the Vampire Inner Council.

"Well not to their faces obviously, but yes," Balor said. "Now we have to change it because of you but we'll find a new name. Perhaps the grumpy old men and the beautiful Kirsa?"

"Before you try to steal her from Ayden, what else are we looking at?" Al inquired.

His cousin was a womanizer, a good natured one but still, he didn't want a vampire pissed at him.

"Tomorrow is the official declaration of her being stripped of name, house and class," Balor replied looking more solemn than anything. "Once that is over with the official sentencing will begin."

"Are they here?"

"All that need to be are here," a melodic voice said.

Kirsa watched as everyone dropped to a knee. She went to do the same but a soft hand caught her chin and kept her standing. Kirsa looked and saw a stunning woman with flaming red hair. She wore a white gown with a halo of flowers around her hair.

"You kneel to no one," Brigid told Kirsa. "We have waited for you."

Al and Balor exchanged a look as the Goddess spoke to Kirsa. "You shall sit with us at the high table tonight," Brigid informed Kirsa. "Alfred will also join you as your guest."

"Thank you," Kirsa said inclining her head slightly.

"You may show them to their cottage," Brigid nodded to Balor before leaving. They waited until she was gone before speaking.

"By the gods, no mortal, immortal or non-god has ever sat at High Table," Balor said as they continued down the path.

Word of the conversation had spread rapidly, by the time they made it to the quaint stone cottage the novices and men were watching Kirsa with curiosity. Kirsa felt relieved when they stepped into the cottage closing all the stares away.

"Who are you?" Balor asked.

"Heir of the sixth line," Kirsa said simply.

"No, you are more than that," Balor said shaking his head. "I will leave now and see you both at dinner."

Kirsa and Al took in their surroundings. The living area was spacious with a place to eat, the fire was already going in the hearth. There were three doors on the back wall leading into two bedrooms and a bathroom. Al placed Kirsa's garment bag on the hanger on the door.

"Why don't you take a bath before tonight's festivities," Al suggested.

Knowing it would be her last chance to relax until they were done in Fae, she went into her room and gathered what she would need for the bath. Titania and Alana were both coming over later to help Kirsa get ready.

As the water filled the claw foot tub, Kirsa stepped into the hot water. She had added lavender to help relax. Leaning back, she began to relax. Kirsa went through what would be going on in the next few days.

After Titania had come to her house and raided her closet Kirsa learned she had nothing suitable for the high court of Faery.

The day after Titania had raided her closet they went to see Ciannan, a fae designer who did all of the Murphy gowns. The Fae's liked to showcase their curves, their features, and their grace. No billowing skirts, or peasant sleeves.

Kirsa felt like she ended up with a new wardrobe by the time they were finished. Ayden would die if he saw her in the attire for tonight. She would have to find a reason to wear it for him, it was definitely out of her comfort zone.

When the water began to go cold she stepped out of the tub and dried off with linen towels. After hanging them on the towel rack to dry she slipped on her robe and stepped into the warm living room. Titania and Alana stood there holding their two dresses, they smiled at Kirsa.

"Ready to become a Faery?" Titania asked.
"Sure," Kirsa said making Alana laugh.

CHAPTER 35

*A*n hour later Kirsa barely recognized herself in the mirror. Her eyes seemed to be more purple, her skin seemed to glow. Alana had let her hair hang in natural ringlets as she finished with the makeup. Behind Kirsa, Titania worked on the ribbons of the corset top that Kirsa wore. It was black with silver brocading over it. Along the sweetheart neck and bottom rhinestones sparkled. She wore a plain black velvet choker and hanging from her ears were her mother's diamond drop earrings. The only other jewelry she wore was her engagement ring and signet ring.

When Titania was done she then helped Kirsa step into the black skirt that just skimmed the ground, it was a straight column of black silk.

"Kirsa you look stunning," Titania said stepping back to look at her.

"I can't believe it's you," Alana whispered.

Kirsa just stared at the transformation before her, Alana snapped a picture with her phone. She turned and smiled at the sisters.

"I can't wait to see what my coronation gown and wedding gown will look like."

Kirsa had loved Ciannan so much that she was having him working on the two gowns instead of going with someone else. Seeing herself now she was thrilled she had.

"Ayden would die if he saw you right now," Titania replied.

There was a knock on the door and Al entered in his family tartan. He went to say something but stopped as he took in the three women who stole his breath. Alana looked young and vibrant in an empire waist dress that went from a deep purple and faded down to near white at the bottom of it. Her platinum blonde hair had been done in a crown of braids as amethysts dripped from her ears.

Titania was a vision in a pale blue with the faintest hint of a shimmer. It was strapless which showed off her shape with the gentle gather and fall of material. Her hair was done in a bun making it look like spun gold. Kirsa looked every bit the heir to a vampire bloodline in her gown of black and silver.

"The three of you could represent the Morrigan's," Al whispered. He walked over and placed a gentle kiss on Titania before recovering.

"Are we ready?"

"What are the plans?" Kirsa asked as Titania handed her the wrap to wear if it got chilly.

"Balor will escort Titania and Alana to their parents, you and I will walk to the center of the room," Al replied.

Kirsa nodded and they walked out into the living area where Balor stood in dress uniform with some of his men. They stared at the three women and blinked a few times before they could think.

"It is an honor," Balor said bowing at the waist.

After that they headed out onto the cobblestone path that was now lit with torches adding a glow to twilight. The novices and apprentices watched in awe as the group headed toward the Keep.

It stood just north of the Tor, the white stone had ivy crawling up it only making it more a part of nature. There was a fountain and the gardens surrounding it were stunning. The large wooden doors stood open and they were ushered into the entry.

When the horn blew, Balor and one of his men opened the door to the hall and Kirsa was speechless as she entered. She had never seen a room as splendid as this. The walls were done in murals of the four seasons, the detail made it seem as if you could see the butterfly flutter it's wing or hear the snow falling. Flowers and candles were everywhere; on tables, in large urns, draped over chandeliers. Tables were covered in gold linens with white place settings.

There were murmurs as the group entered. Balor bowed to the head table before escorting the sisters to the table where their parents were.

Al squeezed Kirsa's hand that lay on his arm, he could sense her nerves. She smiled slightly as they walked to the center of the room. Al went down on one knee in respect, when Kirsa went to curtsey twelve chairs were pushed back as the twelve gods of the Tuatha De Dannan stood and inclined their heads to Kirsa. Nervously she did the same.

"Welcome child," Lugh said. His voice filled the room with ease. "It is an honor to have you grace our home just as it was when your father came thirty years ago."

Kirsa looked at Al, they both didn't know her father had been here. "Thank you," Kirsa whispered.

"You embarrass the child," Nuada bellowed laughing. "Come forward so we can see you. Now

Lord Moore please explain what brings you and Lady Adulwulf to us."

Al nodded as they moved closer to the head table that was draped in white. It held thirteen golden chalices and place settings though only twelve sat at the table. The center setting was for if Danu came.

"We have come to ask that a sentence and punishment be placed on the water faery Susannah Murphy," Al explained.

"And why should we place judgment when her crimes were in the realm of man?" Lugh asked.

"Not all her crimes were in the realm of man," Kirsa said and took a step forward. "Her crimes also stretch into the realm of dreams and the realm of demons."

There was stunned silence as the word demon was spoken. The twelve studied Kirsa before discussing amongst themselves.

Brigid spoke next. "Then it is decided, we shall pass judgment and sentence on to her."

Her word was final as she spoke for Danu as well. "Now we invite you Lady Adulwulf to sit and dine with us as well as your escort."

Excited murmurs filled the room as two settings of gold were added to the head table. Al and Kirsa were escorted and positioned at either end.

Lugh poured wine into Kirsa's chalice and smiled kindly at her. "You did not know that Hagan came here did you?"

"He never spoke of it," Kirsa told him as a server placed lamb stew in front of her for the appetizer.

"He was a great man," Lugh said reminded of the young mortal that impressed him. "He came to ask for help with writing the paranormal laws. He did not want to make an error with the Fae part. We were doubtful, but he would not step down. It is then that Hugh volunteered to assist him. Hugh's line is most distinguished and respected amongst our kind, we allowed it."

"He rarely spoke of that time period."

Lugh waived the server away as he ate some of his stew. "It was not an easy time when the world learned of the paranormal, though they were certain we existed."

"It's one thing to have an idea it's another when you are told that the idea is correct," Kirsa stated.

"Well said," Nuada replied as he drank his stout. "And you are correct, when their suspicions were confirmed some did not react well. The Middle East and Africa became a slaughterhouse. Those that we were able to save were placed elsewhere. But that area lost nearly all of its paranormal."

"Is that why there is no line there? No pack?" Kirsa inquired. No one talked about the reason.

"All the were's were slaughtered, we were unable to get to them in time, the vampires were nearly wiped out," Nuada explained. "Those that survived refuse to ever return to their home. It had been decided to cut off the paranormal from that area. The amount of loss was staggering."

Lugh laid a hand on hers for comfort, her empathy was great. "After the massacre it was decided an organization needed to be created to enforce and police the paranormal laws, your father helped create it."

"Your family seems to have a way of being involved in doing great things," Nuada pointed out. "Now let's discuss happier things, like that shiny ring on your hand?"

The rest of the night was filled with entertainment, food and drink. No one dwelled on the events of the next day.

****

Kirsa dressed in the corset from the night before, she added black trousers that swished when she moved. This was to conceal her ankle holster and knife sheath.

She slipped on an elegantly tailored black jacket edged in black satin. Kirsa slipped into black heels and pulled her hair back before stepping out into the living room. Al was waiting in a black suit with black shirt, he wore a silver tie with a shamrock pin on it.

"You were up late," Kirsa replied straightening his tie.

"Titania and I had a lot to talk about," Al replied knowing his bald spot was probably pink.

"Talk? Is that what you kids call it these days?" Kirsa said laughing at his embarrassment.

"All right smart ass, you ready?" Al asked.

"Yes," Kirsa said. The sooner they were done, the sooner Susannah was handed over, the sooner she could leave and no longer live in fear.

Nodding, they left the cottage where Balor awaited with eight guards. Balor placed Kirsa and Al in the center of guards and once again they made the trek to the Keep.

This time it was early morning, there were no torches or moon to guide their way just the bright light of the early morning sun. The large doors of the keep were closed and Balor pulled the bell pull. The doors opened and once again they were brought into the entry.

Everyone was patted down and weapons were checked before the doors to the hall were opened. When they were Kirsa was amazed at the transformation. The murals from the night before were hidden behind pale blue and green drapes. The tables were gone, replaced with a small group of chairs. The high table wore a black cloth with silver chalices and no place settings.

Balor escorted them to where the they waited for the twelve to enter and for Susannah to be brought it. Kirsa gasped when the floor in the center of the room opened up and watched as the cage Susannah had been brought in was raised up through the opening. Her hair was matted, her gray dress torn and dirty. She looked at no one as the cage clicked into position.

When Kirsa turned to look at the head table she saw that the Twelve were there. Hugh was called to stand before the head table.

"What is your wish Prince Hugh of the Water Fae?" Lugh asked.

"The house of water, the class of faery, and name of Murphy ask that the water faery known as Susannah Murphy be stripped of name, class, and house," Hugh replied.

His voice showed no emotion, nor did he look when Susannah let out a shriek in protest.

Kirsa saw that shock on Susannah's face as the words sunk in. She had always believed that who she was would protect her, that her blood would keep her safe. Now that protection had been stripped from her and from the one person she thought would never turn from her.

"You are aware that once these are revoked they cannot be given back?" Brigid asked softly.

"We are."

"Very well," Brigid replied. They had made a decision when the petition had been sent. But it had to be presented orally to be sealed. "We the thirteen shall grant the request."

Brigid now turned and stared at Susannah. "Susannah Murphy you are no more. Your name will be stripped from our lore and your memory forgotten."

"I exist!" Susannah bellowed shaking the bars. Smoke formed where iron met skin. "I will not be forgotten!"

"You will be silent!" Nuada roared.

Kirsa began to react the moment she saw the change in Susannah's eyes. She was already on her feet grabbing her gun as Susannah yelled.

"You will be the ones silenced!" Susannah threw her arms up and the iron cage that held her exploded.

Iron flew everywhere as the fae dove for cover. Kirsa fired her gun as she threw her jacket over Alana to keep her covered. The bullet caught Susannah in the side but she didn't notice.

"You will not erase me," Susannah stated. "I shall erase you all."

Kirsa felt her begin to pull power, running faster than most could see she tackled Susannah as the twelve began to issue orders. Susannah punched Kirsa in the jaw, Kirsa bashed her head into the floor.

In a rage Susannah grabbed the knife at Kirsa's ankle and pulled it on her.

"Your blood will kill them all," she howled as she dragged Kirsa to her feet. She braced the knife along Kirsa's neck.

"I will drain her," Susannah said calmly. Everything stopped, as demons began to appear surrounding Susannah. "She will die if one person moves."

"Susannah," Brigid said just calmly. "We can resolve this. Please, child, do not do this. There is no return once you do. She has been marked and even you would not be safe if you killed her."

Susannah laughed the laugh of a crazed individual it echoed off the walls. "It's too late for that."

With that she dragged the knife across Kirsa's neck and caught the first drop with her finger tip. She brought it to her lips and smiled as power consumed her. "I call on the power of blood to aid me in this fight. No one shall bind, no iron shall kill me, I shall be unstoppable."

As Kirsa fell to her knees gagging on her own blood Al fired off shots while the fae went to arms. Alana skidded to a halt in front of Kirsa. Grabbing the scarf, she was wearing, she wrapped it around Kirsa's neck. Propping her up against a chair, Alana was trying to stop the bleeding but froze as she and Kirsa watched in horror.

Al had rushed Susannah, she summoned the sword of Nuada and ran it through him. They heard Titania's anguished scream as she ran to Al falling to the floor. She caught him and laid him in her lap.

Kirsa pushed herself off the floor, the battle was going on around her but all she saw was Susannah dueling Brigid. Kirsa caught the sword that Alana threw to her and blocked the killing blow aimed at Brigid. Susannah was stunned when the goddess stepped back and bowed to Kirsa.

"This isn't about blood," Kirsa rasped. "This is about jealousy and never growing up."

Sparks flew as their swords hit. Everything faded as Kirsa focused on Susannah. There would be no prison for Susannah, only death. Kirsa knew that now and accepted it.

As they fought she ignored the noises, the screams, and the smell of burning flesh. With a brilliant move she disarmed Susannah. When she raised the sword to kill her, Susannah shoved a silver stake into her chest. Kirsa looked down at it then up at Susannah.

"I am not a vampire," Kirsa replied with a snarl.

She pulled the stake out and threw it to the floor. She then nodded at the person behind them and stepped back. Susannah went to say something but nothing came out.

She stared at Kirsa with a confused look on her face as an iron sword came out her forehead. Susannah sank to the ground revealing Titania standing behind her holding the hilt of the sword. Kirsa nodded one more time before blackness took over.

CHAPTER 36

Kirsa woke to a familiar cool hand holding hers, Ayden sat next to the bed staring at her, she smiled weakly at him as he helped her sit up. Her throat felt like it was on fire and her chest ached as if she been hit with a ton of bricks.

"Where am I?" Kirsa asked her voice barely a whisper.

"Avalon, Lance and I came after the battle," Ayden told her.

He kissed her forehead, relieved that the fever had finally broken. One of the novices entered, she smiled at Kirsa.

"Your man has refused to leave you," she said as she checked her temperature and bandages.

"He's stubborn," Kirsa whispered.

"Don't talk," the novice said. "I'm Sienna. Ayden says you can communicate through your mind, do that for the next forty-six hours."

"She wants to know what's wrong with her," Ayden said.

"You have bruised and almost severed vocal chords from the knife wound," Sienna replied. "You have some silver poisoning, but the fever has broken so that should be done with. She attempted to stake you but failed, the hole is deep but healing."

"Al?" Kirsa whispered.

Sienna and Ayden looked at each other grimly. Kirsa feared the worst. Sienna finished changing bandages before speaking.

"He lives."

"She wants to know how."

Sienna took the seat that Ayden offered. "Danu appeared at the end with Dagda. They cleansed the area and saw what you and Al had done to save and protect us. They were able to heal him enough so that he lives. But the rest is up to him."

Kirsa raised an eyebrow in question. Sienna smiled as she filled a tea cup with tea and handed it to Kirsa.

"He is alive and awake; the injury though is severe and he might never heal completely from it but he will live a good long life."

Ayden thanked her, Sienna nodded then left. Kirsa looked at him, he pulled her close and held her while she cried.

After lunch with the help from Sienna, Kirsa bathed and sat on the sofa in the living area with Ayden. Lance stood outside on guard. There was a knock on the door, Sienna opened it and tsked at the person.

"He insisted," Titania said. "He heard she was awake and has been annoying all morning."

"He can talk for himself," Al snapped already fed up with being injured.

"An hour then naps for both," Sienna said leaving the cottage.

Titania wheeled Al into the cottage in a wooden wheelchair. Kirsa went over and held him as they both reveled in the fact that they had both survived. Titania and Ayden smiled at each other with understanding.

He was glad that they got along because with the bond between Al and Kirsa if they didn't it would be a problem. When they were done, Kirsa sat down on the sofa and Titania passed the tea around that Sienna had been preparing.

"We are lucky," Al said raising his mug.

"That we are," Kirsa agreed in a whisper.

Ayden looked at Kirsa. "Titania, she wants to know what happened."

"I killed Susannah. We committed her body to a pyre at sun rise and buried the ashes in the sacred well," Titania said simply.

"She was your sister," Al said holding Titania's hand.

"I have another sister but there is only one Al," Titania replied looking at Al.

"She says that she just threw up in her mouth," Ayden laughed. "She wants to know if Danu and Dagda really came."

"They did, they brought Ayden and Lance with them," Titania said.

"Al how bad are you?" Kirsa whispered. She knew she was straining her voice.

"I have four bruised vertebrae, one that is fractured, my spleen has been removed," Al said. "I am strictly paperwork now, no more chasing bad guys unless it's a paper trail."

****

Titania stood with Kirsa on top of the Tor; they would be leaving the following day. Kirsa could talk without being yelled at and Al could wiggle his toes. Kirsa looked out onto the waters that surrounded Avalon, separating it from the world of man. She noticed that in the mist one could make out movement and shapes as if they were glimpses as to what was going on in the other realm.

"Lance took a pinch of ashes just to make sure it was her body we cremated," Titania said.

She laid a small bouquet of flowers at the memorial stone. Kirsa studied the woman she had become close to over the last few days.

"You don't really believe that you have a spare sister, do you?"

"I killed her, Kirsa. I saved Al but killed my sister," Titania replied. She let out a long sigh, Kirsa allowed her the moment. "What do you remember of that day?"

"All hell breaking loose, Alana was keeping me from bleeding out, Balor and you were working on Al, and there were demons everywhere," Kirsa recalled. "But it gets hazy around the time I get staked."

"In that moment, you and Al knew you had to bring down Susannah, you were both focused on that task, what you did not see was Susannah turning guards against guards, that even our twelve gods were fighting alongside with us,"

Titania explained. Kirsa just gaped at her not even knowing what to say. "There was fear that we might not make it. There was a moment when you were staked. Nuada looked at me and summoned his sword that had been removed from Al. It appeared in my hand, we nodded, and I knew then. That if there was ever a moment to stop her that was the moment.

I might have shoved the sword through her brain, but she killed herself when she tried to escape."

"What happened to her, Titania?" Kirsa asked. "What changed in her?"

Titania looked at her, surprised. "You don't know do you?" she said then smiled slightly. "Do you remember when she became banned from your house?"

Kirsa nodded so Titania continued. Kirsa's voice was still tired. "Susannah truly did not know that her blood could kill a vampire. She never did pay attention when dad talked of our heritage."

"She never was good at listening in general," Kirsa replied smiling as she remembered when Susannah had been a good friend.

"That is true," Titania agreed. "After dad grounded her for two weeks she came to me crying. She knew that there was the blood thing that might make you a vampire, she was terrified that she might hurt you without knowing. Or what happened if she fell in love with a vampire, would she have to walk away? I couldn't answer them," Titania said.

"She was determined to find a spell that would protect her blood and yours. But magick like that tends to be on the dark side and I think as she researched she became enchanted herself with the power it could unlock. Then when Alana began to show gifts and your ability was blossoming the jealousy clouded her."

"I always wondered what the catalyst was," Kirsa replied.

"Good intentions that got away from her."

CHAPTER 37

There had been a media circus at Newark airport when flight information had been released by accident. It was a good thing that Kirsa had arranged a charter flight which did not land in Newark but in Sussex County. Five cars waited for them to disembark from the plane. Ayden and Lance were the first two down the steps, Kirsa followed with Louis pushing Al's wheelchair. Colin stood with Tony and Dietrich on the tarmac and watched the group of five make their way to them. Tony walked over and hugged Kirsa tightly, he kissed her forehead before releasing her to greet Ayden with a hug, while Dietrich enfolded her in his arms and just held on to her for a moment. When he was sure she was fine he released her.

"No Sabrina?" Kirsa asked kissing Colin on the cheek.

He laughed, "She's planning your surprise welcome home party."

"Anything earth shattering while we were gone?" Kirsa inquired as they headed to the cars.

"None that can't wait until we're home," Colin assured her as he closed her door.

He shook hands with Ayden who slid in the other side and Lance took the wheel.

Tony signaled for the first unmarked car to begin to head out with Lance following. Louis helped get Al into a car and they closed the door on his protests about being helped. Dietrich went in the car with Al.

It was only a thirty minute trip and Ayden pushed Kirsa's head down as they neared her road, it had been closed off to keep the media out. The cops opened the barricade to allow the cars through all while flashbulbs and reporters scurried to get a shot.

It was hard to get one when all the cars were tinted so only outlines could be made out. Instead of pulling into the drive to the house, Lance continued on down the road to the Black Rose Ranch and pulled into the private drive.

Sabrina and Laura stood in the front door waiting for them to arrive. When Kirsa got out of the car they rushed her and just held on tight.

Al had been positioned in the dining room with everything within reach; Mrs. Hanson was hovering over him making sure he was alright. Colin and Ayden felt bad for the guy but knew better than to say anything. There was food on the table and on the buffet table, Ayden sipped his wine as Colin and Dietrich filled him on what they had missed.

They had been gone for almost two weeks in total and a lot had happened in that time period. When the women came in everyone sat down at the table and began to pass food around. Eileen Brewster showed up out of breath and took her seat at the table.

Colin raised his glass, "To Kirsa and Al for coming back to us relatively in one piece!"

"I can't believe I'm running OPIA until Kirsa is back in a month," Eileen said. Kirsa just laughed at her running the offices without shooting someone.

"I'm planning on staying there so I can help," Al said.

He couldn't go back to his apartment he was on the fourth floor with no elevator.

"Absolutely not," Eliane replied shaking her head. "If you stay on campus you will be a thorn in my side. As Director I refuse it."

"Fine then I'll crash on Kirsa's sofa," Al said wanting to stick his tongue out.

"No, you'll stay in my pool house," Sabrina said tossing him a set of keys. "Brian lived there before he bought his town house. Colin has been updating it but it's all one floor, you'll have access to the main house, use of the home gym and pool."

Al went to say something but couldn't, words failed him. Instead he nodded to Sabrina who smiled understanding.

Lance poked his head in the room, "The lab called. The ashes are a positive match."

There was a moment of silence before anyone spoke. "You two going to tell us what happened?" Sabrina asked.

"There were gods, demons, iron and Susannah," Kirsa said nonchalantly. "They didn't mix well."

"In other words, no," Bridgette replied. She bounced in her seat staring at Phil as if she was brimming with excitement. Phil smiled and nodded. "But I have exciting news!"

"What?" Ayden asked. He liked Bridgette she reminded him of his youngest sister.

"I got a full ride to Grabenberg University!"

There were hugs, high fives and lots of questions as they all congratulated the young girl who had blossomed after tragedy.

When the dinner was over and most of the guests had left, Sabrina sat in the parlor with Dietrich, Ayden, Kirsa and Colin. Lance had wheeled Al over to the pool house, so he could take a look at his temporary home.

"Young lady you have caused us some problems," Dietrich began as he stared at Sabrina.

"I wish I could go back and change it all," Sabrina replied.

"By you breaking numerous laws you also helped us uncover some information regarding Victor who is now being closely watched," Dietrich added. "Eztil was killed by one of our men while Kirsa and Al were causing mayhem in the Fae. We also were informed that the idea of going to the prison was not your own."

"Does this mean her punishment will be light?" Colin asked.

"With the exception of Victor, your punishment is one year banishment from the vampire world starting May 6th," Dietrich told her. "Since Kirsa is not a vampire you do not have to cut ties with her for a year."

Sabrina got up and hugged him. She knew her punishment could have been more severe. "Thank You."

"Now I need to talk to Kirsa and Ayden, so we will be leaving with Zero," Dietrich informed her.

It took a few minutes before they headed onto the path that connected the two properties. There was a chill in the air and the scent of snow to come. They walked in silence as they headed down the path, they passed the frozen pond and the guest house began to appear.

"What's going on?" Ayden asked Dietrich as they neared the house.

"Dimitri, Shamus, Sebastian and I have decided to keep the news of your family a secret," Dietrich informed Ayden.

"Why the secrecy?" Kirsa asked.

"Two reasons; the first is we are unsure of Victor's loyalties at the moment. If he knew of Ayden's family it could be used against him. The second is the vampire responsible for Ayden's death has never been caught, we don't want to jeopardize his family by informing the vampire council about them."

"Because the vampire world only knows me as Ayden O'Brian," Ayden said.

"Exactly," Dietrich replied. "Your family will be protected and safe, but no official declaration will be made until we know it's safe."

****

Kirsa's head lay on Ayden's stomach as he stroked her hair. It was late when they had gotten back to the house and played with Zero. She rolled off of him and looked into his eyes, he saw the grief in them, the hurt and the anger.

"I couldn't save her this time either," Kirsa said. Ayden rolled onto his side and ran a hand down her arm kissing her shoulder as he did.

"No, you didn't." He saw the surprise in her eyes as he kissed her jaw. "It's hard to save someone who doesn't want to be saved."

"Have you lost many that you thought you could save?" Kirsa asked running a hand down his back.

"Enough to know that there are people who truly don't want to be, that they would rather face the unknown then be rescued," Ayden told her. "She made her choice, Kirsa. She could have listened and heard her punishment. Instead she chose to take as many as she could down with her. Susannah knew the only way out was death, the only thing that surprised her was it wasn't you who killed her."

"That's harsh Ayden."

"I've lived for over a hundred and fifty years and death is always harsh," Ayden said. He then smiled at her. "However, trying to make a new life is always a thrilling experience."

Kirsa laughed as he nibbled down her body. She was home, alive, in love, getting married. For the moment all was well, and she would accept that.

Author Note

When I started this journey with Kirsa and the gang, I was a new mom. That was only eight years ago and, in that time, I have grown as a person and as a writer.

When I opened Bohlander House Press in 2016 one of my goals was to bring my first three books over to my press. I decided that if I was going to re-publish them then I was going to read through them again and make changes and if need be. One of those changes was there are a lot of people in Kirsa's life. Almost too many to keep track of.

In the original *Shadows of a Past*, Jeff Cliver survived. In the retelling of the tale in *Shattered Past*, he was not so fortunate.

And that brings us to *Shattered Dreams. Shadows of a Dream* and *Shattered Dream* was extremely personal for me. I poured a lot of past experiences into the book twisting them with a bit of paranormal. It was while reading through *Dreams* that I realized that Susannah need to crueler than she already was. I sobbed writing Sara's last scene, I sobbed writing Kirsa speaking about her. It was one of the toughest decisions as an author but overall it makes for a better tale.

Now I start the process with what will be *Shattered Ghost*.

Dreams

I will admit this, Susannah is still one of my favorite characters I have written.

Thanks,
Meg Castro

www.ingramcontent.com/pod-product-compliance
Lightning Source LLC
Chambersburg PA
CBHW051533250626
47157CB00001B/32